LOVE MUST ALSO WEEP

LOVE
MUST ALSO
WEEP

A Novel Lucidly Intimate
With Awakening's Alchemy

Robert Augustus Masters

XANTHYROS FOUNDATION

Published by XANTHYROS FOUNDATION

Printed and bound in Canada

ISBN: 0-88925-980-1

Again I break, my need dissolving my pride
Again I spill, my hurt streaming, streaming wide
Again I die, letting grief and joy burst and fly, fly, fly
Again I whisper and roar, swimming through the dreamy door
And again I join what's above with what's below
And again I recognize the One behind the show

Again I bulge, feeling murder snaking, snaking down my arms
Again I pray, my dungeon walls swallowing my bloody calls
Again I die, releasing all that I took to be mine
Again I exult, bounding through forests of palm and pine
And again I join what's above with what's below
And again I recognize the One within the show

Again I remember, and open my innermost wounds
Again I remember, and rise where I once lay ruined
Again I'm aflood with force, riding wild green waters down to the sea
Again I face my delusion, and take the mind out of my confusion
Again I break and again I die, again I break and again I die
And again I rise and again I awaken
And again I fall, forgetting the Sacred Call
And again I remember, and again I include it all
And again we are here, already free, not to have, but to be,
To form and unform, to be lovers with the calm and the storm
And again I join what's above with what's below
And again I recognize the One present as the show
And again everything's aflame with the Holy Glow,
And again I move on, uprooted until I find a truer ground
And again I stand where there's room for every joy and every pain
And again we've nothing, nothing to attain,
Only this Wonder to know, this Wonder to forever live,
This gift to give...

Contents

PART I

1.	ANUSHET	3
2.	AMULA	11
3.	AT SEA	19
4.	CAPTURED	30
5.	INSINUATING ITS WAY ACROSS HIS FACE	38
6.	WITH EZPARYA	45
7.	CALLED TO BIRTH	52
8.	HER ROBE A LIQUID PROMISE	61
9.	WHEN ESMELANA WAS BUT THREE	68
10.	TO UNWRAP HIS ONE GIFT	71
11.	A FIRE HE COULD ONLY WELCOME	77
12.	HOW COULD HE NOT RETURN?	88
13.	HIS TO EMBODY AND EXPRESS, HIS TO LET FLY	90
14.	TO PLUNGE DEEP INTO HER, DEEPER THAN FLESH	98
15.	ANTICIPATION WINGING HER STRIDE	110
16.	ARTAKIAB	114
17.	TRUTH CANNOT BE REHEARSED	126
18.	BACK TO THE CITY	131
19.	MORE THAN A DREAM	140
20.	EVEN HE MUST RETURN TO HER	146
21.	SHE HEARD THE SOUND OF SOMEONE CRYING	154
22.	GIVING THE GIFT WITHOUT GIVING HIMSELF AWAY	164
23.	THE BROKEN MUSIC	178
24.	COMING THROUGH THE GATES	188
25.	PASS THROUGH IT WITH OPEN EYES	193

PART II

26. AN APPARENT INTERRUPTION   201
27. RETURNING TO AMULA   209
28. BELOVED STRANGER   216
29. ITS VIRGIN AIR AWAITING HIS INHALE   225
30. XANDUR'S STORY   235
31. I WILL SEE YOU AGAIN   246

PART III

32. THE GREAT FOREST   253
33. COME LET THE SOBERING JOY BLOOM   262
34. TO BE LOVERS WITH THE CALM AND THE STORM   268
35. UNTIL THE FIRE IS BUT LIGHT   273
36. I HAVE BEEN WAITING FOR YOU   279
37. LET ME SHOW YOU MY LAND   283
38. ITS HEARTBEAT SHAPING OUR TRUEST GROUND   294
39. ROOM FOR ALL   298

Part I

When the night pulled back the bedcovers
And I sat knees-up lightly ashaking, hoping for a sign sublime,
My mind looking for the time, my body athrob with eternal rhyme,
The windows, the windows did bulge with something unborn
Something I could neither name nor contain

O When the night pulled back the bedcovers
And outside and inside were lovers, and exhale was inhale
And I knew a love that could not fail,
I did cry out for having so much, and for wanting more,
And for having done all this before

O When the night pulled back the bedcovers
And my breath was not mine, and I knew the Holy Design
And the dark stormed my room so sweet and so blazing bright
And my spirit was a stem of light, so green and so, so white
I did, I did give the night my hand
And let it lead me through every face of every shadowland
And my whole being did shiver and shake
Until my frame of mind did break
And I was in body what I was in spirit,
Embracing the great night shining, shining so wild
The great night forever full of child

1

Anushet

One.

Heavy were his legs, heavier still this axe, its rough black shaft almost
as thick as his forearm, its huge stone blade pockmarked and red.
Sunlight glinted crazily from a quartz triangle inlaid in the middle of
the handle. Such a strange sky this was, pale and icy, almost metallic...

Two.

Not an easy axe to swing, let alone lift. Not like the ones at home, with
their smooth, light shafts expertly shaped for a man's grip, and their
finely balanced, hand-sized heads. Hoisting the axe, he squinted back
and forth along a blurred arc, his face knotting with both fear and
determination...

Three.

Three breaths counted, three quick, shallow breaths, three little
impotent harbingers of reassurance, so desperately chained to the
upcoming registering of breath number four. It was hard to believe he
was actually here. A narcotic softness suddenly permeated him,
sweetly soporific and opaquely consoling, caressingly inviting him to
disembody, to dissolve, to float free... No! Squinting even harder, he
shook off his dreaminess, blinking rapidly, sweating and shivering,
now, brutally naked now, hearing the crowd scream.

Five. Or was it four?

Desperately, he tightened his grip, as if to counteract his wobbling concentration. The crowd, the wraparound, suffocating presence of it! Such a demanding, horribly eager shouting and screeching, engorged with perverse appetite! Now he had the axe over his shoulder. He bent his knees, poising himself for the attack he was certain would come — what else could this howling mob be so hungry for?

Seven. No, it couldn't be seven...

He had lost track; no longer could he distance himself from what was happening. His efforts to achieve stillpoint lay in ruins around his painfully throbbing heart. He stood ready as he could be, half-crouched in the center of this alien amphitheatre, in front of this roaring audience, this thousand-mouthed bloodthirsty monster — how ugly their one voice, how subhuman! No, he would not let them penetrate him! No! A violent surge of power filled him in an instant, streaming up through his torso, snaking down his arms, thrillingly intensifying his grip.

Let the beast come! Some starving carnivore, likely maddened by well-practiced means. Let it come, whatever it is, but O let there be only one! A stabbing yet exquisitely tender sadness rushed through him — he didn't want to die here, so far, far away from his child, so far, far away from his land. He mustn't die here! It wasn't his time; it couldn't be! Let the beast come! He crouched even lower, the axe balanced on his shoulder.

One.

The crowd's tone grew shriller. The beast had arrived in a fury of dust and coarse shouts, dragged out in a rope cage. Red-eyed it was, white-maned and full-fanged, straining from side to side, its bulging ribs precisely curved shadows on a silver shore...

Two.

The ropes were cut. Three.

The beast threw back its massive head, then charged him, faster and faster, bellowing and snarling, its mouth wreathed with yellow foam...

Four.

He no longer heard the crowd. The beast was now but a few strides from him, every detail of its face incredibly vivid to him. In less than a heartbeat, it would be upon him, its eyes such sad bloody pools, its scarred black lips stretched so wide...

In one fluid motion, he leapt to his left and swung the axe, roaring with his effort. The blade sank deep into the side of the beast's neck. For a long moment, all he could see was blood and dust; then he jerked the axe free, raising it high as he could, bringing it down with all his strength on the writhing beast. A geyser of blood briefly rose above him, its gleaming stem drooping over his head, petalling out and out, showering him crimson.

The crowd was cheering. The axe slipped from his hands. He felt dull and heavy, drained beyond rejuvenation, far too exhausted to be impressed by what he had just done.

One.

He wavered as though in a ferocious wind, his knees buckling...

Two. Flat on his back he lay, swooning into unconsciousness. The last thing he saw was trembling sky, cloudless yet barely blue, fringed with a faint violet, a sky that seemed to descend upon him, layer upon fuzzy layer, smothering without end...

He awoke in a room with no light, having no sense of how long he had slept. His dreams fled his recall, leaving in their wake only a fleeting trace of warm, silken green. How coarse were these furs he lay upon, how suffocatingly acrid the air! He could hear nothing, except faint, plaintful birdcries. And something else now. Footsteps, growing louder...

The door swung open, the sudden light hurting his eyes. Over him stood two women, side by side, backed by five or six spear-clutching men. One of the women immediately began speaking to him in his language, with a wetly guttural accent. Dimly, he wondered how she could possibly know his tongue.

"You did well today," she announced, smiling coldly at him. On her forehead were painted four vertical black lines. "My name is Tornellas. I will serve as interpreter for you. I trust that my grasp of your language is sufficient. A strange tongue is yours, appallingly crude, yet not without some merit. You, lowly one, are the honoured guest of Ezparya, ruler of Anushet." Gesturing toward the other woman, she added, "This is Ezparya. You must bow to her before you address her, and when you first see her."

He didn't move. Though the room bulged with heated anticipation, he felt chilled by Ezparya's glistening black eyes. The guards, at a nod from Tornellas, kicked him in front of Ezparya. Gasping, he bowed.

"Excellent!" laughed Tornellas. "Perhaps next time you will be a bit quicker. I suspect that slowness and stupidity are virtues in your land, but they are not here! Now, what is your name?"

"Glam."

"Ezparya wishes to question you, Glam. I will translate for her."

Ezparya's voice was similar to Tornellas's, but much fuller, far shapelier, punctuated by bird trillings, pervaded through and through by a pantherine ease. Such a strange music it contained, strident and purring, cruel and bright, a lush mingling of sun-dappled day and prowling night, catalyzing in him both fascination and repulsion...

"She says," began Tornellas, "that you showed some courage today. She also says that she wishes you well in your next test of courage, which she will personally administer."

He started to speak. A heavy blow to the side of his head informed him that he wasn't to talk, at least yet. Ezparya continued, her sounds harsh yet curvaceous, adorned with sibilant flourishes. In place of her eyebrows were brilliant red bird feathers. Her mouth was painted black. Her face was unlined, yet her hair was white. Out of her mouth slithered and flew her words, croaking and hissing, cooing and moaning, growling and whispering...

"How old are you?" asked Tornellas.

"Thirty-one." His voice seemed to emerge from faraway, almost echoing, as if emitted from some lofty mountainside cave.

"Do you have a family?"

"Yes."

"Give us the details."

"I have a child. A daughter."

After a long, strained pause, Ezparya snapped out a bolt of sound that startled him. Giving him a scornful look, Tornellas said, "Do not presume to hide anything from Ezparya. Now, lowly beast, tell us who else is in your family."

"No one!" he blurted. Then, seemingly against his will, he murmured, "One flower." Why was he telling them this? Why?

"Flower?" Tornellas leaned closer to him, studying him intently, her face a mixture of curiosity and distaste.

"Yes." Slowly, the words marched out of him, obeying a command utterly alien to him. "My flower. A young woman, just past fifteen years, deemed by our elders to be ready for sexual initiation, which I have given her." Abruptly, his words halted, standing at attention.

Tornellas spoke quickly, and Ezparya laughed. "Tell us more!" grinned Tornellas, with mock urgency.

With considerable effort, he took charge of his speech again. "When they are ready, all of our young people spend one month with an older person of the opposite sex, as lovers. After, they spend another three months with their initiator, but without any sex. Then they go. My particular flower left less than seven months ago." How strange it was to be thus reciting these facts, but at least he had not fleshed them out...

Ezparya's laughter was distinctly derisive. She wiggled her body seductively in front of him, spitting out a meandering stream of words. He looked down, feeling anger kindling in his belly.

Raising her eyebrows and thrusting her head forward, Tornellas gave him an icy smile. "Ezparya wants to know if she is ready to be a flower. Perhaps you could tell us?"

He reddened, but said nothing. Several hard kicks in his back, and an even harder blow to the back of his neck, didn't break his silence.

"You must answer Ezparya!" shrieked Tornellas, her face a taut mask, her mouth a bloodless slash. "Answer now!"

He wouldn't speak. He mustn't further degrade himself. Anger coiled within him, swelling furiously with every breath. More kicks. More laughter. How dare they! Now, there was a hand in his hair, its fingernails gouging his scalp, jerking his head from side to side with viciously rhythmic force. Not caring about the consequences, he seized the hand, twisting it as sharply as he could. Ezparya fell to the floor, screaming, holding her wrist. Up he sprang, but immediately the guards were upon him; he tried to escape their grasp, but in vain. With brute ease, they pinned him on his back, spreading his legs wide. Turning his head to his right, he saw Ezparya rising, yanking a small dagger from a sheath at her waist. Hissing and swaying, her eyes blazing black, she approached him, gesturing with her dagger at his crotch. He knew without a doubt her intention, and struggled to free himself.

"Now you will pay, imbecile!" sneered Tornellas, folding her arms across her chest. One of the men began pulling down Glam's trousers, and Ezparya bent forward, readying her blade.

"No!" he screamed with tremendously explosive power, freeing one of his legs, driving his heel right into Ezparya's face. Twisting his torso, he freed an arm. Again, he twisted, roaring with stunning force, breaking away from his captors. He stood untouched, seeing in an instant the entire room, the sprawling guards, the shock on Tornellas's face, the prone figure of Ezparya, the dirty white furs on the floor, the crimson walls, the open door! Without any hesitation, he grabbed Ezparya's dagger and fled from the room, fear pumping speed through his legs. Already, he could hear Ezparya shouting, her voice seeming to claw at his back. Down a long, dimly lit hallway he sprinted, barely keeping his balance. The walls were purple, the ceiling black. The hall seemed to suddenly narrow, to be closing in on him, like a great throat about to swallow...

But see! There was a window at the end of the hallway, a large, oval window, now but a dozen strides away. And now but six...

Through the window he saw the night sky, fresh and vast, studded with stars and a bleached sliver of moon. He could not go back, he could not turn and fight — he must go on, he must!

He fell for a few moments, then hit something hard and solid, feeling as though he'd cracked several ribs. Moaning, he rolled and fell further, landing in what felt like mud, cold, sticky mud. He lay exhausted, his breath frantic, barely noticing that he was crying. He must not stop! See, yes see, the horizon, jagged with tree-tips.

Forest. That's where he would go. Yes! Forcing himself to his feet, he ran, almost oblivious to his pain. The forest arrived sooner than he'd expected, receiving him with stately silence, muting his broken panting. Between trees and through bushes he ran, stumbling and falling, veering wildly, not hearing the staccato snapping of twigs underfoot, not feeling the prickly spring and scratch of the often-dense greenery through which he was pushing. Finally, he collapsed in a graceless heap at the base of a large, hollowed-out stump. A strange forest this was, with its pungent smell and low-slung, looping canopy of darkly matted branches, drooping down and down, its finger-thick tendrils seeking the ground. Nevertheless, it was home for now. As his breathing slowed and settled, thoughts of his homeland flickered through him, brightly beckoning for his attention — feather-soft, welcoming greens rolling oceanward, wave after sunlit wave of friendly eyes and joyous cries, embraces of heart-rooted kinship all around, love steady and shining deep, love so sweetly, so richly, so fully embodied, love...

What was he doing? He must get up! He must keep moving! Yes, he could have burrowed beneath the stump, curling up into cosy sleep, but what a trap that might have been — buried alive, soft flesh sniffed out, unerringly located, inviting the stabbing of probing spears! Shivering, he struggled to rise.

In one hand, he held Ezparya's dagger. What a beautiful and wicked thing it was, its handle subtly serpentine, jewelled aquamarine and gold, its crescent of blade so shapely and razor-sharp...

Grimacing at first, he began to trot through the barely visible trees, brushing through crowds of head-high ferns, sometimes having to drop to all fours to pass under places where the branches sagged particularly low. Gradually, the forest thinned, yielding to ever-widening slices of meadow, cool and mossy, streaked with starlight. Then, open air, at last!

Mountainous horizon. Horse-star constellation now rearing overhead. There seemed to be no pursuit of him. Perhaps he was already at the edge of Anushet. He must keep moving. It would be folly to try to cross to the mountains in daylight. On he ran, slowly and steadily, not considering stopping, at least not until after sunrise; then he'd find some sort of shelter.

Remembrance of Anushet's black-eyed ruler drove him on, her voice chilling the back of his neck. Now he was on open ground, treeless, rocky and rough, eversteepening. Again and again, he stumbled, his ribs howling as loudly as his feet. He must keep climbing! Sometimes, it was so steep that he had to use his hands. He must keep climbing, he must, he must... Several times, he paused and wept, overcome by the intensity of it all, overcome with longing for his homeland and his child.

By sunrise, he was asleep in a cave high up in the mountains, the dagger by his head.

2

Amula

In Glam's land, Amula, the rains were brief and heavy, the sunlight long and warm. It was a glory of gently undulating greens, shade upon succulent shade, rolling back from the eye soft and velvet, smoothly easing into ever bluer shades of green, then ever paler shades of blue, then, at the extreme reach of vision, a gauzy mauve, almost pearly, steadfastly reassuring in its diffuse curvaceousness. There was a sweet comfort to the terrain, a luxuriant maternal depth, an unabashed fecundity, a texture and feel bonding both land and human intent. Teardrop lakes glistened in many a valley, their creamy turquoise waters asplash with swimmers young and old. Most of the trees were brilliantly, even extravagantly, flowered, some aburst with red blossoms twice the size of a man's head. Yet for all their beauty, these trees did not compare for Glam with those that he, sight unseen, knew existed deep in the interior of Amula...

These innermost forests, commonly known as the Great Forest, formed a dense ring around the base of the towering mountain rising from the very center of Amula. This was Mount Aratisha, visible from all points in Amula — unassailable Aratisha, the Unclimbable, the Seat of Lantar, its immaculate peak higher than almost all clouds. No one, as far as it was known, had ever climbed Aratisha, or even attempted to, for to do so was not considered to be Lantar's Will, Lantar being the purest name of the Source and Substance of all. To approach Mount Aratisha, one would have to penetrate the Great Forest, and thereby encounter the beasts that supposedly dwelt there, including snakes of immense size and appetite; and not only such creatures would greet one, it was said, but also the dark, mesmerizing, multi-mouthed presence that was believed to permeate the entire forest. Nonsense, said some, mere superstition. Literally so, claimed many. Legend, declared others, an update of ancient shadowland myths, no more than an interesting metaphor...

However, regardless of what they said or thought about the Great Forest, almost none even considered entering it. Those rare few who actually wanted to explore the Great Forest were strongly counselled to not bother. Why go there? Why risk the peril of such darkness, when the rest of the land was so hospitable, so consistently nourishing, so richly abundant with what was necessary for survival? Why hanker after the mysteries of the Great Forest, when the soil beneath one's feet was, at essence, just as mysterious, just as deserving of profound examination? Why escape into faraway adventure, when right before one there was the adventure and wondrous challenge of living one's life heartfully and passionately, right in the very midst of one's current circumstances? Why seek elsewhere? After all, wasn't the fundamental challenge the same wherever one was? Nevertheless, no argument, however persuasive or intelligent, could convince Glam to fully withdraw his attention from the Great Forest.

Amula was an island, a plump, sinuously indented oval fringed with hundreds of soft golden beaches. For those who craved risk, the surrounding ocean provided countless opportunities; sometimes it became a magnificently foaming fury, a towering sleekness of brilliant power, casting against the shores waves four or five times the height of a man. Such waves were the delight of an adventuresome few, who rode the churning, peaking waters with graceful abandon, their will deeply aligned with the forces governing the waves. Most of the time, though, Amula's ocean was but a peaceful expanse of sparkling blue and indigo, ideal for simple watersport and easy fishing. Amulans were water-wise, as capable of swimming through surf as they were of skilfully handling an ocean canoe. It was commonplace even for infants to spend much of their time playing in the ocean, not only in the shallows of its sun-drenched lagoons, but also just inside the leading edge of shore-climbing waves. The waters of Amula, especially in the smaller bays, were generously supplied with fish, crustaceans, and all sorts of molluskan delicacies, the most highly valued being the flesh of ivory-shelled abalones, iridescent creatures no larger than an adult's thumbnail.

In many ways, the ocean offered the same primal comfort as the land, the same maternal reassurance and embrace, but with one important difference — its boundaries were unknown. From the shores of Amula, no other lands could be seen, although some adventurers who had ventured out far enough from Amula to be able to only see the uppermost tip of Aratisha's peak (to not be able to see the peak was considered to be extremely inauspicious) had said they'd glimpsed signs of land on the horizon. A few had gone, so it was said, so far that they could no longer see Aratisha, but none of these had ever returned...

Most Amulans were involved in farming and fishing. A few also worked as natural healers, under the tutelage of the priests of Lantar. For every thousand Amulans, there was one priest of Lantar, and for every fifty priests, there was at least one high priestess. For every six of these, there was one oracle of Lantar, usually female. And, for every twelve oracles, there was a Sirdhanan. The Sirdhanans governed Amula; their numbers ranged from seven to nine, always including at least three women.

Every Amulan family had a priest overseeing it, serving as final judge in their squabbles and questions of appropriate behaviour. Glam as a child had rarely enjoyed the presence of the priest; by his seventh year, he had decided to become a priest himself, so that he could do without such an annoyance in his house-to-be. His decision, though, was based on more than childish ambition, for, from his earliest years, he had displayed a remarkable aptitude for the very qualities deemed most desirable in a priest of Lantar — he was intelligent, deeply intuitive, and capable of exerting considerable force of a non-physical nature...

He often knew what his parents were thinking, and frequently spoke their minds to them. At first, when waist-high Glam had clearly demonstrated his ability to more than occasionally know the contents of their minds, they had felt both frightened and proud. Not for long though did they indulge their fear; most Amulan parents would have retreated somewhat from such a child, raising up a psychic shield of some sort, but Glam's parents chose otherwise, learning to delight in their son's gift, to care for it with the eyes and hands of a loving gardener. In many ways, they let him grow wild, encouraging him to again and again test his limits. At the same time, through their example, they imbued him with a strong sense of integrity and compassion — gradually, he learned that every increase in freedom was no more than caprice, unless it was accompanied by a corresponding increase in responsibility, such responsibility being not a burdensome, joyless duty, a glum collage of squareshouldered shoulds, but rather a sobering joy, an open-eyed participation in what was needed, a guilt-free accountability serving as the very *ground* for real freedom. And so did Glam's parents tend his growth, neither uprooting him, nor leaving him unpruned, letting his expansion stretch and enliven them.

He matured quickly, growing headstrong and heartstrong, ever eager to test and explore his boundaries. Often, he gazed at the pure white peak of Aratisha, imagining himself climbing it, chafing at the taboo against doing so — how could the priests, oracles, and even Sirdhanans forbid such a potentially magnificent adventure? But they did. To Glam, their reasons only decorated their nay-saying. Eventually, he stopped asking why, keeping his fantasies about ascending the Mount to himself. Even his parents, for all their generosity of spirit and openness of heart, would hear nothing of his yearning for Aratisha. Thus did he begin feeling like a stranger in his homeland...

But at least there was the ocean, the sweet, deep, fierce ocean, so bright and ravishingly wild and welcoming, so magically true to itself! Almost every day, he swam in the rolling waters, playing with the waves, soaring on the rise and bubbling rush of the surf, letting himself at times be tossed about like a twig in a storm. Rising to the dazzling crest of a great wave just before it broke was joy enough to make him forget Aratisha. How he loved these mountains of water, these ecstatic shapings, these brief yet timeless upcurvings of virginal power and grace, falling, crashing, breaking, ever-resurrected, roaring so deep, climbing so, so steep, up through instantly eloquent arabesques of wavespray, reaching, reaching, achingly blue and smooth, stretching high, so, so high...

Sometimes he would feel as though he were but ocean inside, even as he was surrounded by ocean, his skin (and sense of self) but the thinnest of veils, porous and tingling, seeming to be but the flimsiest of barriers between two long-separated friends; the two would pour into one another through him, rapturously merging through his almost disappearing sense of self, their union singing ancient, silent songs that reverbated through his very being sometimes long after he had left the ocean. Yet in this deep surrender, this apparent dissolution of self, his individuality blossomed. When he began his priestly training at the age of thirteen, such oceanic experiences served him well, for some of the training concerned the deliberate creation of experiences of going beyond one's everyday self...

The training was, at first, tedious and difficult for most, for it required the cultivation of extraordinary concentration, through the focussing of attention on objects of all kinds, both physical and mental. This willful redirection of attention was for some no more than a repression of their desire to do otherwise. For others, such repression did not arise, or was ably transmuted into *available* Life-Energy, so that its energies could be harnessed to the deepening of concentration. The purpose of such conscious, finely-honed concentration was, explained the teachers over and over again, to be able to hold one's mind to one thing, and one thing only, to, in other words, keep one's attention from mechanically straying from object to object, inner or outer. There was often a dryness, a spare solemnity, an emotional barrenness, to such an intensity of mentalized focus, but, for most, it was not unpleasant. In fact, for some, including Glam, the practice was occasionally very pleasurable, even blissful, especially when the act of concentration seemed to be happening all by itself, without any apparent effort. At such times, there was sometimes a fleeting, almost unbound awareness of attention itself...

After the prerequisite concentration had been sufficiently mastered, further steps were taught, most of which concerned the art of learning a non-stressful maintenance of awareness, both during the waking and dreaming states. This task didn't trouble Glam, for he already had a keen sense of its goal, unstated though it was by his teachers. With minimal instruction, he repeatedly opened himself, level upon level, to the essence of this goal, letting it become not so much something that he was reaching for, as something that was foundational to him. About this he said very little, partially because he did not have a language for it, and partially because such realization was not the intention of the training. He was not as desperate as most of the other priests-in-training to grasp the prescribed progression of steps, since he already intuitively knew he did not truly need them. Still, the exercises seemed useful to him, and he did his best to master them as quickly as possible.

Early in his training, his teachers had told him that he could easily become an oracle, and that he was, in a sense, already such a one, perhaps even a potential Sirdhanan. This, to the surprise of his peers, did not interest him; it was not that he was without ambition, but that his ambition lay elsewhere. Everything that was required of him, both in the training and in Amula in general, came easily to him. Again and again, he created challenges for himself, seeing how rapidly and inventively he could respond to each, carrying out unusual intentions in his dreams, or maintaining awareness during deep sleep, or entering the ocean during midnight storms to ride enormous, dark waves, or...

Yet no matter how absorbing a particular challenge was, no matter how profoundly and lucidly he was able to relax, no matter how much praise he received, he was restless, undeniably restless. Only in the savage white passion of huge waves did he feel at peace, and then only for a short time. Yes, he could rise above his restlessness, or relax around it, or skilfully diffuse its intensity, or artfully counteract it, but he could not uproot it. Furthermore, he wasn't even sure that he actually wanted to uproot it, for it seemed to him to be much, much more than just an everyday pull toward novelty, much, much more than just mere dissatisfaction, far, far more than just a craving for some kind of sublime deliverance! The less he fought his restlessness, and the more he listened to its depths, its hidden reservoirs of condensed potency, the clearer he felt about where his interest really was.

Mount Aratisha.

In his deepest meditations, the great mountain's flawless triangle blazed behind his forehead, seeming to speak to him of a knowingness beyond all knowledge, a knowingness effortlessly intimate with Lantar. At times, his entire body seemed to be but Aratisha. However, this was more than obsession, for it did not obstruct or dilute his daily life. In fact, his passion for Aratisha expanded and enriched him, leading him not into withdrawal from others, but into fuller and fuller intimacy. How clearly his love for Aratisha reminded him that, no matter what his circumstances, he was not to merely settle into them, thereby solidifying himself, nor was he to bind himself to their repetition...

Even in the midst of his deepest pleasures, he maintained an alertness; this was not a separation from feeling, a dissociative witnessing of self, but rather a *foundation* for it, a primal base as balanced and solid as that of Mount Aratisha. His intense longing for the great mountain didn't darken his days, but illuminated them — for Glam, Aratisha was the purest form of Lantar, the most sublime shaping of all. It stood seemingly inviolable, its virgin peak rising above all his doings.

Three times between his twenty-third and thirtieth years, he set out on journeys toward Mount Aratisha, without telling anyone of his destination. Lonely journeys they were, for to make them, he'd had to push aside the rest of his life. Each time he left, the pull of what he was leaving tore at his heart, imploring him to stay, half-melting his resolve. As well, his actual feeling for Aratisha decreased as he neared it. Nevertheless, he forced himself on, until his will to continue simply collapsed. On each journey, he went a little farther, but he never came close to Aratisha. Only on his third trip did he glimpse the edge of the Great Forest, and, more importantly, that which made him stop...

His turning back was neither in response to the call of what he had left behind, nor to the common-mind fear of the Great Forest. It was, he had to finally admit, as wrong for him to continue as it would have been to slay his own child — however, it was not a wrongness in the realm of moral judgment, but rather in the realm of timing. He was definitely out of rhythm with the Great Current of Being, substituting for It the rhythms of his own spiritual ambition. Did not his impatience merely prevent the ripening of truly auspicious timing? Despite his mind's exhaustive protestations, he could not deny these realizations; he felt crushed yet oddly refreshed, for his very disillusionment revealed his next step, the one that he could now see had been there all along, obscured by his determination to reach Aratisha...

He was, he knew without a single doubt, to sail out from Amula in search of new lands! Mount Aratisha was not the only challenge! In fact, the great mountain's essence pulsated in him with exhiliratingly spacious force at the very moment he fully embraced his desire to cross the ocean. Yes, yes, yes — he would go, and go very soon! How wonderfully obvious, how beautifully sudden! He would go, whether or not he received the blessings of the Sirdhanans. With deepening joy, he knew, and knew with his whole being, that this journey to come was truly his, that it only awaited him for its fruition, that his entire life had been but preparation for it — there were no arguments within him for or against going, for there was no sense of choice in him, no victory of one aspect of him over against another, but only full-bodied surrender, throbbing with an exultation beyond all enthusiasm. Two or three months, maybe four, and he would have a canoe ready, a magnificent ocean canoe with two full sails...

Lantar, Undying One, *this* is what You truly want of me, that I cease dawdling on Your shores, and cross Your vast waters to territories unknown! How easily have I muddied Your Will with my misguided footsteps and lofty aspirations!

He was ready.

All he needed was the canoe. Already he could see it, a shining, sturdy arrow in streamlined flight across the waiting waters...

3

At Sea

Glam's canoe was the largest ever built on Amula. From its tightly woven, multi-roomed shelter to its sparkling oarlocks, it sang of superb craftsmanship and art; everything, right down to the outriggers, was painted bright green and gold, except for the immaculate white sails, which were bordered with filigreed violet. Four months it had taken to build, four months that were for Glam one long, intense day. As he'd expected, the Sirdhanans had stated their disapproval of his journey, but had done nothing to prevent it. Most of the oracles had warned against his going. Just over the horizon, one had said, lurked gigantic serpents, each of their black and red scales larger than the canoe. Others did not speak of serpents, but only of mesmerizing influences and extreme danger. Glam doubted such talk — he'd not seen serpents or any other such thing in his visions, and he welcomed danger. What would a journey be without danger? Of course, he would be risking his life, but that was merely peripheral to a deeper danger, one that he could at times vaguely intuit, but not articulate...

Three others accompanied him, all men. They left on a full moon, to the cheers of several hundred Amulans. The first three days of sailing passed smoothly, but, early in the fourth morning, the sea began heaving and bucking, rocking and shaking the great canoe as though it were but a strip of driftwood. From the frenzied tips of the waves leapt a rough wind, making it very difficult for the men to keep the canoe stable. Glam wasn't worried, for he knew they'd easily survive this aggressive uprising of ocean. At the same time, waves of sadness churned through him, turbulent and broken, as he remembered his daughter Esmelana saying goodbye to him, her seven year old face covered with tears and quivering longing. During his last month on Amula, he had subtly distanced himself from her, persuading himself that he did so for her benefit, all the while knowing that he did it for *his* benefit, so as to make their parting less painful for him. What foolishness! All he had really protected was his well-masked detachment, his less-than-full participation in their love for each other. She had not directly challenged his pulling back from her, but the hurt of it clearly showed in her eyes, especially at their parting...

Now his heart-hurt softly burst, streaming through him, rising to his throat, and he cried out her name over and over, casting it into the face of the gale and across the frothing hillocks of raging blue, his sounds full of both anguish and thanksgiving, his emerging purity of feeling rapidly dissolving the distance between him and Esmelana. None of the others noticed him sobbing and singing as he worked alongside them, steadying the canoe through the stormwhipped waters. No longer did he feel separate from Esmelana, yet how deeply he ached, his everything exquisitely and painfully alive, saturated with a dying nostalgia for what was...

Not until much later in the day did the sea settle, and the sky lighten. A refreshing wind, soft yet strong, took hold of the sails with a grace as intimate as it was efficient. Glam's companions repeatedly shouted out their relief and pleasure, laughing and joking. He watched them with tenderness, occasionally joining in their exuberance. Two were but youths, and the third, Merot, was his age. But only I, thought Glam, have any notion of what we are headed toward. The oracles, beneath their ritualized theatrics, glimpsed it, as did the Sirdhanans, though none spoke of it *directly,* not even Xandur, the only Sirdhanan who seemed to truly understand Glam's need to leave Amula. Like the others, Xandur had voiced his disapproval of Glam's journey. But had it really been disapproval? Glam's last memory of Xandur was of the old man smiling at him, his eyes bright with love and unshakable knowingness. Yet there had been something else in Xandur's glance, something that Glam could now see had actually made light of his seeming disapproval of Glam's adventure-seeking...

The wind remained favourable, and the days passed quickly. At last, they could no longer see even the tip of Mount Aratisha. Another week, and a wrinkle appeared in the horizon, taking on more and more substance as they approached it, slowly yet surely settling into the shape of a small, flat island, easily seizing the imagination of Merot and the two youths. Land, land unknown, now but a day or two away!

Glam shared little of his companions' exultation; he was strangely unmoved by the sight of this land, even slightly uncomfortable, though he did not fully reveal his mood to the others. At the same time that he was enjoying their high spirits, he kept noticing a vague foreboding bristling somewhere within his lack of excitement, but he, with some hesitation, simply dismissed it as just a bit of negative mind-creation, an exaggeration of caution, a byproduct of a mood downswing, perhaps generated by the hazy azure sameness of the last dozen or so days...

Finally, they were there, running the canoe into a muddy shore. The sky was a polished, taut blue, the trees dull green, their trunks almost black.

What an unusual breeze, its scent almost fleshy...

Turn back, pleaded something in Glam, but he remained silent. The dirty green of the trees swayed in the breeze, and so did some of the trunks. The canoe was still, the waters around it an opaque turquoise, streaked with pale brown. No, the trunks weren't moving. Or were they?

For an excruciatingly long moment, none of them stirred; then, as one, they rose to step out of the canoe. A low whistling shattered the silence, the air abruptly pierced by speeding spears, already halfway to the canoe. Two found their way through the chests of the youths. Frantically, Glam poled the canoe away from the shore, keeping as low as possible. No more spears came.

On the floor of the canoe the youths lay dying, their bodies jerking like netted fish, their breathing a spasmodic rasping, their eyes rolling with shock. Glam looked back. At the edge of the forest fringing the shore stood more than a dozen hunched-over creatures, barely human, rhythmically bellowing and pointing. An urge to murder swept through Glam. Look at these beasts, naked and covered with black hair, their mouths gaping and red, their eyes but slits! Look at them, crouching and babbling, coming out to line the shore!

He shook his fist at them, screaming out his fury and shock. His voice, which was even stronger than a Sirdhanan's, drove back the spear-throwers. Long after they had retreated into their forest, he continued to release a powerful torrent of sound, now not just outraged and fierce, but also rich with woundedness and grief.

Why had he so easily shoved aside his intuition about this land?

When they were well out into the sea, Merot pulled out the spears from their dead comrades, flinging them over the side of the canoe. Struggling to speak, he finally said, "Let us return home, Glam."

"No!" roared Glam, angry not so much at Merot's words, as at the helpless tone of his voice. Such impotence, such slouching resignation!

"We cannot go further." Merot's face was a quivering plea. "Our food supplies are low. And so too is our water. You know just how low, don't you? We've just enough to return..."

Glam stared at Merot, softening a little — he was right, unless they found another land where they could replenish their supplies. Perhaps even another part of the land they'd just left. A very flimsy perhaps... Glam wanted to continue, even though he could find no reason to convincingly support his desire. And why should Merot have to succumb to *his* impulse to go on? After a long pause, Glam sadly said, "Let's wait for a while, a day at the most; if things are the same at that time, I will go by your decision. It would be foolish not to, most foolish, wouldn't it?"

Looking at Glam with both relief and appreciation, Merot nodded, then slowly bent, gently running his hands over the two bodies. Glam did the same, immediately feeling better, riding in the bittersweet warmth streaming out of him. Soon, his and Merot's hands were softly dancing just over the surface of the corpses, tracing fluid patterns in the air, simple yet elegant gestures full of deep feeling, shaping and expressing level upon level of grief, of remembrance, of love, of magical ordinariness, all of it spontaneously interwoven by sweeps and curls and subtle bendings of palm, wrist, and fingers. Now, brightly weeping now, they could *feel* their comrades in spirit, hovering so near and so, so vivid, trembling violently, obviously still in shock, but nevertheless starting to settle into their current condition, not as visitors, but as full participants...

Dancing and dancing, dancing free the knotted self, dancing bright the sacred doors, outdancing every distraction and outbreathing every contraction, dancing free the heart of one's true ground, unspeakable Ecstasy tributaried all around, dancing and dancing, dancing fuller and fuller the death that illuminates Life...

At the very same moment, they both began accompanying their hand movements with low, humming sounds, interspersed with occasional rising notes, ever deepening their communion with the invisible yet powerfully tangible presence of their two companions. They wept freely and expansively, their tears only further empowering their ritual. How seamless was such grief, how holy and how vast! How luminously thorough its purification, how richly human its sky of sobering joy! Glam didn't notice the waves slapping at the sides of the canoe, nor did he notice the spears of sunlight raining down on his back.

Eventually, he and Merot began singing, their hands reaching up and up with unpremeditated grace, precisely and artfully outlining bird shape after bird shape, newfound wings aflutter, bodies aimed skyward. Glam's voice soared into a crescendo of pain and ecstasy and intimacy with the Source of All, the Everlasting Unknowableness, the Breath of every breath, and the four hands flew open, the fingers spreading wide, the bird-shapings suddenly gone, seemingly carried aloft by the great voice. Their comrades' way was now lit — would that they recognize Lantar in the midst of *all* they were experiencing!

Often had Glam entered realms comparable to the after-death realm; well he knew the seductive power of the dream-like scenes and possibilities that mushroomed in such locales — a flicker of mind, an unconscious yielding of attention to some desire, and, with marvellous mechanicalness, vivid imagery and persons corresponding to that particular leaning of mind, or to the object of that desire, would almost instantaneously appear, utterly substantial and convincing to those who were asleep to themselves. Only the flame of true awareness could make transparent such conditions, and if that flame was not lovingly tended during one's life, it would not suddenly appear, burning brightly, just because one had died! If communion with the truly essential had not been practised *during* one's life, it would not magically occur after one's death — and how could it be otherwise? Was not Death continuous with Life? Was not Death but a multi-dimensional transition, a gateway of sorts?

The quality of one's death had to do not only with the practice of wakefulness, but also with how one made transitions, big or small, during one's life. Every letting go was a death. If one's letting go was partial, said the Sirdhanans, then what was left over would, sooner or later, automatically create circumstances that could not help but demand the very same letting go! How common was this partiality, this chronic half-heartedness, and how very insidious! It spoke of a lack of genuine trust in Being Itself, eloquently demonstrating an unchallenged compulsion to remain in control. Glam had long ago recognized the delusion that animated this obsessive partiality — it was but the *assumption* of separation from Lantar, the turning away from Lantar. And once Lantar had been turned away from, then Lantar became reduced to a mere goal, an ineffable something to strive toward, a sublime promise dangling just out of reach, eluding every ambition, ever creating the false light of hope...

Death would not necessarily deliver one to Lantar! In fact, for the unprepared, Death was but a crucible for physical reembodiment, for refacing whatever was avoided or clung to during life. So taught the Sirdhanans, but few Amulans truly embraced such insight, finding it much easier to just mouth the words.

Letting go, letting go now, letting go throughout now, and Now... Death, the inexorable fleshing out of dreams, first in mind, then in body. Or the deeper death, the arrow's release into welcoming Light, the pure recognition, the infinite joy, the ever-virgin Homecoming, the limitless embodiment of Undying Mystery, forever pregnant with form...

Glam and Merot threw the two bodies overboard, then lay down, happily exhausted. The only sounds left were those of waves softly beating against the sides of the canoe. Glam hoped that when he died, someone like himself would clearly sing out the line of flight for him, sing out the very essence of the path he must tread, the pathless path, that profoundly individual yet transcendent journey not from here to there, but from here to a *deeper* here. But he was not ready to die, not at all!

During the night, the sea flattened. The wind had died. The canoe lay upon the water like a piece of bleached shell on an immense, deserted beach. The sails were down; beneath one of them slept the two men, their breath coming slow and heavy. Just after dawn, Glam awoke and peered out from under the sail, seeing only glassy green sea; all around him spread the motionless waters, like an endless mirror, unpleasantly, almost nauseously bright with reflected light. The hostile land of yesterday was but a humped blur, a hazy jog in the horizon. Back to sleep went Glam, dreaming of crawling along an ever-narrowing corridor, black and purplish-red, at last being forced to slide, with considerable difficulty, along on his belly, his arms outstretched in front of him, his fear powerful, his will to move forward only slightly more powerful.

"Glam." It was Merot's voice, seemingly from far away, hesitantly yet insistently present, knocking on a spectral door, knocking and knocking. "I still want to go back. Let's begin now. We will row until the wind comes —"

"So be it," muttered Glam, yawning himself awake, stretching out of his dream. "It's probably for the best." How hollow his words sounded, how suffocatingly defeated! Everything seemed dull and thick, far too solid. So back they would go. A colourless anger stirred in him, then collapsed beneath his sluggishness. So back they would go. It was probably for the best — just another letting go, right?

Glam set the canoe on course for Amula, guided by the sun's position. When the stars emerged, he'd set the course more precisely. The thought of resuming his life in Amula saddened him. Had he only travelled away from himself? Had he but put sails on his ambition? Never had he felt so alone, so painfully alone. The day seemed to last weeks. What could he do? An inconsolable longing silently throbbed in him, its rhythms excruciatingly out of tune with everything else about him. Night came, and the sky was a storybook of stars; he read them, but didn't feel them. Resignation lodged itself in his shoulders and back, helplessness in his heart, inertia in his belly. However, he had not fully succumbed — something smouldered in him, slowly eating away at the paralytic grasp of his despair...

Just before daybreak, a low, sharp breeze blew in, and they put up the sails. A short time later, the sea reared up violently, with barely a warning. A thickly folded curtain of clouds, black and puffy purple, descended over the sky; only Venus, just above the horizon, peeked out under the curtain. Suddenly, the wind changed direction, powering in from the direction of Amula, whistling shrilly, drenching Glam and Merot with seaspray. Boiling faster and faster, the clouds billowed and bubbled, darker and darker, like blankets frantically trying to cover an epidemic of grotesque births, even as lightning tore through with jagged brilliance, seemingly igniting the wind to new heights of fury.

Glam and Merot were transfixed. They could only watch as the gale seized the sails, shooting the canoe like an arrow in the direction of the land where their comrades had been speared. Neither man attempted to resist the flight of the canoe; to have fought such a wind would have been almost sure suicide.

Dawn did little to lighten the sky. The sails moaned and shook, their support poles curving close to breaking point. Yet the canoe's course was smooth and sure, ferociously graceful, piercing the waves with an intensely focussed abandon. Already they were within clear sight of the beach where the youths had been murdered. Then, within ten breaths, they were past it, the wind now even stronger. Rain blew almost horizontally over the madly dancing waves. The sky appeared to be about to erupt...

"Glam!" hollered Merot. "Can we not do something about this? If we go much further, we'll be too short on provisions for our return home!" Seeing Glam straining to hear him, he raised his voice as strongly as he could. "I'm afraid to take down the sails! If I stand, I'll probably be blown overboard! I don't even know if we can take down the sails! The wind has them in her grip so strong —"

Merot lifted his head just above the edge of the canoe, and was immediately stung by a thousand tiny darts of rapid fire saltspray, the wind effortlessly snapping back his head. Down he crouched, laughing and yelling at the same time. "No way I'm going to try anything!"

"No point!" screamed Glam, feeling along with his fear a growing joy, a fiery exultation. How magnificent was this storm, how exhiliratingly auspicious! It both drove him, and cradled him, its breath howling overhead, wailing with an intoxicating wildness. Here he was, on all fours in the canoe's shelter, feeling overwhelmingly helpless, and yet somehow protected. He remembered dreams he'd had of being in extreme peril, dreams in which he had shed his urge to remain in control, allowing himself to yield everything, especially his assumed identity; at such times, he'd almost invariably felt a joyous knowing-ness, a fathomless intimacy with That which governed all. His dream body would dissolve, and he'd then spontaneously assume a much more expanded body, or form, with barely defined contours, sometimes seeming to be nothing but unbound Light — O to let the entirety of Existence be one's body, to thus embody Lantar, in and out, everything shining with Ecstasy's Shout! In his surrender to the storm, he felt a tremendous sense of freedom. Not freedom for, nor freedom to, nor freedom from, but just simply freedom, the beginnings of unspeakable freedom, the first stirrings of a seed that had long lain dormant...

He began singing, softly at first, a song to Lantar:

> *O Father of my all, O Breath of my breath*
> *Taking me through death after death*
> *O Guide me on, guide me, guide me free,*
> *Guide me, guide me on, guide me into Thee*
> *O May I be a vessel for Your Light*
> *As I sail through the night*
>
> *O Mother of my all, O Cradle of my every birth,*
> *O Green, green heartbeat of my earth*
> *O Guide me on, guide me, guide me free,*
> *Guide me, guide me on, guide me into Thee*
> *O May I make room for Your Embrace*
> *And may I awaken to You in every, every place*
>
> *O Lantar, O Great One shining so true*
> *You do not make me right or wrong*
> *But only point me to my own true song*
> *You are the Undying One, the Everlasting Sun*
> *O Guide me on, guide me, guide me free,*
> *Guide me, guide me on, guide me into Thee*
> *As I return to You, to You, to You!*

Merot soon joined Glam, and they sang together for a long time, filling every phrase with heartfelt passion and delight, occasionally improvising on the content; they'd repeat one line many times, until it was so full that they could literally feel its essence pulsating through their entire body. Their singing didn't counter the storm, but celebrated it. At times, all that seemed to exist was a numinous dance of elements, with Glam and Merot but rapturous voicings of its sublime choreography...

Finally, the canoe was almost still. The wind had dropped, settling down as softly as a lover's last sigh. On the horizon squatted a faint, jagged tracing of bluish peaks. Seeing this didn't excite Glam; in the midst of his singing, he'd known land would appear, strangely familiar land. "Well," he slowly said, "not more than two or three sunrises away, is it?"

"Looks like a big land," added Merot. "Bigger maybe than Amula."

"I remember hearing something about the land that this may be," murmured Glam. "It was at an oracles' gathering I attended, a long time ago. Xandur sat among them, silent as a stone, his eyes looking at nothing. Yet I felt him looking at me — I'm sure he knew of my desire to leave Amula long before I did.

"Anyway, the oracles eventually sat in a circle, holding hands, swaying as one, chanting until their voices blended in perfectly with the sounds all around them — birdcalls, waterfall, wind. Then they stood, still in a circle, dancing now, graceful as breeze-stirred flowers for a while, then wild as the whitest waves, their every gesture tracing out such magic as has rarely ever been seen! Eventually, their arms gradually rose up unbidden, soft as water, rising like fire, blue, blue fire, rising up and up, until their fingertips met above the circle's very center, forming a peak. Then I understood, really understood, that they were now, without a doubt, Mount Aratisha. Its very form was written into their bodies — how clearly I could see its slopes!

"The Presence of Lantar was brilliantly intense, more concentrated than at any other oracular gathering I have attended. The oracles all began screaming and wailing, beautiful, surrendered screams, radiant with tears and minddissolving laughter. And some chilling sounds, too, pure and deep, sharp with labyrinthine terror. Xandur had not yet moved.

"At last, the oracles stopped, all at once. I remember there being a long silence, a great, shimmering silence, powerful in its own way as this storm we've just ridden. Then one oracle spoke, her voice low and steady. 'In less than two years,' she said, 'Amula will be in great danger, from within. Only the Great Mountain will not be affected. It is not time for us to speak of the danger, nor of its exact form, nor of the manner whereof it will come.'

"Her voice rang true, but not her words, at least for me. Then Xandur walked into the circle, into its center. Turning very slowly, he passed his right hand over the foreheads of all the oracles, his movements almost making me weep. The oracles' heads fell back, like wide-open flowers on wind-curved stems. Their mouths opened seemingly effortlessly, and once again their hands began to rise, trembling as if holding an enormous, unstable weight. In a very loud voice, Xandur at last spoke: 'Now say it!' And with one voice, they all cried out, 'Anushet!' As they did so, I inwardly glimpsed an unknown land, dense yet oddly attractive..."

"Never before have I heard that story," said Merot. "Do you think Anushet's the land we are approaching?"

"I'm not sure," softly replied Glam, "but I know we're not far from finding out. I did ask Xandur about it several times, but his only response was to look at me as though I'd asked the stupidest question possible."

4

Captured

The new land! Glam counted more than forty peaks, looming ever larger, some perhaps almost half the height of Aratisha. A few appeared to be extremely precipitous and dagger-sharp, seemingly impaling the almost colourless dawn. How flatly silent was this hulking landscape, and how very harsh! Its stillness conveyed more of repression than expression. Or, he wondered, was he but carrying forward the feeling of the previous land, and draping it all over this one? Was he already shielded behind dire expectation?

At last, they guided the canoe into a sandy beach, hastily moving it into the thick forest that backed the shore, remembering what they'd received a few days earlier. Towering were the trees, densely clustered, their rough black trunks disappearing up into choppy green seas. Piny and subtly pungent were the smells, sweetly resinous too, veined with meandering currents of woodrot and just-stretching greens. All over the forest floor were fat little mushrooms, glistening blue and orange, scattered in oddly meaningful patterns — ritualistic encodings of a forgotten language, mused Glam, stooping to pick up a handful of the mushrooms. He sniffed them and tossed them away, exclaiming at their stickiness. Probably poisonous, and certainly inedible... They sat down against the tree behind which leaned the canoe. Damp was the ground, and remarkably soft, almost spongy.

"Strange place," said Merot, after a long silence.

"Yes," muttered Glam. "Something strange about it."

"I hope we can find some food here." Merot's words flattened out, as though crushed by the thickly matted branchings overhead.

Glam sighed. "I'm too tired to even think of that. We'd do best to put together a shelter and get some sleep. Come sunrise, we'll find us some eating. The sails will make good cover."

Merot laughed loudly, too loudly. "We've slept a few good nights under them already, haven't we? What's a few more nights?"

"A few more nights," said Glam softly. "A few more nights. I know, Merot, that you spoke in jest, and even more in discomfort. But you need to know that exactly when you said those words, I saw the image of a reddened sword raised high by a huge, disembodied hand."

"And what does that mean?"

"We may soon know. In a sense, I already know, but I feel driven to keep that knowing hazy and indefinite, for I cannot now face more than the fact of our being here and needing to build ourselves some sort of shelter." But that was only a reason, however well-dressed — why was he speaking so formally, and why wasn't he saying more to Merot?

"And what else do you see?" blurted Merot, staring at Glam.

"Your fear." They both looked down, neither wishing to talk further. Ordinarily, they would have talked until they were fully at ease, confessing their inner whereabouts with defenceless honesty, being as sensitively empathetic as they were potent, engaging in what the Sirdhanans called "truthtalk" — lucidly and feelingly exposing inner holdings and sanctuaries of self-obsession, letting emotion freely speak its mind, letting frozen yesterday become fluid now. Glam especially had been trained in the use of such speech, but now he felt an overwhelming urge to not speak, not even of his desire to remain silent. With axe and knives, they quickly fashioned a rectangular shelter, neatly arranging it between the trunks of two massive firs. After drinking almost half of their remaining water, they slept. Not until after dark did they awaken.

"I don't like it here," whispered Merot, his voice a relief to Glam. "The sooner we can get food and water together and leave, the better for me." He hesitated, then, with considerable effort, continued. "I just dreamt that I was trapped, Glam, horribly trapped. Trapped in a small, fleshy room. The light kept getting dimmer, until I could see nothing at all. But, even though it was totally black in there, I could feel the walls oozing hatred at me, a thick, vile hate! I called and called for you, but you were gone. Gone! I'm still shivering from the feeling of the dream — it seems to be still hovering around me —"

Glam moved closer to Merot, hugging him tightly. "I too feel a sense of being trapped. If we don't feel differently tomorrow, after we've gathered enough food and water, we will definitely leave."

Glam didn't tell Merot that he too had dreamt of such a room, except that in his case the room was full of swaying swords and a heavy metallic chant. Listening closely to the chant, he'd heard its syllables with a shock of recognition — An-u-shet, An-u-shet, An-u-shet. Such information would probably be too much for Merot right now; it was terrifying enough for himself. Yet it was not just terrifying — he felt a deep inner excitement, a delicious fieriness, its flames a coupling of will and fascination.

"I'm going to go look for some food," said Merot, almost stammering, rising very hastily. "Some small animals, some tree-fruit, maybe some berries, or... In places, there's bound to be enough moonlight to see by, so..." He stood in the middle of the shelter, a short spear in one hand, hesitating, shifting from foot to foot, his eyes simultaneously blank and pleading.

Glam grunted his assent, wondering why he didn't say more. He didn't think it wise that Merot now go food-hunting, but he wouldn't speak his intuition; a deeper intuition held him silent. Something was already in motion, Merot's departure being but part of its fabric. Nevertheless, Glam was uneasy about his silence — a faceless shame wriggled through him, a shame that he tried to shrug off as no more than his discomfort with his surroundings. The memory of the oracles crying out "Anushet!" throbbed in him with a dull, dusty light. As Merot left the shelter, Glam didn't move. How inert his body felt, how horribly cramped his mind, how vacant his heart! The very air seemed to have congealed. Everything was far too solid. His breathing gradually became very slow and shallow, an almost imperceptible stirring in the dark.

A long time passed. He didn't know if he'd slept or not. It was time he arose. A good stretch, a satisfying spinal crack or two, and — he could not move! Not even his hands, nor his face! But he was awake! This was not the paralysis of some nightmare, the exaggerated dramatization of some fearful impotence from the waking state — he was not sleeping, not at all! In vain, he tried to scream. His voice! He must let it loose! Open it out, let it stream and surge and flower from his throat! Let it sing free! Let it carve a spiralling funnel through space, a bright passageway for what was essential in him...

Silence, silence turgescent and black, silence...

He tried to deepen his breathing, but couldn't. Bizarre shapings of panic madly ricocheted inside him, finding no outer expression. Perhaps if, after the next exhale, he stopped breathing for as long as possible, the eventual inhale would, in its sudden force, push out and thus free his rib cage. But he could not stop his breathing. Again and again, he struggled to make a sound, just *one* sound. O Lantar, free me! Unbind me! Come to me, come outbreathe this horribly breathing silence, come shine Your sacred Light upon me! Come to me, come now, come...

Nothing happened.

Finally, a scream came.

At first, Glam thought it was from him. No, it originated from somewhere outside the shelter! A heavy panting, carrying pullulating shreds of the broken silence, burst into the shelter, hotly stumbling. Then something very heavy crashed down on Glam, something warm and sticky-wet, something smelling of blood and sweat, drenched with terror —

It was Merot, sputtering and moaning, shaking violently. Still, Glam could neither move nor speak. Merot bled over him, gasping, barely coherent. "Glam! Glam! They are coming! Soon, very soon! We must go!"

Suddenly, Glam was able to move a thumb, then a hand, a shoulder. He inhaled deeply, but was still unable to make a sound. There was no light in the shelter. He could hear the crunch of approaching footsteps, many footsteps. Gently, he rolled Merot off him, while fumbling for his spear. Merot sobbed in great spasms, trying to get to his knees.

Footsteps encircled the shelter, dense and thudding. It sounded like ten men at least, maybe more. Glam gripped his spear, rising into a crouch, a deep rage burning through his stiffness of limb. A light flickered outside, brownish-yellow and splotchy, probably a torch or two. Boughs snapped, the walls rippled and shook in the half-light, and down came the shelter, falling in a heap to one side. More than a dozen men surrounded Glam and Merot, tall, grim figures, all aiming spears at them, speaking in a strange guttural tongue that sickened Glam. They gestured to him to drop his spear. He did.

Two of them leaned over Merot. Torch-light revealed his wounds, one in his chest and one in his neck, both bleeding heavily. Merot screamed once before they thrust their spears through his heart. Merot, speared like a fish, Merot, dying so, so fast, going now in one great shuddering paroxysm...

The men seized Glam and held him against the ground, roughly binding him with a coarse rope, so tightly that he had difficulty breathing. Merot, gone already, disembodied, gone far from here, gone so quickly, now weeping over Amula... For a while, Glam's captors stared at him. Repulsive and foul-smelling were they, their faces long and narrow, their eyes dull pits. None had any ears — obviously, they'd all had their ears severed, probably to mark them for some hierarchical purpose. His fear and shock receded before his disgust. What did these look-alike subhumans want? These angular and obscene creatures, with their miasmic eyes and misshapen features? O To eviscerate them with a rage of spears, to leave them face down in their own vile blood! O To send their eyes the way of their ears!

He still was unable to make a sound. They hoisted him upon their shoulders, emitting a few bolts of phlegmy laughter, then marched away from Merot's corpse. The ropes sawed away at his flesh, both burning and numbing it. Several times, when his captors paused to rest, he was violently cast down to the earth and sat upon, his breathing all but stopped. He must not panic, he must not make his helplessness his only reality... Finally, the darkness lightened a little, and he could see that they had left the forest. The air grew chillier as they climbed the slope of a mountain; at moments, Glam could see its peak, and other peaks, jagged and black, easing into purplish blue...

At last a bloody sunrise stained the sky. Glam felt weak and very thirsty. Most of the day was spent marching through a pass high up in the mountains. No trees or bushes here, just huge, bare chunks of uprising rock. A few birds, too, flying so, so free, their wingprints seemingly tracing out messages for him all across the sky, messages that helped him, however slightly, to soften and expand around his pain. His thirst was immense; when he moved his mouth in sign of needing water, he was only spat upon. By sunset, they were out of the mountains. He drifted in and out of sleep, yielding to his numbness, dreaming of crystalline streams turning a viscous, undrinkable scarlet...

Sometime during the night, they entered what appeared to be a city. Everywhere there were voices like those of his captors, thick with corrugated, saliva-heavy sounds, almost clanging with consonantal dissonance. He felt himself being carried down steps, many steps. Through a door they went, and down, down he was thrown onto a hard floor. The door was slammed shut, and he was alone. Over and over he rolled, writhing and gasping. The floor was wet and uneven, saturated with the smell of urine and excrement. He could see nothing. Here he was, such a grotesque, opaque here — smooth stone walls, no bed, no food, no water, unyielding ropes eating toward his bones, delirious thoughts parading through his pounding skull, sleep coming, coming, claiming his body, dissolving his agony, sweet, deep sleep, deeper than dreams...

He awoke to rough hands unbinding him. In the dim light, he could see harsh, emotionless faces — the eyes slits, the mouths rigid slashes, the heads stony oblongs, rough-hewn to the point of deformity, showing no signs whatsoever of intelligence, none! Such ugly creatures, jerking and yanking the ropes from his body, not bothering to turn their faces away from the spurt and spatter of his blood! When they had untied him, they left without a word, leaving him a large bowl of vegetables and meat, fresh-smelling and faintly steaming. Painfully, he sat up, breathing raggedly.

"Merot," he said brokenly, staring at the bloodstains on his chest and belly, "Merot, your death was an insult to you!" Anger rushed through him, swelling and loosening him, driving heat into his fists. But see his wrists! His torn flesh, his wounds! His ankles, wrists, shoulders, and lower thighs were chafed raw, wreathed in bloody hoops, stinging now, stinging horribly sharp. His anger soon gave way to sadness, his sadness to hunger. Clumsily, he crawled toward the bowl, salivary streamings bringing an exquisitely biting ache to his cheeks.

Maybe the food was some sort of poison, but who cared? It smelled wonderful. The bowl was brimming full, and warm. Tender was the meat, seasoned with a bitter salt. Good vegetables, too, plenty of them, firm and juicy. All of it was flavoured with some kind of herb, a dense, aromatic mint, tinged with a subtle sweetness. He ate quickly, not noticing the daylight brightening bits of his room. When he had emptied the bowl and licked it clean, he moved to a corner, unwilling to stretch out on the floor, which he could now see was layered with dried human excrement. There was a window, but it was at least the height of two men above his uppermost reach...

Closing his eyes, he eased himself into remembrance of Lantar, humming very softly, letting his attention's focus gradually broaden. Warmth seeped through his torso, flowing into his limbs. His spine began to straighten. Suddenly, the door swung open with a loud thump, shattering his fledgling equanimity. Five men, all waving swords, stood over him, laughing and spitting, baring their large yellow teeth at him. One placed a bowl of food in front of Glam, pointedly gesturing that he was to eat it right away. The others snorted and smirked, running their tongues around inside their cheeks, while crossing their eyes. The largest of them dropped down on all fours before Glam, flaring his nostrils and snarling ferociously, his tongue almost touching Glam's face; then up he jumped, and they all left.

Glam had no trouble finishing the second bowl, for he was still hungry. He had a sense of being fattened for the kill, like the pigs back on Amula, but perhaps it was just the workings of his fear. Thinking and thinking — yet a thought was just a thought, whether it was of being killed, or of being in embrace with Lantar. Granting any attention whatsoever to his thoughts now was a total waste of time, was it not? When he'd no more to eat, he leaned against a wall, distancing himself from his mind's disaster-filled commentaries, skilfully unknotting and dissipating the dread that kept stirring in his body, readying himself...

Some time later, the door again opened, and five men, seemingly no different than the previous five, pulled him to his feet, and marched him out of the room, into almost blinding sunlight.

One.

He didn't resist the shoves of the men.

Two.

Pink stone underfoot, cool and slightly porous.

Three.

In the distance, the pale, fuzzy distance, he could hear, clearly hear, a crowd roaring...

5

Insinuating Its Way
Across His Face

He awoke late in the day in the mountain cave, one hand gripping
Ezparya's dagger, the other stretching overhead as he inhaled deeply —
had it been only two days since he'd slain the beast in that howling
amphitheatre? Groggily, he slipped into a wobbly remembrance of its
crimson-eyed charge, its bony fury, its gleaming fangs, its tightly-curled
white mane, a white not quite as creamy as the white of Ezparya's
storm-spun hair... Ezparya, strange black flower turned toward an
unknown sun, so fiercely rooted, petalled so sharp and lush — but why
think of her? Why think at all right now? Why...

He must move on! All over the cave's walls sprawled the largest spiders
he had ever seen, bodies broad and mottled, bulging as though about
to burst, with knobby legs thick and furry, almost as long as his fingers.
And who knew what else dwelt in this cave? With some difficulty, he
sat up — what searing stiffness, what a noisy crowd of aches and
bruises! He barely noticed that his pain was desensitizing him to a
deeper pain, a pain from which he willfully withdrew his attention;
after all, he needed all his strength for movement now, didn't he? It
even hurt to turn his head, let alone roll forward into a squat. The sun
hung low in the sky, slightly squashed, more white than yellow. On the
other downside of this mountain was the shore where he had arrived
at this accursed land; perhaps his canoe was still there...

But why should he bother returning? A sudden spasm of terror raced
through him — how could he, Glam, even formulate such a question?
It didn't seem to be *his*, not at all! How could he even consider not
returning? And what was this slight yet definite grin that was now
establishing itself on his face? Shivering, he felt his face, his fingers
crawling almost spider-like across the faintly quivering terrain of his

features — it was the same face, yes, the same mouth, same nose, same contours and same texture of skin, but the very sameness of it, the well-worn familiarity, was oddly *unfamiliar* to him. How could that be? Unfamiliar to whom? He had a fleeting sense that his primary frame of reference was severely warped, shifting shape as though viewed from underwater. Or was it just that he was disoriented from the sheer intensity of the past three days? Was this all just a hallucinatory byproduct of his exhaustion? After all, he had been under extreme strain, hadn't he?

He couldn't think clearly about what was happening, though he could, with considerable effort, disidentify with his mind enough to witness his thoughts — how misshapen they were, how alien their content and tone! The majority of them seemed to be someone else's. Of course, he reminded himself in a teacherly fashion that almost completely failed to reassure him, most of one's thoughts were actually not one's own, in the sense that they merely reflected and mechanically resurrected various influences from one's past, but these particular thoughts were apparently not of that category, for they had no resonance with *him*, positive or negative. So what *did* they resonate with? What generated them? Or *who*? They did have a definite rhythm of sorts, a discordant, vaguely attractive rhythm, tinged with dark promise...

He steadied himself. Why should the appearance of these thoughts concern him? Thoughts, common or uncommon, were fundamentally but thoughts, mouthings of mind, mental automaticities, not to be taken seriously. Yes, yes, very true, but why, oh why, did his very *witnessing* of all this carry exactly the *same* unknown, strangely compelling flavour?

His grin came and went, insinuating its way across his face. Perhaps it was just reflecting an aspect of him that had never surfaced. Or perhaps not. Perhaps, perhaps, perhaps! Here he was, thinking about thinking, grasping for a convincingly consoling *something*, however abstract, gradually losing his foothold in the virgin terrain of pure observation...

What was happening? How could he be losing touch with the center of being he had been so firmly moored in for so many years? How could *he* be so easily drawn into collusion with such alien thoughts, when even his own thoughts rarely interested him, except as objects for meditative focus? Amulan fool he was, madly scrambling for a secure inner positioning, desperately looking for somewhere to stand, to take root, somewhere to reestablish himself!

Whose ravings were these? Enough of such foolishness! He picked up several rocks, viciously hurling them down the mountainside. As he watched them roll and bounce, he realized with horror that he'd just revealed his general whereabouts to anyone who might be below. Come get me, come get me... Surely there must be a search party pursuing him. The voices of Tornellas and Ezparya grew louder in him; he struggled to silence them, but couldn't. His priestly powers of concentration were not working properly. And why? Simply because he, apparently against his will, was *sabotaging* his very capacity for such concentration! As he realized this, he began to weep, momentarily slipping into an undeniable wholeness of being — how good it felt to feel such undividedness of spirit, however transitory it was!

Distant human forms were approaching him from below.

Up the mountain he fled, his heart pounding, his face bright with tears. He ran not only from his pursuers, but also from the seemingly alien quality that had taken root inside him. Taken root? Yes! And was he the soil, or that which was now taking root? Both! He had experienced, sometimes many times in a day, states of being in which he had either radically altered or dissolved his everyday sense of self, but *this* was different than that, *very* different, not only because he appeared to be without any initiatory volition in it, but also because the very position from which he viewed it, the very foundation of awareness fundamental to his being, was no longer the same...

His knowing of this was inviolable yet exceedingly diaphanous, and hence now of minimal use to him. A cousin of witnessing the witness, a blurred sense of the root of attention itself, an aborted... But so what? What use was all this to him now, what use at all? It was too faint, far too faint; there was too little of it, and too much of him!

Now men, or something like men, shouting and growling, were after him! Men, dense clusters of them, gaining on him, spear-points above their heads, waving and jabbing like the alien energy now pervading him — burrowing into him it was, cutting new channels for itself, or so it seemed. He remembered slicing open certain fruits and seeing fatly writhing worms inside, translucent and apparently blind, bulging in their moist little tunnels; this, however, was no worm, no gorged parasite, nor was it necessarily blind. Already, *it*, madly branching it, looked through his eyes. It? I...

He ran clumsily, stumbling and further bruising himself. Desperately, he looked for a pass, or some sign of a pass, but saw none. In fact, he was fast nearing a precipitous wall of rock, at least twenty times his height. Trapped! There was no way he could climb it. Yes there was, pleaded something within him, a familiar but rapidly shrinking voice, yes there was! He could do it! No, it was too steep. He hesitated, losing all drive to attempt the wall.

Spinning around, he saw his pursuers closing in on him with shocking rapidity, their spear-tips ahead of them. He bent to pick up some rocks to throw at them, but thought better of it — they could kill him as easily as he'd squash a fly, if they so desired. A faint sneer arranged itself on his face, so faint that he only noticed it as it left. Standing tall, he made a dramatic show of dropping the dagger and holding up his arms. Moments later, he was surrounded. A dozen or more spearheads hovered a mere handsbreadth from his torso, bristling with barely restrained puncturing intent.

The man who appeared to be in charge began shouting furiously; in his dense ravings, Glam heard the word 'Ezparya' repeated many times. How rabid and disgustingly phlegmy was his speech, how foul its spewed odour! There was actually foam, dirty-yellow and frothy, gathering along the inner perimeter of his lips...

Now the spears were touching him. One multi-armed thrust, and...

Looking directly at the one who was shouting, Glam said, "Anushet." His captors stood motionless, as if astonished, and the spears withdrew ever so slightly. It was because of how Glam had spoken the word; he'd infused its syllables with a power he'd ordinarily reserved for certain sacred occasions on Amula. There was an ancient beauty to his voice at such times, a spacious and sweetly poignant texture and tone that evoked long-forgotten memories in those who listened, memories of timeless moments, vivid not so much in detail as in feeling. After a brief pause, the men shook their heads and blinked forcefully, as though emerging from a dream. Quickly and efficiently, they bound

Glam, but not too tightly. Nor were they unnecessarily rough. Clearly, they had orders to not kill or damage him. Thus would he be preserved for something far worse. Ezparya's face floated before him, half-shadowed...

Toward the lowlands they went, running and walking, with their captive bouncing about upon their shoulders. Through forest they marched, giving Glam a thickly netted sky, and, eventually, the dark dampness of the forest night. He remembered being pinned in Ezparya's presence. So he was returning. What would they do to him? Torture, probably, slow torture — they must have ingenious methods. But why think of that? He was far too tired to fully feel his fear. In and out of sleep he drifted, dreaming of gazing into wildly tilting oblong mirrors and seeing only Ezparya's smile, black and ever-widening, revealing a glistening forest of teeth and a rolling sea of soft red tongue, its waves sparkling with fragments of moonlight...

He was deposited in a room similar to the one he'd been in three days ago. The same foul smells, the same dank floor. This time, however, no food was brought to him, nor any water. Daylight came and went. His inexplicable smile and corresponding body sensations occurred sporadically, but with increasing power; he felt as though he were being pulled out to sea by an undercurrent that had an unbreakable grasp on him. Yes, he fought it, but only half-heartedly...

How hungry he was, how thirsty, how crazed, growing weaker and weaker, both inwardly and outwardly, unresistingly buffeted about by bizarre exaggerations of his senses, especially in the realm of vision — the walls seemed to be crawling with maggot-fat shapings of his fear, occasionally embellished by scenarios sprouting from runaway nostalgia, the juxtaposition of the two both sickening and fascinating him. Succumbing he was, allowing himself a kind of numbing, but not fully; the flame of witnessing was almost absent in him, but not extinguished, not truly smothered, but only covered, blanketed by exhaustion, waiting for rekindling, waiting for his return...

In the middle of the night, thoroughly satiated by his phantasmagoria, he gathered his will, both concentrating and illuminating it, gradually withdrawing his attention from the demands of his appetite, bringing it to a point just above and a thumb's length behind his eyes. When his attention was at last steadily and clearly focussed here, brightly and restfully condensed, he deliberately remembered Esmelana, feeling her touch, her love, her depth of bond with him. He immersed himself ever deeper in his feeling for her, forgetting his hunger and thirst, forgetting that he was bound, forgetting his pain. Gradually, she grew more substantial, filling out his heart and easing his mind, playfully lightening him.

Esmelana! Since he'd left Amula, he, with very few exceptions, had not intentionally thought about her, so as to render his journey more single-pointed, more resolute; sometimes, however, remembrance of her had penetrated his determined onwardness, both enriching and softening him. What lunacy to so turn from her! She was his grounding in many ways, his earth, his Amulan depth and compassion, his innocence — she was not just his daughter, but his spirit-companion, his ally, a deep, crystalline pool both reflecting and clarifying his longings. Except for his longing to leave Amula...

Her love did not fuel this journey. How could it? She was not happy to have him leave her, though her goodbye had been very loving. He recalled her crying face, so open and naked, so exquisitely vulnerable, her eyes alight with almost unbearable tenderness and yearning. Esmelana! Her name rang in him, its echo both widening and soothing his hurt...

Suddenly, he felt as though he were raining inside, as though he were a lush green valley, a deep, abundant bowl of a valley, beamingly fertile, receiving a vast, warm cloudburst that flooded his rivers, his terraces, his very self; he felt himself merging with Esmelana, blending more and more deeply, expanding and yielding at the same time, surrendering to an embrace that was unmistakably much, much more than just his or hers, an embrace throbbing with the Obviousness of Lantar. How profoundly refreshing were the streamings and rushings of spirit-force cascading throughout him! How powerful this communion, how limitless this knowingness, and yet how very, very fragile...

Eventually, bodily achings started eating into his reverie, drawing him back into sensory involvement with the room. Reluctantly, he opened his eyes. A pale, sickly light filtered through the window, splattering against a wall, revealing a mottled brown surface dotted here and there with dull green. O Lantar, how came I to be here? What is Your Will? And what's this stuff about will, all this precious questioning, this stupidly earnest inquiry? Now he struggled to remember Esmelana.

"She is *not* here," muttered a blurred voice somewhere inside him. "Let go of her, and see this, this, this, seeee thisss..."

He felt nauseous. He could not help but recognize the voice as *his*, but with a slight difference, like an apple tree that had had one branch of a different variety of apple grafted onto it. However, his alien branch was now more trunk than branch, rapidly growing in all directions.

And not so alien.

6

With Ezparya

"Despicable creature!" Tornellas, hands on hips, loomed over him, her voice dispersing his half-sleep. It appeared to be late in the day. Now three guards materialized, lumbering forward, bending down, untying him.

"You assumed you could escape, didn't you?"

He didn't move. A low, weak groan crawled up out of him — if only he could pinch himself awake from this nightmare! If only Lantar would intervene! But maybe, just maybe, this *was* the Work of Lantar... And just what kind of idiotic statement was this, since *everything* was the Work of Lantar? What delusion to make Lantar into a super-parent, an omnipotent fulfiller of childish, self-obsessed yearnings! What folly to reduce Lantar to a super-doer, a Creator, a Great Somebody behind the scenes! How very easy it was to make Lantar responsible for it all, and then sit back in resentful or grovelling dependency! And how equally easy it was to turn away from Lantar, proudly deifying one's *apparent* independence...

"Your behaviour was and *is* unpardonable. But, in her generosity, Ezparya wishes to see you before you are killed. Do not feed your hope, for your death will be a very slow one, a work of art, during which you will many times plead for a quick death. Of course, your pleas will at best only amuse your executioners, perhaps even further sparking their ingenuity."

She laughed, toying with the dagger at her side, her eyes faraway. "Only a select few will be present, to witness what happens to one who is foolish enough to strike a queen."

"I am exceedingly hungry and thirsty."

"Fool! You would only vomit it all up when the first implements were applied to you, so you will not eat!" She smiled coldly. "On the other hand, there is a chance you might eat, a small chance — yes, perhaps you might, just before all your teeth are hammered and removed. You, in your ignorance, probably don't know that removal of different body parts is a *beginning* ritual of every criminal's death."

He looked down, hating the lewd cruelty sparkling in her eyes. The horror of his circumstances throbbed strongly in him, but not so strongly as his intuition that all might not be lost. The seemingly alien quality that had established itself in him was growing with abandon; he could feel its strength multiplying, wildly streaming through him, staining his thoughts and emotions, making itself at home with careless precision and a power far beyond mere force. Somehow, it fit this occasion, including within itself whatever Tornellas voiced or did, gathering itself with sinuous ease, now more a *him* than an *it*...

"Come, lowly one! The queen is ready. As I have done before, I will translate for you."

"How do I know you will do your best to be accurate?"

She spat at him, thrusting her jaw forward, her eyes a little less faraway. "Do you really think I'll even consider answering such a question?"

He stared at her, letting his powers of concentration intensify his gaze. He despised this caricature of a woman — how sweet it would be to shut her up for once and all! If only he had his strength and a sword... But how could *he* so easily consider murder?

"You have the eyes of a cornered rat," she sneered. "Or should I say that your mask of bravery does not conceal your fear? You stink of fear! I do look forward to personally witnessing your torture — I may even administer a few of the delights you will receive."

"That would be an honour," he muttered, lowering his eyes to her crotch. Such an act was utterly uncharacteristic of him, but now it seemed quite natural. "Enough of your insolence!" snapped Tornellas, her mouth twisting into a wet, faintly quivering smile. "You who are not fit to eat the excrement of pigs! Come!" Held tightly by the three guards, he followed her, his every step agonizing.

She turned once, saying, "The queen is looking forward to your visit. Do not disappoint her, or your death will be even worse." Her words only glanced off him, the black stripes on her forehead dully gleaming in the eye-searing daylight. The air was musty and clamorous, clogged with the twinned stenches of lust and fear, bustling with a miserably corralled chaos. Nausea bubbled and bobbed in him, but he fought it down; his ribs could not stand a vomitous contraction. Corridor after corridor they passed through, each one dirty and narrow-walled. Overhead were interwoven vines, thorny and purplish-green, through which he could sometimes see birds circling in lazy, patient flight, odd birds, with long turquoise tail feathers and scarlet-beaked, sharply crested heads. Tornellas walked smoothly ahead, her hair piled high, her back an arrogant slenderness, her hips tight...

Through a large, ornately carved door they walked, into a seven-sided room carpeted with bluish-grey fur. In each corner stood tall, spiky bushes with fading mauve and indigo blossoms. The walls were black, the ceiling magenta. In the center of the room was a waist-high platform covered with a shining material that Glam guessed to be silk; its iridescent greens shimmered as though viewed through a heat wave, reminding him of Amulan valleys on certain days...

"Sit here." Tornellas pointed to a spot about two body lengths from the dais. "The queen will be here shortly." She stood motionless, her eyes half-closed. Ezparya entered with five guards. In silence, she sat upon the silk, looking down at Glam, her eyes unblinking, her snowy corona of hair in brilliant contrast against the fuchsia tones of the ceiling. He felt her gaze penetrating him, probing and searching, insistently fingering its way into him. Though he knew he could resist her entry simply by shielding himself in ways he'd learned long ago, he only resisted partially, feeling deeply fascinated by the subtly inviting, definitely enticing sensations generated in him by her gaze.

The corners of his mouth slid in and out of a slight smile. What was he doing? To what was he yielding? Why was he not resisting more vigorously? But just see her clear brow and great black eyes, lit from within, oval pools as radiant as they were dark, pools whose hidden currents tugged at his very core... And see her fierce yet delicate face, so deeply gouged by the rich black line and curves of her mouth... And yes, see and feel her body now pouring through her eyes...

What was he up to? He could not feel Lantar's Current of Being, unless *this* very feeling was it! But how could that be? Were not these exaggerations of sensation simply but a distortion, a merely titillating self-encapsulation of that Great Current? Just stimulation masquerading as genuine feeling?

However, all of his self-questioning was only *superficially* urgent to him, no more than peripheral to what he was experiencing in response to Ezparya. At last, she spoke, her tongue darting and undulating between the corners of her mouth. Her voice was low and sibilant, punctuated by a sound similar to that of breaking sticks, not a sharp or crisp breaking, but a muted, wet breaking. Every movement of her face was in harmony with her vocal tone, all of it seemingly ignited by the energy emanating from her eyes.

"Lowly beast," began Tornellas with exaggerated slowness, "Ezparya reminds you of your behaviour with her." Only now did he notice the purple bruise that disfigured the left side of her face. "You dared to kick her, an unpardonable crime, an unforgivable act. Still, she says she is curious about you. Perhaps you will amuse her. She says you are hiding something from her. What is it?"

"I don't know," he stammered. Ezparya obviously felt his resistance, and probably even his uncertainty about his resistance. Now he fully shielded himself, condensing his Life-Force in his belly, fortifying it by giving it all the conscious attention he could muster.

Ezparya muttered, and Tornellas said, "She says you are lying. She says you do know what you are hiding from her."

"How could I hide anything from one so powerful as your queen? Surely she can see through me!"

Ezparya smiled as she heard Tornellas's translation. After a long silence, she slowly spoke, staring at Glam's abdomen, her tone making him shiver. "The queen," announced Tornellas archly, "is amused by your little game, pig of pigs. She does, nonetheless, grow impatient with it — she claims you are now protecting yourself with a primitive concentration technique. She asks if you want her to show you just how very ineffective your little ritual actually is.'' Without any hesitation, he nodded, letting his focus dissolve...

Almost immediately, he felt a finely honed, flaming power leap from Ezparya's eyes. Burnt-red shapes, fluid in form yet solid, seemed to congregate at his belly and throat, quickly piercing every wall of his will, swallowing up more and more of his attention. Ezparya was inside him, deep inside him, redirecting his intentions, forcing her way in, further and further, sinuous and meltingly warm, making room for herself within him with devastating power. She was much stronger than he'd imagined, almost as strong as a Sirdhanan. He could not withstand her invasion.

Or could he?

He yearned to keep her out, but couldn't help noticing that he also longed to give in. Finally, with a tremendous inner collapse, he succumbed, yielding himself totally, not just to Ezparya, but also to an unseen insistence that permeated the room, a vague amorphousness that demanded his trust. In a moment, a shadow-rippled flood of pleasure had filled him, a pleasure pulsating with harnessed fear. Ezparya's presence coiled within him, its ebony head swaying beneath a bloody sun. His fear fell back before the onslaught of his excitement, his explosively rearing exultation and engorged thrill — his heart thudding, his head falling back, his flesh consumed by a thousand almost unbearably sweet rupturings, his very being ravishingly naked in a lush, twilight-hued landscape, a curvaceously billowing terrain, pinkly involuted, teeming with itself...

Yet he did not fully forget himself. At the bottom of a chasm he might be, his feet caught in a seductively suctioning grip of exotic mud, but his hands held a fraying strand of awareness, a thinning thread of alertness that he strained to draw himself up on — he could surrender to this terrible, intoxicating pleasure, but he need not close his eyes! He mustn't! Was not the key to be awake *in* the very midst of all this, rather than over against it? Witnessing must not be an avoidance of *full-bodied* participation in one's circumstances!

It was so easy to go into meditative hiding, so easy to emotionally dissociate from certain conditions, especially the unpleasant, so, so easy to retreat from feeling, so, so easy to righteously dwell in luminous little caves of bare-bones awareness, inner or outer! The real art was *not* about detaching from passion, but rather about allowing passion open-eyed and joyous rein, yielding oneself to its *true* course, not just passively, but *consciously,* trusting it so deeply that its very momentum *illuminated* one inside and out! What madness to separate awareness and passion! In their togetherness, their sacred, lusty union, they both deepened and purified each other, emanating something beyond both... yes, yes, lovely to consider all this, lovely to reflect upon it, to freshly articulate it for some future imagined audience, but something more was required now, something more than this strange surrendering and its offspring awarenesses — Ezparya was in him, serpentine, intelligent, insistent, her movements sensuously calculating, swooning with colour, her presence incandescent ice. Was he but her playroom, an empty space in which she could do as she pleased?

Suddenly, without deliberately intending it so, he gave voice to what was happening to him, letting his passivity turn inside out. He didn't just reflect Ezparya back to herself, but directed her energies, including her hidden qualities, through the gateway of his own being, with a spontaneous integrity and passion far, far greater than he could have ever summoned on his own. His wordless speech filled the room with oceanic sounds, dark and expansively deep, rolling and splashing with hypnotic power, simultaneously murmurous and thundering, sweeping and sailing into Ezparya with irresistible abandon. Never before had he used his voice like this, not even in the most blissful moments of oracular gatherings; this was clearly the expression of something else.

The two women said nothing. Wonder and shock filled their eyes. Glam felt Ezparya's presence leave him, almost shyly, although he still felt her inside him, as though he were psychically branded with her. Gradually, his sounds softened, becoming more and more river-like, but still without any words, pouring into every crevice of self with an immensely soothing ease. Not until he attempted to bring the name of Lantar to his tongue did he stop. Lantar — how was it that he could not speak the name of the Great One? Back rushed his everyday mind into the spaciousness created by his sounds; back marched his doubts, his ambivalence, his dizzying disorientation...

The room spun crazily. Lopsided, enigmatic eyes studded every indigo blossom. The walls were Ezparya's lips, the ceiling the last moments of Merot's life, the two women blurred dream-beings. Trembling with fatigue, he struggled to remain upright.

After a long pause, Ezparya spoke, her voice full of rain and distant thunder, her eyes only faintly probing. Tornellas's voice was barely audible. "The queen will see you again tomorrow. You will not die today. Such is her mercy." Ezparya and Tornellas left, seeming to drift out of the room, and he was eventually escorted back to his room, where food and clean clothing were waiting for him.

He was not surprised.

7

Called To Birth

Shortly after his twenty-second birthday, Glam had met Oma. Almost immediately, an easy, full-bodied love had flowed between them, a friendly intimacy remarkably free of friction. Where he was fire, she was earth; where he was frontier, she was hearth. She was not at all inclined toward complexity or esotericism, yet she was surprisingly capable of articulating hidden levels of being, with an elegant economy of language. Though the psychic and higher causal realms held no fascination for her, she did not deny herself access to them, her receptivity to such matters being just as natural and unpretentious as her bright-spirited resonance with the land. Glam loved watching her work the soil or tend plants, marvelling at the grace and fertile magic with which she infused the seemingly ordinary.

More than a few times, he'd entered her garden and stood concealed behind its palm grove, seeing her naked and lithe, bending amongst her plants and flowers, sunlight and shadow dancing atop her smoothly muscled, lightly perspiring back, his eyes sketching bright garlands around her waist, his hands quivering with heated reach — behind her he'd tiptoe, his body flooded with blissful anticipation, until at last she'd turn, not always in surprise, turn slowly and lushly to face him, her breasts rising with her full-blooded inhale and delighted smile, the mossed soil behind her soon to receive their fluid embrace...

At the end of their first year together, they both simultaneously felt a strong desire to bring forth a child. Glam was a little surprised at this, for though he dearly loved Oma, he didn't feel fully bonded with her, at least not yet; certainly, they had met at profoundly nourishing depths, but there was a curious lack of risk-taking between them that sometimes troubled him. Oma was not merely passive, but neither was she challenging. He pushed aside his dissatisfaction, making inner jokes about his fear of settling, of taking root somewhere — after all, if not with Oma, then where? Why make a problem out of her ease? Why look for trouble? Having a child was definitely a risk, wasn't it? And was not their desire to do so very strong?

As was Amulan custom, they made an appointment to see a Sirdhanan to discuss the matter. No Amulan couple would have conceived a child without first consulting a Sirdhanan and getting his or her approval, or spirit-blessing. From an early age, all Amulans were taught the significance of birth. None were permitted to have children merely out of biological urge, nor out of romantic inclination; a steady, well-rooted love between the couple was considered to be of primary importance, as was the *consistent* demonstration of their love and longing for the child to come. The arrival of children was, in other words, not some kind of strategy, sentimental or otherwise, to bring a couple closer together, but rather a completely natural outcome of their *already* love-bonded togetherness...

Children born without Sirdhanan approval were so few that their arrival was usually not a matter of concern, although their parents were on rare occasions ostracized for short periods. Such children were ordinarily given an unusual amount of loving attention during their first four or five months, as well as two or three sessions of psychospiritual purification from a Sirdhanan. There were a few Amulans who took the coming of these children as a hidden boon for Amula, for their uninvitedness brought a touch of uncertainty to the steady, predictable fabric of Amulan culture, a potentially enlivening touch. However, the great majority of Amulans regretted the occurrence of such births, fearing the questionable quality of beings that might incarnate through such haphazard and irresponsible conception — in short, they wanted the security of a good feeling about the beings to come. This feeling, which was actually in substance more of a belief than a feeling, was primarily sustained by the well-communicated intuitions of the Sirdhanans, who were believed capable of conversing with those as yet unconceived or unborn. This belief was very firmly entrenched, for the Sirdhanans had often correctly predicted many things about a child long before its conception or birth.

No predictions had been made about Glam, for he had been conceived without Sirdhanan approval, his existence having been kept secret until two months after his birth. His conception, however, was no accident, nor was it ill-considered; his parents' desire for him had been deep as it was pure. They had feared that their extreme youth might dissuade the Sirdhanans from giving the needed approval, and so they had lived in a remote, almost uninhabited part of Amula from early on in the pregnancy until a short time after Glam's birth.

As a child, Glam had sometimes felt envious of playmates about whom predictions had been made. He spent much of his time making predictions about himself, donning many adult garbs in his fantasies. During his priesthood training, he tired of his futurizing, granting more and more of his attention to the qualities of the present moment, both inner and outer, as consciously as possible. This use of attention was at the core of the Sirdhanans' teachings — it required both deep concentration and an equally deep, accompanying relaxation. Few were adept at this, for it was much more than a technique; it was all too easy to lose oneself in the dynamics of activity, or to isolate oneself in the stillpoint of meditation. To be truly awake in the midst of action, without distancing oneself from one's desires or passions, *that* was the art of arts! To not meditatively separate out during the play of desire, but to actually *embody* and thus become the desire so totally, so purely, so vulnerably, that the awareness *inherently* present at the very heart of desire could spontaneously and luminously emerge, *that* was the great art! Such deep trust it took, such a raw yet intelligent welcoming of chaos, such love and balance, and yet it could be so easy...

As he matured in his capacity to enjoy the interplay of passion and alertness, visions of his future sometimes came to him, utterly unpremeditated, astonishingly vivid in detail, far clearer than his preadolescent fantasies. Some of the visions came true, though none extended for more than a year into his future. Shimmering in the background of almost all of them was the great triangle of Mount Aratisha, its slopes a rose-tinged gold, its apex blazing white...

About a year after he'd met Oma, Glam had a vision that he knew without any doubt was of events to come; rarely had he felt so shaken by precognition, and rarely had the details of a vision been so vibrantly compelling... As usual, Mount Aratisha dominated the background, its immaculate geometry pulsating with a light both faraway and tantalizingly near. Between it and him there briefly bobbed a much smaller triangle, closely resembling the sail of an ocean canoe. He gave this little attention, for he was transfixed by what was right in front of him — an amorphousness of swirling brilliance, bulging and bursting with madly writhing forms, grotesquely beautiful, spiralling in and out of breathtaking shapings, dancing so savagely and so nakedly — how sudden its lacerations and eruptions, how ferociously voluptuous its twists and turns, its multi-layered undulations! It seemed to have hands, many hands, with long crimson and ivory fingers stretching toward him, stretching and stretching, each fingertip wildly fibrillating, almost shapeless for a moment, then lucidly crystalline, whorled with masterful precision, reaching for him, reaching and reaching...

He withdrew from its touch, feeling both revulsion and awe. His senses were swooning, his heart crazily thumping, his body thrilled beyond its usual boundaries; with some regret, he further distanced himself from the chaotic wonder in front of him, until it was but a spinning blur of colour and sound. Suddenly, Oma entered his vision, kneeling beside him, her love pervading and steadying him, broadening his base. Then, just as suddenly, she was gone, her presence lingering briefly, with the same verdant fragrance as the Amulan valleys and hillocks that now billowed before him — soft and comfortingly ethereal were they, hazily infused with a sweetly stabbing nostalgia, a yearning of numinous green, so, so green, soaked in green...

How tenderly mesmerizing was the call of the land, how reassuringly enticing its fecund embrace! Again, he pulled back, breathing deeply, resolute in his movement, yet not pushing away his sadness. No, not sadness, but grief — how very wounded he felt, how strangely homesick! He didn't fight his hurt; the more room he gave it, the looser and truer he felt, the closer to...

Now his vision took yet another turn, blossoming with significance. In front of him sat a child, an infant girl, surrounded by a pale golden light tinted with delicately curling pinks and blues. Her body seemed lit from within. "Esmelana," he said, his surroundings shaking with each syllable. "Esmelana..."

Slowly, she gazed up at him, her eyes round and ancient, shining blue and violet, overflowing with mind-free emotion and a depth of recognition that made him weep with joy and gratitude. She was coming to him! And she was *here*, with him now! Her body was transparent, yet her presence was remarkably substantial. She, *she* was here! Rainbowed fountains of light danced behind her forehead, wings sprouted from her throat, oceans skimmed and stormed her skin, but the visual marvel of this, the grace and meaning of such appearances, was secondary to the overwhelming sense of reunion he felt with her, the unspeakably deep spirit bond between them, a bond unpolluted by any sense of sentimentality. "Esmelana," he repeatedly whispered, more and more softly, until he was silent. There was nothing more to say or see, just this silence to breathe in; his eyes started to close —

But what was that behind her? He looked over her shoulder and, some distance back, saw another child, also an infant, its face blurred, its body half-veiled by a rapidly swirling mist that thickened as he tried to see through it. Then there was only the throbbing amorphousness that had dominated the earlier stages of his vision, fading quickly, leaving nothing of itself behind. Only the feeling of Esmelana persisted. Thus did his vision end.

When he told Oma about it, she immediately embraced him, laughing and crying, joyously confirming that Esmelana was their daughter to be. Glam shared her delight and enthusiasm, but not fully. Of course, it was quite obvious that they were to receive Esmelana as daughter; he had no doubts about that, none! What he'd felt in his vision regarding her was far too strong to be denied or postponed — but what about the second child? Maybe it was just that, a second child, its distance and indistinct features suggesting a considerable span of time before its conception. The mist around it, though, was disturbingly similar, at least in feel, to the pulsating chaos that had danced before him early in his vision. He decided to ask Xandur about it; if anyone knew, it would be Xandur, whom he considered to be the wisest of the Sirdhanans. Besides, he was the one they both wanted to see to discuss the matter of having a child...

A short time later, they met with Xandur, who readily gave them his full approval for conceiving a child, saying not only that he personally felt very close to Esmelana, but that her name meant blessed gift, and that she had been with Glam in spirit since he was but an infant.

"But what of the rest of my vision?" asked Glam. "The great, spinning circle of colour and sound, with all its shapings? And the second child?"

"What is it to you?"

Glam sighed. "I think it has to do with me opening myself to new possibilities, especially ones that I have no control over. But that's just what I think; I really don't know."

"The surrounding chaos was of all colours?"

"Yes."

"And was the dominant colour red?"

"Yes," replied Glam, with some surprise. "All shades of red." Only now did he realize just how red-hued his vision had been.

"That's all," said Xandur. "Your vision speaks for itself; it is much larger than your scheme of things. Interpretation now would only corrupt the rhythms of what is being called to birth."

Glam wanted to say more, but didn't. He watched Xandur's eyes close, then he and Oma left the room, walking out hand in hand into the brilliant green morning. Swallows swooped through the cloudless sky, their compact exuberance of flight appearing to sign the air with 'Esmelana.' Glam and Oma began skipping and running, laughing and shouting like ecstatic children. Truly blessed was this day, this gorgeously alive day! They would have a child! A specific child, an ancient intimate, a beloved ally! Esmelana! Glam's heart surged with rejoicing — what a fine glory of benediction this all was, what a surpassingly sweet wonder, what a soaring exultation of yes, yes, yes! Through the dewy freshness they strolled, moving as one, enjoying every step; everything seemed to be celebrating with them, magically participating in their joy...

Toward the end of their walk, the blurred face of the second child floated in front of Glam for a strained moment, but he gave it minimal attention. "Let it go," he said to himself, "simply let it go, let it pass, do not feed it with worry or analysis — just let it go!" In his good feeling, he easily distanced himself from his vague forboding about the second child and the reddish chaos. Why should he indulge such concerns? Why nourish his anxiety? Why take so seriously every idiotic ripple of discomfort or doubt? Why not simply pass through distress, right to the heart of the Unspeakable Wonder That animated it all in the first place? But was he actually passing through it, or only *bypassing* it? Away, doubts, away! Why waste time rummaging around in his mind now? There was so, so much to celebrate, so much to enjoy, so much living to do!

A jubilant, multidimensional yes filled him, lifting him to overflowing, elasticizing and lightening his stride, softly yet dynamically intensifying the touch between his body and Oma's, effortlessly evaporating his thoughts. Soon, very soon, they would make love with nothing held back, their flesh but a delicious, wondrous veil for their love, their passion both uninhibitedly lusty and spiritbright, their coupling a conscious welcoming of Esmelana, as well as a surrender into Lantar...

Two months later, Oma was with child. The days passed quickly and harmoniously; never had Glam felt so happy, so richly fulfilled. He forgot Mount Aratisha. His subtle dissatisfaction with Oma and their cosy familiarity seemed to have all but disappeared. The pregnancy was enough, more than enough! Many nights as they lay together, they sang to the child to come, strong, playful, improvised songs ringing with warmth, longing, and readiness. Sometimes, they sang wordless sounds, letting their voices carry them into realms where Esmelana's being was clearly revealed to them; at such times, Glam saw the Esmelana of his vision, light-filled, simultaneously formed and formless, unquestionably aware of him.

During the final month of the pregnancy, Glam and Oma, as was Amulan custom, stayed in a small, comfortable hut overlooking the ocean. Nearby lived two midwives, almost always available to them. As much as possible, Glam and Oma became as one, merging ever deeper; almost every day, he bathed and massaged her, especially delighting in touching the great globe of her belly. How moving was the play of the child within, the tiny elbowings and kickings, the swift turns, the fluid rhythms, the seemingly deliberate pressings against the firm spread of his hands — how he loved to massage and kiss all these shifting contours! At times, he felt as though he himself were in womb, afloat in a cushioned bubble, his limbs waving slow and pure in velvet currents of warmly throbbing night, his torso bulging with heart, his spirit cupping the little hut in its palm...

He often sat in meditation for half the night while Oma slept, guiding his attention into ever deeper levels of being, purifying himself for the birth, clearing out psychic space throughout himself, establishing himself as securely as possible in the very core of his love... One night, not knowing why, he focussed in on an area a handsbreadth or so behind his forehead, something he had not done for a long time — it was a practice engaged in by the oracles when they wished to pass into particularly subtle visionary realms. It was not easy to do, for arrival there was more a matter of surrender than of journey; all attention had to be withdrawn from bodily sensation and feeling, as well as from all activities of mind. He had once mastered this inversion of attention, but had soon ceased doing it, for he had found that it all too easily interfered with his vitality, and with his sense of connectedness to the ordinary and earthy...

Now, as he entered the inner reaches made accessible by this practice, his everyday sense of self all but gone, he sensed a vague warning coming from elsewhere, like the distant cry of a gull through a stormy fog. Nevertheless, he allowed himself an ever-deepening absorption in the optical wonders of Consciousness Itself, until they were almost completely unobstructed by the apparitions ordinarily generated by the mind and the outward senses. But *what* was the presence he felt here? It was not at all characteristic of this locale — it was far too coarse, too rough, too dense, too —

Abruptly, the reddish chaos of his vision of a year ago was all around him, crowding his sublime inner sky with madly boiling clouds, bloody and far too gross for this domain, far too solid, swirling and twisting, arching and bubbling and leaping into startling shapes veined with dark promise, growing thicker and thicker, obscenely pulsating, overgrown with wildly waving tendrils reaching, reaching, reaching for him...

He could not see through it, nor could he dissipate it. *Where* was he? With a supreme effort of will, he contracted his awareness, joltingly reembodying himself, returning to the world of his physical senses, struggling to deepen his breathing, which had grown extremely shallow during the exercise. Shaking violently from the extreme suddenness of his exertion, and feeling shocked by his forced return to bodily awareness, he pushed the still-thickening reddishness away from him, until it was no more. But had it gone, or was it merely waiting for him, establishing itself in some unknown corner of himself? Doubts and questions, be gone! Soon, he was at ease, settling into the simple observation of the flow of his breath, his attention riding every nuance of sensation created by inhaling and exhaling, inhaling and exhaling...

By morning, he'd almost totally forgotten about the disturbance; the traces of it left in his memory seemed to disappear in the sparkling sunlight and salty breeze. How beautiful Oma looked! Why should he trouble her with what might have just been hallucinatory, a morbidly dramatic fleshing-out of his fear? Green was the day, easy and rich their eye contact, warm and full their touch, generous and ripe the swell of the land, gracious the Source of All!

His happiness had been torn, but he'd adeptly stitched it up again, reentering the joy and intimacy he shared with Oma. The midwives told them the birth could happen any day now. Any day now.

The birth was short, a great, pulsing wonder of powerful, fluid rhythms, a thrill of sustained intensity and deep peace, a soft brilliance of orgasmic pain and breakthrough, an uninterrupted labour of love... No matter what she was feeling, Oma yielded, screaming and weeping and growling and laughing, her eyes heartbreakingly receptive pools for Glam, pools he coloured with his own love and passion and need, as he poured all his strength and joy into her. Slowly came the child's head, stretching Oma wider and wider, its scalp wrinkled and wetly glistening, pushing against Glam's palm. A little further, and out was the head, turning now, turning up, the little face, so pinkish-blue and delicate, making Glam cry. Then out slid the body into his hands, a slippery, exquisitely tender jewel, so perfectly formed, so magnificently vulnerable!

It was a girl. Esmelana. He lay her on Oma's upper belly, her head between Oma's breasts. Then he lay beside Oma, placing one hand on Oma's forehead, and the other on the baby's back.

Esmelana! She opened her eyes and looked directly at him, a long look uncluttered by meaning, yet saturated with significance. He felt an immediate love for her, an overwhelming tenderness and protectiveness, as well as a deep ease.

Her eyes were full of ocean...

8

Her Robe
A Liquid Promise

Glam rested in his room, wondering what Ezparya wanted from him —
was it only to toy with him a little longer, to further test him, to
psychically gut him? No, it was definitely more than that, more than
the squirming possibilities paraded before him by his fear, more than
just a matter of serving her amusement. He could not help but be aware
of a growing sense of belonging here, strange as it was. And was he not
becoming more accustomed to his peculiar smile? It animated far more
than his face — the actual sensation of it kept rippling and spreading
throughout his entire body, steadily disrupting his sense of familiarity
with himself...

Ezparya, standing black and creamy-pale, diaphanously draped with
incandescent reds and pinks, so vibrant and — he half-gagged on the
word — beautiful! What was he up to? Beautiful? How could *he* even
see her thus? How could he submit to such a perversity of attraction?
His questions multiplied rapidly, jostling with one another like
gawking spectators all around the seemingly impenetrable boundaries
of a solidly alien point of view — his! Whose eyes was he looking
through? Who was doing the looking? And whose mind was this that
refused to take these questions seriously?

Thoughts of torture gnawed at him. Hopefully, Tornellas had been
exaggerating the cruelty of the queen and herself. But what could he
do? How could he survive this? Obviously, he was at Ezparya's mercy.
The arrogant bitch! What did he have to offer, to bargain with, what?
Damn her! He had to stop indulging! Was there not more here than this
useless seesawing? Was there not something significant a mere arm's
length away, something far more substantial than his fretful concerns?
Beside him, yes, beside *him*, was clean clothing, neatly folded and

sweet-smelling, its fresh, colourful symmetry easing him, its mere presence inflaming his hope.

Slowly and smoothly, he removed his clothes and put on the new ones. His old clothes he tossed into the darkest corner; bloodstained and dirt-matted were they, a torn and crumpled mass of greyish-brown, looking like little more than an eruption of the floor. Soft and silky were his new clothes, pinkish-yellow streaked with iridescent blues, loose-fitting and very comfortable. What an excellent fit! *His* clothes! Around and around the room he walked, in loopy circuits of varying speeds and sizes, repeatedly pivoting, enjoying his deepening balance. The material felt good against his skin, except where it was raw. His eyes kept returning to his wrists — what a mess they were! Torn and bumpily red, covered with overlapping scabs, wrists that had shot gleaming through the downcurling spill of great waves, wrists that had been clasped and caressed in love-making, wrists from which Esmelana had often excitedly dangled in games with him...

Esmelana! How could he keep on forgetting her? With some strain, he attuned himself to her, until he could see her sea-green eyes and open face floating just in front of him — wise beyond her seven years was she, and yet still a child, unmarred by her precocity, unburdened by unnatural demands, exuding the luminous yet earthy signs of a heartfelt, passionately *embodied* commitment to both freedom and responsibility, such commitment being not some sort of mentalized resolution, nor a submission to outside authority, but rather an utterly natural expression and companion of awakened love, a surrendered yet dynamically individuated participation in both Life's limitations and transcendent dimensions — and just *what* was it that he was committed to? Saving his skin? Who cared? Wasn't a spectral Esmelana now gazing back at him with tender compassion?

For a few moments, he basked in her look, not caring if it was imagined or not; then, with a sharp shock, he noticed unmistakable horror staining her eyes. Hastily, he disconnected himself from his vision, roughly shaking off the overlapping after-images of her shock-filled eyes. *What* was happening? Whose clothes were these? Was it that he saw himself the way she did? Her seeing felt to him to be much deeper than the product of mere imagining or worry-projection; she seemed to be a true witness to him, simultaneously ghostly and substantial, undeniably psychically and spiritually connected to him. And if she saw him with such wide-eyed fear, then just what could it be that was creating her horror?

There were no mirrors in the room. He stared down, blinking violently, at his wrists; scabby and pus-beaded were they, in stark contrast with the satiny pinkish-yellow sleeves. Desperately, he felt his face, his fingers moving too fast, searching for some sign of whatever had frightened Esmelana. Nose, chin, cheeks, mouth, forehead, sticky with accumulated sweat and dirt, lumpy here and there, bruised, tense, but nevertheless *his* face, displaying no evidence of some bizarre metamorphosis...

What an idiocy of logic! To have even considered that such a change might have occurred, he must be mad, or swaying on the verge of it! Spinning and spinning, with no sky of stars, inner or outer, to guide him, but only this filthy mud ceiling! He couldn't right his deeply imbedded wobbling, his seemingly bottomless disorientation, and, worse, he didn't know if he *really* did want to right it! This was what Esmelana saw, of course — this hideous working in him, this distorted machinery, this oozing insanity, this shapeless something that was reshaping *him* from the inside out!

His confusion billowed and stormed, squeezing itself into rabidly righteous articulations of his contractedness of being, blanketing him with all its voices and apparent choices, eluding his every effort to figure it out, to somehow grasp it and hold it still. He didn't notice that he was still walking, round and round, in ever smaller circles, nor did he notice that his efforts to understand his condition were only making things worse. Again and again, he tried to see himself through others' eyes, particularly Esmelana's and Xandur's, but found no stability, no reassurance, nothing even remotely consoling, in what he imagined they saw. The very ground beneath his feet seemed to be disappearing with vertiginous ease; this, unfortunately, was no nightmare from which he could forcibly awaken...

At last, he stopped moving, standing slouched in the center of the room, his eyes unfocussed, his breath erratic, his hands in cold fists. Lost, lost was he, lost to himself, sucked into a vortex, down and down, round and round, knotting up into a self-obsessed condensation of fear, a babbling personification of lostness — yet was he ever *not* lost? Had it ever been *truly* otherwise? When he'd felt that he belonged

in Amula, or that he was in communion with Lantar, he had not felt
lost — but he *was*, even then, even dreamy then! And so what?

He laughed harshly, throwing his head back again and again. Let his
stupid mind race around, trying to figure this all out! Let it bleat and
scold and unknowingly contradict itself! Let it impale itself on the neat
angles of all its tidy little categories and fact-crushed stories! Let it
argue itself into informational oblivion! Why should he not enjoy these
fine clothes? Why should he bother wading into his memories? Was he
not just suffering the consequences of clinging to what was passing?
Was it not so that losing one's balance gave one an opportunity to find
a deeper balancing? Was it not...

Enough! His laughter, less harsh now, sank into the walls. Sitting down,
he closed his eyes, gradually relaxing into the now welcome darkness,
intentionally dropping below his turbulence and confusion, below the
clutching insistence of his pantingly reasonable, earnestly zigzagging
thoughts, breathing more and more loosely, not looking for meaning
or understanding. Fear still coursed through him, dense and blind, but
he didn't dive into its streamings, nor did he listen when it spoke its
mind.

He knew he was at a crucial edge — one false step, and madness would
claim him. There was no way he could resolve his inner conflict, at
least for now, so he might as well do whatever he could to accept it, to
somehow make room for it, to soften around it. Yes, he was changing
on terms that didn't feel like his own, but why make a problem out of
that? His earlier laughter was alien to him, and yet now it didn't bother
him that such sounds had emerged from him — was not the familiar
but a mechanically ritualized superimposition on Beingness? Whose
words were these? Perhaps Xandur's, except that his language was less
dense. Steadily and resolutely he sat, finally slumping against a wall,
still inwardly alert, passing into sleep.

In the morning, he was taken before Ezparya and Tornellas. "Beast!"
shouted Tornellas, her eyes dramatically narrowed. "Bow to the
queen, you who are not fit to see her shadow! In her concern for you,
she has given you food and clean clothing. Do not assume you will live
another day!"

Was that a faint smile crossing Ezparya's face? Tornellas did seem funny to him, with her nastily consistent tones and rigidity of carriage; he bowed, giving her a quick grin, baring his teeth. "I would —" A hard kick in the back of his neck silenced him.

"How dare you speak before the queen has addressed you! One more such insensitivity, and you shall lose a hand. And, lowly one, your smirk of a moment ago has not gone unnoticed by me. Soon, very soon, we shall see just what sort of creature cowers behind it."

Glancing at Tornellas, Ezparya spoke to Glam. "She says," announced Tornellas in a stiffened yet slightly quivering voice, "that she wishes to know if you like your new clothes."

"Yes," he said, his heart racing.

"She wonders if there is anything else you want."

"A bath and a clean room."

Ezparya now looked at him with sudden force, her eyes sharp and round. Speaking with a lilting power, she gestured with her hands that he was to stand. Wavering a little, he arose, avoiding her eyes, hearing Tornellas say in a distinctly troubled voice, "The queen wishes to examine you. Remove your clothes."

What was Tornellas so bothered by? Why was she not enjoying the play of her queen with him? Three guards moved behind him, their swords unsheathed. Another five stood behind Ezparya as she approached him. Awkwardly, he took off his clothes. She stood directly in front of him, gazing at his face. Though he wasn't looking into her eyes, he could feel an intense force emanating from them, and something more, something pulsating with reach... Thin was her nose, yet full-nostrilled. Black-painted were her lips, surprisingly well-formed, trembling ever so slightly above the delicate mound of her chin, parting once as her tongue slid glistening and pale red between the corners of her mouth.

He felt her gaze descend to his chest, and then to his belly. Fear and excitement churned in him; it felt as though her looking was unlocking his torso. Now her hand was on him, on his belly — a light touch it was, alert and probing, precise and sensitive, knowing and easy, a faint pulse in each fingertip. Hard as it was to admit, he liked her touch. It was soothing, even relaxing, full of presence. There was a coldness too, not of temperature, but of compassion, and below that, a warmth, a wild heat, a luxuriant depth of desire, and below that, a frozenness housing something that —

Suddenly, she let one hand drop down to his genitals.

At first, he was frightened, remembering the castrating intent of her dagger of not so long ago. Her hand, however, carried no trace or promise of such violence; in fact, it cupped him with deliciously compelling force, firmly yet fluidly receiving his rushing heat, his swelling size. For a moment, he tried to withdraw energy from his genitals, to somehow ice his desire. Then, as if drawn up by an irresistible force, he lifted his eyes and looked directly into hers, his penis rapidly rising into a full erection, throbbing up and up, aching with an almost painful pleasure and urgency, thrillingly engorged with longing, filling out her hand.

Half-smiling, she stepped closer, placing both her hands along the shaft of his erection, letting its head lie against her upper belly. Her eyes, bright with black flames and knowingness, drew him in, and drew his desire out, further and further; he felt her enwrapping him, sheathing and inflaming him, riding with him the waves of rapturous insistency now permeating his entire body. Looking down, he saw that the thin silken fabric of her robe was thrust out by her stiffened nipples, its almost transparent, pale turquoise sheen rippling with her every breath, shimmering and undulating with sensual invitation...

Never before had he felt lust like this — its heat was not just toward release, nor was it, as far as he could tell, simply generated to fuel some spiritual or psychic technique. It was a lust free of any activity of mind, a lust intimate with more than its own imperatives, a lust that in its very intensity somehow transcended itself, without losing any of its force. It was a lust charged with ascent, with a sense of rising brilliance. But...

Ezparya withdrew her hands, and closed her eyes. A coolness, spacious and snowy-blue, slowly descended over Glam, and his entire body relaxed, letting go of its orgasmic yearnings with remarkable speed. However, this was not a repression of passion, but rather a diffusion of passion, an expansion, the release of an awareness that had been coiled *within* the fire of his lust!

All of his flesh tingled with a blissful, unsedated ease, even as a remote revulsion nibbled ineffectually at the edges of his mind. Gracefully, Ezparya turned and left the room, her robe a liquid promise in the dancing shafts of morning light.

"You may dress now," said Tornellas at last, her voice almost inaudible. "The queen will see to it that you are bathed soon."

She started to say something else, then stopped, and quickly left, her back rigid, her stride brittle, her robe a dark blue storm, full of fisted lightning and twisted fury. As she passed through the doors, she snapped at the guards, and Glam was taken to a clean, well-lit room.

It had definitely begun.

9

When Esmelana
Was But Three

When Esmelana was but three, Glam made the second of his three trips to Mount Aratisha. His turning back was even more disappointing than the first time. The peculiar inertia that had invaded him as he neared the Great Forest was maddeningly immune to his will; at a certain point, there'd not been anything more he could do to take another step. Bitter he was, but not so bitter as to obscure his sense that he was no mere victim of some external force, but rather a participant, however unwilling, in something that required not only right timing, but also impeccable intent.

And what was his intent, his true intent? Was it other than to reach and ascend Aratisha? Yes. Perhaps it was more hidden than true, but it could not be denied — was he not, the smooth-domed words slowly crowning as he grimacingly birthed the question, half-wanting to look away, was he not, the question now skywide and naked, its cord pulled tight around his chest, was he not, in fact, actually *hoping* to be somehow magically altered by such a feat as climbing the great mountain? To be delivered once and for all from his suffering? What supreme foolishness to thus burden his potential climb with the obligation to somehow transform him! Hope, ever addicting one to mere possibility; hope, the mind-riddled romance with Later; hope, nostalgia for the future...

During his return, he felt both restless and bone-weary. Although he looked forward to seeing Oma and Esmelana, he felt more disinclined than ever to continuing his life on Amula. What he yearned for lay not just in the rearrangement of his lifestyle, but *outside* it; knowing this brought him no relief, for the *how* of it was consistently vague to him, and besides, how could he even consider leaving Oma and Esmelana?

Late one afternoon, he reached his house, exhausted and gloomy. Esmelana ran out to him, crying and stumbling, and he picked her up, immediately feeling better, loving the uninhibited passion of her little arms around his neck, the pure pressing of her need against his flesh — he had sorely missed her, and she him, but why was she trembling so violently? His heart shuddering, he asked her where Oma was.

She didn't answer.

Gently, he pulled her head back, telling her to look into his eyes. There was such pain in her gaze that he began to weep, knowing exactly what she was going to say...

"Oma all gone!"

"Gone?" he whispered, summoning his disbelief. "But...

Then he noticed two priests standing in the doorway. "She drowned yesterday, late yesterday," said one of them softly. "Her body is in your bedroom."

He stood wobbling, utterly speechless, feeling waves of ice-blue shock slamming him against a barren, rocky shore. Not unkindly, he motioned to the priests to go, observing his gesture as though from a great distance, a frozen distance rigidly calm and deadly still beneath its sagging sky of barely-contained blues and blacks. Let it rain, let it break and burst, burst open! No tears came, but his numbness loosened a little, thawing here and there, until he could again *feel* Esmelana in his arms, shaking with great sobs. Breathing deeply, he carried her into the bedroom he had shared with Oma, the bedroom where they once had...

For a long time, he stared at Oma's body. Beneath its silvery garment, it was bluish-pink. The face was lightly bruised, the eyes closed, the lips parted, the hair golden-brown, so soft on the pillow, so very smooth between his trembling fingers — her sweet, loving body, once so brightly animated, so graceful and easy beside him, now but an empty shell, totally abandoned!

Empty was the room, dead its silence, enlivened only by Esmelana's sounds. Where was Oma, where was disembodied she? Better ask, where was *he*? Wandering through the feeling of no-feeling, all but oblivious to Lantar, registering no more than mere information, yet how could such neatly noted facts cast such thick, crazily bulging shadows, shadows howling with dizzingly bloody fissures, shadows squashed and gutted in the horribly compressing silence, this silence so oppressive and screaming for its own death...

It was too, too much, too sudden, much too sudden!

The broken music of Esmelana's crying finally broke through his shock. A huge wave of emotion, churning wild and thunderously blue, burst through him, flooding away his hearthold, undamming his hurt, and he slowly sank to his knees, his head falling beside Oma's. Still holding Esmelana, he let himself weep and wail uncontrollably, allowing himself to fully remember Oma — her love, her earthiness, her ingenuous smile, her eyes soft yet direct, eyes that now, sobbing now, bright and excruciatingly painful now, seemed to be gazing at and into him with infinite tenderness and sorrow. "I am gone," smiled the eyes, "yet I am not gone. Feel me now, feel me with you. Be with me now..."

Now he yielded even more fully to his grief, letting its currents possess and cleanse him; he cried for his loss, and for Esmelana's, and finally he wept with gratitude for his time with Oma, especially when she'd been pregnant with Esmelana. His tears both mourned and celebrated her. When the ache of his grief had subsided, he deepened his communion with Oma's spirit-presence, singing it toward the Light of Lights, the Great Flame of Lantar, his instructions melodic and precise, passionately threaded by his goodbye, a goodbye both wounded and joyous, seeded with an eternal hello...

In silence he sat at last, a luminous, ecstatically sobering silence, resting in Oma's depths, feeling himself lovingly enwrapped, cradled like a newborn baby. Gradually, what was left of Oma faded, leaving him in an even deeper silence. Esmelana slept in his arms. From now on, he would be both mother and father to her...

10

To Unwrap His One Gift

In her room, Tornellas wept bitterly and silently — how could Ezparya do what she had just done with the stranger? How could she allow herself to engage in such a disgusting display of lust? Admittedly, Ezparya's was not commonplace lust, but it had been such a flagrant *exhibition*! And the stranger, repulsive beast, of course had almost *immediately* succumbed to the heat of the moment — why hadn't Ezparya had him killed? Why? Over and over again, Tornellas asked herself this question, viewing it from many angles, even though she knew the answer.

His voice.

There was not only power in it, but something else, something vaster, something that Ezparya wanted, and didn't Ezparya always get what she wanted? Always! Did she not have full use of Tornellas's gifts? After all, without her, she wouldn't be able to converse with the despicable alien, although she could probably probe her way into his speech patterns easily enough to grasp much of what he said...

Tornellas felt a surge of hate for Ezparya, hard and icy-sharp — how calculatedly and how cruelly the queen used her, how insensitively! Ezparya, with infuriating arrogance and nasty delight, even used Tornellas's hate of her to serve her own ends, while tacitly *daring* Tornellas to expose her venom, to, as it were, fatally slip. But how sweet it would be to have their positions reversed! Then, delicious then, they would see who would squirm!

Tightening her jaw and neck, she arose and went to her mirror. For a while, she critically studied the long, slender face staring back at her, especially noting its full, almost protruding lips and dark, wide-spaced eyes with their slight tilt. Maybe it wasn't as curvaceous or striking as Ezparya's face, but nor was it as showy! All in all, it wasn't a bad face, though the nostrils could probably use a little more flare, and the jawline a little less definition. Her hair, of course, needed no alteration whatsoever; it was thick and gleaming black, just curly enough, its ends tipped ever so slightly with red. Carefully, she painted her lips and eyebrows a shiny indigo — at least she had eyebrows instead of bird feathers!

The vertical black lines on her forehead needed no touch-up of paint, for they were stained deep into her skin, signs of attainment in the arts of interiority practised most profoundly by Ezparya and the temple-masters of Anushet. And, as well, her abilities as a torturer were second to none, were they not? A bolt of pride stiffened her spine, pulling her head back just enough to please her eye. If it was up to her, as it ought to be, she would torture the stranger, introducing him to a fear beyond any fear he'd ever known! The thought gave her pleasure — she would surely enjoy seeing him writhe and slobber for release!

Her mouth watered, its lips unconsciously parting, quivering and swelling with caged hunger — the stranger, the loathsome beast, exposed as he truly was! His everyday facade gone, his *real* face squirming and frantically pleading, its naked agony only driving her to further inventiveness, to even more brilliant creative twists and cuts! Flesh-hooks, barbs, eye-pins, and fire-probes were musical instruments to her, tools whose proper and aesthetic use both thrilled and focussed her, sometimes bringing her an exultation deep and diffuse, a hot, melting swoon streaming through belly, groin, and skull, reducing her tension and worries to luxuriant lagoons of exhilirating calm — such a joy, such a fine treat, were these cascading starbursts of sensation, orgasmically inflaming, then soothing her, so dark and rapturously peaceful, so...

Her teachers had often praised her cleverness, though they had occasionally admonished her for losing herself in the pleasures she felt during torturing sessions — what blindness to so accuse her, what a silly, stupidly conventional narrowness of perception! But why fret about this? Rarely did she even get to apply her torturous arts now, since she was so busy being Ezparya's translator and obedient ear. Her gifts of translation were considered to be far more valuable than anything else she could do, especially given the steady influx of strangers to Anushet — fools, all of them, disgusting barbarians, cowering and begging, stunned by her mastery of their tongue, bulgy-eyed in the amphitheatre or, far too infrequently, in what she liked to call her toolshed. She hated serving as Ezparya's translator and, even more so, hated knowing that she had no choice; it was either be translator, or be put to death. Unfair as these were, they were the conditions set forth by Ezparya and the temple-masters.

Tornellas fumed — how much longer would she have to speak the ridiculous language of this latest stranger? It was a soft, lilting language, a real strain for her to speak. Its extended vowels and overly sibilant moments of punctuation and emphasis infuriated her; she wanted to crush the velvet undertones, the green waves of it, to hack off its tongue...

Harshly, she cut off her musings, watching her reflection smooth over its fury of thought, efficiently arranging its features into something more composed; nevertheless, she couldn't entirely calm herself. Soon, she reminded herself almost aloud, she would be meeting with Ezparya and the head temple-master, Artakiab. She must ready herself!

Ezparya sat with Artakiab in a dark red room, awaiting Tornellas. Neither spoke. She appreciated his company; he was one of the very few who wasn't afraid of her, perhaps the only one. Several times, she glanced at him; his eyes were closed, his body still, his presence all through the room, his energy heavy yet extremely agile, resolutely unblinking, steady and hard as the gnarled wonder of his body. None in Anushet, including her, had taken their open eye to such depths as Artakiab — his center of knowingness was an unmovable anchor, densely encrusted with his triumph over the forces that kept others asleep to themselves. He had been her main teacher, and in some ways, still was...

The door swung open. Tornellas entered and sat, her face expressionless.

After a long pause, Ezparya said, "Our subject matter is the one called Glam. Ordinarily, we do not keep our aliens for long. They feed our beasts or, when necessary, the hunger of our torturers." She smiled at Tornellas. "But I do think we should keep this one a little longer."

"For what purpose?" growled Artakiab, half-opening his eyes.

"There is an uncanny power in his voice. Not in his regular speech, but in response to my mind-touching."

And your hand-touch, thought Tornellas, tightening her lips.

"He attempted to resist my entry," continued Ezparya, "but was only partially successful, due to his use of a concentration ritual, through which he balled up his attention in his belly. Then his resistance shattered, and he sang out in a voice that drew me toward something unknown and oddly attractive, something of mysterious radiance and even more mysterious significance."

Artakiab creakingly turned his gaze to her. "Attractive in what way?"

"That I intend to find out, and that, my dear Tornellas, is why you are here — I want you to befriend Glam, to do whatever you can to uncover the more important, or shall we say intimate, details of his life, without, of course, revealing the purpose of your little visits."

Tornellas visibly stiffened, her cheeks suddenly crimson. "Does it matter at all that such a course of action goes totally against my wishes?"

"You already know the answer to that!" snapped Ezparya. "I am surprised you would even ask! You should remember that it is not in your best interests to let your hostility toward me slip through so blatantly — do not assume, my charmingly hateful Tornellas, that you are indispensable. Valuable, yes; amusing, yes; indispensable, no!"

"I will do everything I can." Tornellas hardened her gaze, trying in vain to still the trembling around her mouth.

"Thank you! I am sure you will. Your efforts will not go unrewarded. You may go now." As Tornellas rose, Ezparya laughingly added, "One more thing: Though you may be tempted to, do not under *any* circumstances engage in sexual activity with Glam."

"Yes, my queen," murmured Tornellas, moving like a gliding statue from the room, her face red ice, her hands curling into white hooks.

After a short silence, Ezparya said, "Her hatred of me serves me well; it keeps her close to me, constantly aware of me."

"That is not what you wish to say to me," said Artakiab, his words slow and leaden, ominously thudding, like the approach of monstrous yet unseen footsteps in some thick, black nightmare.

"Your insight is most admirable! I simply wanted you to bear witness to Tornellas's agreement, and to give me your opinion about what I have asked her to do."

"Will my opinion make any difference with regards to your intentions?" The footsteps grew much louder, almost metallic, oozing with bloated violence.

"Not necessarily, but I still want to hear it."

"As you request," muttered Artakiab, smoothly shifting his body to face her. "You are making a mistake." The footsteps thundered closer and closer, saturated with claustrophobic echoes, then halted outside a suddenly bloody door, panting inhumanly.

"How so?"

"By enslaving yourself to a whim." The door, even bloodier, began to throb and rattle.

"And why would I do that?" Now she was straining to maintain center, feeling fear blossoming in her, its bouquet starting to poison her ease.

"That, Ezparya, is for you to discover." The door blew open, revealing a gigantic black shaping of her fear, its eyes yellow-red and melting, its fangs leaping forth from all over its pullulating flesh, its fingernails long and jagged blue, almost touching her throat...

No! She looked through the apparition, no longer giving her fear any attention, though its byproducts still ate into her body. With some effort, she smiled broadly, declaring, "So I'm making a mistake, am I? Perhaps I am just chaining myself to a fascination, creating a gap in my power, as you would put it. Nevertheless, I am going to go ahead anyway. I am well aware of the risks."

"I'm not so sure you are." His eyes began glowing with a dull reddish light. "I can see you have already admitted some of the alien into yourself. An infection has begun. There is still time to cleanse it, and be done with it. Such is my counsel."

"Thank you, Artakiab. I shall do my best to not get infected! But, before you go, please just tell me how you can be so sure that it is a disease that Glam brings?"

He stood, his body twisted into a dense harmony of unnatural curvings and knottings; storm-winds seemed to circulate around him, almost as if shaping him, yet held firm by the great force that emanated from him. "It shows in you, Ezparya. Even now, you are defending its entry in the very way in which you are addressing me."

"But perhaps I am defending its entry because I sense its value."

"I will not argue with you, queen."

"I wish you to see Glam at some point."

"As you wish." He left the room, limping slightly, his brokenness of movement somehow increasing his stature.

Crippled with wisdom, thought Ezparya. They had differed before — why should this be any different? It was her will that Tornellas study Glam, and her will was supreme, regardless of how much or how little she tempered it with Artakiab's advice. She wished, though, that he had supported her desire; that he hadn't both bothered and excited her. Naturally, there was a faint danger, a remote possibility of danger, in keeping Glam, but she had more than enough power to handle whatever dangers might emerge. Was she not the queen of Anushet, with as much power as any temple-master?

Glam was no match for her. So what could be the danger?

She only wished to unwrap his one gift, and then she would give him to Tornellas as a gift! Tornellas would be more than ready for such an offering by that time, wouldn't she? For a long moment, she lingered over the image of Tornellas applying all the arts of her cruelty to Glam...

So much for the danger.

11

A Fire
He Could Only Welcome

"Up you get!" Tornellas, without knocking, pushed open his door, followed by three guards. "We can talk for longer this time."

He sat up on his bed, surprised to see her — the evening before, she'd come to his room for a brief stay, asking him in very formal language some questions about Amulan geography and customs. He had answered her concisely, then she'd left without saying anything more, her exit cold and brisk...

"About what?" he yawned, making a show of stretching.

"About whatever *I* want you to talk about! I will ask the questions, and you will answer. Is that clear?"

"Yes, but why do you want to know anything about me at all?"

"I said *no* questions! Any more, and I shall have the guards teach you the meaning of obedience. Now, tell me about your early years, from the very beginning, in detail."

He coughed, saying nothing, acutely aware of her discomfort in making such a request. She tapped her feet impatiently, then hissed that he was to speak immediately. Dropping his head, he remained silent, bracing himself for the attack he was sure would come — he must risk this! Perhaps there was something to be gained by withstanding her; it was possible Ezparya even expected him to! These were, however, just reasons, hastily arranged presentations of poorly anchored logic, much shallower than his actual impulse to defy Tornellas, an impulse he knew he must trust, however uneasy he was with it...

At a word from Tornellas, the guards grabbed Glam and stretched him out on the floor. He didn't resist.

"Speak," said Tornellas, "or you shall regret it."

"What is your interest in me?"

"Enough of your insolence!" Kneeling, she removed the ring from her little finger, and began grinding one edge of its sharpened stone into his temple, dragging it down toward his ear, twisting it in a zigzagging pattern. She worked slowly and carefully, panting slightly, her breath aromatic and warm. He pulled away from his pain, confining his attention to his exhalations, making them as long and even as he could — but why bother, when it was so obvious that he couldn't outlast her? Already she, with her hair rhythmically brushing his forehead, was starting to cut into the flesh that joined his ear to his skull, throatily whispering, "Speak, or you shall lose your ear, and more. This is only the beginning, an unusually gentle beginning, a mere taste of the feast to come..."

"I will," he groaned, and she stopped, signalling to the guards to release him. Dizzily trembling, he sat up, blood running from his wounds, its rivulets fanning all over his shirt. How smug Tornellas looked, how nastily intoxicated! How he would love to just take her flushed face and quivering little grin and give her —

Away rage, away! This was no time to cut loose! Besides, did she not see his fury, and was she not actually deriving undisguised pleasure from it? He watched her slip her ring back on, its translucent purple stone meticulously and efficiently wiped clean of *his* blood, while he calmed his face, letting his anger recede, gradually reducing it to a far-off, dreamy squall poised above a midnight sea, fragments of moon dancing atop its velvet waves...

"Your parents. The conditions of your birth. In full detail!"

Fighting to steady his voice, he described his parents and birth, listing fact after fact, feeling no interest in his list. Tornellas, though, seemed remarkably hungry for his information. On and on he talked, without any emotion, but suddenly —

With no build-up or warning, there was something here to be spoken, something he had not even told Oma, and here he was unable to stay silent about it, in front of this heartless caricature of a woman, this subhuman who kept looking at him with unbridled scorn!

The story demanded that he tell it.

"My sister," he stammered. "My sister, my twin sister..."

"Well, what about it?"

He shivered, feeling the words assembling in his chest and throat; an overcast sadness seemed to be about to engulf him. "My twin sister, if you could call her that, followed me out of my mother's womb, stillborn. The midwives told my parents that she'd been dead for at least seven weeks."

He hesitated, and Tornellas narrowed her eyes. "Come, lowly one! What was done with this darling twin of yours?"

"The midwives consulted with a Sirdhanan, who commanded that it be burned as soon as possible. The cremation occurred when I was three days old."

"It?" sneered Tornellas. "*It*? Just *it*? Then why such a display of emotion? I can read you, you know. That little lump of cold flesh was, and *is*, clearly much more than a corpse to you."

"That is true."

"And how could that be?"

Again, he felt an urge to not speak, but at the same time, an even stronger urge to speak arose in him, accompanied by a lithe, strangely powerful confidence that, apparently without his bidding, effortlessly filled him almost to overflowing. Softer now was his focus, more spacious the room, easier and easier his speech...

"Partway through my priesthood training, we were guided into recollection of our distant past, beginning with forgotten yet significant events from infancy and birth. At first, our remembrance was but

superficial, no more gripping than everyday fantasy — it was as if the
viewed scenes featured someone other than ourselves. Then, with
masterful skill and care, our detachment was thoroughly shattered,
broken beyond all mending, so that we had to feel, really *feel*, the stuff
of those memories.

"The very depth of our emotional response created a very strong sense
of continuity with the *essential* self of the memory; it became quite
easy to see how we had, and still were, *literally* embodying our past,
especially our wounded or unresolved past —"

"Yes, yes!" Tornellas glared at him. "Enough of your little lecture!
What about your sister?"

"I fought remembering her. I didn't even want to recognize that there
might be such remembrance. Other events, many of them clearly prior
to my conception, came to me, sometimes magnificently fleshed out,
populated by oddly familiar beings, some of whom I knew to be — "

"Get on with it!"

Her irritation glanced off him. Look at her, leaning forward, shadows
lightly prancing across her too-earnest face, her eyes glistening and
taut, and behind the tautness, far behind it, a child, vague and almost
faceless, trying to scream... Look at her, caressing her purplish
cutting-stone, her fingers like ivory snakes, probably hoping for
another opportunity to hurt him. But why would she do that when
she was obviously so interested in what he was saying? Was not her
impatience but the corset of her curiosity?

"At last I let myself remember her fully. Xandur the Sirdhanan guided
me through the necessary trance and cathartic states." For a moment,
Xandur's unwavering yet tender gaze flickered before Glam, like a star
in a misty night. "My memory of my twin was a tremendous jolt to me,
a little like the feeling in the midst of a nightmare when you realize that
you are actually dreaming. My parents had never mentioned her to me,
but they did confirm the accuracy of my memory when I told them of
it. I was in agony in my recall, feeling her as I did beside me in our
mother's womb — it was a terrible intensity of pure feeling, unrelieved
by any protective numbness! I could not escape her dead flesh, her
suffocating inertness!"

"But when she was alive?"

"Joy! Joy deep and unbound, a joy that I only remembered *after* fully feeling the hell of all my weeks of being pressed against her corpse... It was a joy of companionship, wonderfully constant, both of us floating and touching, swooning to the rich beat of our mother's blood. We had an almost uninterrupted communion of spirit, a lovingly shared awareness that extended far, far beyond our bodies. It was a time I cannot now forget, no matter where I am. It was exceedingly painful to recall her death. She simply left. Left without warning, without any warning..."

He paused, sighing. How strange this was, to be telling such matters to this odd, unfriendly woman, with her painted forehead and hard eyes; she was, however, listening intently, her eyes not now so hard. "I remember," he continued, "suddenly not feeling her presence. There was no life-force left in her body, though it still moved about in the womb, probably because of my movements. Her absence ate into me; in my own way, I began searching for her, but in vain. I, still not born, could neither locate nor sense her spirit — it too seemed to have vanished.

"As I said before, my grief upon remembering my loss was overwhelming. I even, for a while anyway, felt responsible for her death, though my teachers repeatedly told me that her death was not my fault. Gradually, they helped me abandon my guilt, saying that her departure was simply a matter of her being called elsewhere; such words comforted me, helping me accept the fact of her death, though I must admit I did secretly yearn to know that elusive elsewhere... The time of that remembering seems long ago, quite vague now, but I cannot forget the one who was my sister, my dark yet luminous intimate, my twin!"

Tornellas laughed loudly. "You are *still* haunted by her, aren't you? You stoop beneath what you have made of her — I doubt that you have truly disengaged yourself from her. Her departure, as you put it, is not the issue! I look at your eyes, unpleasant as that is for me to do, and I see a romantic. You are the type who slobbers meaningfully before their heart! Disgusting isn't it, this ardent grovelling before mere emotion?"

"And you, what do you *do* with your heart?" he asked heatedly. Her words had burned into him, corrosive and icy; they wouldn't have hurt him if he hadn't been so stupidly open, so unguardedly vulnerable. The smug bitch, with her wasteland of a face and nasty slash of a mouth! The cut on the side of his head throbbed painfully.

"I do not let it control me," she replied scornfully. "That is but one of the differences between us. Now, before you get too upset, do continue, and please, please spare me the sight of your tears!"

"One of my teachers said that only those who fear the power of the heart seek to control it."

"Garbage! Sentimental, simplistic garbage, masquerading as wisdom! Teachers? Pitifully inept, ignorant of real mastery, though no doubt well-meaning, as are all fools. Now, foreign beast, do continue with your tale, and know that if you insist on resisting me, you shall regret it! I have neither the time nor the desire to lower myself to argue with you — I would only consider doing so if you displayed more than rudimentary signs of intelligence."

He struggled to control his rage — he mustn't let her get to him! It was very difficult to not scream at her, almost impossible. Then, in the midst of his temptation to let loose his fury, a knotted trembling bolted through him, rippling rock-hard, and he smiled at her, feeling the upturned corners of his smile clawing the heart out of his eyes, quickly sucking and squeezing the life out of his vulnerability...

Still smiling, he said, "Of course! How extremely inconsiderate of me to try to engage you in dialogue! Thank you for reminding me of my position. Now, shall I continue with my history?"

"Yes." Her compressed, quick smile only partially masked her confusion. How gratifying it was to see that tiny flicker of uncertainty in her eyes! Speaking smoothly, he described his early adventures with the ocean, emphasizing the beauty and power of its waves. He had only been talking for a short time when she almost embarrassedly interrupted him, saying in a loud, flat voice that she had heard more than enough, and that he should be prepared to tell her more the next day. She looked at him closely for an instant, then left. Never before had he noticed the dark green streaks in her eyes...

The following morning, he again talked to her, insulating himself from her coldness, making sure he didn't reveal himself any more than he wanted to. Her motive in seeing him wasn't clear to him; it was quite obvious, though, that she wasn't enthusiastic about coming to him. She did very little to disguise her scorn for him, repeatedly yawning and grimacing with irritability.

Yet there was more than scorn, more than disgust and distaste, more than a nastily unwilling ear — there was undeniable fascination, wriggling around behind her display of contemptuous sophistication. He was, he knew, actually addressing her fascination, however clumsily, however inadvertently! He must let his speech be an arrow, a straight, muscular flight right into the very core of her curiosity! Inwardly, he asked for the guidance of Lantar a few times, but his prayer rang hollow, rapidly shrivelling to nothing. He could not feel Lantar, nor did he know if he even *wanted* to feel Lantar — but then what *did* he feel? Only this meandering struggle with his hate-filled interrogator? Only this urge to survive?

Yes, and something more, a deeper urge, another passion that was growing day by day, strong as the stormiest lust, but much richer, an ever-swelling current that was compellingly winding its way through him, smiling his face and shaping his stride, catalyzing and directing more and more of his intentions, empowering him in unusual ways, *changing* him, radically changing him! Yes, transforming him, but *only* because he cooperated with it, only because *he* allowed it!

And should he do otherwise? Ought he to act as if he were just an unwilling host who, at any opportune moment, would, in the name of his supposed integrity, unceremoniously eject his strange, apparently uninvited guest? Yet *he*, this particular he sitting here now, *was* the guest! Yes, he the intruder, the uncoiling stranger, no longer so unwelcome, now the guest, now *literally* making himself at home! But what of the host? A rapidly receding presence, to be sure, but certainly not about to actually disappear — he was not only the guest, but also the host, the one who could not *fully* resist opening his doors, the one who so convincingly played the role of victim, the one who clung to the *Amulan* meaning of the name Glam!

Host and guest — their discomfort with each other was but his primal struggle, his deep disease, a multidimensional battleground made all the more muddy by his insistence on taking sides — but exactly *who* was taking sides?

And, furthermore, what of the dwelling, the living space wherein both host and guest took their respective stands? What of *that* realm? Unnoticed it was, almost completely unnoticed in the seesawing heat, confusion, and maddeningly opaque complexity of this self-induced struggle, this rabidly automatic identification with one side or the other! Unnoticed it was, unseen, unfelt, amidst all this inflated, self-obsessed drama of back and forth, of in and out, this inner war that was blindly *trampling* the green, the seedling green, of his *true* ground! His true ground, his ever-virgin heartland, uncomplainingly housing both guest and host, ever asking only for his *undivided* attention...

What a perverse feat was this obliviousness to the obvious, just as miraculous as the fact of him in the midst of all this somehow managing to speak to this glaring torture-lover, as though he had been doing so for years!

On and on he spoke to her, fluidly and dynamically, acutely aware of what he was doing, trusting the deep inner expansion now radiating throughout his body. Insights, many of them transverbal, arose in him, blooming brightly, their significance both exciting and calming him — for the first time, he fully accepted his being in Anushet, fully accepted his condition, inner and outer, not passively, but passionately. Fiery it was, hot and unrelenting, terribly consuming, but now it was a fire he could welcome, a fire of necessary purification, nakedly blazing, dancing so blue and wild — no longer would he flinch from its flames, no longer would he merely bemoan his circumstances!

Had not Xandur once said that we can only have our heart's deepest desire when we stop fighting the preparatory fire?

Whatever it was that was surfacing in him, however dark or unseemly its expression might be, was clearly none other than *him*! The obviousness of this made him smile — the entire matter was just too simple, just too, too basic for his mind to get its teeth into! Better to let his mind just keep on churning out well-dressed information for Tornellas! With pleasure, he noticed that his smiling coordinated perfectly with what he was saying...

"Well," yawned Tornellas at last, "you certainly have enough things to say about your precious Amula. I am tiring of hearing about your childhood — a tedious tale it is, full of barbaric novelties, barely amusing. Now, I wish to hear of what led you into your so-called priesthood, how you were selected, and so on."

As he spoke, she watched him closely. The creature was surprisingly intelligent; this morning, his speech was almost hypnotically smooth, infused with an easy elegance. The sound of his voice actually pleased her, though she took care to not show this. Of course, pleasure was nothing special to her, especially this sort of pleasure — was it not just a sugared surge of energy, a wavy little tickle, a slightly exaggerated sensation that, for so many, carried within itself a disgusting begging for its own repetition? There existed a deeper pleasure for her, an unnamed thrill created and sustained by the tantalizingly precise application of her torturing talents. Unfortunately, this required subjects, most of whom interfered horribly with her special pleasure by slopping their fear all over the place, instead of simply resisting her, like any courageous person would.

"Yes, yes, yes!" she finally exclaimed, leaning forward. "But just what was it about you that caught the priestly eye? Did you by any chance show signs of some unusual gift?"

"Not particularly. I was a quick learner. I suppose that might have impressed those who tested me."

"Fool! That is not what I mean, and you know it! Though your intelligence is minimal, you are devious. Do not assume you can conceal anything from me! Now, tell me what I want to know." Moving closer to him, her hand upon the hilt of her dagger, she gestured to the guards to surround him.

"I had a gift," he said quickly, but not too quickly, "for seeing the future." As the guards, at a signal from Tornellas, backed off slightly, he began describing several precognitive visions he'd had as a youth. Tornellas listened attentively; nothing had been said about his voice, yet she could not bring herself to ask him about it directly. Soon, though, she must question him about it — surely he must know what she was after! Torture might work, but Ezparya had forbidden it. Mustn't damage the dear creature! His descriptions of his future-seeing sounded quite convincing. Vaguely, she remembered times of precognition for herself; then, to her dismay, she realized that she was actually feeling a sense of kinship with Glam! Her fingers still played with the handle of her dagger, but without any sign whatsoever of threatening intent. The gap between her and him was little more than a blur to her now, a clouded warmth, a soft, richly resonant —

Viciously, she yanked herself from this encroaching cosiness, this uninvited intimacy, straining to sever the link that seemed to be forming between her and this maddening foreigner. No! she screamed at herself over and over, driving the inner sound of it through her entire body. No! It was not her will that there be *any* association between this pig and herself! No! Was it not enough that she had to be in the same room with him? She had listened to his drivel for far too long!

"Stop!" she shouted, shaking her head. "I have heard more than enough from you! Your fanciful tales are but perfumed excrement to me. Do you really think I don't have better things to do than sit here with you?"

"I appreciate your company," he said, half-smiling, still feeling something between them that was not entirely hostile. "I am sure that you have far better things to do than spend time with me, and I am sorry that you find me so burdensome to be with."

"Yes," she said, suddenly feeling very tired. "But, Amulan beast, do not seek to please me; your pitiful doings do not even remotely approach the realm wherein I am pleased." Standing, she turned and moved toward the door, followed by her guards, trying to disguise her hesitancy, but without complete success; an unaccustomed inertia slowed her step, subtly yet unmistakably disturbing her balance...

"Thank you." His voice was soothing and melodious. He knew he had touched her, however briefly. How, he knew not. Nevertheless, he definitely had gotten to her — just look at her, having trouble leaving the room! Carefully, he concealed his exultation, only allowing it expression through the relaxed intensity of his gaze.

"One last thing," announced Tornellas, her profile to him, a study of sharp, precisely drawn lines, except for the faint swell and droop of her lips. "Do not be so foolish as to assume anything from these talks."

She paused, then looked directly at him. "And, despicable one, do not again toy with me, as you have done so well today. Tomorrow, I shall return for you, to take you, at Ezparya's request, to where you will have the good fortune to view certain customs of Anushet."

Smiling tightly yet triumphantly, she left.

12

How Could He Not Return?

Again and again, the waves reared up, sometimes high enough to block her view of the canoe-dotted horizon. Each wave roared in, churning furiously, tumbling and frothing, bubbling all turquoise and shining white, finally flattening, silkily transparent, its scalloped gossamer edges lightly and almost dryly touching her feet. All around her sparkled tiny snail shells, extravagantly coloured turrets and twists and swirls of endlessly inventive artistry, each miniature spiral, however beach-worn, a brightly polished tapestry of possibility. In one hand, she held a few shells she'd gathered earlier, all heart-cockles, each one no more than twice the size of her thumbnail, burnished ivory and creamy mauve in the afternoon sun, casting tiny, ribbed shadows on her palm.

A few children were playing nearby, but she paid them no attention; another day she would have, and gladly, but today she had no time for them. High in the cloudfree sky hung the ghostly disk of a half-moon, near and yet so far away, just like Glam. A long, long time ago, he had left, sailing away in the biggest ocean canoe she'd ever seen. She had felt very close to him when he left, and very sad...

Esmelana sat still, occasionally weeping, her arms wrapped around her knees, sometimes hoping that the next great wave would bring Glam back to her. Over and over, she imagined that a far-off wave, an immensely powerful but friendly wave, was carrying him, and that it would be coming to shore this very day, any moment now — passionately, she visualized this wave, this vast rolling wonder, urging it on, asking it to safely transport her father. Her hope, however, was starting to fade; she had kept it alive as best she could, terrified to be without it, but now it was becoming more and more of a burden, rather than a spirit-booster.

When the other children talked about Glam's possible whereabouts, she always told them that soon he would be back. How could it be otherwise? How could he not return? How could he not come back to her? He must! He was, of course! He was, he was...

The tide began to recede. She was alone on the beach. The shells had fallen unnoticed from her hand. Overhead, a few iridescent green birds soared in graceful ovals, their long black beaks occasionally opening wide, emitting sharp cries that sounded sorrowful to her.

The waves rolled in, glittering goldenly with fragments of setting sun, gloriously arching, crashing, and foaming, rolling in and in, achingly beautiful, fire-crested and dancing so pure and empty, rolling in and in, rolling in Glam-less...

13

His To Embody And Express,
His To Let Fly

How uncomfortable Tornellas looked, how writhingly and resolutely stiff! How absurdly ill-tempered she kept herself, sitting so unhappily upright beside Glam, perched atop the best seats in the amphitheatre, her face a disdainful mask, her narrowed gaze seemingly holding her neck-cords taut — if only she knew she was being watched!

Ezparya laughed. Her viewing place was concealed from all, less than a bodylength from Tornellas and Glam, in front of and slightly below them. Glam was such an interesting specimen, remarkably, perhaps even excessively, transparent in his expression — he appeared shocked and very hurt. No doubt he had never seen such spectacles in his homeland; the only carnage there was probably the slaughter of creatures for their meat. Tornellas was much less fascinating to observe, almost boring; she spoke to Glam as if he were but a dog, even less than a dog, rigidly and meticulously maintaining the distance between them, her flesh like stone...

Ezparya decided she would instruct Tornellas to be much friendlier to Glam. Most of what she'd told Ezparya about Glam had been too dry, too ordinary, too consistently flat, little more than a tedious recitation of facts. Her blatant hostility was, mused Ezparya, giving Glam an unnecessary sense of certainty, perhaps even confidence — he could in all likelihood easily arrange himself around the predictable nastiness Tornellas so insistently displayed, thereby gaining an immunity to surprise...

Slowly and knowingly, Ezparya ran her hands over her face and neck, her fingertips lingering along the wetness of her lips, caressing them looser and fuller, her breath gradually deepening, tinged with a finely-tuned thrill — how deliciously familiar this sensation, how wonderfully enlarging, and oh how sweetly potent with upcoming surprise!

Now Glam looked genuinely frightened. He could not hide his fear and revulsion. Ezparya gazed at him more closely — his lips were parted, and there were tears in his eyes. Involuntary grimaces skidded across his face, stormy and jagged blue. And his hands, his exquisitely formed hands! See them tremble! See them infold and bulgingly fist, squirming so sinewy tight and purplish-white, then suddenly radiate out, wider and wider, blossoming with ambivalent intent — what would those hands like to do? Strangle Tornellas? Or her? They stretched and sang with rage, frustration, helplessness, agony, longing — what loveliness to feel their need! Their naked need, their pure greed! Such long, stronglooking, yet oddly feminine fingers, so crazily and ferociously intertwining, just like the beasts and their human prey in the bloody dramatics far below...

In the center of the amphitheatre, three lions were mauling a man. Even in her enclosure, Ezparya could hear his shrieks. She had heard the same sounds thousands of times, the same jarring music of horror and hurt, the same tedious tune. Glam, however, certainly did not appear bored; he was shaking all over, his face bright with tears, contorted with extreme emotion. At last, the screams ceased, and the crowd applauded. The next victim would probably be tied in place, and then presented to more ravenous carnivores, and so on, and so on, the whole idiotic matter merely serving to sate the appetites of the spectators, to feed their psyches, to flood and plug up their hollows, they the beloved populace of Anushet, her ever loyal subjects, so, so unquestioningly chained to their troughs...

She was far more interested in Glam. She watched him shut his eyes, and saw Tornellas order him to keep his eyes open. Still shaking, he turned to face Tornellas, but she abruptly looked away, obviously telling him to not look at her, probably insulting his show of emotion. Little did he know that the show had just begun.

He squirmed. Spearpoints jabbed at his back, reminding him to keep still. Beside him sat Tornellas, like a smug rock, coldly yet lasciviously viewing the obscenities occurring below — damn her! Damn this godless place! His revulsion at the applauded bloodshed gradually coalesced, condensing into rage; a smile twisted about somewhere inside him, unable to make it to his face, which was now dominated by his surging anger. Once again, Tornellas commanded him to keep his eyes open.

Not only could he not avoid seeing what was below, but he could also not avoid *feeling* it. The crowd seemed to experience it as a great thrill, a marvellous stimulation, a juicy feast, but he could not help but feel the pain, the fear, the agony, the brutal shock of those who were being slaughtered and eaten — the sheer degradation, the subhuman depravity, the incredible heartlessness, the horror, the unspeakable damage! Suddenly, the smile crossed his face, briefly and brokenly, almost limping, baring his teeth...

Now a man and a woman were carried into the amphitheatre. With exaggerated ceremony, they were tied upon a waist-high wooden platform, their limbs spread wide, strips of sunlight falling across their open-mouthed faces. Then a lion appeared, roaring and grotesquely thin, apparently oblivious to the hooting encouragement of the spectators. The cheers grew even louder as the lion began ripping into the neck and chest of the man. His screams, for the short time they lasted, were strong, but the woman's were much stronger; her terror, her horrified anticipation, seemed to please the crowd, to further fuel its hunger. The entire amphitheatre pulsed for Glam, rhythmically thudding beneath its hazy dome of sky, as if readying itself to burst...

Thudding and thudding, beating steadily and dreamily, all time seemingly cupped within a viscous yet membranous silence, a silence imbedded with vaguely meaningful sounds, drowsily droning round and round, thudding slower and slower...

Then it all shattered.

Another scream was heard, far, far louder than the woman's. It was a screaming full of terror and something else, something senior to terror, something that both included and transcended all terror. A huge, ringing sound it was, shivering with pure power, blazingly penetrating.

It came from Glam. Without willing it so, he'd been so completely pervaded by the suffering of the two below that it had become *his* pain, his to embody and express, his to magnify back and out, out into the bloated excitement of the crowd, piercing and cracking their thickness, wedging into and splitting wider and wider every fissure of awareness or empathy — the terrible hurt of the pair upon the platform poured forth from him, wildly and rapidly flaming through the stands, effortlessly seizing all attention, wailing with a searing eloquence, sailing into everyone present.

The spectators were suddenly silent. All eyes turned toward Glam. Vibrating with waves of tremendous force, he stood, his screaming now a fluid singing, high and reaching higher, a singing rich with untainted longing, bright and achingly clear, suffused with the echoes of an ancient sadness, the primal hurt that almost all human doings were but distractions from...

Though his eyes were open, he saw little more than the play of colour and form, for he was profoundly absorbed in his sounds, simultaneously witnessing and *being* them; the archetypal currents of his voice were not so much his, as they were *him*... Abruptly, he stopped and pointed down at the lion, dramatically gesturing that it should be stopped immediately. The crowd shifted back and forth, smoothly, almost mesmerizingly, rippling; some stood, as though ready to do his bidding. Again, he pointed, hurling a thundering shout across the stadium. Tornellas still sat beside him, unmoving, tears on her cheeks, her eyes glassy. Now he ran toward the bottom of the amphitheatre. None opposed his path. No thoughts intruded into his intensity, no doubts, no self-dividedness.

Halfway down, Ezparya appeared, wrapped in shimmering black and turquoise, her hair flaming white. She stared at Glam — already, he was past her, his shoulders wide and swinging, his hips loose and free, his head high, as though an invisible hand were pulling it up by the hair. The crowd bulged sharply at its lowest edge, nearest to the lion. A group of men appeared ready to spear it.

Ezparya knew exactly what she had to do.

She could have done otherwise, and easily so, but she had, a long moment ago, already made her choice. There was no turning back now, none! What joy to *totally* obey this lucid excitement that raced through her, and what relief! In a commanding voice, she told the group of men to kill the lion right away. Their instant obedience perfectly fit the line of Glam's approach, the way an arrowhead fits its shaft. She knew she had but lent her authority to what was already in motion...

Glam momentarily halted as he watched the men attack the lion. Already, a dozen or more spears protruded from it. He could see that there was no life left in the sacrificial man; his neck was more than half-gone. However, the woman was very much alive. He ran to her in long, floating strides. Ezparya, from high above, gestured that none were to interfere with him, then asked that Tornellas be brought to her.

Tornellas, the earnest fool, looked very upset; the corners of her carefully made-up mouth were crazily twitching. "This is madness," she stammered, blinking rapidly. "Sheer madness, my queen! Do you not see what you have allowed to happen?"

"Come now," said Ezparya softly. "You allowed him to begin. I didn't see you try to stop him."

"But —"

"Silence, you hateful fool! You have *no* vision! If you did, you would readily appreciate this, and perhaps even understand it — look at him with *more* than your eyes!"

Quickly yet sensitively, Glam untied the woman. She glanced up at him, her eyes rolling slightly, red with exhaustion and trauma. Her face was badly bruised — she had obviously been beaten prior to her appearance in the amphitheatre, and probably raped. Her skin was the same colour as Esmelana's. Not bothering to fight back his tears, he gathered up the woman in his arms, as though she were but a young child, and began carrying her back up into the stadium seats. Though he knew not where he was going, his steps were certain. The spectators looked like stunned cattle, clumsily frozen in place, dumbly awaiting a miraculous thawing...

"Come, Glam!"

It was Ezparya's voice, clear and surprisingly refreshing. She stood above him, with Tornellas beside her. Her calling out his name only deepened what was already astir in him. Easily and strongly, he went straight to her, briefly meeting her gaze. A warm throbbing filled her, and an even warmer silence, as she watched him tenderly put down the injured woman. Then, as he glanced up at her as if for information, she saw both caring and detachment in his eyes. This, *this* was it, this very moment — now, electrifying now, she *must* sever any remaining possibility of turning back!

"Do not concern yourself now with this woman; I give you my word that she will be taken care of, well taken care of! Perhaps you, and of course Tornellas, are surprised that I can speak your tongue. I always had the capacity, almost to the degree that Tornellas has. She did, however unknowingly, greatly assist me in gaining fluency, for which I thank her. Let us hope she is not overly jealous of my ability to speak your tongue!"

After a short pause, she continued, in a much softer tone. "I am taking you from the city, Glam." She was not surprised when he nodded his assent, his nodding in no way lessening his stature...

Ezparya glanced at Tornellas, who stood stiffly wobbling, like a statue about to topple. "I don't think we'll take Tornellas with us," she said. "I can see no need for her presence. Do you, Tornellas?"

"Not unless you wish it so." Tornellas's face was ashen.

"You may go now, Tornellas," smiled Ezparya. "Your services have been invaluable. I'm sure they will be again."

As Tornellas haltingly walked away, Ezparya turned to Glam. "Let us not talk now; there will be much to say later. Come with me, and we will ready ourselves to leave." He followed her from the amphitheatre, looking back just once, seeing the lion on its side, asprout with spears, the dust around it fatly blooming with dark crimson petals, each one faintly brightened by a few shards of sun...

The outskirts of the city were heavily treed. Little stone houses occasionally peered out through cracks in the dense wall of foliage; smoke drifted up from some, hinting at a hearthside warmth, but they all looked cold and resignedly forlorn to Glam, seemingly uninhabited.

But so what? Their barrenness of being was not his concern. As he rode along in the covered chariot with Ezparya and seven guards, he breathed easily, sensing no threat. Ezparya had said no more to him, but he had felt her open and receptive to him since they had left the city, even when she had imperiously arranged the details of their departure.

Two other chariots followed theirs, both pulled by huge white horses with curly beige manes and extravagantly hairy forefeet, stunningly muscled, prodigiously sweating beasts almost twice the size of Amulan horses. Through the open windows of the chariot came a cool breeze, carrying a fresh green scent, sweet and faintly pungent. How very refreshing this was, to be bathed and in clean clothes, to be well-fed, smoothly rocked by the steady gallop of the horses, sitting upon cushions in a speeding chariot, caressed by a fragrant wind!

He stopped his pleasurably reflective list short — he did not take Ezparya lightly. Somewhat tentatively, he included her on the periphery of his sense of well-being, savouring her presence with both the desire and the caution of a very thirsty man who discovers a water source that may very well be poisonous. She sat close beside him, though not so close as to be touching him, gazing out of the window on her side. No sign did she give of being aware of him, yet he could feel her attention all around him, sinuously and almost casually enwrapping him. Again and again, he remembered the pair in the amphitheatre, carried in and bound, exposed to carnivorous jaws, the drama of it now like a dream to him, a shimmering, slightly warped trapezoid collapsing with time, crumbling and coming undone, its boundaries eddying and dissolving... The power, however, that had possessed him did not in any way feel like a dream; he could still feel it in him, at rest, peacefully coiled. But was it actually *in* him, or was he in *it*?

Then they were out of the city and its environs, and in open country, a rough, rolling, rock-strewn muddiness, stubbled here and there with pale, stunted shrubs, its dreariness only occasionally interrupted by patches of farmland. At last, more forest appeared; its trees were sturdy, straight and tall, each one with enough encircling green to conceal almost all of its trunk. How far apart were these trees from each other, each seeming to proclaim its selfsufficiency, its independence! Between them stretched bits of reddish meadow, streaked with the late afternoon sun, apop with clusters of small, silvery bushes...

The trees seemed like sentinels to him, ever-watchful, keeping an unmoving vigil, rigidly peering out from above their intermeshed hoops and angled loopings of foliage, unquestioningly on guard, persistently suspicious, trusting only their mistrust, so, so unlike the forests of Amula, which were, almost without exception, welcoming and friendly. A broad green embrace was theirs, easy and intimate, generous and wonderfully lush — Esmelana loved to lie back on the forest floor, gazing up into the trees. He did, too; often, they had lain together beneath a sky of swaying branches, their spirits swimming together up through all the feathered layers of enchanted green, higher and higher — now an image of Esmelana flooded him, her eyes overflowing with grief and bafflement, her little arms reaching out toward him, reaching and reaching, her fingers spread wide, stretching with heartbreakingly pure need. Open was her mouth, but he couldn't quite hear her sounds. There was a definite urgency about her, a desperation, a yearning that ate into him. Sadly, he watched her image gradually fade...

"What are you thinking about?" Ezparya's voice cut through the last strands of his reverie.

"About Amula."

"Amula must seem to you to be purer, more innocent, sweeter and more intimate than Anushet. Look at these trees! They stand sullenly apart, as if there is no bond between them, except their common bondage to the earth they are so firmly rooted in."

"And what is the bondage of Anushet natives?"

"The very same as that of Amula's inhabitants," she smiled. "Only the appearance is different."

He was about to say more, but a fleeting glance from her told him to not bother. Closing her eyes, she let her head fall back onto the raised cushions at the back of the chariot. The trees were now very sparse, and shorter. Turning around, Glam saw great white horseheads behind him, snorting and huffing, nostrils wide and moistly black, eyes flecked with burnt red. Sunset was near. A wave of exhaustion swept through him. As the sun sank squat and dusty-pink, he dropped into sleep, seeing nothing, luxuriously yielding himself to the gently rolling lull of his breath...

14

To Plunge Deep Into Her,
Deeper Than Flesh

Barely visible figures, cowled and deferentially bent, materialized out of the dark to lead the chariots through a pair of enormous gates. Once inside, Glam was immediately led to a spacious, candle-lit room, and left alone. Soft orange furs on the floor, fatly-stuffed cushions piled in the corners, ceiling a flickering blue dome seemingly pregnant with stars, candle-flames disappearing before his heavy-lidded breath, his deliciously pervasive drowsiness...

He awoke late the next morning, unable to remember any dreams. One wall, all window, offered a view over a red hexagonal courtyard bordered with yellow-blossomed trees. Yawning and stretching, he readied himself to go out for a walk, sensing that doing so would be safe. As he strolled across the courtyard a short time later, he saw many guards, but none of them paid him any attention, except to abruptly nod as he passed.

Satiny and pleasantly crisp was the air, smooth and cool the tiles beneath his bare feet. Centering the hexagon was a small oval pool brimming with water of an unusually dark blue. Each tile around the pool bore a slash of black paint, a short, thick curve that dominated its surrounding red. Into the water he edged his foot — it was surprisingly cold, and oddly dense, too, unlike any water he'd ever known. Kneeling, he peered into the pool, but couldn't see his reflection; there was only the indigo sheen of the surface, showing no forms, rippling sluggishly, stirred by the breeze crisscrossing the courtyard. A few yellow blossoms lay scattered nearby. Scooping them up, he brought them close to his face, inhaling their fragrance — a pale, lemony aroma it was, slim and watery, faintly tattered, veined with a sweetly undulating echo, a dappled curvaceousness, an ancient promise...

With a start, he looked up, hearing a strange, deeply muted creaking. At the far end of the courtyard loomed a huge silver-black door, almost imperceptibly moving back and forth. A flurry of fear burrowed all through his belly, clammy and blind, frantically gnawing out niches for itself, almost instantaneously coupling with his mind, spawning thoughts supportive of its continuation. How horribly compelling fear could be, especially when one submitted to its point of view! Breathing deeply, he detached his attention from his fear's paralytic grasp and cast of phantoms, giving it space to become something more life-giving — such an unnecessary knotting of aliveness was such fear! It was but a reflex, a survival mechanism, badly mishandled by almost all, harnessed as it all too often was to automaticities of thought, past or future, its mind-generated offspring guilt, doubt, and anxiety, its presence spurring those who *feared* it into the security-riddled haunts of full-time distraction...

Through the door he strode, surprised at how easily it yielded to his push, his burst of fear now but a rising excitement. Before him gently stretched a pale green land, blurring back into bluish hills. Lanky grey clouds hung limply all across the sky, as if waiting to be filled out. Spongy and finely textured was the soil, lightly pebbled and moist — how fertile-feeling was this landscape, and yet how empty, how widely sad, how quietly dismal, how very lonely, as though craving but despairing of impregnation, like a woman marooned from her capacity to bear children...

He walked on for a while, his steps short and sure, then finally stopped, closing his eyes. Although he stood upon earth, he felt as if he were on a boat, a long, graceful canoe with golden sails whistling taut, atop a gloriously rolling sea. There was, however, no Merot here with him, no enthusiastic search, no clearcut hunger for arrival somewhere; the boat only spun in place, its horizon but the circumference it traced. In its center he stood, his hands trembling by his sides, flimsy flickers of breeze caressing his skin, shuddering walls of emerald seaspray encapsulating him. Stuck, stuck was the he of the fantasy, jammed tight with lofty inertia, and even tighter with an urge to escape, to somehow travel on — but, in truth, there was actually *nowhere* to go! Nowhere at all!

His fantasy had but painted the negative side of this, revealing his habit of making a problem out of the whole notion of getting somewhere. In terms of awakening, there was *fundamentally* nowhere to go, no ocean to cross, no ultimate goal in the face of which to neatly play hero, or master explorer, or God-realizer! His journey, his essential journey, not only preceded and transcended *all* its would-be maps, but, more importantly, was more a matter of *open-eyed* surrender than of sequential or progressive experience — yes, such experience would of course *naturally* arise from time to time, but it must *not* be merely reduced to a spiritual ladder, with evaluation reports eruditely babbling from each grasped rung! Were not all such ladders just mirages, systematized structurings of mind clung to and *believed in* by those who were obsessed with altering their spiritual condition? And, to the point, did not this very *obsession* with bettering their state not only make them more and more miserable, but also *actually* blind them to their *true, already*-present condition? That very condition which required not *seeking*, but rather full-bodied *recognition*, now and now, ever *now*!

How ruthlessly these realizations (which were more of feeling than of cognition) kept crumbling the edifices of his spiritual ambition! Yet out of this crumbling, out of the ruins of what he took to be himself, there arose a profound intuition of his fundamental nature, eloquently and stunningly obvious — That which animated everything, inner and outer, called in countless voices for his full intimacy, Its formless Face undressing and exploding his heart, all the rainbowed fragments streaming out and out, blossoming in endless sky, the Consciousness of All once again continuous with his consciousness...

He felt the ground beneath his feet, wiggling his toes into it. Yieldingly moist it was, subtly throbbing, gently conveying the currents of what was far below it. The joy-bright knowingness of untrammelled being welled up in him — what deep kinship he felt with his surroundings, what eternal unity! They seemed to be as much him as that which referred to itself as him; there were no boundaries, yet there was diversity, there was individuation, all of it paradoxical only to the periphery of what was occurring. Slowly, he lifted up his arms, his palms aimed skyward, letting his head fall back. On his forehead he could feel a touch of mist.

Let it come! Let it rain, let it thunder, let it pour down and down! Laughing and weeping, he raised his arms even higher, his entire being filling out his gesture. Lantar! O Supreme Unknowableness, see me blinded by my search for Thee! I cannot *reach* Thee, but I can express Thee! I cannot become Thee, but I can *be* Thee! Does not Your Heart *now* breathe me, right now? Does not Your Love *now* shape me? Does not Your Eternal Mystery now invite my embrace, my forever's face, my awakening from my assumed living space? Lantar, O Name of the Infinite Unnameable, Great Source effortlessly *present* as all of this, everlastingly existing where love cannot lie, Your sublime Ordinariness ever intuited in the uncharted depths of Now, calling to me, calling and calling...

He stood thus absorbed for a long time, letting the forces of sky and earth expand and nourish him, burdening none of what was happening with any meaning.

It simply was what it was, an unbound Wonder with Which he felt an overwhelming intimacy and identification — there was nothing to figure out, and *everything* to live! Everything! Not through cumulative experience, but through undiluted, *passionate* resonance with the Great Wonder wherein everything arose. What joy to relax into that Wonder, with clear-eyed attention! Yes, *attention* — was there a greater art than that of giving one's full attention to Unsleeping Consciousness Itself? And when attention thus *dissolved* into its Source, then, sacred, sexy then, then...

He felt a hand on his back.

Firmly placed it was, right between his shoulderblades. Its arrival had been so smooth and sure that he had not been startled. The pressure of each fingertip was distinct and pleasing. Gradually, he lowered his arms and turned around, opening his eyes.

Ezparya.

Her eyes were the same colour as the courtyard pool, perhaps even darker, yet transparent, clear in their depth, bright with vitality. Silently, she took his hand, leading him back through the courtyard. He didn't see the billowing clouds above, nor the fire-coloured tiles below; only the oval pool caught his eye, and then only for a moment. An unhurried excitement streamed through him, lightening his step. Up several long flights of stairs they went, and into her quarters, passing between two rows of guards. There were, however, no guards inside.

She closed the door, then sat, motioning for him to sit across from her. The twin arcs of tiny red bird feathers that served as her eyebrows fluttered slightly, as though in a light breeze. A scent of jasmine hung in the air, laced with a vanilla'ed afterswirl. Along one wall was a trough of orchidaceous plants, flamboyantly petalled, with creamy-pink, succulently-lipped centers. The walls were blue, the ceiling a paler shade of blue. The floor was of highly polished wood, dark brown and swirlingly grained. Throughout the room were large cushions of all colours.

Steady and powerful were her eyes, rich with command and authority, and yet also inviting. He accepted the invitation and, at the same time, felt a sobering caution. Yes, she radiated a very alluring welcome, a welcome of lust and something beyond lust, but it was surrounded by the jaws, the razor teeth, of her power; the woman in her was, it seemed to him, servant to something else...

Nonetheless, he felt pulled to her, more and more strongly, and she too was drawn to him, was she not? Was she not breathing him in, and her desire out? Was not the heat he felt from her, the flushed radiance, the lush glow, a sign of her passion for him? Just then, she smiled at him, as if acknowledging his awareness of her. He had not seen her smile so fully before; now he felt even more intoxicated, pervaded through and through with a fiery throbbing, his flesh engorged with a rapturous hunger.

She watched his eyes cloud with desire, then brighten soft and clear, without any weakening of passion; so he did not lose himself in his lust, and nor did he flee it! It was strong, as was hers, but apparently not enslaving, nor obsessive — suddenly, she remembered Artakiab's warning, hearing his dense, careful voice. But this encounter was hers to risk, hers alone! Artakiab, for all his baleful certainty, could not hold her back! Nothing could, and nothing would!

Now Glam's eyes were penetrating hers, happily and deeply, slowly surging into her, undressing her depths; her very flesh seemed to be parting, spreading and melting ever wider, moistly yielding to his entry, his deliciously sustained thrust. Sweet was this hotly tingling knowingness, this succulent fire, sweet the feel of its flames, and sweeter still its vast, pulsating sky! This intensity of longing, in its very fieriness and thrill, not only consumed her body and mind, but also richly illuminated her very being...

There was no need for detachment from her longing, so as to witness it, for did it not carry within its very momentum, its very aliveness, an *inherent* awareness? And was not Glam also afloat in this effortless alertness, this vibrant lucidity, even as his body beckoned lustily to hers? Was he not breathing in rhythm with her now, his growing smile saturating his entire body? For a long time, they sat unmoving, ever expanding to include more and more of the other, allowing stillness to both permeate *and* magnify their mutual desire...

Standing in front of him, she undressed, feeling his eyes following the slow descent of her robe. Her skin was exceedingly pale, yet healthy-looking, almost satiny. Everything about her body fit with everything else; there was a pleasing balance to it, a symmetry both of form and essence. Interlacing her fingers behind her neck, she raised her elbows up and back, arching her back and breathing deeply, inviting him to merge with her, to plunge deep into her, deeper than flesh...

He lay back, reaching up to her, no longer driven by his passion, but abiding in the very heart of it. Gracefully, she came to him, taking his hands and placing them over her nipples, then on either side of her face. As his touch began to roam her body, travelling freely but not superficially, returning again and again to where she was most impassioned, she undressed him, kissing each new revelation of flesh, hungrily, almost hypnotically, absorbed with him in the all but simultaneous intensification and relaxation of their blissfulness. At last, their mouths met, playfully at first, lightly and teasingly, then hungrily, fiercely, wildly, their bodies intertwining, pressing together with such force and abandon as to eliminate any distance between them. In full embrace they lay, gazing into each other's eyes, doing nothing to deliberately heighten or maximize stimulation — the sensations and feelings that *naturally* arose between them were more than enough.

Waves of pleasure, arching and peaking, insistently surging, spilling and then lusciously rupturing, wave after wave, rolling through and through, each one luminous with presence, wondrously transparent to the Undying Mystery that silently persisted through each wave's shorecoming and blue-white death... Wave upon wave, lull upon lull, beating together, no matter what the weather...

Now, with both hands, she guided him into her, enwreathing him with her warm, fluid welcome, drawing him in deeper and deeper, her voice melodically filling the room, blending with his sounds, their speechless music both embroidering and deepening the silence in and around them. Together they flowed, riding in and out of ecstasy, surrendering to motiveless rhythms, large and small, becoming more and more sensitive to each other, losing face without losing touch, their bodies but a cascading, flowering communion of primal wonder and spirit-joy, choreographed by an unseen yet deeply intuited current of pure being. Finally, an almost unbearably sweet, roaring glory of an orgasm exploded in and rose up all through him, carrying her into an equally powerful and enlivening release. As their movements gradually subsided, they again looked into each other's eyes...

"Well," murmured Ezparya after a long pause, carefully introducing her voice into the silence. "Something has begun."

"Yes," he said, "and we're at its mercy."

She propped herself up on her elbows, letting her head fall back. "Surely you don't mean our appetites?"

"No. It has little to do with the play of pleasure, though it certainly includes it." How stiff his voice sounded, how guardedly formal!

"So you are wise, too, are you? You are quick to speak learnedly after the sating of your lust!"

"And you are quick with your tongue!" It pained him to speak thus — how rapidly they had distanced themselves from their intimacy! But had not this distance been there all along, merely obscured by the sheer intensity of their sexplay? Yes and no...

Her gaze knifed through his thoughts. "I would be even quicker if I had the voice you sometimes have."

She stopped, waiting for him to reply. He appeared hurt and defensive, yet remained open-eyed, as if sensing a similar pain in her — but how could she, Ezparya, even permit herself the possibility of such empathetic pangs? How could she even consider entertaining such a weakening of self? "Thrice," she said coolly, "I have heard you sound your voice with a power beyond power, a seemingly unmatchable force. Tell me, what is the source of this power?"

"That wherein all arises." Hollow did his voice sound to him, lonely, emptied of their closeness, panoramically barren, impotently pleading for some sort of greening, for a reestablishment of the depth they had shared...

"Yes, yes, yes!" she snapped. "Do not treat me like a fool! Tell me how you speak this sound!"

Was *this* the purpose of their meeting? He disengaged his body from hers. "I cannot explain it." Seeing her eyes beginning to storm, he matter-of-factly added, "All I do is make room for it, but even doing that doesn't necessarily guarantee its arrival. It comes when it wills it so, not when I do; otherwise, I'd likely abuse it, hooking it up in some way to less-than honourable motives. So I am grateful that *I* cannot control or will it."

She laughed. "So you are its vessel, its humble medium! But please tell me, just *how* do you make room for it? How do you invite it in?"

Suddenly, he felt afraid. "By remembering it."

"I am sure you will want to say more later! But for now, that's enough. Are you upset that I might be talking down to you? Don't look so ruffled! Do you know that I could have you killed in an instant?"

"Then why don't you?"

"Because you are of use to me."

"Is that all?" He reddened with anger.

"Why should there be more? You should consider yourself lucky! Very few are the men who have lain with Ezparya."

"And when I am no longer of any use to you?"

"A foolish question!"

"Do you only lay with me to take from me? Do you? Do you know nothing besides manipulation? Answer me!" No longer did he suppress his anger.

"Again, a foolish question." Derision stained her smile.

"How distant you keep yourself, queen of Anushet! How very yielding is your flesh, and how very reluctant, and frightened, you are to *give* yourself along with it, except when it suits you! How fearful you are, how unnecessarily protected right now, how arrogant and cold! Do you not remember our warmth, our depth of meeting?" Now he was shouting. "Do you not remember the *fullness* of our passion, and the brilliance, the joy, the wonder, in which it took wing? You, Ezparya, are far more drawn to *me* than you will admit, in spite of your words to the contrary!"

"Make your point!" she hissed, her eyes burning.

"Dare you confess that you actually *care* for me?" He let his eyes soften, feeling his anger transmuting into a deep, dynamically poised receptivity.

She laughed scornfully. "Impudent creature! You shall —"

It was impossible to complete her sentence. To her astonishment, Glam was starting to weep; there was, however, no trace of self-pity, sentimentality, or weakness in his tears, nor was there any sign of helplessness or manipulativeness. As he wept, he looked directly at her, his gaze powerful in its very vulnerability. Several times, she tried to speak, but couldn't — despite her resistance, she could not help feeling as though she were floating upon his sadness, soothed and rocked by his sobs, held lovingly, yes, *lovingly*...

Many memories arose in him, memories of past hurts, misunderstandings, confusing difficulties, painful shrinkages of being, stubborn denials of self, heart-wounds every one of them, searing heart-wounds, but now only *secondary* to his sadness itself, all of their content, however dramatic or compelling, of no *real* import. His crying was more a celebration, a heartfelt acknowledgment, of loss than it was a bewailing of it. Because of the inevitability of change and death, love, if it was authentic and unshackled, must weep! Real love could not stand apart from suffering, human and otherwise, and nor could it wallow in the dramatics and blind reinforcing of that suffering. Real love did not rise above human hurt, but rather felt it, *fully* felt it, without getting lost in it.

Love must weep.

Weep, and simultaneously shine right through its weeping, never compromising its purity of being, never limiting its reach, even as it opened itself to the unavoidable pains of *necessary* limitation...

Gradually, his sounds steadied, rolling into a music that was half-hum and half-lovecall, gently yet potently welcoming, irresistibly receptive. Something of Ezparya entered him, leaping to his throat, flowering out into tender, bittersweet bouquets of sound, and he sang her longing back to her, not just the longing he had already felt and seen in her, but also a more hidden longing, one trembling with vulnerability.

As she listened, she felt afraid; her everyday power seemed to be disappearing, evaporating into something she knew well, but always before from a safe distance. She could not stand apart from this something now, nor could she bear to deafen herself to its call, a call that echoed not only all around her, but also inside her, beating insistently, drawing her in, and in. Seeing her fear, Glam reached out his hand to her; without any hesitation, she took it, and he pulled her to him, still singing, but very softly. In silence they lay together, not moving for a long time, their embrace firm yet delicate; they were each aware of every breath both took. Eventually, a strong, affectionate passion stirred in them, its fire more of light than of heat. Slowly surrendering to its imperatives, they gratefully glided into a long, exquisitely subtle lovemaking...

Ezparya didn't leave Glam until late that night. She felt wonderfully nourished, as if she'd been at some magical feast, resplendent with the choicest of the choice, bountiful to the most delicious extreme! However, this encounter with Glam, this richly textured meeting, this deep greeting, was much more than mere appetite, much more than exhiliration, much more than the thrill of sensual novelty or skilful satiation. There were tears on her face, tears she didn't remember crying. As she touched this unfamiliar wetness that stained her cheeks, she sighed, marvelling that such a sound could come from her...

He was still asleep, lying on his side, his mouth slightly open, his face like a child's. She halted an impulse to stroke his hair — the waiting tenderness in her hands confused and surprised her. She must go! She was weakening, losing her power! How strangely difficult it was to leave! She must concentrate, she must stand firm! A sensation of unmistakable caring arose in her, threatening to overwhelm her, until she, with a considerable effort, chilled it to a standstill. She must go, now! Fiercely, she surrounded her softness, gripping and compressing it, subjugating it to her will, forcing it down into a familiar hardness. This hardness, however, was not totally familiar; there was definitely something different about it now, something that had the flavour of Glam. No longer was she alone...

Nevertheless, she was still in command, was she not? Glam only added to what she already was, did he not? He only fed what was already thriving in her, did he not? He only enriched *her* soil — her earth, her land, her queendom! Hers! Artakiab would certainly disapprove of her actions. Let him! She knew what she was doing! Was she not clear about what she wanted, consistently clear? Somewhat reluctantly, she noticed an exaggerated urgency in both the tone and the content of her thoughts, an undercurrent of excessive and almost desperate self-convincing, but passed it off as no more than a byproduct of her passage back into her personal power, a mere mental realignment...

For an intensely unpleasant moment, Artakiab's face hung before her, warped and darkly unyielding, its eyes smouldering and sparking. Shaking herself free of the image, she leaned over Glam, letting her hair brush his face, no longer so concerned with leaving right away. Slowly, he stirred, yawning himself awake, glancing up at her.

"You sleep like a child," she said, surprised by the softness in her voice.

"Did you enjoy watching me?"

She slipped into his arms. How warm was his body, how muscular, and yet how very soft! "Yes, I did. But not as much as this!"

"You sound very different than you did earlier today."

"I could still have you killed," she said, with more than a hint of self-mockery.

"I yield to your need to reassert your power!" he laughed. "But do not think I make light of you!"

Brushing aside a fleeting sense of disorientation, she murmured, "Enough talk. Soon, I will go. Until then, let us converse in other ways." Bringing her mouth to his, she deepened their embrace, sure of her passion, sure of his.

15

Anticipation
Winging Her Stride

"Come in," said Xandur. "You can sit in front of me."

"Thank you," murmured Esmelana, feeling very shy — she'd never been alone with Xandur before, although she had occasionally seen him from a distance. Often she'd listened to other children noisily whispering about him, excitedly inflating themselves through association with their seemingly precious information, repetitiously creating wide-eyed drama out of their parents' assertion that Xandur was, besides being perhaps the wisest of the Sirdhanans, none other than Lantar in human form. Even more fascinating for them, however, were the reports of his strange powers, especially his ability to enter the sleep-dreams of others, in order to instruct them, or to draw their attention to some personal matter to which they were blinding themselves — to do this, he had to know such dreamers' deepest thoughts and feelings, somehow being more intimately involved with their depths than they were!

Of course, his appearance in another's dreams was not always a literal visitation of his spirit-presence, but frequently only the automatic creation of the dreamer, merely expressing some unresolved parental or authoritative force or difficulty in the dreamer's everyday life. Xandur sometimes spoke the dreams in which he had projected himself, *before* hearing the dreamer's version, which had already been meticulously recorded by the family priest; the correlation between the two, both in detail and in feeling, was astonishing, leaving no doubt as to Xandur's ability to be present in the dream-life of another.

Such a profundity of intuitive power was not unfamiliar to Esmelana, for she too could often view the inner workings of another, though she was not able to actually establish her presence within them, except under extraordinary conditions. Rarely had she demonstrated to others her capacity to thus see and know, for it usually made them uncomfortable, too faraway from her, and such distancing pained her, especially since Glam had left. It was much easier to convey her knowingness indirectly and unobtrusively, through the structure and dynamics of the games she played, or through the multidimensional subtleties of touch...

Only with Glam had she been uninhibitedly knowing, happily immersed in his obvious appreciation of her and her gift of true seeing. Often had she sat or lain with him, deeply absorbed in wordless understanding with him, not only on meditative occasions, but also in the very midst of the most mundane circumstances — how fine and how very satisfying it was to *feel* his love-bright understanding while they did something not normally considered to be at all conducive to such understanding! Intense he was, playful too, wonderfully adept at entering her world, inner and outer, passionately and creatively participating with all its inhabitants, giving them both a mythic and a comic feeling...

Away he had been swept by the waves, away he had gone, far away, and now here she was in front of Xandur. She had simply been told that he wanted to see her. She had not asked why.

"Do you know why I've asked you to visit me?" His voice was low and relaxed, each word precisely yet softly shaped.

"Yes," she replied, looking directly at him. "Because of how I sometimes see." Such large, soothing eyes he had! Pale brown they were, gentle yet immensely strong, not so much in emanation as in depth and spaciousness, their expression now both sorrowful and peaceful. But was it sorrow? And if it was, was it his, or hers? Both! Now she saw laughter, and behind that, a deep peace — no, not peace, but passion, a vast passion, wound round and round a blueflamed intensity, the core of which *nothing* could disturb! The everlasting Core, blazing so, so white, the Heart of Hearts, the Great Stillness, the fluxing, vibrant Stillness, ever pulsing out shape after shape, pulsing out and out as love, undying love, Lantar's Love, love incarnate, shining through every form! She began to cry, feeling a sudden and overwhelming heartache...

"Do not wait for Glam to return," said Xandur.

"But I want him to!" she blurted, sobbing loudly, forgetting what she had just seen in Xandur's eyes. "He must come back! He must!"

Tenderly, he placed his hand on top of her head. Her body wilted, and she sank into his lap, immediately comforted by the warmth and intelligence of his touch. After a while, he said, "Glam is gone. He is far, far away. Do you not see that?"

"I don't want to," she whispered, nestling in closer to him.

"Have you dreamt of Glam?"

"Yes! Many, many times! I used to see him in his canoe, crying for me, all covered in blood, screaming and screaming! Then, later, I kept seeing him chained in a small black room, screaming even more, his eyes all gone!" She cried some more, hugging Xandur as tightly as she could.

"And what about your dreams of the last few nights?"

"The black room keeps getting bigger, almost like it's breathing. I go to Glam, and he sees me, or seems to see me. Then his face changes, and he looks strange."

"In what way?"

"Well, he's twisted and ugly, and smiling at me, a horrible smile! I hate it! His teeth are very long and sharp, dirty red at the tips. I feel scared, and leave the dream."

"Was he alone?"

"Yes," she replied, then suddenly remembered more. "No, he actually wasn't alone! A thick, eerie thing was near him, sliding closer and closer to him; it had the same shape as his smile, the same horrible feeling. I couldn't stop it, even though I wanted to! Once it looked at me, not with its eyes, for it didn't have any, and I felt frozen —"

"You need not say more, Esmelana." He began stroking her hair, humming softly, cradling her in his love — she was such a beautiful child, so vulnerable and transparent, so unassuming in her precocity, so clearly aflame with Lantar! She had the same luminous passion as Glam, the same resolute integrity, and the same uncompromisingly adventurous spirit...

When she was still, he said, "You are to be an oracle. I myself will train you. When we need to, we will talk of Glam, but, much of the time, we will be busy with other matters."

Excitement rushed through her — an oracle! She could hardly wait to begin! And Xandur would be her guide! His hand was sure and warm, just like Glam's. How would Glam's hand feel now? What would it say to her?

"Do not worry about Glam," said Xandur, sitting her up. "He is far away, and we are here."

She looked at him, feeling deeply included in his brightness, which was almost as white as his hair. Then he smiled at her, a full, childlike smile, and an earthy jubilation surged through her, breaking up her remaining sorrow and doubt. For a while, she basked in his glow, then, feeling the words forming in his mind, knew it was time to go. Silently, she arose and left, relief and anticipation winging her stride...

16

Artakiab

Glam lay in his room, gazing at the ceiling through half-focused eyes, letting thoughts waft through his mind, few of which claimed enough of his attention to take on any substance. He could still feel Ezparya's body beside his; it had been at least ten days since they had first made love, ten seamless days of ever-deepening intimacy. Such a glory of pleasure it had been, such an abundance of ecstatic discovery! The unstressed yet potent lull, the waiting waves, the lush warmth and blissful currents, the rising heat ashiver with luminous intensity, the storm and the calm so lovingly intertwined, consuming and ever rejuvenating him...

It seemed, however, that no matter what Ezparya did with him, she did not relinquish hold on her personal power, not fully — she was vulnerable with him, especially during times of breakthrough passion, but never so vulnerable as to meet him where she was utterly defenceless. Almost always, he could sense an observance in her, a resolute witnessing of her actions. This witnessing of hers was to him like an undying flame, seemingly immune to the laws of change, but there was, most of the time, *effort* in it; it was clearly fueled by her will, not having its own life, as it appeared to have in Xandur —

But so what? Was she not doing what anyone must do who was awakening to their true condition? Yes, but only *partially* yes — there was too much tension in her self-observation, too rigid a grip, too fixated a focus. A brittle fortress of witnessing was hers, stiff with humourless sentinels, ever-suspicious and untrusting, unnecessarily encapsulated — where was the ease, the fluidity, that was essential for the Great Understanding?

And there was fear in Ezparya; he could sometimes feel it, even as he watched it cringe before the whip of her rule. She had mastered it, but not uprooted it; its very incarceration kept her bound to it, stuck in the jailor's position, ever-watchful for a breakout. Even more interesting to him was the amorphous sadness which hovered behind her fear, a sadness which she, when questioned by him, claimed did not exist, except in his mind's eye. He had not pressed her further then, deciding to wait for a more auspicious time to probe. All this aside, however, Ezparya was an amazing woman, a marvel of labyrinthine depth, unlike any he'd known on Amula...

Amula. So far away, so gone. Oma was but the shadow of a memory for him, and barely that. With a concentrated effort, he recalled her face feature by feature, carefully assembling it in his mind — was it only in a dream, an earthy, convincingly solid dream, that they had been together? The place in him where he could feel her was no longer shaped to hold her form. His love for her now seemed to belong to someone else, a simpler someone whose eyes he had once looked through...

Someone who had been the father of Esmelana. And still was! He could not leave her, regardless of what was happening to him — were not all his changes, however radical, only secondary to his bond with her? He couldn't leave her, no matter what he was or became! This was not his choice; it was a fact, an endless act. Without her, he'd likely disappear into Ezparya. Without her, he'd likely be harder, denser, meaner, cleverly frothing in savage caverns and sophisticated traps, obsessively and inventively *exploiting* his capacity for experience, letting the very heat of this wondrous fire he felt obscure its light...

Quickly and commandingly, Ezparya's presence flooded him; she seemed to have walked right into him. How elegantly passionate was her stride, how bright her greeting! Closing his eyes, he awaited her, a smile toying with the corners of his mouth, his breath moving in pleasurable waves, long and soft, faintly tingling — it was becoming easier and easier to sense her before she actually appeared physically.

Abruptly, she entered his room, clapping her hands loudly. "Come!" she said sharply, her voice gouging him.

"What for?" He sat up slowly. She looked very severe, as though she'd never been at all intimate with him. Her sudden distance frightened him — how stonily angular her face was now, how unnervingly distorted, how drained of heart, how cut off from him!

"Artakiab is here, with three hundred warriors. He awaits us now."

Glam began to speak, but she interrupted him. "It is enough for you to know that Artakiab strongly disapproves of me being at all involved with you. Now come!"

He stood, his voice shaking. "What does he expect of me? And what do you expect of me in this meeting?"

"You, my dear Glam," smiled Ezparya, her eyes fiercely glittering, "are but a disturbance to him, an annoyance, a mere plaything I've indulged long enough. I knew he'd come here, even before we left the city."

"But are you not his ruler?"

"Of course! But he has immense power, and is held in reverence by the populace. I cannot deal lightly with him; his obedience is not necessarily a given. As well, my rule has been deeply influenced by him. You might even say that he has, to some degree anyway, ruled through me, although that certainly hasn't been true since your arrival in Anushet."

Fear thrashed around in Glam, blindly extending itself throughout him. Ezparya seemed so remote; it was difficult to believe that she'd lain in his arms only a short time ago. There was no tenderness in her eyes now, no signs of love. "I am afraid," he said. "You appear distant and hard, and somehow at Artakiab's mercy."

She laughed harshly. "I am at no one's mercy! No one's! Do you think I am going to let him have his way with you?" Feigning playfulness, she hugged him. "I am not yet done with you!"

He felt stung by her touch, suddenly sobered. With quiet force, he said, "How well you cover your fear, Ezparya! The proud queen, clinging to her power so insistently that she squeezes the life out of her heart! You so efficiently pull back from me, no doubt preparing to show Artakiab that you are actually quite detached from me, unstained from contact with me."

"Perhaps, and perhaps not. I will do what I must. I cannot protect you from Artakiab."

A subtle sadness passed across her face, so light and brief that he barely saw it. Out of the room they walked, him following her; he wanted to walk beside her, to take her hand, as they had done so often in the past ten days, but now the distance felt appropriate, even oddly supportive of their bond. Together they were again, not so much in intimacy as in common purpose, gathering strength with every step, saying nothing, converting their fear into excitement and readiness. Her bare back was but a body-length in front of him, its finely muscled symmetry almost free of lateral movement, her arms swinging freely, her stride loose and sure. This was no dreamy corridor they were passing through, but rather an achingly real portal...

Soon, all too soon, they were in the courtyard. Artakiab sat on a chair beside the oval pool, dressed in a white robe. His forehead was bright red. Behind him stood at least a hundred motionless men, in a thicket of spears. Ezparya and Glam stopped just in front of Artakiab. He raised one hand, and the spears bristled; he lowered his hand, and all was still.

Then Ezparya spoke: "By whose command are you here?"

"By my own." His gaze sent a shiver through Glam.

"It is not my wish that you be here!" Her shout sent a shudder through the spears. "You are here against my wishes! If you do not *immediately* give me a more than excellent reason for your appearance here, you shall suffer the consequences of such flagrant disloyalty!"

"It was against my counsel that you came here in the first place." Artakiab's voice was thick and metallic, deceptively leaden. "I am not here to supply you with reasons, queen. I am here to put an end to your neglect of your duties as ruler of Anushet. Your indulgence of your appetite for this pitiful creature cowering beside you has harmed Anushet."

"What do you care for Anushet?"

"Such a question only reveals the extent of the degradation in which you now wallow and root."

"You are not indispensable, Artakiab," sneered Ezparya. "In fact, I now strip you of your position. You will have to earn it back."

"Foolish woman! Power is yet but a toy to you, a mere intoxicant. Perhaps this miserable excuse of a man trembling beside you finds your power fascinating, perhaps even erotic, but definitely suckable! You stink of him! Shall we now rid ourselves of the stench?"

Standing, Artakiab pointed his palms at Glam, exhaling noisily, and Glam gasped, feeling an icy shock slam into his belly. Though he understood little of the language of Anushet, he had understood Artakiab's intent right from the start, and had prepared himself for an attack. He had not, however, expected such force; it was more than he could withstand. Groaning, he bent double before the fisted might of Artakiab's will. With a great effort, he lifted his head for a moment, seeing Ezparya tightly guarded by Artakiab's men, her face all but hidden to him.

"Ezparya, you are in my grip now," growled Artakiab, his voice inhumanly low. "I suggest you closely observe the reaction of your creature to my probes. Let us see if he is truly worth keeping." Something remotely resembling a smile dragged itself across his face, exposing his teeth; all were yellowish-brown, except for his cuspids, which were white, and sharpened to fine points. In two steps, he was standing over Glam, who lay curled up on one side, his hands over his belly.

Glam didn't resist when Artakiab roughly rolled him onto his back, nor when he felt Artakiab's fingers pressing into his neck and chest, as if searching for something. It was an uncanny touch, full of presence, extremely sensitive, yet without a trace of tenderness. As the fingers and knuckles worked more and more deeply into his flesh, he felt like screaming, but wouldn't — searing, jagged bolts of pain scraped and rushed through him, seemingly deboning him, turning his muscles into flaming currents of Life-Energy, not for purposes of liberation, but of malevolent preparation for... At last, when a tiny moan escaped him, followed by a huge sigh, his tormentor leaned directly over his face, his eyes less than a handsbreadth away.

"A whimpering animal who masks his fear with a show of bravery," announced Artakiab, pressing his knees into Glam's chest. "He is but a child! A grovelling plaything for the bored queen! What a pity that she has so lowered herself as to be influenced by him! Such weakness, Ezparya, does not serve you or Anushet well, and therefore must be extinguished, wouldn't you say?''

Glam felt crushed by Artakiab's gaze. The eyes above him were saturated with accumulated power, bulging with unswervingly bright focus, their blackened irises webbed with tiny red fissures. The fingers seemed to be inside his rib cage, like a mass of ravenous iron snakes, writhing and striking, again and again...

A question came to Glam: Where was Artakiab vulnerable? Then he saw Artakiab grin — he had seen the question! A cruel grin it was, more snarl than smile. There was tremendous hate in Artakiab, but it was obviously subservient to his power. And such power! The contours and lines of his face proclaimed victory over all emotion, an unyielding masterminding of feeling, a triumph of self-manipulation. His mouth was a compressed slit, its lips almost non-existent, oozing darkly, seemingly eaten away by his achievements. Lumpy and faintly purplish was his skin, as if bruised from within. The red on his forehead was blood, fresh blood...

Glam retreated far into himself, away from the pain of Artakiab's touch, away from the penetration of the dark eyes, away from the invasion, the arrow-sharp entry of Artakiab's presence. Further and further away from his body-feeling he fled, concentrating himself into a tiny node of consciousness, all the while knowing that Artakiab was fully aware of his flight.

"You see, Ezparya," said Artakiab, standing over Glam, "how your precious creature runs from facing me. Now he hides, numbing himself to me, but I see him, all curled up inside himself, like a frightened snail gone to the darkest spiral of its shell. And *you* let this abjectness influence and copulate with you! Shall I now squash him? Or shall I pluck him from his shell?''

He pulled a small dagger from a sheath at his side. "But first, we shall see just how effective his withdrawal is."

As he watched the blade approaching his face, Glam called on his voice, inviting it with all his will. A short, dense scream burst out of him, briefly startling Artakiab, and then another scream, stronger than the first — but, unfortunately, they were only *his*, carrying none of the force of the sounds he'd released in the amphitheatre.

"So there *is* some life in Ezparya's plaything!" snarled Artakiab. "And this is the voice I've heard about? This bit of noise is what all the fuss has been about? Shall I now show you the source of his sounds?"

He brought his dagger down toward Glam's throat. "Are you not going to command me to stop, Ezparya? Is this all you care for this dear bed-companion of yours?"

"Do what you will," she said quietly. "It is at your peril. There is no turning back now, for any of us."

Again, Glam summoned his voice, making a supreme effort to be a medium for it. Over his throat swung the dagger's point, in a slow, teasing arc. His screams and roars were very strong, but carried no unusual force; desperately, he called on Lantar to help him, but nothing happened.

Nothing!

Suddenly, he realized that it was not his to make happen — these circumstances were not *his* to alter or master, any more than the weather was his to change. He was helpless. Helpless! His only power was in the acceptance of his helplessness, the heartfelt, full-bodied acceptance, the acceptance that, in its very expansiveness, transcended *all* resignation! As he realized this, and realized it with his entire being, he felt more spacious, more at ease, even though his screaming and fearfulness continued; there was now room in him for something more than *his* intentions, something rippling with potency, something about to birth...

The dagger-tip lightly stroked his neck. He remembered Merot's death. Although he could have easily dissociated from his physicality as his own death loomed near, he chose to remain in *feeling* contact with all of himself, whatever the coming pain. Escape was no longer attractive to him. Above, he could see the twisted cords of Artakiab's neck, backed by a billowing grey sky. It was raining.

Raining hard and pure.

He stopped screaming, and a great sadness filled him, an ancient, multi-faced grief for all the unnecessary hurt delivered from human to human, all the torture and revenge and greed, all the misguided need, all the abuse, all the destruction of love's creations, all the turning away from...

With soft yet overwhelming intensity, he looked directly at Artakiab — into the black eyes he gazed, pouring into them with the insistency of a rain-gorged river, rapid and wild, exquisitely savage, churning with unshackled feeling, acrash with a thousand melodies, overflowing with a love both fierce and tender, animated by a power, a vast wonder of a power, that he knew was not merely his own, a power free of all ambition.

No sound came from him.

He felt Artakiab's surprise. Then he could go no further — Artakiab had stopped him, damming his entry. But it had not been *his* entry! What Artakiab had managed to block was none other than the feeling-force, the capacity for compassion, the need for empathetic communion with all other beings, that he *himself* had had to extrude from his being in order to manifest his particular kind of power.

As Glam understood this, he looked at Artakiab with something resembling pity. Growling and spitting, Artakiab slapped his face hard, over and over. "Your creature has made his effort to overpower me! I will not waste any more time on him!"

He pushed his dagger-point just into the surface of Glam's chest, slowly dragging it up toward his throat in a widening red groove. Glam struggled to free himself, but could not move. Again, helplessness, and an even more potent acceptance of it, a sudden, effortless expansion of being, accompanied by a sublime sense of immense, almost limitless embodiment...

Death now so, so close, Death the passageway, Death the so-familiar outflowing winged by inner knowing, Death the luminous door — before him hovered Esmelana's face, transparent with love and recognition, her eyes his sky. Into the Light that so clearly shaped her face he would die. Die *into* Life, deeper and deeper into Life, die without regretting any goodbye, die free, die in love, fly, fly, fly through the holy doors with open eyes, without clinging to any disguise...

"No!" A finely-honed shout, ferociously female, arcing near.

Artakiab fell aside, a spear through his shoulder. Over him stood Ezparya, her eyes wet and savage. With a great, hissing sound, she spun around once, encircling herself with a command that none touch her. The armed men all stood as if frozen.

"I am your queen! None of you shall be punished for supporting Artakiab if you will now obey my orders!"

"Seize her now!" bellowed Artakiab. Some of the men hesitantly approached her.

"He is a traitor!" she spat. "Bind him before he rises!"

A few moved toward Artakiab, but fell back before the withering contempt and authority of his gaze. Still sprawled on the tiles, he said, "Now we shall see who is master. I taught you well, but I didn't teach you to overpower me."

"Do you dare to challenge me?" she snapped, driving all fear from her voice.

Down smashed the rain, unnoticed.

Wavering slightly, Artakiab stood, blood gushing from his wound, his face shadowed. Ezparya shivered as she watched him summon his power, seeing a tangible condensation of attention all around his head and abdomen. Like a huge monument he stood, rooted more and more strongly, almost unbearably solid, weathering the situation, frighteningly alert amidst the crepuscular erosion of his body. Once she had seen him naked — there was a preternatural shaping to his body, a premeditated and horribly fascinating marring of its natural contours, made all the more repulsive by his skin, which was asquirm with fatly bulging veins and raw, crescent-shaped scars.

Artakiab stared at her, his eyes aflame, and tore the spear from his shoulder; blood leapt from his wound, then stopped at a word from him. The warriors were now but gape-jawed children, their eyelids irresistibly pulled back, their spear-points passively gutting the sagging blacks of the sky. Glam lay unmoving, his hands over the cuts in his flesh. Ezparya's fear grew — she knew she could not match Artakiab for long, for whatever she could command in herself he *already* was. Were not the thrusts of her will merely glancing off him?

"Seize him now!" she yelled, but no one moved. Artakiab took two quick steps toward her, the bloody spear in his hand. As if in a dream, Glam sat up. He saw Ezparya tall and trembling mightily, her head high, emanating a ring of intense force all around herself, and he saw Artakiab, spear held aloft, advancing toward her, his face an elemental mask, hard and jagged, sweepingly desolate, burning with an unearthly fire, his eyes incandescent ice. Gathered near were the armed men, seemingly paralyzed, vague dream-beings mechanically awaiting animation...

He took in the courtyard, noticing its tiles glistening with dancing rain, quickly scanning the viscous indigo of the oval pool, glancing once at the sky, seeing its puffy greys smeared and erupting with black. The silence was deafening, the leap but a heartbeat or two away.

Now Artakiab was directly in front of Ezparya. She shook like a tree in a storm. Smoothly and almost hypnotically, he swung the spear's shaft against the side of her head, with a dull, wincing crack that shattered the silence. She fell, appearing to float to the ground...

Raining slow and sure.

Artakiab raised his spear over Ezparya's throat, the sinews of his forearms thickly writhing — such a long, elastic moment it was, almost done, yet not fully completed, as though awaiting interruption, no, not awaiting, but needing, needing...

Now — *now*!

He sprang at Artakiab, knocking him away from the crumpled figure of Ezparya. With thunderous fury, Artakiab whirled to face Glam. Again, Glam leapt at him, feet first. With astonishing speed, Artakiab lunged aside, so that Glam missed him completely.

As he landed on the tiles, slipping crazily, he felt Artakiab's boot drive deep into his upper belly. He shrieked with pain, seeing the foot now coming toward his neck, its arc quickly picking up speed. He knew he couldn't stop it — but what was that ghostly shadow behind Artakiab, just over his right shoulder? That bluish phantom, suddenly fleshing out, so pale and miraculously solid behind the veils of falling rain?

Ezparya, dagger in hand.

Already, she had brought it down into Artakiab's back. As he turned, howling, she drove her blade into the base of his neck. Before he could strike her, she fell in front of him, just below the fountain of blood spraying from his throat, then rose up like a surfacing diver, thrusting her dagger up into the underside of his jaw, her free arm extended straight up, like a released arrow. Artakiab stumbled, violently shaking his head, almost losing his balance. There was still life in him! Snatching a spear from the nearest man, she drove it into Artakiab's chest.

Ripping out the spear, he charged her, seemingly oblivious to his wounds, but before he could reach her, he fell heavily, with Glam on his back. Quickly, Ezparya grabbed another spear and, as Glam moved aside, thrust it down between Artakiab's shoulderblades.

It was over. She and Glam moved away from Artakiab, watching his final shudders. At last, he was still, the spear rising from him like a lone tree atop a stark hill. The courtyard shimmered slightly, like the landscape of a lucid dream. For a long time, no one moved or spoke. Down poured the rain, down in dense sheets, down and down, spreading Artakiab's blood over much of the courtyard, its sounds exaggerating rather than breaking the quivering, enervated silence...

Finally, Ezparya spoke, her voice low and firm. "Take his body outside the gates. Cover it well, so that no animal may touch it. Tomorrow at sunset, burn it completely. Those who attend the cremation are to wash their clothes afterward, and to bathe."

An inaudible sigh rippled through the men. It was over. Glam watched seven of them pick up Artakiab's body and carry it from the courtyard. The others remained, looking at Ezparya, their faces sporadically flinching.

"Do not punish them," said Glam.

She looked at him, her eyes sorrowful yet strong, her face very young, her hair stained with Artakiab's blood. The side of her head where he had struck her was swollen, the bruising extending down to her cheek. Breathing deeply, she said, "None of you shall be punished. After the cremation, you shall return to the city with the news that Artakiab is dead, and that he died a traitor."

Silently, she and Glam left the courtyard, slowly walking out into the surrounding countryside. The rainfall was but a drizzle now, refreshingly cool. Bits of blue were breaking through the dark grey slabs of sky; a few sunrays fanned down, each pearly shaft, however pale, gladdening them. Tears poured down Glam's face. At last, they stopped walking. Wide-winged birds circled in the distance, their sounds thin yet sweet.

"Artakiab was my teacher," she whispered.

"Yes." He took her head between his hands, and brought her to him.

"He guided me. He knew me like no other."

"And he controlled you."

"Perhaps," she said softly. "He was a master of power — but let us not talk any more. I don't want to think of him now. I need to have my wounds tended to, as do you, and I need to rest."

He took her more fully into his arms — how welcome was this relief that kept sweeping through him, how blissfully sobering! Over her shoulder, he could see misty greens, here and there swelling up into vague hills, and, further back, the even vaguer blur of the horizon, almost the same colour as the sky. Comforting was this gently-layered blurriness, softly diffusing the intensity of the encounter with Artakiab. Everything seemed looser now, more benign, more blessed, more rounded, kinder...

Ezparya stood a little stiffly for a while, then let her forehead rest on Glam's shoulder. A few sobs escaped her; it was the first time he'd known her to cry. At last, she let her entire body droop like a spent flower, giving all her weight to him. For a very long time, they stood unmoving, intertwined and breathing together, infusing each other with a tender warmth, before returning to her room.

17

Truth
Cannot Be Rehearsed

Blackened plumes of smoke rose into the evening sky, pinkened here and there by the fading fires of sunset. The smoke sprang from faraway flames, only the tips of which Glam and Ezparya could occasionally see from the terrace where they sat.

"Are all who die in Anushet cremated?" he asked.

She nodded, her eyes on the uppermost reaches of the smoke. "Do you not also do the same on Amula?"

"Yes, except for those known as Sirdhanans. They are buried in the sides of certain cliffs that face out over the largest valley in Amula. The corpses of Sirdhanans do not usually rot like ordinary bodies; their flesh remains intact and fresh, for as long as a year after their death. Their bodies are closely guarded, to prevent them from becoming the meals of animals, birds, or insects. It is considered to be a great privilege to guard the corpse of a Sirdhanan. Many Amulans make regular pilgrimages to these burial sites, for purposes of rejuvenation and remembrance of —"

"But what stops the bodies from rotting?" interrupted Ezparya, turning to face him.

"The presence of the Sirdhanan, which is, in some ways, much more powerful after death than during physical life. For a Sirdhanan, death is not what it is for everyone else; for them, *all* experiences, including death, are but dream-play, endlessly inventive shapings and expressions of the Consciousness in which they are so deeply established. They are no more disturbed by death than is the ocean by the activity of its waves."

He paused; this wasn't what he would have said on Amula. Now, it didn't seem as true, not as clearcut — how did he know that they weren't disturbed? And, moreover, was it not true that the majority of Sirdhanans were more than a bit corpse-like in appearance, having already apparently abdicated all but the necessary minimum of physical embodiment well prior to their death? Were *they* really the pinnacle of human possibility? Or were they just adepts at dissociating from the passions and difficulties of Life, making a religion out of their capacity to hide out in the stillpoint's infinite bubble? Xandur wasn't, though. Xandur...

"The bodies don't rot," he continued. "I myself have seen this. The absence of decay reminds Amulans of the One Who gives them life."

"And who is that?"

"Lantar. But Lantar isn't a particular who — Lantar is the name for the Source and Substance of all that is, created and uncreated. Lantar is both Infinite Being, and Consciousness Itself. I, however, don't mean consciousness in the ordinary, thinking sense, but rather consciousness that is *inherently* self-aware, *forever* self-aware, depending on no object, person, or experience for its existence. Such Consciousness is, paradoxically, also the great Life-Force Itself, and is therefore not just the apex of witnessing — at least that's how Xandur, my main Sirdhanan teacher, sometimes described Lantar. Sirdhanans, some of them anyway, are so intimate with Lantar's Essence, so deeply aligned with Eternal Being, that they literally *are* Lantar in human form, not in the sense that everyone is, but transparently, obviously, consciously..."

Again, he felt uncomfortable with his words. They sounded hollow to him, lifeless, a merely *factual* reporting, devoid of any Truth, far too burdened with information to be truly alive; put another way, the informational had usurped the position of the essential, instead of being in peripheral harmony with it. Was not Truth far more than facts? Was not Truth uncompromisingly alive, fresh, and spontaneous, always both illuminating and transcending its content? Truth could not be memorized, nor parroted, or it was not Truth, but only information. Truth could not be rehearsed, but only expressed in *empathetic* correspondence with *all* the qualities of Its moment; Truth's content could only emerge newborn, again and again, with each new encounter, creatively mixing its information with That out of which all information arose...

"So these are people of great power," murmured Ezparya, her profile to him.

"Yes, but not power like Artakiab's. More like the power of a shoot breaking up green and slender-straight through hard, stony soil. Or the power of waves, or wind. It is a natural power that expresses itself through them, a force free of personal ambition. They do not exploit this power, except perhaps in the service of their own bodily decomposition, and even that is intended to nourish the spiritual well-being of Amulans."

A little better, but still somewhat hollow, still too carefully arranged. He could have been speaking to almost anyone — *that* was it! He was but delivering a report, and it didn't really matter *who* heard it, as long as there was someone to hear it. What would he have said if he had spoken *specifically* to Ezparya, instead of to a faceless listener? His word-play, his tone, his gestures, his emphases and pauses, his flights and dips, would have *all* spontaneously synchronized with his moment-to-moment experience of her, both accurately *and* feelingly reflecting the qualities, whether obvious or subtle, of their contact, thereby enriching rather than just filling up their time together. In other words, he would have been empathetically *present* with her, in responsive communion with whatever epitomized each moment, allowing his speech to honour whatever was occurring between their beings...

No longer could Ezparya see the smoke. Venus blazed in the rapidly darkening sky. "You speak eloquently of these Sirdhanans. You praise them, speaking of them as though they are where you assume you ought to be. They sound like gods, and not cruel or capricious ones. So why did you want to leave Amula?"

"I had to go."

"Why?"

"My going was deeper than reasons could make it — does a wave need to supply a reason for its shoreward pull? Does a fir need to know why it grows the way it does? And even if it did have reasons, what good would they do? They would only drain energy from the very activity they sought to explain!"

"You do have a clever tongue!" she laughed. "Nevertheless, there are reasons deeper than any thought, hidden motivations that make their presence known in many ways. You left what sounds like a peaceful, happy land, wisely and benevolently overseen. Maybe it was all too childish for you, just too easy, too naively innocent, too rigid in its softness, without truly worthy challenges — but what does Anushet have that you could not get, or create, in Amula?"

"You."

"Do not flatter me! And do not insult me with your facile answers! You are fascinated by more than me here; you are not just adding Anushet experience to your Amulan experience. A lot more is going on than mere accumulation, wouldn't you say?"

"So what *am* I doing?" Now he was angry.

"Asking a foolish question, instead of uncovering *who* is asking such a question! Just who is it who insists on asking such a thing? *Who?* Who is it that now glares at me, all red and ruffled? Or, more to the point, *what* is it? And is there more to you than this urge to defend yourself?"

She paused, then, seeing him starting to smile embarrassedly, continued in a much softer voice. "You have spoken quite learnedly of your Sirdhanans, portraying them as the very heart and pinnacle of Amulan culture, yet you seem peculiarly disinterested in them, almost bored! Is it not true that you have all but forgotten Amula?"

He stared at her. Moonlight lit her hair, making a starkly beautiful landscape out of her face. "Maybe I have, Ezparya. Maybe I have — the man I was in Amula died on the shores of Anushet. I know not who I am now."

"You never really did."

"And I suppose you do?" he retorted, surprised at his edginess and unwillingness to pursue their conversational line — what good was it doing him to obstruct their flow together? And what was this urge, this violent urge, to crush her?

"Let us not argue," she smiled. "Seriousness of this sort does not

become you. I'm quite sure Tornellas will be glad to argue with you
when we return, for soon we must return. But now, sweet, rich now,
let's enjoy *this*! Artakiab is dead, and we are alive. Let's step out of
your past and mine, and enjoy ourselves, now!" She took his hands,
squeezing and caressing them, her eyes bright with both mischief and
longing.

"Still," he said slowly, only partially responding to her touch, "I don't
feel like celebrating. I don't know if Artakiab is really gone — all day
I've had a feeling of him hovering around us, like a stench at the edge
of a pleasing scent. I don't think he will let you go easily."

"Do you really think he has any power over me, Glam? He cannot
haunt me, nor influence me any more. I simply won't permit it!"

"He is still here," Glam said quietly.

"For you, perhaps, but not for me."

"How can you be so sure?"

"Because I spilled his blood and sent his spirit fleeing! I know I am not
deluding myself. Whatever is left of Artakiab has no power to invade
me, for I have made myself impermeable to it. Yes, the subtle
embodiment of what he is now *is* here, definitely here, looking for
openings, quite insistently. I, however, am well-guarded against such
parasitic intrusion — he himself trained me in such matters years ago.
He is for me now like a breath of air trying to pass through a solid
wall."

"So he *is* here for you! Do not take him so lightly —"

"I will do what I will do."

"I am sure you will," he muttered, smiling a twisted smile, a barely
perceptible knotting quickly passing through his body...

18

Back To The City

Five days after Artakiab's cremation, Ezparya and Glam returned to the city, where they were greeted by a large, noisy crowd. As their chariot slowly wound through the welcoming throng, Glam studied its bobbing, shouting rows of faces — whether thick or thin, wide or narrow, young or old, almost all looked uniformly and disgustingly coarse to him. Such a raucous chorus, such braying enthusiasm, such gross insensitivity! Such a sickening exhibition of force-fed patriotism and frothing mechanicalness, such a cheery slosh of degradation, such a slopbucket of unswerving mediocrity!

This poor mob had all the alertness of cattle busy with their cud — just look at them, so dumbly waiting for Ezparya to tell them who he was to be to them! The drool of their anticipation seemed to be enveloping the chariot, seeping in here and there, bubbly green and viscous, shapelessly reaching for him. How he hated this frenzy to be fed, this obsession with being filled! Did they not remember him from that long-ago day when he'd faced the white-maned beast in their shrieking amphitheatre? Did they not remember lusting for the spilling of his blood? Thick-fleshed savages, so busily gobbling up their gory dollops of entertainment, concerned only with satiation!

At last, he turned from his scrutiny of the crowds; perhaps another day he would look upon these beings with a kinder eye, but today was not the day. Ezparya sat close beside him, occasionally glancing at the onlookers, never smiling. She felt Glam's revulsion and anger, and took his hand in hers — soon, she thought, he'd learn to be indifferent, to be no more bothered by the natives than he would be by pigs or goats or any other animal. Yes, their coarseness would soon cease to irritate him; in fact, it would one day undoubtedly please him, when he realized just how valuable such unwavering vulgarity could be, insofar as governing was concerned. Since Anushetites, in general, didn't think of themselves other than as their appetites, their loyalty was easily bought, given how predictable and easily satisfied their appetites were — all she needed to do was be in *full* control of all that they had been trained to lust for...

She laughed to herself — this very afternoon, the amphitheatre would be packed with them, row upon hungry row, voraciously eager to hear her announcements, and to watch the following displays of human slaughter. Unquestioning spectators they were, just about all of them, wonderfully predictable, always seeking to be viscerally associated with the objects of their lust, without any interference. Freedom for them was to be fed when they were hungry, or, more precisely, when their hunger was catalyzed according to her strict directions. Her art was to train their yearnings toward behaviours reflecting and reinforcing the lowest possibilities of human adaptation, thus teaching them to equate being themselves with being established in the most perverse pits of their desiring self.

The inculcation of this association between self-security and lust-satisfaction had not been difficult for her to implement and sustain, except for rare occasions in the realm of religion. She did whatever she could to align her people to deities who demanded the very qualities that *already* characterized Anushet; those who dared stray from such allegiance were either crippled with guilt, or, much more commonly, provided as amusement fodder for the rest. Of course, the deities of Anushet didn't really exist, except as bizarrely exaggerated personifications of the prevalent behaviours of Anushetites. The hierarchy of these gods and goddesses was modelled after that of Anushet itself — the chief god was simply the biggest and most powerful, a six-headed giant who not only was partial to human flesh, but who also had been thoroughly implanted in everyone's dreams, thanks to the relentlessly efficient application of trancebased suggestion and imagery given periodically to all, regardless of age.

Absolute loyalty to the chief god, and to Ezparya, was required; the slightest transgression was rarely forgiven. Artakiab's power had been great to break through this taboo, but, thought Ezparya, so then had Glam's...

As they passed through the last strands of spectators, he sighed, turning to her. "How do you think they will take the news?"

"Like everything else. They'll digest it easily, and just as easily forget it. I didn't see any mourners for Artakiab. If they hesitate a little to accept you, it won't be out of doubt or concern, but out of dullness."

"They're a lowly bunch to you, aren't they?"

"They have their use. They are remarkably dependable."

"You mean obedient!"

Earnestness marched into his voice. "Have they no aspirations for a less degraded life? How can they not want to rise above the muck they inhabit?"

"They don't consider it muck."

"But it is!"

"A mere *interpretation*, and one that not many of them would appreciate hearing. And for those who might be foolish enough to really listen, it would only increase their misery."

He checked the headlong surge of his reply — why should he side with these savages? Why should he argue for their betterment? Out of misguided loyalty to his and their common humanity? Or out of that pseudo-caring, that false tolerance, that aberrated humanitarianism, indulged in by those whose egoic makeup relied on such supposed compassion? Real compassion was much, much more than the repetitious mouthing of the innate goodness of all people; in fact, it was unburdened by any sort of romanticism. Not only were sentimentality and hope transcended by real compassion, but their opposites, cynicism and despair, also were. Authentic compassion made room for distaste, as well as for joy — its caring was passionate and ruthless, its eye unseducible, its heart open to feeling *everything*, no matter how painful. In the very core of that capacity to freely feel, that ever-spontaneous, mind-free capacity, was an awakening force that he yearned to be more intimate with...

He was not willing, however, to *fully* feel the inner lives of these
half-humans, fearing that such an intense contraction of being might
damage him in some way. No, that was not it! Such a gloomy forecast
was but an excuse to hold back the fullness of his empathy. It was
simply not time to do so — a premature pushing back of his reactivity
and disgust would do him and them no good at all. Just look at them!
They were obviously suffering, and just as obviously numbing
themselves to their suffering; their entire presentation of themselves
only served to camouflage, and therefore deepen, their suffering...

Even if he were to eloquently and convincingly point this out, what
use would it be? Their concern was *not* about awakening from their
lot, but rather about *exploiting* its possibilities! They were *not* mere
victims of a tyrannical superstructure — they were, moment-to-
moment, making a choice, were they not? Yes, yes, their *conditioning*
was making the choice, but *that* was also a choice, was it not? Their
lack of awareness of this did not in any way excuse those who had
dulled them in the first place, but nor did it totally excuse *them* — all
in all, they seemed to be but an easily controllable and exploitable mob
whose sole reason for existence was to be pleasurably distracted...

Suddenly, he felt closer to Ezparya, understanding more clearly now
her detachment from her people, even as he turned away from his
seeing of her role in their condition — why should he side with
anyone? Why bother? Was not everyone getting *exactly* what they
most needed? Did not their very actions and reactions keep setting in
motion corresponding forces that both reflected and exaggerated their
current condition, forces whose very structure and dynamics literally
invited insight and revelatory breakthrough? Yes, but...

"So," said Ezparya, "how shall we raise these poor beasts up from
their manured ruts? What noble aspirations shall we indoctrinate them
with? What great insights shall we ladle into their troughs?"

"Let's change the subject."

"No!" She thrust her face at him, with caricatured earnestness. "Let's
not! Maybe you're right — maybe I've been too hard on my people.
Should we begin by inviting them to visit my quarters? They could
bathe there, ten at a time, and gawk, and then they could listen to your
passionate pleas for a higher way of life! You might even attract a
following!"

"Enough!" he laughed.

"You see, you're as fickle as them! One moment, you ardently support a cause, in this case, the downtrodden of Anushet, and the next moment, you've abandoned your position. Are you actually going to sit back and permit the masses of Anushet to remain in what you term their muck?"

"Yes!" He blew at the tiny red feathers above her eyes.

"They're a lowly bunch to you, aren't they?"

"I can see you'll use anything!"

"I'm afraid I have to," she said. "Otherwise, there's a danger you'll incite the populace into unnecessary stupidities."

"But that's impossible, Ezparya! How could they possibly rise up when you've done such a thorough job of crippling them?"

"I'll let you think about that for a while. Just don't be too quick to judge me for what you see in this land! The conditions of Amula may seem to you to be superior, far more humane and caring, but please consider the fact that you *left* such a supposedly wonderful place, and that you don't appear to want to leave here."

"That has far more to do with you than with the natives of Anushet."

"So it seems," she murmured, her eyes both piercing and sad. "So it seems. But look — here we are at the gates of my quarters. Tornellas will be awaiting us inside."

Open swung the towering black gates, and their chariot passed through, stopping in the center of a small, rectangular courtyard. Quickly stepping out, they walked through several long, dark corridors, at last entering a brightly lit room, bare except for a thick black carpet. Tornellas was there.

"Don't look so startled, Tornellas!" declared Ezparya, motioning that all should sit. "Did you hear the details of Artakiab's death?"

"Yes."

"And what did you hear?"

"That you, with Glam's assistance, killed him."

"And what else did you hear?"

Tornellas sat even more stiffly, her lips twitching; Glam had never before noticed just how thin she was. Her hands lay half-clenched in her lap, purplewhite and rhythmically writhing, as though, thought Glam, she were strangling two vipers. "It was said, my queen, that you and Glam were intimate, and that you and he spent much time in each other's company."

"Does that surprise you?"

"You will do as you must."

"Come, Tornellas! You know you can speak freely."

"I already have."

"You are such a proud one, Tornellas, even prouder than me! You need not fear my punishment if you voice something I don't like. So, tell me, what do you think of my so-called intimacy with Glam?"

"I, I —" How very awkward she felt, how horribly frozen! Curse Ezparya for putting her in this position! Did not the queen care at all how *she* might feel? And what was this nonsense about being able to speak freely? "I half expected it, I must admit, but only in the service of your pleasure. And I did feel some concern when I heard how much time you were giving him, though of course I'm sure you knew exactly what you were doing."

"Just as I'm sure you handled your jealousy well!" smiled Ezparya.

"I was not, and am not jealous!"

"The very force of your denial speaks otherwise."

Tornellas's face reddened, sourly puckering. Then Glam spoke: "You need not make her squirm, Ezparya. She has served you well. Is it not obvious that she is baffled by the depth of your interest in me?"

"And are you too thus baffled, Glam?" exclaimed Ezparya, playfully nudging him, then wetly kissing his cheek.

"Baffled beyond all hope!"

Ezparya took Glam's hand in hers, breathing deeply, then turned to directly face Tornellas. Though she had total command over Tornellas, she wanted more from Tornellas than mere obedience, or forced agreement — how odd it was to have such power over another, and yet feel vulnerable at the same time, even *caring* — how very unfamiliar were these sympathetic pangs she felt for Tornellas, and how strangely nourishing! "This very afternoon, I am going to announce that Glam is my consort, and that he is to assist me in my rule. Also, I will ask that he be given the same respect as I am."

Tornellas stared at Glam, seemingly unable to speak, shock and fury competing for control of her face. Finally, he stood, saying to her, "I do not impose myself on you. You need not hate me, Tornellas, and you need not view me as Ezparya's biggest mistake, though I may well be! Ask me whatever you need to ask me now, though not necessarily in the manner you adopted when you stooped to interrogate that lowly Amulan beast!"

She continued staring at him, her anger bubbling with hurt. How excruciatingly difficult it was to speak! It was all she could do to not cry... "Are you in agreement with Ezparya's announcements?" How she hated this trembling in her voice!

"It's not a matter of agreement, nor of disagreement — it goes much deeper than that. All I know is that I must stay with her, and that I want to."

"Do you not feel out of place?" If only this trembling would pass!

"Yes," he replied, enjoying the stumbling intensity of her gaze. "But I don't mind, not at all!"

"Are you content to be with Ezparya?" How she hated this!

"No! Not content, but excited, challenged, warmed, thrilled, moved! I am deeply affected by her, and she by me, as you must have by now gathered — we have met in a land you have never travelled."

"And what land is that?" What pleasure it would be to eviscerate him!

"Let's say it's a place where love outshines fear, a place where passion has a heart." Even though she wasn't really listening, he knew he must go on — this was not the time to strip bare her hostility, nor to shatter her shields.

"How fascinating." What a gross outrage to have to submit to such a conversation! Now the trembling was even worse, claiming the left side of her face...

"Ezparya loves me —" Now he'd had enough! An urge to strike her rushed through him, hot and insistent; with some effort, he directed the force of his violent desire into his voice. "Listen to what I'm saying, and stop trying to hold yourself together! What you are now fighting in yourself is *exactly* what is happy to hear that Ezparya *loves* me!"

"And how do you know that?" A huff of incredulity halted her trembling. How could Ezparya just sit there, eyes all aglow, and let this ugly foreigner utter such garbage? How could she?

"I feel it!" The words rolled heavily from his mouth, drawing back the corners of his lips into a wide, tight smile, half-baring his teeth. Without warning, a powerful current of sensation, fiery and thickly twisted, jerkily passed through him.

"You feel *what?*" asked Tornellas, surprised at her sudden calmness; it was as if his spasms had relieved her of her distress...

"That Ezparya — " He tripped over his words, feeling as though two very different phrasings were fighting for the use of his tongue. The smile, though now less taut, still lingered on his face.

"What is it, Glam?" asked Ezparya.

"I don't know. I felt confused for a moment. Somehow I forgot what we were discussing."

"Do you remember now?"

"Yes. I was saying that you love —" Again, he felt the surging, hotly knotted sensation, seemingly entering him through his forehead and lower abdomen. With a tremendous effort, he cut off its entry, and continued speaking — the interruption had been strong, but brief — "*me*! An obvious, wonderfully undeniable feeling!" He could not help but notice that his voice, though potent, sounded peculiarly empty.

"I have no more questions," said Tornellas, smiling slightly.

"Then do I have your support?" asked Ezparya. Tornellas nodded. "This is no whim of mine," continued Ezparya. "It is *not* a matter of love, but of fortune, of unparalleled opportunity. Artakiab wanted to deny me this opportunity, and he paid for his opposition with his life. I must warn you, Tornellas, to not fall prey to the assumption that I am making a mistake."

Her eyes swung in a slow, luminous arc. "Do not forget that I am queen. And do not think that I forget it when I am with Glam. You may go now."

As Tornellas left, Glam felt a sense of gloating, of perverse triumph, followed by an intense flash of stabbing fear and horror. Ezparya's body came to him, warm and pleasingly firm, richly reassuring.

"Do not," she softly said, "be concerned with your uncertainty. Tornellas will undoubtedly take some time to adjust to your new status.

"And one more thing: Tornellas is Artakiab's sister."

19

More Than A Dream

Densely packed was the afternoon sky, crammed with plump, jostling clouds. On a white dais in the center of the amphitheatre sat Ezparya, flanked by Glam and Tornellas. Finally, she stood, raising her arms overhead, the folds of her purple robe dramatically rolling with her words.

"Citizens of Anushet, listen to me! Artakiab is dead! He died a traitor's death! Never again is his name to be uttered!" She paused, waiting for the ripples in the audience to subside. "Beside me is the one called Glam, the one who helped me slay Artakiab! He is dear to me, and is from now on to live as my male, and also as assistant to me in rule!"

The crowd buzzed and rumbled, undulating like water in a suddenly jostled pail.

"Hear me!" she shouted in a high, penetrating voice. "I will not repeat this! You are from now on to recognize Glam as my consort and assistant in rule! Such is my command!"

All was quiet. Ezparya sat, her palms turning up and moving apart exceedingly slowly in a gesture of giving, not so much to the audience as to the forces governing everything. Let the spectators make what they would of this utterly uncharacteristic movement of hers, this fluid mudra — why not let them look upon her gratitude for what was happening for her? After a long silence, she left the dais, followed by Glam and Tornellas, walking up to seats in the uppermost section of the stadium. When they were seated, the dais was ceremoniously removed, and four men were dragged feet-first to the spot it had occupied. One of them was crying noisily. Another was screaming like a baby. Two gaunt lions approached them, growling.

Ezparya squeezed Glam's hand, as if in warning. The lions ripped into two of the men, to the roaring approval of the spectators. Back to normal, thought Glam; he felt nauseous, but not upset, nor outraged, as he'd been when he had last witnessed such carnage...

The lions were hungry. So was the crowd. Both were being fed; both were enslaved to the demands of their appetite. And was he really any different? Roughly, he slapped away his question, turning his attention to matters more visual — why be concerned with such worrisome abstractions? The bloodletting below seemed very remote to him, almost phantasmal, just more drama, just another variation, another play upon the basic Condition in which everything, however sublime or sordid, inhered. It was an unpleasant circumstance, to be sure, a nasty piece of barbarity, appallingly crude, but, all in all, fundamentally no more than just another splash of colour in the entrapping pageantry of Existence, no more or less significant than anything else...

But was it *actually* so unpleasant? Did he *have* to dislike it? Was there some irrefutable logic that demanded he display distaste for such spectacles? Abruptly, he no longer felt nauseous. Ezparya's grip lightened. To his surprise, he laughed — the whole thing was so thoroughly ridiculous, so predictable, and so incredibly tedious! All these rabid onlookers, so fixated on the slaughter below, so busily fascinated by it — and, more to the point, fascinated by *their* lower life, the meaty thrill of their own bestiality, the murderous heat of their own loins! Lust-ridden automatons they were, so cheaply enchanted, ugly and yet also not ugly, filthy yet obedient clay in Ezparya's hands. She was their will, their brain, their headquarters...

But then who was their heart? He giggled at his question, visualizing a gigantic body with nothing between its head and belly except for a desert of undifferentiated grey. A barren, oppressive place was this zone, screamingly lonely — only a fool would try to start something growing in it! Only a fool, an utter fool, would attempt to establish a heart, a center of love, in such a wasteland! Yes, only a fool salivating for the glory of rescuing others from their self-imposed hells, a fool of insincere sincerity, eagerly campaigning for spiritual applause! Far be it from him to even consider such foolishness! Again, he laughed, so loudly that Ezparya jumped.

"What do you laugh at?"

"At all of this!" The left side of his face drew back in a contorted smile.

"Does it please you?"

"No, but neither does it displease me." His tone suddenly softened, and he blinked forcefully. "I only wonder at my part in it all. I am neither them, nor the spectacle upon which they now feed, nor am I —"

"Nevertheless, you *are* here, Glam! You *are* part of this, a functioning part. You belong here. Your role will take clearer shape with time." How unsatisfying and subtly disquieting was this conversation to her, but he was obviously adjusting, and clearly needed room to do so, didn't he? Nonetheless, she was not at ease with him...

"But I don't know where I belong." His face pulled itself into an exaggerated frown. "And, moreover, my not knowing bothers me mightily. I am still a stranger here, right?"

"Possibly," she replied, staring at his brow. "But you would be a stranger in Amula, too."

The cords of his neck briefly stood out, erasing the form of his frown, but not the feeling of it. Turning his face from her, he asked, "Do you enjoy watching the lions take their meal?"

"Rarely. I have seen such scenes far too often." What had gotten into Glam? It must just be a temporary aberration, an awkwardness of adjustment; she must be patient with him...

"I suppose you have." His voice was hard, his body suddenly filled with a turgid, tightly tangled sensation, cold and powerful. "But tell me, Ezparya, is it not worth it? Is it not satisfying, scrunchily delicious to the spirit?"

"Look," she said, leaning forward, struggling to ignore his bizarre behaviour, breathing more and more life into her patience. "Look below. What is next will really please the people."

"But will it please you?" he grinned. Seeing her surprise and barely repressed anger, he very quickly added, "You need not answer; my question was not serious."

Far below, three men with spears were facing three men with swords. All were naked. Glam let his gaze soften and widen, taking in as much of the amphitheatre as possible; for the rest of the afternoon, he simply observed the events below, detaching himself from all empathetic inclination. There was something spectral yet solid settling in him, something he did nothing to resist — its serpentine, fiercely energetic knotting coursed through his body, with a flow as calculating as it was exhilarating. Once, he felt an unpleasant heat on the left side of his face; turning, he saw Tornellas looking at him. As their eyes met, a shiver raced through his neck from front to back, and he remembered Ezparya stabbing Artakiab's neck...

Dropping his gaze, he felt a wave of hatred for Ezparya.

That night, he dreamt he was standing on a sandy, desolate plain, a spear in one hand, a sword in the other. Though the sky was dark, it was not night. A low but steady thudding filled the air. He was alone.

His spear and sword were wet with blood.

Then the horizon quivered and bucked, slowly erupting, shaping itself into a great face, first Esmelana's, then Xandur's. The Sirdhanan's face, transparent and sorrowful, loomed before him, its forehead emblazoned with the blue-white peak of Aratisha, its eyes overflowing with vast compassion, its every feature calling to him, calling and calling. He strained to hear, but couldn't make out a single word.

Nor could he move.

The face vanished. Looking down with more than a little reluctance, he saw that the spear and sword were now actually growing from him, like branches from a tree trunk. The thudding gradually intensified, beating against him, hotly panting, pushing at him from all sides. He must escape!

Suddenly, he found himself in a long, narrow room. No longer did he have the spear and sword. His hands were bloody.

The walls began pulsing.

His hands were very bloody. He saw no windows, and no doors. But look — on one wall there hung a mirror, ornately framed, beckoning to him. He walked toward it, feeling as if he were crawling, vaguely wondering if he was dreaming. For a moment, he saw nothing in the mirror. A sinuous dread crept into him...

Then a face appeared in the mirror. He had a moment of relief, then, with an electrifying shock, realized that the face was not his! A scream froze halfway out of his throat.

It was Artakiab's face.

Suffused with a purplish glow it was, horribly disfigured, with burning black eyes. The face snarled and grinned, thickening and deepening, stretching out the mirror until it covered the entire wall.

Glam stood paralyzed; at last, with a tremendous jolt,he realized that *he* was actually looking out of Artakiab's eyes at himself! Screaming, he burst free of the dream, immediately sitting up on his bed, looking out his window, gulping the air.

The night was bright with stars, the air breezily cool. What a dream! Now, some of the amphitheatre scenes from the afternoon came to him, and he felt angry and disgusted — but why hadn't he felt anything when he'd been there? What had happened to his heart? What was he becoming?

He had left Amula, and he had also left himself. Yet had he? Like a battlefield he felt, hosting hordes of blind, viciously patriotic fighters. On and on went the warfare, bloodying his soil, trampling whatever seedlings had taken root in him, leaving him muddy and barren, bereft of green, a graveyard for unillumined deaths...

He began to weep, welcoming his tears. Yes, Artakiab was definitely around him. Tornellas knew. But did Ezparya? Seemingly not. Even now, he could feel Artakiab psychically probing his places of softness, the long, spectral fingers passing through his flesh. He knew he didn't have to let Artakiab enter him, but he'd *already* let him in, had he not? Did he not feel Artakiab throughout his body and mind, like a triumphant plague, inexorably infusing him with his will? But no more! Out Artakiab must go, now!

Glam curled in on himself, crying more deeply, feeling easier, feeling closer to Ezparya, vowing to tell her of his dream tomorrow morning.

Yes, he must tell her!

But on the other hand...

20

Even He
Must Return To Her

"Get to the point!" fumed Ezparya.

Fingering the folds of her robe, Tornellas looked down. "I just thought you might wish to talk about what Glam is up to with you."

"And just why would I want to do that?"

"Because you need to."

"And how do you know that?"

"Does it really matter how I know it? I am concerned about you! Do you not notice what is happening to Glam?" Tornellas hesitated, absorbing Ezparya's angrily quizzical look, then continued, adding more urgency to her voice. "Artakiab is alive in Glam, with Glam's *cooperation*. He is permitting Artakiab to guide him. Wait! Let me finish! Consider this: if Artakiab were fully embodied now, and laying beside you in your bed, what do you imagine his intention might be?"

"My dear Tornellas! Do you miss Artakiab so much that you make yourself see him in Glam?"

"You are blinding yourself, my queen! Do you not feel a change in Glam since Artakiab's death?"

"You are persistent! Perhaps you are counselling me to doubt him. I must admit I do at times, but not in the area you're suggesting — he sometimes makes too much of a virtue out of his more tender feelings, almost prostrating himself before them. This both touches me, and inspires my caution, not to mention my humour."

"But," said Tornellas dramatically, "does not that very vulnerability make him all the more susceptible to Artakiab's influence?"

"Of course! And to all sorts of other influences as well! Yet he is no wall-less room receiving all winds — he is too strong for that. He is influenced by me, but he is clearly no slave to my influence —"

"That," interrupted Tornellas excitedly, "is *exactly* what I'm getting at! He *is* strong enough to choose what he lets in, and he *is* letting Artakiab in! It isn't that he is just a helpless medium for Artakiab's presence! No! *He* is a more than willing medium!"

"Do you have proof?" asked Ezparya coldly.

"Yes — look closely at him. You are so enamoured of him that you don't see him as he actually is; you only see the Glam who won you with his voice and his... whatever! You have let yourself be betrayed by your lust!"

"That is enough." Ezparya drove her gaze into Tornellas, who immediately wilted; certainly, Tornellas had permission to speak freely, but this was a gross abuse of that privilege, was it not?

"You can overpower me," said Tornellas, trembling and pale. "You can close your ears to me, and override my counsel. That is your choice."

"And just what would you have me do?"

"Consider what I have said. Observe him closely. See for yourself."

"I will," murmured Ezparya, staring at the black lines on Tornellas's forehead. How firmly Tornellas had stood her ground! She seemed convinced of what she was saying — she had undeniably seen something, but was her interpretation correct? No, it couldn't be! Glam was merely adjusting, wasn't he? Besides, it was obvious that Tornellas was burning inside; there was a virulent stabbing occurring within her, a crackling of searing ice, a vicious, multi-taloned heat that one could easily view as evidence of a desire for revenge. Of course, she had hated Artakiab, but he was *her* brother, her only brother. It was therefore natural, for this and other reasons, that Tornellas should try to separate her from Glam. Still, Ezparya felt uneasy with her logic, more and more uneasy, wishing that she could just simply dismiss Tornellas's statements...

"So I have let myself be betrayed by my lust, have I?" Now it was a terrible strain to thus act; if only she didn't know!

"You speak as if in counterattack, my queen. What you do with your desires is your business. My concern is over a possible danger to you."

"I said that I will see for myself!"

"Do not delay. Did you not —"

Tornellas stopped. The door was rattling with a very loud knocking.

The two women stood motionless, watching the door slowly open. Ezparya wasn't surprised to see Glam enter. He looked as though he hadn't slept very well; his eyes were dull, his lips flecked with bits of dark red, his shoulders hunched, his hands white claws.

"You have interrupted us," said Ezparya, with forced calm. He gave no sign of having heard her.

"Look, Ezparya!" hissed Tornellas. "Do you *now* see?"

"Speak, Glam!" shouted Ezparya. "What are you doing here?" Again, he acted as if he hadn't heard her. Angrily, she took a step toward him. "Fool! I have no time for your obdurate silence! *What* are you doing here?"

"Don't you know?" he sneered. "Hasn't Tornellas already warned you? Haven't you already decided something about me, something horribly unpleasant?"

Tornellas spoke quickly. "I haven't said a word to him."

Ezparya shivered, then gathered herself. "Leave the room, Glam."

"No! Am I not your consort and assistant in rule? Am I not your camouflaged beloved, your partner in juicy bliss?" He laughed harshly.

"You must see now!" urged Tornellas. "This is what I warned you about!"

"Is it? All I see is vulgarity of the most disgusting sort — but that is enough for me to take action against him!"

"Him? *Him?* You dare to speak of me as 'him'?" He strode toward Ezparya, his eyes aflame with a far-off light, his hands bulging, as though gripping unseen weapons. As fear and disbelief collided in her, he bellowed, shoving her backward. She fell, her head smacking the floor.

"Get up!" he snarled, his voice crawling with hate. "Get up, or I will see to it that you never stand again!"

Out of the corner of his eye, he glimpsed Tornellas reaching for her torturer's knife; as soon as her hand grasped its hilt, he took a step back, swinging his hand in a sizzling arc that caught her across the mouth, knocking her to the floor.

Ezparya rose, screaming and hissing, dagger in hand.

"Just like our initial meeting!" he grinned, kicking her dagger away with shocking ease, simultaneously gesturing at her belly. Immediately, she felt a broad, jagged pain in her middle, as though the head of a spear had been driven into her.

"Foolish woman! You do not control me! And you cannot seduce me!" Over her he now stood, quivering with grim exultation, alert and frighteningly poised. Blinking hard, she stared up at him, seeing the twin trunks of his powerful thighs rising up into the dark, fiery column of his torso. A psychic storminess, webbed with purplish-white lightning, both revealed and obscured his face. His arms were conducting all his force; their swollen, gleaming sinews were sheathed with silvery reds and swirling violet. And all around him, thickly teeming, were the grotesque shapings of the allies of the greatest of all temple-masters, bloated with his force...

Tornellas stirred, then heard him say not to move, or Ezparya would die. She lay still, feeling the sensation of rough fingers around her neck.

"You tried to warn our dear proud queen, our amazingly blind queen, and, as is her marvellously enlightened custom,she wouldn't listen to you. Dear sister, your efforts shall not go unrewarded!"

"So, Glam," croaked Tornellas, tightening her throat and puckering her lips, "you have succumbed. I did not think you would so easily let Artakiab in."

"I have not succumbed!" he roared. "*This* is *my* will! Artakiab has no power over me! He merely serves *my* will!"

"And what is your will?"

"It is taking its course. Bring me your knife."

She didn't move. "Go!" he shouted, glaring at her. Contemptuously, she looked away from him, readying herself for his blow. As he lashed a foot out at her, she caught his ankle, but only for a moment — he spun around, shaking her loose, slapping the side of her head. As she fell, he hurled a long, wailing shout at the center of her forehead; she tried to rise, and he again shouted, dropping into a crouch. She crumbled, and was still.

Ezparya sat up, gasping with pain. Summoning all her strength, she brokenly whispered, "Glam." For a moment, he stared at her, then leapt upon her, laughing and grunting, easily pinning her beneath him. With his face almost touching hers, he encircled her neck with his hands.

She looked into his eyes.

Artakiab gazed back at her, his eyes molten fists... There was, however, more than Artakiab in those eyes, something larger and even stronger, even more fierily veined with venomous intent. The fingers tightened slowly. "Glam!" Now she was choking. "Glam —"

Soon her face was crimson. She could not stop him. It couldn't be! It just couldn't be... Nevertheless, she couldn't stop him.

Without intending it so, she stopped resisting. He was going to kill her; that she didn't doubt at all. There was no hope. He was going to kill her, and there was nothing she could do, nothing at all. Her entire body spontaneously softened, seeming to lose its boundaries, as in deep lovemaking, and a vast, subtly thrilling warmth flooded her, bringing tears to her eyes, effortlessly dissolving her fear of dying.

No longer did the fact of her being strangled disturb her. Her surrender, however, was much more than mere submission or resignation; it empowered her in a way she'd never before known, creating in her a deep sense of elemental and spiritual continuity with all that existed. Up at Glam she gazed, her unbound heart streaming through her eyes...

Her look, in its very softness, pierced him. The murderous intent in his hands vanished. Her eyes, her great, loving eyes, took him in, their dark, shining depths seemingly bottomless and almost unbearably soothing, full of immeasurable compassion and sacred silence, full of mother-force, full of pure woman, full of innocent yet wise child, so, so full of Death and undying Life, so unwaveringly rich with rise and fall, all of it lit from within by something he could feel pulsing through him and her and the entire room. All of him, even the blackest corners, suddenly coalesced in the center of his chest, beating out an eternal unity of rhythm, a vibrantly alive wholeness of being, a heartbreakingly sweet reunion of everything that he was...

Releasing what remained of his grip, he collapsed on her, sobbing with unstoppable grief. She closed her eyes, letting his hurt seep into her, like rain into earth, happily absorbing his nakedness of feeling, receiving and replenishing him, again and again birthing and cradling him, letting herself rest in the loving silence that pervaded the room. Tenderly yet firmly, she pulled him closer to her. For the first time in her life, she felt utterly content.

Finally, some time after Glam had ceased crying, Tornellas spoke, her voice seemingly faraway. "What will you do now, Ezparya?"

"I don't know." Glam lay beside her now, his head upon her breast. "What would you suggest?"

"It's difficult for me to think clearly right now," said Tornellas, gingerly sitting up. "He almost killed you, showing as much power as Artakiab ever did, perhaps even more. He may be resting peacefully now, but he is, in my opinion, extremely dangerous, and should be treated as such."

"Are you recommending I imprison him?"

Opening her eyes, Ezparya watched Tornellas nod, then sighed. "More has happened in this room than we know, much, much more than the events we can recall. Don't look so hostile, Tornellas. Can you not feel what has occurred?"

"I don't trust it, my queen. It is too sudden."

"But can you not feel it?"

"Yes, but it still does not ring true for me." Her voice shook slightly as she spoke; the palpable softness and peace of the room was eating into her. Never had she seen Ezparya look like this — her imperious, arrogant queen, she of the scathing tongue and ruthlessly assertive presence, now so open-faced, so pinkly vulnerable, so spaciously... maternal!

As far back as she could remember, Tornellas had secretly longed for Ezparya's warmth and affection, and now that it was here, or at least partially here, she felt frightened of it, doubtful of it, threatened — it was too unfamiliar! Her whole manner of being was tailored to a very different Ezparya than this one, an Ezparya from whom she sought no more than crumbs of approval. And Glam — stranger from afar, lying beside the queen, seemingly defenceless, breathing as though in deep sleep, all curled up, hands and mouth slightly open. A faint but inconsolable loneliness drifted through Tornellas, its almost inaudible moans dungeoned deep, its tiny fists beating against the inside of her chest...

"Did Glam injure you?" asked Ezparya.

"No," replied Tornellas, feeling fragile and very small. "The sides of my head hurt, but that's all."

"I assume you are afraid that Glam may repeat his actions of today."

"That's true."

"Well, so am I, but I'm trusting that he won't. Do you think I've gone mad? But this is what I want, to stay with Glam, whatever the risk. Doing so is far more important to me than worrying about whether or not he's going to murder me."

"As you wish." Tornellas pursed her lips, looking at Glam. "I suppose I ought to go now." Ezparya nodded, and Tornellas left, her stride stiffly forlorn.

The entire room seemed to exhale. For a long while, Ezparya stroked Glam's hair, gently rocking him from side to side, humming lightly. Finally, he opened his eyes. "Hello, Glam," she whispered, bending low over him, kissing his forehead and eyes. "How fresh you look, like a baby."

A wide smile brightened his face. "You need not say anything," he said, reaching up for her. "I heard everything you and Tornellas said. I am no longer disposed to admit Artakiab; his presence only intensified something that was already astir in me. Now he has gone, drawn far beyond himself.

"His power snapped when I was strangling you; it could not tolerate your look. His position had been established in opposition to *all* mothering, and through your eyes shone the gaze of the Mother of us all, including Artakiab. Even he must return to Her..."

Gently, he encircled her neck with his hands. For a moment, she felt afraid, and then, feeling the caring in his touch, relaxed. His desire to say more subsided. It was more than enough to be with Ezparya now, to feel her inside and out, to let his insights about what had happened evaporate in the meltingly warm love of their embrace.

21

She Heard The Sound
Of Someone Crying

Tornellas sat in her room, motionless except for sporadic eye-scans of the walls. Glam and Ezparya, Glam and Ezparya, Glam and Ezparya — her mind was horribly overgrown with thoughts of them, scabby, obsessively repetitious thoughts, tangled and sophisticatedly frantic, thoughts and thoughts, buzzing and fussing, each one pleading and hollering for her attention, each one only further tightening and complicating her knottedness of being...

A short month ago, Glam had almost killed the queen, and she, with that idiotic leer of the lovestruck smeared across her face, had been with him ever since! How could she? How could she so blithely announce that she was happy, that her trust for the alien beast was getting ever stronger?

Yes, yes, of course she looked happy, but what was the virtue in that? The sloppy glee of the apparently happy didn't fit her like it did the populace of Anushet; their intoxication with the ritualized fulfillment of their pelvic leanings admirably suited them, but *Ezparya*? Glam, precious Glam, was *her* addiction! With his wide, knowing looks, his loose arrogance of stride, his soft sweep of shoulder — O would that he were strapped upon her torture-bed, pinned atop its immaculate granite, slobberingly anticipating the application of her instruments!

Bitterness filled her. Across her floor lay strands of moonlight. In through her windows floated a thin, tattered wind, cooling her face, but she only felt hotter and hotter. True, Ezparya was treating her more kindly — that is, whenever she had a few moments between copulations with her beloved Amulan! Yes, swooning with bed-lust was Ezparya, again and again emptying herself of vital energies that could be put to far better use!

Tornellas shook her head violently — never would she stoop so low, never! She was virgin to man, and would always be! To submit to such coarse, heatedly groping touch was as unthinkable as it was laughable. Momentarily, she imagined being the recipient of such carnal touch, then disdainfully crushed the image. The very thought of sexual embrace disgusted her — was it not, other than for procreational purposes, a mere indulgence, just a pleasurable means for discharging stress? A mechanistic throwing off of tension? Such a gross waste of Life-energy! Except, of course, in the case of the masses, for whom it served as an eminently practical regulatory device, controlled and catalyzed by the pronouncements of the temple-masters...

The masses seemed to accept Glam, but give them their meat and blood and sexing and amply-rewarded rules, and they'd likely accept a squealing hog as assistant ruler of Anushet! She almost smiled, in spite of herself — the royal consort, madly oinking, shoving his noble snout wherever he pleased! What did, and yes, she'd had the thought at least a thousand times, what did *he* know of Anushet? At least Artakiab, unpleasant as he was, had known Anushet intimately, and had wisely counselled Ezparya. And what of Glam's counsel? He was advising Ezparya, he must be! His influence was poisoning Anushet, wasn't it?

Several days ago, she'd been told by Ezparya that she seemed lonely. She had not responded. Lonely? Was she not sufficient unto herself, given the right circumstances? And, moreover, did she not take great care to ensure that she had the right circumstances? Glam, however, was a hindrance to that auspicious arrangement of conditions, a definite obstacle! And so was Ezparya! But what could she possibly do? Their mutual presence disturbed her; she had begun to shake almost uncontrollably when she was near them, especially if they were in any sort of embrace. Something had to give. If only Glam wasn't here!

Murderous thoughts flocked in her mind, then, bleating incoherently, fled before the sudden upthrustings of her fear — he was very powerful, and very unpredictable, appearing stronger every time she saw him, stronger than Ezparya, just as strong as Artakiab had ever been. He carried his strength easily. He had left her alone. But for how long? Was she only to be crushed when he finally willed it so?

Abruptly, an extremely compelling desire to see him arose in her, almost completely overturning her mood of a few moments ago. She had not been alone with him since those long-ago days when she'd questioned him at Ezparya's request. She resolved to see him the next day if at all possible — they must talk! But about what? About her? There was no point in thinking about it; all she knew was that she needed to clarify *her* relationship with him, so she could...

Early the following morning, she saw Glam walking alone; usually, he was with Ezparya. He was moving slowly and loosely, his gaze turned slightly upward. The sky was a moist, tattered grey. A sword swung at his side.

He stopped when he saw her, nodding as she greeted him. Concealing her nervousness, she said, "Could we talk together for a few moments?" He smiled yes, and they walked side by side to a small grassy enclosure near her quarters. She awkwardly hesitated, then sat across from him, silently cursing herself for creating such a situation.

"Go ahead," he said.

"I'm not sure where to begin."

"Do you need to be sure?"

"Of course not," she said briskly, hating the dewy itch of the grass. "But what I want to say is not simply on the tip of my tongue."

"You are very cautious around me."

"There's some truth in that."

"And you have difficulty admitting that you're afraid of me, don't you?"

"What makes you think I'm afraid of you?" she retorted.

"The way you so tightly grip yourself when you are in my company! The way you are looking at me right now! The way in which you are moving your body backward ever so slightly!"

She stiffened, then tried to hide her hardness, to somehow unfreeze her facial expression, all the while knowing that he saw her efforts.

Curse him! "Perhaps you find me amusing," she muttered, looking down.

"Not at all! The more you manoeuvre and fidget behind your pride, the more bored I become with you. How can you possibly talk sanely with me, when you won't even admit your fear of me?"

"Would such admittance please you?"

"Your question gleams with hate! You are still desperately trying to arrange yourself, to somehow position yourself above or away from your woundedness, which only tells me just how frightened you really are."

"Must I let you pin me down in order to talk with you?"

"*You* have already pinned yourself down, Tornellas! The trap you squirm in is your own, your very own! You only *imagine* that the nets you gasp in are mine — they are actually yours!"

"Why should I take such abuse from you?" she snapped, appearing ready to leave. "Why should I listen to *you* telling me what I'm doing?"

"Do you trust me?"

"Am I supposed to?"

"Do you *trust* me?" he shouted. As she shook her head in vehement denial, he angrily added, "And just what is it that you don't trust about me?"

"Why should I reveal that to you?"

"You have cornered yourself," he said slowly, "and are shielding yourself with all your supposed questions. But I tire of this, Tornellas! Are you at all willing to tell me what you came to talk about?"

"Of course!"

"Then go ahead." He waited, but she said nothing, staring down at her

whitely writhing hands, vainly searching for just the right turn of
phrase — none of the phrases that came to her, however, seemed sufficiently representative of what she wanted to say.

Finally, he said, "I am waiting."

"I know." Her voice was sullen, and barely audible.

"I will not wait any longer!"

"There is nothing for me to say to you then!" blurted Tornellas, her
gaze still fixated on her hands, which were now turning purple.

Glam started to speak, then decided not to — why flog this tedious
dialogue through another useless round? He had better things to do
than draw out Tornellas! Quickly, he stood, and left, his stride full of
anger.

She sat unmoving, righteously spinning amongst her thoughts, feeling
outraged. Slime that Ezparya lay beside! Foreign filth! He had humil-
iated her, embarrassed her, made her squirm — never would she yield
to him, never! Never would she disarm herself for him, never! If only
she had slain him that day he tried to murder Ezparya! She fingered
the handle of her dagger, lingering over its jewelled inlay, imagining
it thick with Glam's blood. A calculating, viciously consoling iciness
slithered through her, even as the sun poured down hotly on the back
of her neck. Yes, it was time to —

Suddenly, she realized she was not alone.

Over her stood Glam and Ezparya. "Are you by any chance having
thoughts of revenge?" he asked. When she didn't answer, he roared,
"Speak!"

"I am sitting here enjoying the morning," she announced, her voice
cold and remote, her eyes avoiding his.

"Liar! Speak your truth *now*, or suffer the consequences! No longer
will I tolerate your clever little sulk!"

"And just what is the truth that you would have me speak? You seem to already know what it is, so why don't you just go ahead and supply the words?''

"I've something else to give you!" Lunging, he shoved her, knocking her onto her back.

"How dare you push me!" she shrieked, reaching for her dagger.

"Don't!" shouted Ezparya.

"Don't what?" sneered Tornellas, sitting up.

Again, Glam shoved her onto her back; before she could rise, he sat on her belly, pinning her arms beneath his knees, grabbing her hair with both hands, holding his face right above hers.

"You are no friend to us," he angrily said. "Your obedience to Ezparya is at best begrudging, and you don't wish me well, not at all. Just look at you! Your eyes brim with hatred, and not just from this morning's events! My overpowering you, brutal or unfair as it may seem, only brings out what is *already* festering in you."

"I serve the queen to the best of my ability," she stammered.

"But what about me?"

"Ezparya seems fond of you. It is her will that you do what you will do, and I accept that." Deeper and deeper into her plunged his gaze — why was she not more bothered by the position she was in? The she who was speaking seemed very faraway, a brittle personification of something *she* was quickly losing interest in...

"Fool! It is *my* will! I am no puppet of Ezparya, and you know it! I require your service, as does Ezparya, but I don't want it if you won't give it willingly."

"Am I to force myself to give it willingly?"

"No!" He brought his face even closer to hers. "Vicious snake! I know that you don't wish Ezparya well, and I know that you'd love to torture me! You are poison to me! Change, or I will have you permanently banished!"

"He means it," said Ezparya.

"I mean change," he said, getting up. "Right now! I will not give you any more time to nourish your treachery! Something in you needs to break, to burst, to come undone, to die!"

She sat up, her face in disarray, her body shaking uncontrollably. Glam stood in front of her like a colossus, his legs planted wide, his arms folded across his chest. Beside him rose Ezparya, tall and slender, but just as solid. She cowered before them — they seemed like wrathful deities to her, towering monuments of eternally punishing parental force, cruel and iron-hard, sternly awaiting her submission. The scabbard of Glam's sword blazed green and blue in the sunlight. All around her swooped and darted multi-voiced birdsong, bright and astonishingly clear, chiming and ringing through her confusion. Ezparya's hair was a snowy hillock, wildly spiked, backed by the quivering blue of the sky, a vast, welcoming blue...

Tornellas convulsed with torso-pain. Grating heaves of raw emotion again and again tore through her, wave upon turbulent wave, capsizing her mind and seemingly fragmenting her body, rolling through every resistance of flesh and thought. She felt as though she had broken into a thousand pieces, all of which were floating on an immense, subterranean pooling of warm water, or something like water. Each piece emitted its own sound, its own refrain of personal pain, deaf to all but its own dolorous song. Yet that was not all — the water itself had a sound, a deep, soft sound, silky and exquisitely round, strong and soothing, achingly familiar, a sound that effortlessly penetrated and illuminated *all* the fragments...

Eventually, she realized that this sound, this lovely, irresistible music, flowed from Glam. Into her it sank, deeper and deeper, thawing her, comforting her, touching her where she could not remember ever having been touched.

Suddenly, all the pieces came rushing together, bursting into one great song.

She heard the sound of someone crying.

It was her. She couldn't stop. Now, she was up off the ground, held in strong arms, rocked gently and rhythmically.

"Open your eyes," he said at last. She looked up at him. His eyes were wild yet steady. She watched the tiny quiverings of his nostrils as he breathed. What a refreshing landscape was his face! How unfamiliar and yet how undeniably significant its mixture of force and caring, its contours of cruelty and tenderness, its luminous texture of thrust and yield...

"Now what do you say?" he asked.

"I don't know."

"You need not fight with me."

"Yes," she whispered, feeling only slightly troubled by her unaccustomed vulnerability. Gently, he lowered her to the ground, and withdrew. Immediately, she missed his touch. And what of Ezparya? What of her queen, who was changing so quickly? She appeared to be in Glam's hands, but was he not also in hers? Tornellas let her thoughts go. The air was fragrant and beaming, the sky tender and gracious, the day marvellously bright, throbbing with delightful possibility. Ezparya was actually smiling at her, and there was no scorn in her smile, no sarcasm, not a single trace of irony!

Tornellas suddenly averted her eyes, fearful of what she saw in Ezparya, but even more afraid of what she felt in herself — a longing, yes, a longing, to be cared for, a deep, passionate yearning that rose strongly in her, threatening to overwhelm her, to inundate her, to sweep her out of control. At the very same time, however, she felt an urge to give in, to fully yield.

"You need not submit to the viewpoint of your fear," said Glam. "Simply trust this great current of feeling that now engulfs you. It is *not* an enemy, except to the you who insists on maintaining control. Trust it, Tornellas! *Be* it! Yield to it, fall into its very core, and you will discover, *directly* discover, its built-in wisdom, its sublime knowingness of flow. But is what I'm saying to you no more than mere exhortation? You look away from Ezparya not like a cringing dog, nor like a sullen servant, but like a child, a child who has waited so, so long for what she *truly* needs, that when it, precious it, is finally available, she is suspicious of it, thinking it to be but a mirage, or a trap! She doubts everything except her doubt, ever turning away from what she most needs, trying to satisfy herself with surrogates of what she longs for! Your sadness calls you to your heart, Tornellas, inviting you to ride its waves. Look now at Ezparya. Look into her eyes..."

Tornellas returned her gaze to Ezparya. "It is all too fast for me," she sobbed. "I know not who you are anymore. I don't know who to be loyal to. No longer do I know what is required of me!"

"It is more than enough for me that you speak thus," said Ezparya.

"But what about —"

"Don't concern yourself about what happened this morning. It is done."

"No," declared Glam, *"do* concern yourself with the events of this morning! Savour them, chew them well, digest them! Learn from them, and then maybe you won't be so quick to rekindle your hostility toward us. Obviously, you don't wish us ill right now, but that is a product of unusual circumstances. When the desire again arises in you to do away with me, as I'm sure it will, I pray that you don't give yourself to it — for *your* sake, Tornellas! If you continue to feed your hatred of me, I will have you banished. Just like that!"

"I don't hate you now."

"I know that. But you will again, and when you do, *that* will be the test of how well you have learned the lessons of today's meeting..." He stopped, suddenly tiring of his voice and his caution.

"Yes," said Tornellas. Across her face flickered a fragment of a smile, ingenuous and very young. He saw it, and felt his heart quicken. She looked like a hurt child to him, bruised with crushed longing, curled in on herself, like a snail without its shell. But there was more than a child here — he glimpsed the woman in her, ephemeral and shyly beckoning, delicately suffused with pulsing blushes. With rosy golds and silvers she was brushed, her features shaped by a silken wind, her every breath heightening all her colours, inner and outer...

"Let us go," said Ezparya, taking his hand. "I suggest you rest here for a while, Tornellas." As they slowly walked away, Glam noticed with appreciation the warmth of Ezparya's hand. So sure and solid. A match for him. So unlike Tornellas, who was a ghost by comparison.

But a ghost seeking fleshy embodiment, even inviting it. She, apparently unknown to herself, was reaching out to him, in a strange, undifferentiated way that appealed to him more and more strongly as the day passed...

22

Giving The Gift
Without Giving Himself Away

He was glad to be alone.

On a hilltop overlooking the city he sat, his arms wrapped around his knees. The city was a lumpy, almost pustulant, conglomerate of reddish greys, a miasmic lagoon of vague, crumbling cubes and even vaguer streets. Strands of bluish mist lay loosely draped around its highest towers. Beyond the city, he could just make out the shape of the mountains to which he had once fled. On the other side of those blurred peaks was the bit of coastline upon which he and Merot had landed. Merot? So, so long ago — could his canoe still be in the forest wherein Merot had been murdered? Such a strange, fear-thick time that had been, swollen with dread and radical possibility...

And further, much further, across the unseen waters, Amula, bright green jewel, sparkling so soft and so dreamy, lying with such lush abundance and sunny ease around Mount Aratisha, the Unclimbable, the Seat of Lantar. Aratisha, where art thou now?

He shivered in the sudden wind. Why was it that he didn't question his being in Anushet? Why was it that he didn't question his being with Ezparya? Had he actually — No! Vigorously waving one hand as if to discourage a persistent delegation of mosquitoes, he laughed out loud. Doubts, get away! Away with you, away with your righteously shouldered concern, your earnest gloom, your heart-shrinking focus! I will not cripple myself by accommodating you, nor by bonding with your point of view! I owe nothing whatsoever to you, with all your dour arguments and naggingly repetitious commentaries and stagnant, miserable chatter! What a fool I am to even *consider* taking your *contents* seriously, when all I need to do is breathe loose the very knottedness that spawns you! A knottedness as much of body as of mind it was, a literal contraction of being...

The only trees on the hill were a few old pines, bent almost double. Around his feet pale-faced little flowers swayed in tiny pockets of breeze. Not one of these little beauties questioned its flowering, nor obstructed it, nor tried to mastermind it; not one of them compromised its blossoming with philosophical considerations, nor with any other such distraction. But he, he who could crush these fragile mandalas of dewy colour with brute ease, kept obscuring his own flowering in all sorts of ingenious ways, again and again burdening himself with doubt's chimeras, more and more subtly undermining his own spirit-awakening, creating limitation where none was needed...

And just *who* did he do this for? Exactly for *whose* benefit? Was it not for the one who took his mind seriously, the one who chronically animated his entrapping dreams, the one who wanted to figure it all out, to distract and comfort himself with time-gobbling complexity and cosy, wraparound explanations? Fool that he was! Was not the tangy, fine-honed scent of pine enough, the pearly fanning of dawn's nacreous light, the cloud-plumped arc of the sky? Was not the flow of his breath eloquence enough? Was not the elemental communion and exchange between him and his environment far more substantial than any meaning that he or anyone else could superimpose on it? Was not all that he needed available in the heart of each moment, if only he would cease looking elsewhere? Was he not looking everywhere but *inside* his looking? Sighing, he shook his head in mock disapproval of himself.

The mists around the towers thickened and greyed. The sky showed only a few slivers of blue. What a strange place Anushet was, barbarous and cruel, unswervingly subhuman, and yet the home of Ezparya. She was, he thought, like a brilliant gem in a field of mud. No, worse than mud — filth, the stinking filth of the lowest of human possibilities...

Ezparya, rare flower, silvery pink, delicately yet voluptuously petalled, rising up so fragrantly on a long, slender stem, rising up from the foulest filth. It was, nevertheless, *her* soil; she drew forth nourishment from it, transmuting its baseness into beauty. She did not try to alter her soil, nor to awaken it to a finer destiny — no, she kept it just as it was, through an impeccably managed blending of fear and pleasure-gratification.

He, however, was a very different soil for her. Her roots had plunged deep into him, as had his into her. He knew not what they were becoming in their union, but he'd no desire to alter its course. Together they were uprooted from what they had been, and what they were establishing themselves in had a will of its own — it was clearly no passive medium for their growth, transcending both Anushet and Amula, infusing them with as-yet undeciphered imperatives...

Again, he gazed at the mountainous skyline. Beyond its purple jaggedness stretched the ocean he had crossed — how far he had come to be here! There was no denying that he felt no urge to leave Anushet, regardless of its culture's shortcomings. Nevertheless, this was not his home, nor could it ever be! One day, he would want to leave; he wasn't waiting for that day, but when it came, he would not resist its invitation...

He stood and stretched. It was beginning to rain. As he walked down the hill, he sang:

> *Lantar, Source and Substance of All*
> *In You I rise and fall*
> *My everything pulsing with Your Call*
> *Lantar, Bright One*
> *Undying Sun, Light of lights*
> *Blazing through all my, all my nights*

His singing brought a smile to his stride — how long it had been since he had sung to Lantar! Several times, he and Ezparya had talked about Lantar; she'd said she conceived of Lantar as Primal Context, as the Condition both existing as, and giving life to all other conditions. She had also said that she saw no need to personify this Condition, nor to worship it. He remembered telling her that such personification *could* be used as a means of actually *feeling* Lantar, and that worship, at its *best*, only served to intensify and celebrate this feeling. Naturally, Lantar was not a somebody, not even the greatest somebody of all, but rather pure Being, eternally radiant, simultaneously empty and full, unmanifest and manifest, unbound to any of Its appearances...

Now, as he sang, he felt crazily happy — how absurd it was to try to define Lantar! How extraordinarily pointless was the effort to grasp the Ungraspable, to somehow pin It down, when It *already* included the very effort to contain It! It was impossible to stand outside the Infinite, impossible to define It over against oneself. The true journey, Xandur had once said, was the shift from trying to know It, or have It, to actually *being* It — yes, yes, words and words, erudite turds, words, words, words! Words without awakened passion, words enslaved to the reinforcement of meaning, words and words, nets of abstraction cast into imaginary seas, words and words, humble or arrogant, braying with self-importance, campaigning for increased attention, committed to framing and naming everything, making a virtue out of thinking about thinking! Yet words could be used to go beyond the merely verbal; words could evoke, words could sing, words could dance, words could, with artful precision, carry one through and beyond the confines of mind — O to be like a pen in the Heart of hearts' Hand, from which undreaming beauty would eloquently stream throughout every land!

Louder and louder he sang, his voice a torrent of ecstatic force, a toe-to-crown thrill, his entire body a cornucopian yes, yes, yes! Down poured the rain in slanting sheets, as if in response to his jubilation. Still singing, he began to run and crazily skip, falling, rolling, leaping and spinning, letting his hymn to Lantar become pure sound. Finally, he stopped, muddy and gasping for breath, wild with laughter. The sky was now a uniform grey, but how nevertheless wondrous! It, for all its drabness, also arose in Lantar, and *as* Lantar — it too was but a texturing of Lantar...

As he strolled through the city toward Ezparya's quarters, he silently sang his song to Lantar, letting the very feeling of it, the devotional intensity, pervade all of him; soft yet immensely powerful was his love now, vast and tender, panoramic in its embrace, at rest in its grace — not only was it within him, but also all around him, cradling and carrying him, like a speck of dust in a sunbeam.

Anushetites thronged through the streets, noisy and coarse, but always making a path for him, for the one who was the intimate of their queen. Usually, he ignored the citizens of Anushet, seeing little more than their outlines, closing himself to their degradation; now, though, he looked intently at them, at the bobbing, colourful turbulence of expressions, seeing both the diversity therein, and also what they had in common, namely a perversity of appetite, a twisted lustfulness, a craving for perpetual distraction from their suffering...

And he also saw something else they all shared, a very different sort of hunger, almost completely obscured by the first, a hunger deeper than appetite, a hunger for love. Love! All these faces, these endarkened, divided faces, had given up on love, and didn't know they had given up; they looked and acted as if love, real love, was non-existent. They had settled for caricatures of love — love of violence, love of desire-satisfaction, love of entertainment, love of food. Love, however, unlike appetite, didn't disappear or fade when gratification occurred, unless it was only appetite masquerading as love, as in the swooning charades of romance. There was no desperation in true love, no clinging, no hope, no delusions, but only an expansion of being that in no way diluted one's passion and empathetic capacity...

Suddenly, he felt too exposed, too open; the crowds seemed to be siphoning Life-energy from him. There was, however, no real danger, but only a temporary drainage which he could easily remedy a little later. Why not permit this empathy, this unexpected compassion, to take him where it would? He could, if he had to, readily protect himself from the condition of these beings — it was no grand feat to psychically shield himself from them.

Turned away from love were they, making a lifestyle out of their turning away and its compensatory addictions, reducing freedom to no more than an exaggerated kind of permission. He could only feel their condition, feel their hidden hurt within himself, knowing that he saw what they didn't see — and how could he possibly convey or effectively translate his seeing for them? How could he? All around him he could not help but see a seething mass of self-perpetuating suffering, an overwhelmingly deep woundedness from which all these beings almost constantly sought to escape...

This was not something that could be fixed by a mere rearrangement of circumstances, a more benign form of government. No! This situation invited transformation, a radical shift *independent* of circumstance and mood, a shift that could not be simply installed from the outside. In fact, it could only begin with the heartfelt recognition of what was *actually* occurring. And could he catalyze such recognition? And even if by some miracle he could, then what? What of his responsibility? If there were signs of some awakening in a few Anushetites, would he *really* want to nourish it along? Would he *truly* want to nurse and guide them through their phasing in and out of authenticity? Was his capacity to guide, to act as trailblazer, pure enough, or had it not yet ripened far enough past the point of mere enthusiasm and egocentric helpfulness?

He smiled to himself, half-ducking his barrage of questions. He had influence, no doubt about it, but his *use* of it was another matter altogether; there were definite consequences to using his influence and power for purposes that he deemed to be good for others, consequences of which he was wary. Anushetites were fast asleep, bustling about in their well-ordered, thick-walled dream. Who was he to hammer on their door? Who was he to act as awakener? He who was not yet fully intimate with the roots of his own motives, he who was getting so interestedly tied up in these noble concerns...

Also, was it not extremely likely that his intervention, however skilfully handled, however artfully embodied, would, sooner or later, be quite unwelcome? Did these people *really* want their sleep disturbed? No! If their dream *had* to end, they would in all likelihood just desire immersion in *another*, perhaps more consoling dream. Even if he were to lucidly and *convincingly* present true transformation to them as a viable option, they would, with very few exceptions, only dreamily arrange themselves within their *mind's* version of such transformation, resolutely *believing* their latest snore to be the voice of Truth!

How to prove to the dreamer that he or she is dreaming? How to call to the dreamer to awaken, without merely appearing as just another dream-being in his or her reverie? Not unkindly, Glam left his questions, walking a little more quickly, feeling an imperative deeper than that which fueled his doubts. Again and again, he watched children squeezing their way through a forest of adult legs. The children's eyes were, beneath their film of savage vitality and quick defiance, more bitter, more *obviously* frustrated than the eyes of the adults. He remembered Ezparya telling him about infancy in Anushet...

Children were separated from their mothers right at birth, usually for a week or two, except for tightly scheduled feedings. At two months, they were abruptly weaned from their mother's milk. At six months, they were taken from their parents for about half a year, sometimes more; displays of upset or fear were severely punished, usually by heavy blows to the temples and abdomen. Overall, a cruel but functionally advantageous approach, Ezparya had said. Seeing Glam's face twist with disgust, she'd quickly added that *all* children in Anushet received exactly the same treatment. Yes, of course almost all of them became predictably servile and appetite-bound, but a rare few used the very adversity of their early years as an opportunity to know and strengthen themselves — she had been one of these. So the process, inhumane though it might seem, actually exposed brilliance, singling out those who were exceptional. Perhaps, he had said, but it also crushed whatever might be starting, albeit a little more slowly, in others...

The faces that he now walked through seemed crushed, crushed beyond all reclamation, battered far beyond repair, utterly spiritless, narcotically treading the tracks of a completely *mechanical* destiny. What they kept obsessively filling themselves up with did not in any way ease their starvation of being, but rather only camouflaged and sedated it, suffocating its cries. And ought he to point this out? And if so, to what benefit? Their allegiance was *not* to their awakening, but to their actual *entrapment* — the repetitive and uninterrupted *exploitation* of its predetermined possibilities was all they aspired to, was it not?

The sky that opened for them was but the ceiling of their hungriest thought. The — what was he saying? Any more musing about their lot, and he'd likely become their smelly old bard, waggling an arthritic yet poetic finger, plucking choice metaphors from the tedious shitpiles of their lives! Yes, an impotent juggler of pleasing phrases, serving to amuse the masses when their desires were at low ebb, providing a bit of music for the dance of toothpicks between bloody teeth ...

Blind to their blindness were they, and he, should he give them eyes, he who was still partially blind? No, *unless* his giving was neither strategic nor partial; only then would it be pure enough, free of inner ambition, free of any motive to collect spiritual approval. His help, if it was to be given, must not be calculated! Rather, it must be a totally *natural* byproduct of his very manner of living, spontaneously and creatively given, without any tactical goodwill or preheated directions; that is, his help would not so much be something he would *do*, as something that he would *be*, something he would artfully, passionately, and potently *embody*!

If he was to be an awakening agent in their midst, the impulse to do so would have to arise from a foundation free of any desire to play rescuing hero, however humble or pious; otherwise, his supposed help would only *further* complicate and reinforce the very trouble it purported to ease! In such a case, *his* need for them to improve their lot would, in its very obsessiveness and goal-fixation, be fundamentally no different than *their* need to keep feeding their aberrated lusts...

He had his own journey. Should he linger here as a myopic, would-be saviour to this festering mob of self-obsessed fools? Should he even attempt to dent the certainty of these beings who were so, so firmly committed to their dark rounds? Turned away from love were they, too lost to lose face, too thick to see their walls. He wanted neither their attention, nor their gratitude, and though he knew their depths intimately, never, never would he send *his* roots down into them! Never! It was enough that he breathed their air and walked their streets. Strong was his disgust, but not so strong as to *fully* obscure his love — it was painful to feel what they were doing to themselves, sometimes excruciatingly painful, but it was, more and more, a hurt he did not turn away from, however strong his distaste for their self-abuse...

What he gave of himself he gave without hope.

His gift to them was the quality of emanation from his own center of being; sometimes, the gift was passively offered, as illuminated presence alone, and other times, it was made available in a more active form, manifesting as a pure showering of deep inner force, as sensitive as it was potent, bright with an accuracy both of content *and* feeling. Giving the gift without giving himself away, *that* was the true art and ever-enlivening challenge...

The crowds thinned as he approached Ezparya's quarters. He hesitated for a moment, then turned left, stretching out his stride, inhaling deeply — *where* was he going? Wherever it was, the impulse to go in this particular direction was extremely compelling, almost irresistible.

Suddenly, he realized he was on his way to see Tornellas.

He didn't question his going. She would probably be alone in her rooms at this hour, no doubt practising some trick of attentiveness, or perhaps just resting. He'd only seen her a few times since their confrontation three weeks ago, brief, easily forgettable meetings of necessary formality. Soon, he stood at her door, knocking with the same rhythm as his heart was beating out...

"Come in," she said sleepily, opening her door.

"Have I disturbed your sleep?"

"No. I am just very tired."

"I am surprised to be here." He sat, half-wishing he hadn't come here. He could leave with some grace now, if he made the effort...

"Why is that?"

"I hadn't planned to come here. Yet here I am — so much for my plans! I'm sure my purpose in visiting you will soon emerge." How incredibly stiff were his words and tone, how very self-conscious! Yet he needed to ease into what he had come to say, didn't he?

"Do you need my help in clarifying that purpose?"

"We need not speak so formally, Tornellas. I am not here politically." After a long, awkward pause, he said, "Do you not remember crying in my arms?"

"Yes." She looked away, reddening slightly.

"I see you are still affected by that."

"Does that please you?" she snapped.

"Yes, it does!" He brightened, feeling suddenly much looser. "And does it please you?"

"Why should it?" She watched him warily, her mouth a tightening line, her body motionless.

"Because, Tornellas, your solitariness is not so gratifying as you pretend it to be."

"A strange answer."

"You only know fighting and struggling, don't you? Even now, you spar with me, test me, elude me, trying to deflect me, to maintain distance between us. But that day three weeks ago, that day when you broke open so beautifully, you stopped fighting me for a while."

"Make your point!" She glared at him, folding her arms across her chest, trying to hide her growing disorientation.

"You were true then. You shone soft and sweet, tender and deep. I saw a dawning woman in you, fresh and untouched, reaching out, delicate as a newborn shoot, exquisitely green, reaching out, welcoming the kiss of daylight..."

"Do go on," she sneered.

"You are young in ways unknown to you."

"As are we all."

"Yes, yes! Must you keep me out now?" His voice rose; he knew his direction now, knew its risk, knew he must go ahead. "Let me be blunt. Have you ever desired a man?"

"I do think we have talked enough," she said brittlely.

"Answer me!"

"No, I haven't!" she hissed.

"Liar!"

"Glam," she said softly but venomously, narrowing her eyes, "do you imagine that I actually desire you?" Seeing him nod, she blurted, in a much louder voice than she wanted to, "It's *not* true! Not true at all!"

"Then why is your face suddenly pink and your breath so irregular, and why are you now trembling so? It's not just from having raised your voice!"

Fumbling for words, she finally said, "Does Ezparya know that you're here?"

"Not as far as I know."

She stared at him, waiting. Now he must dive deeper, or somehow create a minimally embarrassing exit for himself. Now!

"I need to touch you." How ungainly these words of his, rigidly marching after one another, gracelessly waving the flag, or at least the outer flag, of his intention! Nevertheless, now there was no retreating at all, no option of escape...

"So I assume you now know your purpose in coming here." Her tone was distinctly condescending. Nodding, he reached out for her hand, as though through a wall in a dream. She sat motionless, offering no external resistance. Now her fingers lay in his, limp and very pale, like bleached lengths of gutted eel, he thought.

"I am very uncomfortable, if that makes any difference to you," she said at last, pulling her hand back ever so slightly.

"So am I."

"So what are you doing here?"

"Not making my discomfort more important than reaching out to something in you that you insist on denying." The sentence, though somewhat ungainly, hung in the air, refusing to go away.

"But what is your interest in all this?" she asked, relaxing a little.

"That is what I came here to discover."

"And are you?"

"A little. There is no life in your hand, no presence, no warmth. Are you really afraid to *touch* me? To *really* let the tightness out of your mouth and body? To let your passion speak its mind and dance its truth? Why not release the hold you have on your hidden excitement?" His words tumbled out smoothly, bright and sinewy, but he still felt ill at ease — what was he doing here, pushing Tornellas, pushing and pushing, when she was making it so clear that he was unwelcome? But wasn't there something else in her that was, however subtly, responding to him as more than an invader? Yes, but...

"Let's stop, Glam. I can guess your purpose. I can smell it! But I am no man's lover, nor will I ever be."

A warning sounded deep inside him. His encounter with Tornellas, regardless of its unpleasant aspects, was definitely drawing forth some sexual heat from him — he knew that the very way in which he was verbally engaging her was actually feeding his erotic interest in her. Was he only here to seduce her? Was he only trying to manipulate forth her admission of attraction toward him, so that he would then feel *justified* in further pursuing his desire for her? His desire, however, was not particularly strong — it was little more than a faintly tingling anticipation, a waiting for her to open, to unguardedly welcome him into her depths...

He pushed aside the warning and, with some embarrassment, said, "Do you not remember watching me naked in front of Ezparya? How did that affect you?"

"I felt disgusted."

"And besides that?"

"Well —"

Abruptly, he squeezed her hand, speaking with a passion that rapidly dissipated his tension. "Why am I quizzing and pushing you so? Why do I so determinedly *seek* your confession of desire for me? You are obviously *unwillingly* submitted to my control, but that is *not* what I wish! Not at all! How very awkwardly we now sit here, me with my untucked desire, you with your caution!"

"What exactly *is* your desire?"

"To be lover to you." How easy the words, how unburdened by drama, how very ripe to be uttered!

"But this is absurd!" she stammered, not noticing that her hand was now tightly gripping his. "You are already lover to Ezparya!"

"If I wasn't, would you view the matter differently?"

"Possibly." She looked directly at him, a pleasing yet unfamiliar warmth now spreading through her body, dissolving her tension.

"And yet you said a moment or two ago that you would never be any man's lover, didn't you?"

"That's true," she whispered, suddenly no longer interested in their dialogue. He released his grip, letting his fingers slowly slide up her forearm, barely grazing her skin; she didn't resist at all. For a moment, he thought of Ezparya, imagining her possible reaction to what he was doing, and to what he might well be soon doing... His actions, however, made him feel not further from Ezparya, but closer to her, especially in spirit; he did not have to exclude her from himself in order to take this leap with Tornellas.

More than lust was driving him now.

The risk begged him to fully flesh it out; all his reasons for proceeding or not proceeding were flimsily peripheral, no more than articulate excuses for holding back, just the logic of inflated prudence, every argument of which was but a confession of a mistrust of his depths. In no way was he deluded or blinded by the swelling thrill rising through his body — in fact, its very heat was, through his use of it, actually self-illuminating, radiant with consciousness, or, more precisely, with *awakened* attention...

He ran his fingers up to the nape of her neck, her slender, satiny neck, gently bringing her to him. Slowly and steadily, they eased down to the floor, embracing more and more fully, breathing together torso to torso. At first, her touch was quite tentative, but soon grew more certain, more openly hungry, as his hands caressed her face and lower back. Her body was muscular yet soft, thinner than Ezparya's. He felt an urge to kiss her deeply, and an even stronger urge to not; though the must in lust might say so, it was not yet time to do so. Looking into her eyes, he saw both fear and longing. Such longing! Surfacing through her fear, breaking through her hesitation, shyly and not so shyly inviting him in, and in...

Now he could not help but feel as though he were her parent — no, not exactly her parent, but her guardian! What she was so sweetly baring to him was his to protect, his to honour, his to safeguard against loveless plundering. However, this awareness in no way diminished or inhibited his desire to embrace her as lover, but only brought more tenderness and refinement to his desire.

How refreshing was her invitation, how lusciously awkward, how intoxicatingly fragrant! How moistly pleasing her seedling receptivity, how nakedly green her expanding welcome! She seemed ready, but he, despite the intensity of his passion, actually wasn't; it was not the right time, and he refused to perform any conjuring of reason that might convince him that it really was the right time. He stroked her lightly, in rhythmic, swirling patterns, without any intent to inflame her with his touch. Her hands and body moved with surprising delicacy, with just enough force to bring him closer to her. Gradually, their breathing grew quieter and more relaxed, until the room hummed with a richly textured silence — how lovely it was to float, seemingly bodiless, in its sublime vastness! At last, he softly eased out of their embrace. So they had not become lovers. She still seemed impassioned, but nonetheless pleased, and more than a little relieved.

"I will go now," he said. "We need not mention anything about this to anyone — yet." She nodded, propping herself up on her elbows, a flushed joy ripening her features. Her whole body seemed to be smiling.

He left, and was soon once again in the streets, walking toward his own quarters. The faces of the crowds, though still revealing long-time commitment to slumbering lust and degradation, seemed softer now, a little more resilient. A song to Lantar found its way to his lips. Almost inaudibly, he hummed and sang it until he was stretched out on his bed...

> *Lantar, in You I rise and fall*
> *My heart beating with Your Call*
> *Lantar, Spring of my soul*
> *Eternal Sun ever making me whole*
>
> *O Guide me on, guide me, guide me free,*
> *Guide me, guide me on, guide me into Thee*
> *Until I only live You, and You me*
>
> *Lantar, may I now open to You*
> *Open to You through and through*
> *Up and down, in and out, round and round*
> *Until my heart's found its truest ground*

23

The Broken Music

Three days later, Glam returned to Tornellas's room, arriving just after sunset. He knocked lightly. A dozen heartbeats later, the door swung open. In the breeze-stirred candlelight stood Tornellas; naked she was, draped only with flickering shadows, her hands over her breasts, her body trembling. Quickly, he closed the door, not hiding his surprise.

Yet he was not so surprised — since he had lain with her, he'd seen her twice, once in passing, and once behind the amphitheatre. On both occasions, she had glanced at him with unmistakable welcome. Of course she knew he was coming to her! Look at her, richly blushing in the fading shadowplay of the candles, her body a gift just unwrapped, smooth and fresh, quiveringly transparent to the thrill permeating it, radiant with longing!

A lithe body it was, obviously supple, and just as obviously unschooled in what she was about to experience. The fluid intertwining of her openness and her artlessness not only excited him, but also brought a deepening care and sensitivity to his approach. A childish yet elegant innocence blurred the sharpness of her features. The light ceased wavering. Her mouth was a waiting curve, glistening and full, her eyes yearning and wide, asking no questions...

He went to her and took her wrists, lifting her hands away from her breasts, watching her nipples swell and stiffen, seeing gooseflesh sweep across and down her torso. Slowly, looking into her eyes the whole time, he stroked her from forehead to toes, feeling her longing sweetly intensifying. How very receptive was her skin, how ripe and yielding her flesh! At last, as he undressed, he watched her watching him, her gaze caressing and inflaming him.

There was no stopping.

Naked they stood, hugging and swaying, their mutual passion needing no stimulation other than being in each other's unrestrained presence. What a delicious urgency this was! What bliss to surrender body and mind into it, without, however, reducing it to a mere *prelude* to orgasmic release! Joy, lust-bright and throbbing with pure yes, was *already* the case, rather than being the goal of their sexplay — how very *natural* this was, especially relative to the desperate search for pleasurable stress-release that epitomized the sexual activity of far too many...

There was no stopping at all.

Still standing, he entered her very slowly, cupping her buttocks in his hands, gently sliding and guiding her onto him, feeling her widen to receive him, her widening pulsating with heated embrace, her breath full of luxuriant sighs and half-broken cries. Finally, when he had fully entered her, they stood unmoving for a long time, both deeply rooted in the currents of their joining, and yet also afloat in a sky oceanic and electric, a sky ever expanding...

Gingerly, laughing a little, they eased down to the floor, rolling over once onto a thick rug, soon intensifying the rhythms of their passion. Eventually, as he rested near the summit of his pleasure, he found himself in a calm within the flames of his desire; he looked into Tornellas's eyes, seeing her swooning joy, her gratitude, her fledgling love, and...

And also a trace of fear, probably just a bit of holding-back, nothing to be concerned about — in fact, it was vanishing just from him seeing it in her, disappearing in the very warmth of their shared emotion. But what was *this*? What was this subtle stabbing in his midsection?

It was his own fear!

He distrusted the situation now, immediately feeling himself removed from the interplay of the two bodies. His motions completely ceased. She kept moving.

"Something is not right," he said in a low voice.

She looked startled. "What is it?"

"I don't know. But I know I cannot continue this, lovely as it is."

"Just a little more," she whispered, putting her hands on either side of his face. "Just a little more."

Dropping his head, he closed his eyes. She held him tightly, moaning and sighing, breathing deeper and faster, some of her sounds like those of a woman in the last throes of labour. Sadness filled him. He didn't mind what she was doing. He remembered the starving faces of Anushet, the loveless horror pullulating and parading behind the unknowing, dully satisfied eyes. Let Tornellas have this! Let her ride it wild, let her ride it all the way! But what was it that he mistrusted? His back felt uneasy, unprotected...

Then he knew.

For a moment, he wished he'd never come to Tornellas's room, never started anything with her, never pursued more — but now there was no turning back, no possibility of some miraculous reversal, no awakening pinch, no relief-drenched ejection from a mere dream, no escape, none! Already he knew that the door was slightly ajar — any moment now, it would burst open.

Into a rapturous climax rose Tornellas, wave upon melting wave, her voice breaking into soaring song. When she was still, she and Glam rolled onto their sides, softly intertwined.

If only there was no one at the door...

The silence bulged and shook, pregnant with its own explosion, stretching its moment just a little farther...

The door smashed open, the sound brutally penetrating, and Ezparya strode into the room, followed by at least fifteen armed men. As she lifted her sword, Glam leapt aside, as he had known he must as soon as the door opened. There had been no time to warn Tornellas of what was now gleaming right above them; he had not expected Ezparya to be so instant in the use of her sword, or even to be resorting to it. Everything was far too fast, too final — there was no time for him to get through to Ezparya, to truly meet her, no time at all!

The great blade, as long as a man's leg, arced down viciously, cleaving the air with a streamlined swishing, cutting Tornellas almost in half at the waist. Before Tornellas could scream, Ezparya brought her sword down again on her throat, then whirled to face Glam, who crouched in a corner, stunned by the extreme finality of her action.

"Seize him!" she screamed.

His shock, though intense, was not so great that he didn't know what she had in mind — their initial meeting was more than vivid to him. He growled at the guards, who stood at arm's length from him. Into their eyes he cast his glare, his demand that they not touch him; they blinked and shuffled their feet, letting their speartips drop.

"Go!" shouted Glam. "Go from this room, or I shall have you fed to a pack of dogs! Am I not co-ruler of Anushet?"

"Take him now," demanded Ezparya, "or you shall suffer my displeasure! He is but a naked man, and you are sixteen, well-armed!"

Glam spat disdainfully. "Listen, and listen well! This is strictly a private matter! It is not the queen who orders you, but only an *insanely* jealous woman! Go, and let us settle this by ourselves!"

Back and forth the men swayed. Ezparya snarled, pushing at them with all her strength. Three fell upon him, their spears clanging to the floor. He took their weight, then rolled out from under them, snatching a spear. For the first time, he caught Ezparya's eye — dense and black was her hatred, cancerously swollen, quivering with unbridled righteousness and intensely contracted force. He could see that she was about to cut open one of the guards, so as to incite the others to obey her. Her sword, all silver and crimson, rose up.

"Stop!" roared Glam. She didn't. As the dripping blade hissingly descended toward the juncture of neck and shoulder in its terrified target, Glam swung his spear as strongly as he could, knocking the sword out of Ezparya's grip. It banged and skidded across the floor, stopping by the corpse of Tornellas.

"See what you have done!" Stepping forward, he drove his hand across her face. She stumbled back, almost falling. Weeping and bellowing

with rage, he slammed his fist into the center of her chest, sending her
to the floor.

"Fool! Is this what you *truly* wished to do? *Is it?* You, with all your
powers and all your opening, so easily giving in, yes, giving in, to the
darkest impulses of your jealousy, yielding yourself to *its* viewpoint!
You have murdered more than Tornellas! Look at her! Can you not see
what you have done?"

"She deserved to die, as do you! Never again will you strike me!"
Speaking words he didn't understand, she stood, shaking her head
violently, her eyes remaining rigidly focussed. The guards, abruptly
animated, took hold of Glam, forcing him to his knees. He submitted
to their grasp, pushing down the almost unbearable intensity that filled
him.

Not now.

Let it grow, let it rise. Let *it* instruct him! He would not prematurely
release it. He must wait, he must trust...

"Now what will you do?" he asked.

"Watch you die!"

"For what?"

"For betraying me!"

"I didn't betray you! But you, you have betrayed yourself through the
indulgence of your murderousness! You have betrayed *your* love,
Ezparya, letting it be strangled by the vengeful demands of your
twisted hurt!"

"Your words do not move me."

"How could they? You are unwilling to be moved!"

She picked up her sword. "I have heard more than enough from you!"

"Back to the old Ezparya, the female Artakiab! Was our time together no more than an interruption of your ugliness? Is there nothing more to you than this impenetrable fisting of jealousy, this hardness, this lovelessness?''

"Empty words buying time."

"And what of *your* hurt, Ezparya? What about the woundedness, the sad wrenching behind your righteous stance? What about the searing hurt, the agonizing sense of rejection throbbing within your jealousy? What about the *you* who is witness to all this? What about the *you* who cannot help but love?''

"Clever to the end, aren't you?" she sneered.

"You won't let me touch you in any way, will you? What a pity! You have killed Tornellas, and now you are quickly destroying our bond, literally killing it! Is this what you *truly* want, to destroy what you most value? *Is it?*''

"Soon you will not have a tongue to blabber with."

How powerful was this intensity, this primal feeling-force, within him! He felt as though he were about to burst. Just a little longer...

Softly, he said, "Is there anything else you want to say to me?"

"No."

"Goodbye, Ezparya."

As his last words ricocheted through her, she wavered briefly, then resolutely stepped forward, her sword aimed at his lower belly, her face shadowed ice, her eyes black suns...

Now!

At last, he could let what filled him speak freely — out and out it exploded, blasting wild and screamingly wide, convulsing his entire body, throwing off those who held him, as if they were but pieces of driftwood in a sea-storm. A pristine howling poured out of him, a howling crowded with immense deserts, a howling that was the raw soulsound of the most barren of wastelands, the most parched and lonely of all desolations, outer and inner. It was the music of naked suffering, the pure cry of orphaned humanity, the wailing of unnecessary hurt, not to be at all muted, buffered, anaesthetized, or camouflaged by *any* strategy, pleasure, or consolation of body or mind...

There was deep mourning in his voice, a blame-free grief, spaciously and turbulently flowing, and there was also compassion in it, a compassion beyond all sentimentality and manufactured morality, a compassion of ruthless integrity and unexploitable love, anchored in the very heart of Being. Tears cascaded down his face. Gradually, his howling flattened into a broad, tranquil river of sober yet joyous sound, sparkling with the dancing reflection of an eternal sun, melodically fanning and circulating throughout the room, soothing and warming all who were there, momentarily awakening them beyond who they took themselves to be.

Ezparya stood transfixed.

The sword dropped from her hand. He raised his eyes to hers, letting the streets of Anushet occupy his voice, letting the spiritless, teeming faces jostle and mingle in him, giving them a common voice, singing out not only their self-satisfied degradation and disease of feeling, but also their hidden longings, their crushed hearts, their collapse of being; the pleasures of the amphitheatre thickened his tongue, shrieking out bloodlust and mutilated passion, slobbering and salivating through him, louder and louder, finally turning inside out, shifting into sounds of shock, horror, and loneliness, and, eventually, grief, the broken music of long-suppressed grief.

The consequences of her entire life rushed through her, almost instantly uprooting all her defences. No rationalization, no insight, no explanation, no viewpoint, had any power whatsoever to comfort her. The floor was covered with the blood of Tornellas. Tornellas...

Glam knelt in front of Ezparya, his face transfigured by deep pain and an even deeper joy. Love for him swept through her. She began to cry.

Rising, he went to Tornellas's body, kneeling beside it, letting his hands softly move just above the entire length of her, his voice dropping into a low humming; back and forth his hands flowed, round and round, undulating here and there as though over invisible contours, his every movement contributing to what appeared to be an almost seamless massage. Finally, he placed one hand upon her forehead, and lifted the other, palm up, high above his head, his voice suddenly pooling out into majestically compelling sounds. Ezparya sobbed with abandon. The guards stood motionless, their eyes dreamy.

"Now," he whispered, "now you can go, Tornellas, go from this place, this fleshiness, this trouble, this time. Know that you are not dreaming. This body is lifeless. Let it go. Do not carry its wounds. Let yourself go, let this go, let go into the Great Brightness that is even now so, so near you. Go, go freely from this place, go where your love takes you. Do not linger here. It is done. Go, go now, go with my love, go now, go..."

He paused, then stood, breathing deeply, surveying the room. Quietly, he asked the guards to leave. As they filed out, he went to Ezparya.

"It is done," he said.

She stared back at him, still weeping, her face in ruins. He knew she understood. Her eyes were helpless with knowingness. There was a bottomless pleading in them, a yearning, a terrible heart-hurt. Glam was leaving. Glam was leaving...

He was leaving! She could not stop him. There was love in his eyes, but it was not servant to their bond. Their separation was starkly obvious to her, not needing to be spoken of at all.

"Forgive yourself," he said at last. "And forgive me, if I have misled you. Recognize that I do not part from you in bitterness, nor in retaliation."

"I know that," she said, her voice breaking.

"You are still queen, Ezparya. You have more than enough power to alter your course, to make good use of the harm you have done today."

"But without you —" She shook with a great sob.

"You are alone. You are already without me. I am long gone, even though I will stand here a little longer. Mourn me as you must mourn Tornellas. And beware the hope that resurrects me! You know I must go — your slaying of Tornellas didn't cause our separation, but only quickened it. We were bridges for each other, Ezparya, not homes!

"Our affinity, our love and passion, our depth together, in no way implies or necessitates a life-long coupling. You know this as well as I do."

"I don't..." She cried freely, her eyes wide open. Never had he seen her so vulnerable. Suddenly, he felt very close to her, much closer than his words suggested, intoxicatingly and poignantly intimate, full of an achingly sweet tenderness; he yearned to touch her, to hold her, to melt into her, to once again let their spirits sing through the blissful blending of their bodies. How easy, how warm, how rich and deep it would be, how thrillingly healing...

How marvellously fulfilling it would be to reestablish the mutual nourishment, the sensual adventure, the spirit-quickening, the fluid magic and joy, of their togetherness!

He hesitated, pulling back from the urgency of his desire. Something much stronger was calling him. Reluctantly and sadly, he stood back, overflowing with longing for Ezparya. Why not just one more embrace? After all, she was in no position to harm or manipulate him now — she was just raw, beautiful need incarnate, superbly intelligent, voluptuously and heartbreakingly open, full-bodied womanliness —

No.

It was enough to simply feel this, all of this...

"Remember our love," he said. "Brief flame though it may seem to you now, it kindles a more fundamental fire, one that your entire life has been a skilful avoidance of — let *it* brighten your sky, and let it *consume* you! But I have said too much; my words sound empty to me now, a little forced. I will not soon forget how much you have given me, how very much..."

His voice trailed off, disappearing in the silence in which they stood rooted, a silence of almost unbearable eloquence and significance.

Goodbye, Ezparya.

She seemed to be pure invitation, nakedly receptive, overwhelmingly appealing, her everything shaped into a gesture of magnificently lucid desire...

Goodbye, Ezparya.

His course was elsewhere. His time with her was over. Without hurry, he put on his clothes, and left, his heart both breaking and soaring, his goodbye lengthening his stride.

24

Coming Through The Gates

Fresh and fragrant was the evening, exhilirating its willowy breeze. Just above the city's towers stared the moon, almond-shaped and orange, crisscrossed by braids of purplish cloud. The sky was the colour of Ezparya's eyes. Glam walked slowly, acutely aware of every step he took, blowing out each exhale as fully as possible. She wouldn't follow him; he was sure of that. Nor would she have him attacked. Ezparya, still in *that* room...

Tonight he must leave. There was no point waiting until dawn. Back in his quarters, he quickly gathered up a backsling of clothes, two daggers, and a small axe that had been a gift from Ezparya. On his way out of the city, he added bread, cheese, and meat to what he was carrying, as well as two spears. He didn't look back.

He walked rapidly and easily, remembering how he had so long ago fled in exactly the same direction. By sunrise he'd likely be at the foot of the mountains that now loomed in the distance. He didn't feel tired. Several times, he broke into a run, stretching out along the flat, hard earth and, eventually, the cushioned floor of the forest just beyond the city's outskirts. It was such pleasure to run like this, to soar with each stride, to precisely plant the fleeting foot, to feel the compressed coiling of muscles, to rock and spring forward with such surging, high-lifting extension, to feel the current of breath coming in great, rhythmic gulps! O the balance and thrust of it, the feline grace, the sinewy exultation, the steaming embrace of speed and stamina, the arrowed momentum, the cooling caress of the breeze!

Had he not just stepped out of a cage? A spacious, uncage-like cage it had been, ingeniously decorated, with many levels, the higher ones of which had almost invariably taken their overseeing of the lower ones as evidence of their freedom. However, a cage was but a cage, no matter how sublime, or cleverly arranged! At the same time, though its latticework be of the sturdiest material, a cage was not truly fixed or positioned — regardless of how solid it might *appear*, it was not so much a thing or even a structure, as it was an activity, a *doing*! How very easily humans took their cages to be themselves! Yet, they were not actually *within* a confining structure of some sort, but rather were simply *doing* it, busily breathing Life-energy and attention into their self-entrapment with unquestioning consistency, madly defending and *believing* in their spirit-negating condition, literally dying for *it*!

Was not Ezparya's freedom but the freedom of an animal to move unhindered through its cage? And he, was he so different? Did he not also create entrapping circumstances for himself wherever he went, however lofty or transcendent, however broad the boundaries? Regardless of its refinement and expansion, it was just a repetitive confinement, whatever its levels, a chronic resurrection of the merely familiar, a self-generated barricading and compensation-crowded encapsulation, existing to produce a *convincing*, or at least predictable, illusion of safety and security. Habit, mere *habit*! The ever-subtler *personification* of habit, especially the habit of self-suppression — had he not just spiritualized his leanings, somehow making *his* search sacred?

But his search itself *was* his trap! Xandur had once told him that his very searching was blinding him, but that to *deliberately* stop searching would in no way remedy his blindness; Glam had then asked what that left him, and Xandur had only smiled. Another time, Xandur had said that searching, no matter how noble its quest or goal, was but another way of occupying oneself, of ensuring and maintaining one's capacity for self-distraction — yet he had also encouraged Glam's seeking, telling him that what he sought would be found only when the very *foundation* of his seeking had been utterly and luminously frustrated, irreversibly uprooted. Xandur! That wily old intimate of Paradox! How he would love these trees, this mossy gallop of mine...

Deeper than the play of insight and questioning, deeper than any working of mind, was the fact of his leaving Anushet. He gradually slowed to a walk, letting his thoughts roam and randomly graze, superficially savouring their ruminations, letting none of them disturb him, including those concerning the *apparent* dilemma of seeking. The trees grew sparser, the ground rockier. At last, he tired of his thoughts — their very crispness and sharpness of nuance was beginning to dull him. Was not their tone of excitement but his excitement at leaving? The unevenness of ground required his full attention. On and on he walked, weaving his way through mazes of jagged boulders, chanting a song to Lantar in a low, steady voice:

> *O Great Heart, I dance in Your Spirit-Fire*
> *You appear as me and the sky and all these trees,*
> *And as the shining Flame of pure desire,*
> *Already here, already alive, already free*
> *Lantar, Source and Light of every star*
> *Ever dying into You am I,*
> *Like a cloud into boundless sky*

Eventually, he increased the force of his chant, improvising more and more of the words, roaring out single lines over and over, letting himself well and glow with full-blooded delight. Though daybreak was near, a few stars were still visible, seemingly urging him on. He let his entire body participate in his singing, allowing the obvious vitality and wonder of all that surrounded him to amplify and enrich his sounds. At last, overcome with emotion, he stopped walking — now, crystalline, glorious now, there seemed to be only beauty, only Existence pouring out its song of being, forever *already* ecstatic, ever shining through the flux of appearances, the birthing and dying of everything and everyone, ever in virginal embrace with Unsleeping Consciousness...

For a moment, he considered expressing his gratitude for such potent revelation, then realized that *all* of this, including himself, was in essence simply an expression of gratitude, utterly motiveless in its thanksgiving. *All of this* throbbed with exactly the same primordial Heart! The same immensity of love, the same eternity of Being! Such love was not apart from Consciousness, not at all! Such love favoured none, and pervaded all! More precisely, it now *was* all, its light transforming Paradox into Truth, its Source revealed in and *as* everything, its call touching all, its innermost cry its joy... Lantar! Lantar! How obvious, how sublimely and forever obvious! How could he go on not recognizing Lantar? How could he go on *acting* as though they were apart? How could he? Laughing and crying, he dropped to his knees, his hands out in front of his chest, palms up, fingers trembling and spread wide, as if offering a gift, a sacred gift...

Not until long after his ecstasy had passed did he move. Dawn reddened the tips of the highest peaks. He began his ascent, winding his way through a dried-out riverbed's almost tubular channel. The vegetation was little more than occasional patches of parched grass and small, thorny bushes. Several times, large, bluish-yellow lizards slithered between rocks in the riverbed as he stepped near, their pale orange tongues glistening and darting. A ragged wind swirled over the slope he climbed, a wind dry and emaciated, forlorn and lonely, faintly moaning. He walked quickly, knowing that very soon the mountainside would be baking in the sun. Sweat beaded his forehead. A few more lizards appeared, smaller, greyer, unmoving at his approach, as if supremely confident of their invisibility. He took out a spear, using its shaft-end to ease and support his climb. At last, he reached a small plateau, a bumpy, partially shaded shelf of damask stone from where he could see, high above, what appeared to be a pass between two peaks — he could be there by noon!

After a short meal and rest, he continued, not minding the ache of his body, nor the labour of his breath. The sheer work of his ascent exhilirated him; he was breathing too rapidly to sing, but he again and again found a music in the pattern of his rise. Whenever he remembered Tornellas's death, he climbed a little faster, as if to outstride the memory — he could not now afford to dwell on what had happened. The mountains invited him up and through, requiring his undivided attention. Had he not already mourned Tornellas, and had he not already sung out her path of transition? Yes, but there was more to feel, more mourning perhaps, more to integrate, but now was not the time...

Snow-sleek peaks, so taut and sword-sharp, I go beneath thee, to the other side. How grand your skyline, though lower than Aratisha's — no foot shall I set in your lofty snows, as through your pass I go... Cool but sweet was the air, tinged with a pristine melancholy, an unfulfilled solitude. The pass was not difficult to cross. Through its troughs of creamy mist he walked with great pleasure, anticipating the view ahead. Long were its corridors, rough its walls, bright its promise. He was eager to be through it, yet he didn't regret its length. Then, finally, he was free of it, ready to begin his descent.

The horizon was all ocean, an exquisitely smooth curvaceousness of sublime softness. The ocean! The brilliant expanse of it, the vast welcome, the unspeakable depth and intimacy of it! Only now did he realize just how much he had missed it. The waiting waters, the rolling steadiness, the thrill of its swells, the white thunder of its spray!

Below him was a rocky slope, slanting far below into forest. Singing and yelling, he ran down, leaping from stone to stone, exulting in his balance, running until he was deep into the forest. The trees were greener and closer together on this side of the mountain, but not so closely packed that he couldn't easily pass them. Green, soaked in green, singing with green, so, so green was this! Fresh, moist, aquiver with stretching jubilation, speechless with green...

Treetrunks, smoothly and precisely columnar, effortlessly supporting feathered layers of gently wavering green, through which filtered sunrays — and was that the smell of salt, mixing with the mushroomy, resinous odour of the forest?

The shore was near!

He sprinted toward it, bursting with excitement. Though he couldn't see the shore, he could feel it, and now he could hear its muted thunder! Through the forest's edge he leapt, running onto a sandy shore against which beat large, shinily ribbed waves, dazzlingly blue, lacy with dancing foam, curling up and up and over, breaking and pouring in, bubbling wildly, flowing in like cloudy satin, calling to him. Ankle-deep in pinkish-white sand he stood, completely absorbed in the play of the great waters. Yellow birds with long green bills lazily floated above the waves. He was here! Taking off his pack and clothes, he slowly walked forward, at last diving into the sea. Cold were the waters, much colder than Amula's, but he didn't care; when he eventually emerged from the sea, his skin tingling, his breath full and sparkling, he felt deeply rejuvenated, cleansed of more than he could name. Though this was still Anushet, Anushet was no more...

Later in the day, he used his axe to fashion a frame just inside the forest, with its roof-slope facing the ocean. He covered the frame with a bedsheet and many boughs, finishing just before sunset. It was not yet fully dark when he fell asleep, his mind afloat on the music of the waves.

25

Pass Through It
With Open Eyes

Late the next day, he found the site where he and Merot had stayed. The shelter they'd built was still there, caved-in, partially covered by the sails of the canoe. Merot's body was not there.

His death was, however. The memory of it barged back into Glam, vivid and harsh, violently flailing. Without any hesitation, he chopped the shelter to bits, swinging his axe with ferocious power, grunting and howling, soon standing sweating and shaking amidst all the pieces, screaming louder and louder, sweeping the entire area clear of Merot's murder, cleansing it and himself, pouring out a fury and a grief and a pure goodbye to the bloodletting of that long-ago time. Deliberately, he reentered the nightmarish cocoon in which he had once lain paralyzed, feeling it fully, at last bursting himself free of it, shattering it beyond all repair...

To a nearby stream he carried the sails, washing them, scrubbing out their bloodstains as best he could. Such a masterful weave they were — how long it had been since he'd touched anything Amulan! And what of his canoe? Had it been destroyed? It was not where he had left it. Perhaps, though, it was close by; what good fortune it would be to have the canoe, instead of having to build another! Eagerly, he searched for it, roaming further and further into the forest. When it was almost too dark to continue, he stumbled upon it at the base of a sharp incline. Maybe its carriers had planned to carry it to the city, and had tired of their task — regardless, it was his again, and, furthermore, it was undamaged! The next morning, struggling with its weight and bulk, he dragged it to the shore, glad that his direction was mostly downhill.

In a few days, he could leave. All he had to do was gather some food and water. The water-containers of the canoe were intact, and easy to fill. The next task was much more difficult — it took him almost a full day to track down a forestboar. A compact, bristly-haired beast it was, with long yellow tusks and tiny red eyes, whirling to face him when he rushed roaring at it, his whole body electric with risk. Its head was massive, its snout long and frothing, its sound guttural and raggedly thick. Deep into its open mouth he drove his spear, knocking it over backward, leaping out of the way of its black hooves. One fast sweep of his dagger across its throat, and it was over...

The forestboar was well over his weight, not at all easy to carry to the shore, but meaty enough to last him for a long time. He could alternate it with fish. A repetitive diet it would be, but nutritious enough. He'd make his bread and cheese last as long as possible. Also, there were plenty of berry-laden bushes all along the forest-crest, inviting his picking.

On the morning of his final day in Anushet, he watched a small group of men appear on the beach, less than a stone's throw from where he sat loading the canoe. When they spotted him, they stopped, but did not raise their spears, nor draw their swords — it was clear that they hadn't come to attack him. Their black tunics reminded him of Ezparya, not so much through their colour, as through their uniformity; he recalled the obedience she commanded and needed, the deep subjugation on which she depended. Such recollection was, however, now just peripheral to what he was doing, little more than the play of thought, but beneath it was...

Ezparya, sad-eyed flower with such a supreme elegance of line, swaying with trembling uncertainty above what she rose from, her creamy black petals now curled in on themselves, drooping and torn, but still emanating the fragrance that had carried him through so many unsuspected labyrinths...

Ezparya! How richly she had opened for him, letting him swoon in her nectared folds, taking him so far into herself that she could never again truly close! Her midnight eyes burning so bright and fiercely tender, her proud heart spilling wide, her succulent flesh consumed in ecstatic dance, her love dying into a deeper love — did she know how deeply he'd taken *her* in? Did she know that his very core of being was branded with her presence? Did she know the difficult yet profoundly enlivening alchemy he underwent with her? Here he was, far from her, busily preparing to leave. To leave! Now he missed her terribly, feeling an overwhelming intensity of longing and love for her, shot through and through with a nostalgia of excruciatingly seductive force.

"Tell Ezparya I left Anushet today!" he shouted, casting his voice over the men. "And also tell her that Glam's love for her does not die!" For a moment, the men hesitated, then shuffled back into the forest. Glam knew they would return straight to the city.

He began to weep, dropping his head onto the side of the canoe. Goodbye, Ezparya, goodbye, goodbye... Do not take my leaving as a tragedy, nor as a burden! I cannot deliver you from your pain; I cannot even do that for myself. All I can do is *listen* to it, and somehow feel my way through it. You must pass *through* your hurt, Ezparya, pass through it with *open* eyes, rather than just dwelling in realms above it. Use my departure, use it wisely! Mourn me deep, mourn me full, but do not drown in your sorrow — ride its waves toward a truer shore. Goodbye, goodbye...

Each time he said goodbye with unrestrained passion, he wept more freely, feeling an inner release that was both painful and pleasurable. His hands gripped the lip of the canoe, as though anchoring the great shudders and sobs surging through him. Now I see you standing over Tornellas, inflated with unforgiving wrath, your sword and arm as one. You did not hesitate to kill her. Use her death, use it wisely! And Tornellas, shy, arrogance-armoured woman, your final days tender with opening — I felt your heart, faraway and tentative, but so beautiful in its birth-stirrings! On the very edge of your humanness you were poised, your ripeness just barely exceeding your resistance...

Now he cried for Tornellas, his tears unpolluted by regret. There was no judgment in his grief, no nostalgia, no contraction of self — his crying was for Tornellas, and for Ezparya, and for himself, a crying that was too true for any thought to penetrate. Not until the ocean was lapping against his feet did he stop. Such a gentle touch it was, silent and motherly, full of satin subtlety. Looking up, he saw the unbroken expanse of the sea, bejewelled by the noonday sun, its azure waters seeming to absorb, cradle, and celebrate his sadness and everything else he was feeling.

Goodbye, Anushet, and hello, wild blue waters, soon to be crossed! Very soon! How intimately intertwined were its currents and his! How unequivocally broad its welcome, how ancient and familiar its call, how simultaneously passionate and detached its flow...

In mid-afternoon, he pushed off from shore, nosing the canoe through the surf, then out onto the barely undulating waters. For some time, he paddled with an oar he'd made the day before, not looking back. So he was returning. Somewhere over the horizon waited Amula. For now, though, this ocean was home, and likely would be for a long time. He was in no hurry, knowing he needed time to fully digest his stay in Anushet, and what better place to do this than on this great ocean?

How clear it was that he was not who he'd been when he'd first arrived in Anushet! He couldn't just resume his pre-Anushet life. The Glam of those days looks at me wide-eyed — he is talented but unknowingly naive, occasionally wise in his communion with the Source, and blind to the deepest roots of his spiritual ambition. He is an adventurer, sealed into his seeking. Now and then he is truly surrendered to the Lantar Who shines above his head and in his heart, but not to the Lantar Who burns in his belly and snakes through his pelvis. Again and again, he struggles to mastermind his own evolution, reducing awakening to a strategy. He, ardent, Amulan he, is looking for an experience that will deliver him once and for all from his suffering, so he artfully exploits his capacity for experience, and suffers the hope-crushing consequences of such tactics, while seeking a remedy for *that* very suffering!

How critical he was of that long-ago Glam! He, he who was not all that different! He, he who was still addicted to *his* search, *his* journey, cleverly ennobling it with supposedly sublime purpose! As if his changes, however dramatic, signified anything more than *change!* As if there was something *inherently* virtuous in changing oneself! Nevertheless, he *was* definitely ripening. His deepest changes, those which were more than just rearrangements of persona, were *not* those *he'd* sought to bring about — all he could claim here was a kind of visceral cooperation with the forces catalyzing his transformation, a begrudging cooperation at that!

He laughed, unwilling to further develop his sequence of thought, smiling at his seeming clarity of mind, a clarity blind to its source, a clarity that upheld itself with acrobatic nuance, weaving multi-levelled meaning into whatever was happening — fool that he was, trying to encapsulate this Wonder! Trying to create and neatly package some understanding, then earnestly presenting it to himself as a precious gift! Tears ran down his face as he laughed, mixing with the spray breezing off the ocean. O but there was a deeper understanding, a full-bodied knowingness, ever lurking in that holy place where insights lose their mind!

At last, he stopped paddling, and turned around. No longer could he see the shore he'd left. Only the mountains were visible. Somewhere past them was Anushet's city and its queen — did she now sit in the stark luxury of her rooms, proud and straight, firming herself with some well-honed manipulation of attention? Or did she lie on her bed, weeping and heartsick? Closing his eyes, he focussed on her, allowing himself to feel her. Almost immediately, he saw her sitting in the amphitheatre, slightly slumped, her eyes faraway, her fingers interlaced so tightly that her hands were white. He wanted to touch her, to contact her, and knew he could psychically, but didn't.

Their paths had parted, like the banks of an ever-widening river. What needed to occur in her could only do so in his *total* absence. There was, he once again told himself, no turning back, and no need to do so, nor was there any hope for such a venture. Had not Xandur once said that hope was but nostalgia for the future?

No nostalgia now, no lingering, no weakening, not even a goodbye anymore — the very passion of his farewell had extinguished itself, its ashes scattered far behind him, swallowed in the wake of the canoe.

A cool wind caressed his face. Opening his eyes, he resumed paddling, not stopping until long after the last flames of sunset had disappeared into the soft black velvet of the sky...

Part II

Look for me
Where storms come uncaged
Look for me
Where the sea carries shattered sky
Look for me
Where black leopards await their prey
Look for me
Where sunlight fans through throbbing decay
Look for me
Where emerald valleys sway in orgasmic trance
Look for me
Where the land is wild with rhythmed Wonder
Look for me
Where jagged shores moan with white thunder
Look for me
Where insights lose their mind
Look for me
Where joy's the ground, and silence the sound
Look for me
Inside your looking
Look for me where joy and pain disappear into sun and rain,
Where we can only once again love ourselves sane
Look for me
Where we can only dance the sacred dance,
The dance whose Heart beats out of time,
Forever surrendered to an ecstatic Rhyme

26

An Apparent Interruption

A week passed, and he saw no land. His speed had been good — the winds, though mild, had been strong enough to fill out the sails, and the nights had been stunningly clear, their stars intimate guides. Rarely did he mind that the days ran together in their similarity; in fact, he welcomed their level steadiness and ease, their soothing spaciousness, their effortless transcendence of complexity and abstraction. Nothing really interrupted the magical ordinariness of the ocean, not his mood-shifts, nor the leaps of porpoises, nor his musings, nor the final shudders of hooked fish upon the canoe's floor. He ate when he was hungry and slept when he was tired, his entire being in deep harmony with the rhythms of the sea. Sometimes he sang to Lantar, but usually he was silent, blissfully yet soberly content, his body the great waters, his mind the sky. There was no hurry to do anything, no real urgency at all, just the fluid, muscular joy of functional grace. It was enough to just be, more than enough...

A second week sailed by, and a third. Near the end of the fourth week, he saw land. Although it was clearly off his course, he aimed straight for it — perhaps there'd be game there. He could use fresh meat, and his water was getting a bit low. Who knew how much further Amula was? Soon, he could see that what he approached was a small island, apparently no more than a half-day's walk in length. Rugged was its coastline, deeply indented with narrow inlets. It was late afternoon when he finally eased the canoe down what appeared to be a passable inlet. The water was still and dark, shaded by the cliff faces rising up sheer from both sides of the inlet. Several times, the canoe scraped against unseen rocks, making him wonder if he ought to try a different entrance to the island. Just as he was about to turn back, he saw a small beach at the end of the inlet. A short time later, quite relieved, he landed the canoe.

Land. Land, so dense and contracted compared to the ocean, so
resolutely fixed, so rigidly positioned, pushing up against his weight...
Taking a spear and his axe, he walked into the land, a little unsteadily.
Its surface was of dark earth and bizarrely sculptured stone, flat and
creamy in places, but mostly caught in rough upthrust, as though
having been frozen in the midst of a small eruption — a choppy sea
precariously held in place, pink and beige, its handiwork seemingly
not that of erosion, but of — what?

Permeating it all was a chalky stillness, a stillness that was more pause
than silence...

His steps shortened. A few clumps of misshapen trees dotted the
landscape. There were no signs of animals or birds. Once, he looked
back and saw his canoe, a dull and subtly wavering sliver, almost
spectral. Dread seeped into him. The silence strained mightily, like a
breath held too long...

Suddenly, he knew he must leave, and began running back toward the
canoe. He'd taken no more than a dozen strides when the ground
rocked under his feet, bursting open halfway between him and the
canoe, squirting up black and red, oozing out thickly braided and
steaming furiously, its molten fingers stretching up high and fat and
then collapsing slowly, drooping over like spent stems, falling and
flooding with shocking speed down toward the very shore where he'd
left the canoe.

The entire island spasmed violently, again and again. He dove down,
stretching out face-down against the heaving earth. The land roared
and shook, moaning and shrieking and spurting in a paroxysm of
release, each great shudder stronger than the last. He clung to the
ground, his heart madly throbbing, his skin singed by fiery waves of air.

Abruptly, it was over.

When he eventually looked up, he saw that the inlet he'd sailed in on
was packed with churning, rolling red, its waters leaping and frothing
and steaming high — the inlet was literally boiling! And what about his
canoe? Probably just a mass of ashes now! He wished he were
dreaming — what unbelievably bad timing this was, what terrible
fortune! Coincidence was too flimsy a label for it — gone was his

canoe, gone was his food and water, gone was his easy journey to Amula! Gone. It was too fast. He had only an axe and spear. Now, the earth was still, but where might it next erupt? He sat unmoving, oblivious to his own safety, shaking his head in disbelief and anger. If only he could awaken from this nightmare! If only...

Finally, he looked around. The sight of a few scattered clusters of trees reassured him — how could they take root in a soil that was constantly erupting? He must go to where the trees were most plentiful! Slowly, he arose, making his way toward the center of the island. Overhead, clouds billowed, black and swollen. The sea sizzled in the distance, grotesque shapings of steam crazily dancing over its surface, seemingly mocking him, their eyes gory white...

He had difficulty balancing, and kept stumbling. The sky held onto its rain. Not so far away there appeared a grove of trees, quivering in the surface heat. As he neared the grove, he felt some relief; there were at least a hundred trees in it, some of them six times his height. Between the trees squatted small, berry-abundant bushes. Blackish-blue were the berries, mealy and sweet; he gobbled them until he could eat no more.

However, his satisfaction was minimal. He was trapped, wasn't he? Trapped! In a rage, he drove his spear into the soft, mossy earth, then violently jerked it out. Cursed island! Would that he had let it pass! His canoe was no more than embers, mere smoke in this suffocatingly oppressive sky!

The clouds burst open, as if impaled with a million spears. The grove provided only the barest of shelter; very soon, he was totally soaked. Then there arrived a wind like no wind he had ever known. Screeching and sharp and immensely powerful it was, stinking of sulphur and rot — each of its howling rushes clawed at him, scraping his skin and punching his head back. Hastily, he lay face down, gripping tree-roots with both hands, but the wind still got under him with long, blindly probing fingers, as though trying to lift him like a sail. He must stay down! Desperately, he struggled to flatten himself, to somehow withstand this malevolent onslaught — yes, malevolent! Could he not feel its intention, its *specific* intention regarding *him*? This was more than wind, more than impersonal force, more than a riptide of air! Did he not feel its murderous will, its primeval hate, its fanged breath? Did he not see its scaly spirit, its writhingly ravenous essence, greenish-yellow and bulging with a dozen bloody eyes?

Creaking and groaning and whistling bent-double, the grove withstood the storm. The rain blew almost horizontally. Massive waves smashed against the shore, rushing up onto the land; a few almost reached the lowest clumps of trees. Finally, the rain stopped, then the wind. Broken branches blanketed him. Very slowly, he rose to his knees, wiping the mud and moss from his face, watching the trees creep back to their original positions. How gnarled and bent were their windward sides, like the backs of paralytics...

He sat straighter, breathing as fully as he could. He must get up! Quickly, for it was near day's end, he built a small lean-to between two of the largest trees, using a tight weave of branches for a roof. Tomorrow, he'd build a better one. Tomorrow...

Just before dawn, he awoke trembling. His body seemed to be twisted into a horribly distorted shape; he had to run his hands over and over it before he felt himself to be physically intact. Whatever it was he had been dreaming was still wrapped around him, like an obscene shawl, lighter than air, yet incredibly smothering, seemingly seeking entry into him. With a surge of will, he screamed himself free of it, dispersing its blurred, groping imagery, eviscerating its deformed intent. He peered out of his lean-to, seeing treetrunks and berrybushes and bluish-white sky. For a dizzying moment, he thought he heard footsteps nearby, huge, padded footsteps, softly yet ominously thudding. Cautiously, he stepped outside, spear in hand, crouched low.

He saw neither animal nor human.

Down to where his canoe had been incinerated he walked, wondering if he was imagining that the ground was shaking. Was he, in fact, still dreaming? Was this but a false awakening, as when a dreamer dreams he is awake? No, definitely no! Nevertheless, the earth did seem to be shifting beneath his feet, like muscles moving under skin. Fear oversharpened his senses, dangling paranoia before his mind. He must settle down! With considerable effort, he focussed his attention on the mechanics of his walking, while remaining aware of every breath he took. Such an eerie landscape this was, with its wavy spurts and twists and crinkled curlings of stone, all these turrets, cones, and drooping spires of half-buffed rock, hollowed here and there, fantastically shaped, some having an uncanny resemblance to the human form. Leering props from an exaggerated nightmare. The visions of a lunatic, unerringly sculpted. One could easily go mad here...

Already he had an urge to talk to some of the landforms — they seemed to be awaiting his animation of them. Instead, he sang to Lantar, his voice weak but steady:

> *O Lantar, whatever I see,*
> *You are here, here with me*
> *All I see and know is but Your Mystery*
> *All of this is but Your Form...*
> *In You arise the calm and the storm*
> *And all that is yet unborn*

Bright and fast rose the sun, gladdening his song, evaporating his sense of mirage, of babbling stone. The inlet's beach was completely covered by lava. His canoe was gone — there was not a trace of it to be seen. He must build another, as soon as possible! He could begin this very day, after he had explored the land. Let these bizarre shapings of stone continue their hallucinatory posing; no longer would they so easily seduce his imagination! Let them insinuate their way into ambulation among each others' shadows, but he, he'd offer neither choreography nor applause. His attention was not theirs, but his, his to focus, *his* to grant!

By noon, he'd crossed to the other side of the island. There weren't any sandy shores here, but only yellowing cliffs plunging straight down into the sea. Nearby was what appeared to be the highest point of the land. Soon, he stood atop it; it was little more than a mound of dirt and lava, untreed. Tiny plants crowded the few crevices of this lowly summit, their leaves compact and succulent, their flowers dull white. The entire island was within his view — its surface appeared to be the same everywhere, the same wildly extravagant sculpturing of stone, broken up only by patches of earth and groves of trees. He saw no lakes, no river. There were, however, signs of ravines, hints of streams. He wished some birds would materialize. Not even an insect had yet appeared...

Eventually, he found a small stream close to the site of his lean-to. Its

waters were clean and cold, and home to an animal of sorts —
miniature snails clinging to the algae-coated pebbles of the streambed,
their shells smoothly textured and remarkably delicate, exquisitely
variegated with mauves and greens. They were far too small to make a
meal out of, but they were company! For a while, he talked to them,
enjoying the sound of his voice. It was the first time he'd smiled while
here. Look at these tiny creatures upon the vastness of his palm! See
their transparent coils full of sunlight, their opercula iridescent pink
and swirling tangerine, their artistry uncompromised by any internalized
eye...

He spent the rest of the day cutting poles for a more substantial shelter,
singing as he worked, happy with the rough touch of the wood. That
night, he slept deeply, awakening at daybreak, again feeling unpleasantly
tangled up in the remnants of a dream. Grimacing, he shook it off, and
was soon back at work on his shelter. By sunset, he'd finished it.

Sleep came painstakingly slowly, even though he was tired and it'd
been dark for a long time — he knew he was readying himself for
another round of the dream whose aftermath had disturbed the past
two mornings. At last, he dreamt he was tightly bound by an unseen
material, a viscous, ropy substance writhing with a life of its own. He
tried to free himself, but without any success. He strained to see where
he was, gradually realizing that his eyes too were bound, covered by a
sour-smelling heaviness. Finally, he stopped struggling, and the binding
grew even tighter, especially around his neck and abdomen. What
could he do? A deep crying churned somewhere inside him, but could
find no externalization.

There seemed to be no escape possible. Everything he attempted only
intensified the binding. Doing nothing didn't help. So there was no
point struggling, and succumbing was useless — what could he do? He
could barely breathe. Helplessness inundated him. And yet...

Of course! He was *dreaming*! He still felt trapped, but now he knew
that he was dreaming! Ordinarily, dreams in which he recognized that
he was dreaming shifted with fluid ease, according to his more
energized intentions; such dreams were often a delight to participate
in, given the sheer breadth of option generated by his wakefulness.
This dream, however, persisted in its form, in spite of his lucidity — its
structure did not alter at all, despite even the most compelling of his

directives, including that of willing himself elsewhere. Perhaps it was more than a dream! However, he could not *convincingly* locate his physical body, nor could he sense the shelter. But was this just another part of the dream? No, definitely no!

Knowing that it was his dreambody that was bound didn't free him at all. He seemed incapable of leaving the dream. The malleability and arbitrariness of his dreambody did not in any way reduce or ease its binding. What if he shifted his attention from his apparent predicament to something else? For example, what about the binding itself? Since this was *his* dream, was he not also *creating* these very strands, and also creating their tightening? And if he wasn't, then *who* was? Panic filled him. He must stop trying to figure it all out, and simply go deeper into *it*! Deeper into now, right now...

With a concentrated effort, he remembered Lantar, and abruptly found himself existing *as* an even subtler body, patterned inside and out with the finely textured energies characteristic of deep meditation. To his horror, however, the binding continued!

There was no escape, or, more to the point, there was no escape for *him*.

Suddenly, he realized with his whole being that this constrictedness, this relentlessly binding *embodiment* that he felt, had almost *always* been with him, whether he had noticed it or not, no matter how expansive or centered he had been, no matter how sublime his meditations. The binding was fundamental to him — it was *not* apart from him. In fact, *it was him*, as he took himself to be! It was, in other words, *his doing*, rather than something that was being done to him! It was but recoil from Lantar, recoil *personified* as him! It was but reactive involution in the face of the Infinite, a self-centered, opaque retraction from the Source of All...

An oceanic thrill of recognition surged through him; no longer did he feel trapped by the binding, though he continued to experience it. And the he of the dream, the he who so adroitly and *solidly* embodied the central viewpoint of the dream, was not *he* also simply *part* of the dream? Yes! And why should everything revolve around *his* position, which was essentially no more significant than anything else in the dreamscape? But if he wasn't the dreamer, nor the awakened dreamer, then *who* was he? Now a deeper recognition briefly penetrated him, a radiant knowingness that both included *and* transcended all that was occurring...

The dream grew more transparent, pierced by the details of the shelter, and then was no more. He lay awake, curled up, his eyes open and unfocussed, his breath a flow of relief and happiness, his heart flooded with rhapsodic silence. All around him whispered the trees — he could literally feel all through him the currents of their sap, the probings of their roots, the playful profusion of their leaves, the uncompromising yet profoundly surrendered fullness of their multidimensional reach.

He felt intimate now not only with the trees, but with the sea, the land, the night, the soft, fecund night, the dark, dark womb of the night, the vast throbbing night with all of its magical doors and luminous birthstirrings! Did he not, as always, have *exactly* what he needed? He would build a canoe, not in bitterness, but in gratitude for the opportunity of being able to do so. Was he not well, and did he not have the tools and materials he needed? How very obvious it was that his being here on this island was not an interruption of his journey, but a *part* of it!

Laughing, he got up, and slowly walked through the grove. A half-moon lit his way. Everything seemed to be welcoming him, to be breathing with him, as if sharing a common heart. He continued walking until he stood at the edge of an inlet near the one where his canoe had been destroyed. Silken wavelets softly splashed and lapped below him. In the moonlight gleamed the leaping bodies of fish, bringing him to tears — he would certainly not die of starvation here. Though his belly rumbled and grumbled with hunger, he was content for now to do nothing except sit and listen to the seasounds, all of which seemed to be *inside* him, steadily and eloquently beating...

27

Returning To Amula

Three months after his arrival on the island, he finished his canoe. The work had been wonderfully consuming; he'd wasted no time, and yet had not hurried. He'd sung to the trees, to the sea and sky, to the rocks and streams, about his journey, about Ezparya and Tornellas, about Oma and Esmelana. Sometimes he, pretending that Xandur was present, had engaged in crisp, intricate dialogue, exaggeratedly playing both parts, conferring powers of audience onto the surrounding greenery and volcanic shapings. A time of healing it had been, a time of profound simplicity, a time of assimilation and regeneration...

The canoe was in length just over three times his height. The most difficult work had been in the last month, during which he'd woven a sail from the fibers of a bush that was plentiful in the grove, finally reinforcing its weave with a latticework of very light yet resilient poles. His last step, however, was much easier, lasting only three days — with chunks of soft stone, he rubbed the canoe's interior free of splinters, then thoroughly applied to it a dense, pungent oil he'd obtained from the seeds of the island's most dwarfish trees.

At last, when the canoe was loaded, and its outriggers securely fastened, he paddled away from the island. Already, the sun had set. He gazed back at the land, remembering his arrival there — what an unbelievable story to tell when he reached Amula! Amula, so blurred, so seemingly undisturbed, overflowing with green, such a dreamy profusion of greens, wave upon plump wave...

He knew not what he was returning to — he could breathe familiarity and fertile promise into it, greening it with pleasant expectation, but chose otherwise — should he resurrect hopeful dreams from what were more than likely just exhausted themes? Ought he to enliven what no longer served him, just so he could float in a mirage of security, fanned by spiritual lullabies? No, a quiet but unwavering no, full of an unshaped yes, a softly spinning yes whose very core was pure Mystery... Between Anushet and Amula was he; there was a territory within him where they overlapped, a turbulent, richly chaotic zone that seemed to be settling, becoming stabler, firmer, simultaneously more solid and more porous, gradually assuming its place as soil for what was to come. It was his ground. Above it wheeled unseen birds, their immense, spectral wings like eyelids, their luminous flight drawing him far beyond the differences of Anushet and Amula, their long, haunting cries filling out his sails...

Two days later, the wind bucked ferociously, whipping the waves into a frenzy, crowding the air with crazily tressed seaspray. He could barely see. As rapidly as possible, he took down the sail. He had anticipated such a storm, knowing that when it came, there'd be little he could do other than not to panic. Now here it was, a rearing, hissing fury with foaming talons, heaving and roaring, clawing the sea into wildly wrinkled troughs flanked by whiteplumed crests that loomed shockingly high, well over twice his height. The sky seethed black and bleeding silver, blistered all over by splotchy, dark purple eruptions, slashed by lightning.

Through the stormsounds, he could hear the the outriggers' binding creaking and groaning; he prayed that they would hold. The wind seemed to be blowing in from all directions. In the bottom of the canoe he lay. Wave after wave broke across the canoe, drenching him. He must not die here! It was not his time! It could not be his time...

There seemed to be no end to the storm. The canoe spun and tipped and rolled, madly veering, its outriggers still somehow intact. At last, the winds straightened out, blowing directly toward... Amula! How he knew this, he did not know, for he couldn't see past the end of the canoe. Nevertheless, he must put up the sail! Right now! The canoe was more than a third full of water. There was no time to lose, no time to waste considering his intuition as to the direction in which he was going. Now!

With a supreme effort, he secured the sail-pole, then raised the sail and drew it taut. Immediately, the wind drove into it, tearing it in a few places, and the canoe shot ahead, skimming over the sea. What a wind! What a thrilling fury of thrust, what unbridled intensity, what a glory of power! It howled out a harsh yet lovely sound that he now sang along with, his voice storming out of his entire body, his thoughts no more than flotsam in the canoe's wake. Sitting up behind the quivering curve of the sail-pole, his face red and exultant, he rode the storm...

Shortly after sunset, the sky cleared enough to reveal a few stars and the twin brilliances of Venus and Jupiter. The wind was still very strong, but much drier. Periodically, he scooped water out of the canoe, using a large bailer seashell he'd found on the shore of the island. The stars' position indicated that he was on direct course for Amula — he could be there in a matter of one or two weeks! Esmelana, your eyes the colour of sunned ocean, your whole body smiling at me, I am not now so far away! Again and again, he imagined leaping from his canoe onto the warm, fine-grained sand of an Amulan beach...

And just *who* was it who was returning to Amula? Glam, *this* Glam, saturated with adventure, weary with experience, profoundly altered, older and younger at the same time, dramatically ripened, wonderfully disillusioned, returning, returning and returning, his skull vast with rising light, his heart broad and weepingly bright, his flesh embodied delight, all the fragments of his being swimming together into a joyously healing reunion...

This return was not the end of his journey, but rather a *deepening* of it, a thinning of its drama that rendered it ever more transparent to its Source. Lantar, Lantar, Lantar! Ever more obvious to me! Eternal Heart, *You* are the Truth of all this, this play of waves, this clearing sky, these doings and these unglueings of mine! No matter what my mood or circumstance, I can turn to You, turn and turn! Return and return! Alway *You* face me, always! You Who beat my heart, You Who are the Everything of this, You Who are not a you, nor a me, You Who simply *are!*

He sang wildly, spontaneously composing songs to the sea and the sky, making no effort to make any sense whatsoever. It was sufficient to be alive, to be sailing through this blazing night upon this magnificent sea...

The wind softened just before daybreak. He sat slumped over, thoroughly and happily exhausted, at last letting himself drift into sleep. When he awoke, the sun was directly overhead, and the breeze just strong enough to keep the canoe moving. He saw no land on the horizon, but didn't mind, for he knew there soon would be. O to step onto twilit Amulan sand, gleaming purple and turquoise with wave-deposited phosphorescence... And back of the beach, rich green forest, palmy and fragrant, lushly hospitable... And back of that, Esmelana and Xandur... A doubt crept into his mind — how did he know he would be well-received? Laughing, he swatted away the doubt; his purpose in returning was much more than just a matter of being warmly welcomed, was it not?

A week later, near afternoon's end, he saw land. The outline was very familiar — a pale peak, barely distinguishable in the clouded sky — Mount Aratisha!

Mirage-like, but no mirage! The wind was sporadic and weak, only occasionally filling out the sail, so he had to paddle much of the way in. He worked without hurry, watching the land slowly grow more substantial. Such a deep-bosomed power it had, such a depth of ease, luxuriantly and smoothly unfolding, its soft, gently rounded contours contentedly sighing...

At last, he reached shore, coasting into a small, deep-sanded beach. There was no one there to greet him, to see him arrive. After he'd pulled the canoe up behind the sands, he sat facing the sea, overcome with gratitude. Again and again, he sighed with relief — he was back! For a long time, he sat unmoving and unthinking, wrapped by the warm, silkily sliding air, absorbed in a silence enriched by the multilayered pounding of the sea. He did not stir until well after dark, and then only to cover himself with the sail. On his back he lay, looking up at the sky through barely focussed eyes. The night danced with starlight. Gently and easily, he slipped into sleep.

The following morning, he was awakened by children's voices. Lifting his head, he saw three children playing in the canoe, their brown, naked bodies lithe and agile. They giggled and squeaked and shrieked, chasing one another with wildly dramatic gestures, flinging themselves about with exuberant abandon and grace. One stood on the bow of the canoe, his little legs boldly astride, his hand curved over his brow as if sighting some nautical marvel, his voice high-pitched, despite his efforts to lower it. His comrades were noisily unimpressed, again and again irreverently knocking him from his perch. All the while, they laughed merrily at everything they did, without in any way distancing themselves from it.

Finally, they all sat in the canoe, looking very serious, taking turns working the paddle, sometimes letting its blade get almost stuck in the sand, grunting mightily to keep their craft going. When one of them began scolding the paddle, Glam laughed loudly.

"A fine morning!" he shouted, sitting up.

The children turned, showing less surprise than he'd imagined they would. He stood, and walked to the canoe, feeling a little stiff. In silence the children waited, their faces open and unafraid. Behind them, just over a wavily rippled rise of pale gold sand, spread the ocean, a violet-stained turquoise, each one of its breaking peaks and curls brightly tipped with sunlight, the great ebb and flow of it all bringing a sudden tenderness to him. He recognized none of the children. They were all Esmelana's age.

"I'm glad you're enjoying my boat," he said quietly, sitting on the edge of the canoe. "It has brought me a long way."

Pausing, he watched their faces widen with curiosity. "Go ahead," he said, his voice so soft it almost broke. "Ask me some questions."

"Where have you been?"

"Across the ocean, much further than you can see, much further than you can imagine."

"But where?"

"A strange land, very, very different from this one."

"Who are you?"

"Do you know Esmelana?"

All three children spoke at once: "Yes!"

"And how is it that you know her?"

"She is the youngest oracle of all time," announced one. "Xandur himself said so. Everyone knows about her!"

Tears came to his eyes, fast and full. "I am her father. I am Glam." He wanted to say more, but couldn't; his whole being was quivering with both joy and grief. Sighing, he lowered his head.

"You are?" shouted the children. "But..."

They ran off, and were soon out of sight; he knew they hadn't run from fear, but out of desire to spread the news. Let them. He wept in silence, gazing out at the sea, knowing that Esmelana had many, many times sat as he was now sitting, watching the waves for his canoe, tiny seashells, bright and empty, dropping from her hand...

Early in the afternoon, a group of men approached him. They appeared friendly, and also a little cautious. "Greetings," said Glam, standing.

"Greetings," said one of them. "You are Glam?"

"Yes."

"Xandur wishes to see you."

"And Esmelana?"

"She'll be there. You can come with us." He followed them. None spoke, though he could tell they were all very curious about him; it was likely that Xandur had requested that they not converse with him. The sun had almost set when they entered the temple wherein Xandur lived. Smiling, they left him alone. Where he stood was achingly familiar to him — the pale pink sandstone, the towering hedge of palms, the undulating, intertwining smells of sandalwood and frangipani, the feline, playful figures sensually cavorting in the frieze above the temple's inner entrance. For a moment, he remembered a very different courtyard, where he and Ezparya had slain Artakiab — how faraway that was, and yet how sharp its memory, how painfully poignant its sky, how brilliantly etched its edges! A place of transition it had been, its drama and breakthroughs now imbedded in his stride, Ezparya's being forever staining his...

He walked toward an arched doorway behind which he knew Xandur would be waiting, as he had in past years. He'd walked these steps before, but they had not felt like this — the man he'd been before he'd left Amula now seemed quite insubstantial, little more than a phantom of mind, a mere fleshing out of personified inclination. He had changed, right to his core, or, more precisely, he was in a truer alignment with his core of being than ever before. The palm fronds and frangipani blossoms were his witnesses.

He whispered his name, and it seemed to hang in the air, subtly altering the mood of the courtyard...

28

Beloved Stranger

"Come in." With mellifluous, resonant ease, the voice floated toward him, full of gentle yet immensely powerful presence.

He entered, and stood in front of Xandur. The room was arranged just as it had been since he'd first seen it — a red vase of white, violet-lipped orchids on the windowsill, a few large, multicoloured cushions, a circular silk carpet of blue and white flames, a candelabrum in one corner. Xandur sat upon the center of the carpet, looking as if he'd been there forever. Glam said nothing, waiting for the Sirdhanan to speak, feeling the ancient eyes probing his entire body with unhurried thoroughness.

Finally, Xandur said, "Your journey is not over, as you know."

"Yes," whispered Glam, feeling a sudden urge to fall into the old man's lap and cry. His time away from Amula welled up in him, demanding to be told — how good it felt to be in the presence of someone who could truly hear! At the same time, he felt soothed and cradled by an unbound stillness, his surge of emotion no longer so headlong, or needing such immediate verbalization. The stillness streamed from Xandur, just as naturally as the elegantly curvaceous, lemony-sweet scent emanating from the frangipani blossoms outside. The Sirdhanan's peace clearly was not at the expense of his passion, but rather *included* it, without any fuss or complication...

Glam had missed Xandur, yet he had needed to be without him — to have constantly been under Xandur's wing would have definitely provided sanctuary for deep inner work, but it also would have *inevitably* shaded him from certain angles and qualities of light that were necessary for his full flowering. It was not a question of dependence or of independence, but of *awakening*, to the point where dependence and independence were no longer in opposition, nor in parasitic collusion, but rather in heartfelt, full-bodied embrace, unleashing through their interplay a profoundly *felt* appreciation of interdependence. There was no inherent virtue in having left Xandur, nor in remaining apart, nor in returning; the key was not to surrender to Xandur, nor to avoid him, but to make good use of him, to love and honour him, to give himself to Xandur without giving himself away...

"You have gained immense power," continued Xandur. "Not only power over, but power *for*, power *with*, power *to*, power *as*, power that's in the service of the truest journey of all. You have been broken enough to emerge whole, having learned, on many levels, that there is much more to Lantar than you'd assumed. You have *lived* depths you never knew you had, strange realms with black suns and labyrinthine passions, wildernesses of being simultaneously sordid and sublime, luminous pits, fertile hells all abloom, shouting up a glory of unsuspected green...

"You have done far, far more than simply gain experience, however. You have accumulated *and embodied* enough power to love under *all* conditions, even when your love *must* wear the face of anger. Allowing your heart to remain thus open, no matter what, no matter how deep the wound of doing so, is your responsibility and sacred need, Glam, and also the *bridge* to your ultimate freedom."

A sudden understanding jolted Glam. It wasn't just what Xandur had said, but *how* he had articulated it — each word, each phrase, each emphasis, resonating with empathetic wisdom, each gap between words a fathomless mystery, all of it imbued with a significance beyond comprehension. Yet it was not even a matter of how Xandur had voiced it; it was how Glam had *received* it. For a brief but breathtakingly vivid moment, he glimpsed a vista beyond all meaning, an inconceivable possibility of being, existing not to be reached, but to be *directly* and *consciously* lived, forever *now*...

"What you have done," whispered Xandur, very slowly, "has been necessary, and immeasurably valuable."

Tears poured down Glam's face as he stepped forward to take Xandur's hands. How firm and knowing was the Sirdhanan's touch, how very sensitive and delicate! What benediction it was to have Xandur in his life again! How could he not be grateful for the presence of such a one? Especially now, when he was so, so ready to make *truly* good use of such rare company...

"I do look forward to hearing the details of your journey." Xandur smiled broadly, radiating a love that made Glam feel like a very young child being tucked into bed by its parent.

"Esmelana is in the next room. She is waiting for you."

"Thank you," murmured Glam. Bowing and turning, he left, his heart seeming to saturate and spill out of his entire body. He walked into the adjoining room. On the floor sat Esmelana, weeping.

Esmelana...

He dropped down beside her, gathering her up in his arms. Tightly she held him, and he her, their bodies breathing as one, their hands eloquently urgent with welcome and need. Soon they were crying together, letting the waves of their emotions pass through them with unresisted intensity — what pure hunger in their embrace, what joy, what fiercely unrestrained love, what grief and what relief, what a communion of hellos! Torrents of undiluted feeling, achingly alive, again and again swept through them, with a yes of turbulent release, a yes that was but space for love. Several times, he recalled times when he'd remembered her while he was in Anushet — and now here she was!

After they'd stopped crying, he sat her atop his folded knees. She seemed to have aged years. She was much larger, her face was more defined, her hair a touch darker. Her eyes, liquid with hurt and happiness, conveyed a knowingness that surprised him. Clear and spacious was her brow, radiating a force he recognized as highly developed inner seeing; had not one of the children on the beach referred to her as an oracle?

Such ancient eyes in a child's face, such a timeless immensity of vision! Such may be your path, daughter, but I pray it's not too soon; premature psychic ascent would only cripple your balance, as it has done in so many others. However, Xandur himself must be your guide — I trust him to be sensitive to your needs, ordinary as well as extraordinary. And do you now sense these thoughts of mine? It seems you do...

He smiled. "Did you know I was coming back?"

"I knew you would try." Her voice was much richer, though still very young.

"I never forgot you," he softly said. He waited, but she said nothing, her gaze suddenly not so intimate.

"How do I look to you?" he asked.

"Like Glam," she replied shyly. "But bigger inside, much bigger. Darker and lighter at the same time, and older. Something inside the bigness is very, very tired."

"Yes," he sighed, "very tired. Even dying. So something else can form." He wished their conversation was less formal-feeling, less adult, but it didn't feel appropriate to play now, to assume an everyday intimacy. Was it not enough that she was here with him now?

"There are ways of meeting each other that'll take some time," he said. "You are beloved to me, and yet a stranger in some ways."

She smiled. "Same for me."

"Well, what can we do about it?" he asked teasingly.

"I don't know."

"Either do I! But just look at us, look very closely! Are we not an unusual pair? You, you're an oracle of sorts, and me, I'm a tired old traveller soaked with adventure. No, not just soaked, but super-soaked, extra super-soaked!" Grunting heavily, he made the gestures of a determined old man wringing out an enormous cloth, which grew larger and larger the harder he squeezed. Esmelana smiled slightly, letting her shoulders drop. Then Glam squinted ferociously, as though within a great canoe, paddling with a ludicrously intense rhythm, grimly panting, urging his boat on and on with a spasmodically exaggerated rolling of hunched shoulders, bringing a flurry of giggles from Esmelana.

Relaxing and dramatically wiping his furrowed brow, he exclaimed, "But let's not get too serious about being grown-up! Let's see who we are, besides an oracle and a tired old adventurer! Do you remember how I used to carry you out into the waves, the really big ones?"

She nodded. "Well," he continued, feeling a little awkward, "I want to do that kind of thing with you, as well as share what you're learning as an oracle."

"Yes," she declared, her eyes brightening, "but let's not get too serious about doing *that*!"

"You are getting sharp! Pretty easy to trip up old Glam, isn't it?"

She laughed with him for a while, enjoying the unwavering fullness of his gaze, then blurted out, "I missed you terribly! I watched for your canoe *every* day!" Her face quivered, and tears came quickly. "Sometimes I dreamt that horrible things were happening to you, black, bloody things. Sometimes I thought you were dead! I waited and waited and waited for so long..."

He reached out to her, and held her in his lap. How strongly she was shaking, as though she wasn't completely sure he was back! He knew there was nothing he could say to completely reassure her of his presence — she simply needed to feel him more, to be touched by him. As he stroked her, he began to sing a low, melodic chant full of her name. Occasionally, he wove in other words, but only to further enliven her name. The more he sang to her, the more he realized that he was also singing to himself, singing himself home. His sounds evoked the dramatics of parting and reunion, the inevitability of change, the bittersweet blur of the seasons, and, finally, the seasonless Wonder that permeated it all... He watched as she drifted into sleep, her lips parted, her hair away from her face, as if blown wide by a stormy wind. When he at last arose to go, leaving her curled up asleep on a cushion, he noticed Xandur standing in the doorway; he'd no idea of how long the Sirdhanan had been there.

"Your house is ready for you, Glam. As you may have guessed, Esmelana no longer lives there. Tomorrow, around midday, she and I will come to visit you." As Glam left, Xandur added, "May you rest well."

Toward his house he walked, feeling confused. *His* house? And he, homeless he, its sole inhabitant. No one in Esmelana's room... Suddenly, his confusion cleared. He felt angry — how dare Xandur take *his* daughter from him? How dare he? How dare he thrust her into oraclehood, and take her so completely under *his* parental wing? Whose daughter was she, anyway? He paused, halting his barrage of questions. He had been gone a long, long time — was Esmelana supposed to merely wait for his return, burdened by a hope-fueled loyalty? He ought to be grateful to Xandur! He was, he was...

So they were both coming to visit him tomorrow. To *visit*. How very lovely — again, he burned with resentment. At the same time, he was shocked at how easily he was upset. Was not Esmelana alive and well? Had he not felt her love for him? Must he make his jealousy more important than his love? Jealousy was just a righteous collapse of heart, an intensely knotted, violent reactivity generated by melodramatic assumptions of rejection — but *who* was rejecting him? No one! It was only his clinging to a particular *form* of relationship that was triggering his contractedness. His and Esmelana's relationship had changed — why should it necessarily be bound to its old structure? Was it written in stone that parent and child *must* live together, or that if they lived apart, it must be because they were incompatible? How very easily a bond, if not permitted room to change form, could become bondage!

He laughed, shaking his head in mock concern for himself, feeling his jealousy dissolving. There was no decision he needed to make; what he needed now was some rest, and some time alone. What a joke! After all his solitude of the past months! Nevertheless, he did need to be alone. Xandur already knew this.

How dare he treat him like a child! How dare — forcefully, Glam uprooted his sequence of thought, knowing that he was in no condition to explore his state of mind. Rest he must...

His house was not far. See it white and blue, perched halfway up a small, pinethick hill, facing the ocean. It was here he had lived with Oma and Esmelana. It was here he had decided to leave Amula. It was here he had left to be with Ezparya. It was here, inescapably here...

The door was slightly ajar. Opening it slowly, he stepped inside. The crusty aroma of freshly baked bread drifted out from the kitchen. He wept, feeling Ezparya momentarily beside him, her eyes delightedly absorbing the rough cosiness of the little house. Everything looked clean and fresh, as though it had just been scrubbed and set straight. Clean clothes were laid out on his bed. Again and again, he walked through the rooms, slowly and dreamily.

It seemed he'd never really left.

Nowhere was there any acknowledgment of his journey. Beside him now was not the feeling of Ezparya, but the ghost of who he had been, growing more and more substantial as he wandered through the house, until it was *he* who felt like a ghost. He squirmed in the grasp of his own nostalgia, unsuccessfully trying to extricate himself, feeling intoxicated by suffocatingly poignant, yet maddeningly hazy recollection, sinking ever further into a tidily positioned sleepfulness. Yet was he not still walking about, eyes open, ears open? Yes, but did not a dreamer also do the very same thing, *automatically presuming wakefulness*, regardless of how bizarre or how nonsensical their particular dream-scenery might be?

He saw and heard only the pageantry of his Amulan past. Was not Oma in the kitchen, and Esmelana on a chair beside her? And he? Was he not gazing out the window at the glittering sea, envisioning a great canoe? Was he not dreaming of distant adventure, vague and darkly attractive, somewhere across the ocean?

He blinked forcefully, noticing that he was sitting on the edge of his bed. His breathing was irregular and shallow, his forehead tense, his hands in half-fists. Shaking his head, he stood and went out onto the porch. Beautiful was the sun and sea and green-sparkle, but still his dreaminess persisted, tinged with narcotic promise. Had he *really* ever left? With considerable effort, he remembered Ezparya, drawing her to him, fleshing out in his mind their mutual passion and love. Suddenly, the impact of his journey broke through his stupor, like a legion of lightning bolts ripping through a dense cloudcover.

A fierce smile lit his face. Everything slipped into place — he was not of Amula, nor was he of Anushet. In no location could he ever *finally* settle; his real roots were *not* in dwelling-places, inner or outer, nor could they ever be! Amula could not claim him, nor could Anushet. His true home was nowhere in particular, just as his true self was fundamentally no one in particular, *except* somewhere in time...

Now the house was but a house, and a fine one, a perfectly good shelter. He felt grateful for its warmth, its lack of pretension, its well-crafted ordinariness. He'd not had the luxury of a room since Anushet. Back into the house he sprang, singing and whooping, sweeping the clothes off the bed, taking enormous bites out of the bread, opening all the windows as wide as possible, touching all the walls with as much of his body as he could, spinning and dancing through every room, until he was happily exhausted. His memories were but memories now, inconsequential wisps unable to capture any of his attention. Sea-air filled the house, mixing deliciously with the bread-smells. At last, he lay upon his bed, gazing at the ceiling, content to simply feel himself lying there, letting sleep come...

He awoke to dawn's light. Upon the horizon squatted the sun, plump and fiery. What a long, satisfying sleep he'd had! Bread and milk and fresh fruit made a very pleasing breakfast. While he ate, he looked through the kitchen window at the sea. Once he'd felt a great longing to cross it; now he didn't, not at all! He didn't know what was next for him, but he knew what *wasn't* next — no ocean journey, none! Just swimming and playing in the waves, as well as the occasional excursion from shore, uncluttered by any notion of grand purpose...

However, the longing itself wasn't gone. It was obviously much more than desire; it was a deep imperative of being, similar to that which compelled a seed to outgrow itself. And the seed had broken its shell! Once it had stirred so busily within its spherical night, compulsively distracting itself from its entrapment, repetitiously dreaming dreams of liberating light, and *now* it was out, clearly out! He paused — was he now simply inhabiting a different shell, a more expansive, subtler seedcasing? Perhaps. Nonetheless, much more had happened to him than just a mere wardrobe change or house-reconstruction! His doubts could not so easily capture him; in fact, they vanished as soon as he doubted *them*!

If the seed didn't possess unfailing faith in what guided it into self-transcendence, into the uncoiling of pure green, then how could it possibly grow?

Such faith was not a matter of naive submission, but rather of *open-eyed* trust, of profoundly committed alignment and communion with what was most essential. As well, it also involved sacrifice, the sacrifice of seed-ness, of position, of whatever identity was currently being assumed. How readily he had, in the name of so-called intelligence and individuality, battled and rationalized away and learnedly postponed such sacrifice, fearing loss of face and place! How easy it was to defend against what *appeared* to be the end! And wasn't the crux of spirit-awakening all about losing face, level upon level? Such an art it was, such an exquisitely vulnerable yet potent art, losing face without losing touch...

The seed had cracked its shell, cracked it beyond repair. He smiled, his eyes resting on the sea, his heart elsewhere...

29

Its Virgin Air
Awaiting His Inhale

At noon, Xandur and Esmelana arrived. Glam welcomed them into the house, acutely aware of it being *his* house — how odd the whole notion of ownership was, how suppressive its moralistic assumptions of possession, how painfully common its obsessive emphasis on *having*, rather than on *being*! Yet ownership itself was not inherently wrong nor even problematic, nor was it, as more than a few spiritual aspirants dogmatically stated, *necessarily* a cause of suffering — what really mattered was what one *did* with ownership or possessiveness! One could take it so seriously that one got lost, perhaps even imbedded, in its dramatics, or one could render it transparent to what was senior to it, thereby simultaneously enjoying and illuminating it, without robbing it of any of its functional qualities...

It was, he thought, all too easy to *blame* possessiveness, anger, lust, jealousy, and other related activities for human ills, as though *they* actually generated suffering, when, in fact, it was *what was done* with them that either brought about or didn't bring about suffering!

Was not the responsible use of anger, not sublimated, repressed, revengeful, or righteous anger, but rather raw, free-flowing, *mind-free* anger, an act of barrier-breaking vulnerability, the very *force* of which could, with potent sensitivity, impassion and enhance intimacy? And was not the same true of possessiveness, lust, and jealousy? Were they not but raw material, however strangely knotted or misshapen, just *awaiting* conscious, empathetic contact? Were they not simply to be entered into and passed through, until their energies were *fully* and luminously integrated with the rest of one's being? There was no point in assigning blame — was not blame just the indignant, compensatory bleating of those who refused to take responsibility for their actions? And did not blame militate against the cultivation of intimacy? Blame was a collapse of being, whereas true responsibility was *commitment* to being...

What was necessary, sooner or later, was to do one's best to stay aligned with one's core of being in the midst of *whatever* one was doing, inwardly or outwardly. Such an intention of remembrance, of wakefulness, did not, however, justify or legitimize all activity; rather, it catalyzed a *natural* discriminatory ability. The very alignment with Lantar created its own morality, thereby making the doing of certain activities utterly unattractive and inappropriate.

Thus, mused Glam, thoroughly enjoying his logic of insight, ownership could, when lived in this light, *only* be benign and life-giving in its effect — it could not help but be consistently sensitive to its environment. There existed an *innate* generosity in such possession, an unforced emanation of goodwill, a deep-rooted humour and trust, a solidity of foundation harmoniously and juicily coupled with an ongoing sharing of what rose from that foundation. Put another way, it permitted a quality of ground, or groundedness, that created sky...

"A fine dwelling this is," said Xandur, after a long, comfortable silence. "It's sturdy and well-built, spaciously friendly, but quite sad as well, knowing that what it loves is but a guest."

"I also grieve," said Glam, "though I don't know if I'd even label it grief. There are tears and heart-hurt, but no regret, no shrinking of self, no blame, just an expansive, wonderfully sad joy."

"Such grief is but acknowledgment, perhaps even celebration, of the necessary passing of all that exists," smiled Xandur. "It is also a deep letting-go of what was, a purification of one's attachment to what once was. Much has happened to you since you left Amula — will you now tell us of your journey?"

Glam looked at Esmelana, both gladdened and saddened by her gaze, then began describing his adventures enroute to Anushet. When he'd finished telling them about Merot's murder, he hesitated, feeling uncomfortable.

"What did you leave out?" asked Xandur.

Glam blushed — he must tell it *all*, and tell it without trying to cast himself in a flattering light! This was not about him looking good, nor was it about him looking bad. "I knew we were in Anushet, but I kept this from Merot, even though I'd already recounted for him the time the oracles called out the name of Anushet. I had a clear foreboding about him going into the forest, yet I said nothing to him, nothing at all!"

"What difference would that have made?"

"He might have lived."

"So you feel as though you betrayed him."

"Sometimes..."

Xandur paused, then softly said, "You need not torture yourself. Your guilt is of no value to Merot, nor to anyone else. Besides, you know it wasn't true for you to speak your foreboding at that time. What you did was not wrong; in fact, it both signalled and catalyzed a deep shift within you. Merot was already committed to a direction dictated by his fear — he was no victim, but a participant, however unwilling, in his own demise. If he had chosen otherwise, he may still have been murdered, but his death would have been utterly different."

Glam resumed his tale, then again hesitated, as he described his inner ordeal in the cave high up in the mountains of Anushet. He expected Xandur to say something, but the Sirdhanan simply smiled at him, offering neither praise nor condemnation. "Something changed in me then," murmured Glam. "A darkness seemed to enter me, a sinister, perversely compelling, and, I must admit, extremely fascinating force — it was very difficult for me to *see* that I not only fought it, but also actually permitted it access to me! I, noble, cleancut I, was welcoming darkness, not to transform it, but to *be* it, to *embody* it!"

His voice widened, gathering power. "I am not apart from that darkness, nor would I now even call it darkness! A great power, *seemingly* malevolent, permeated me then, though it took some time to make itself obvious. At first, I felt possessed, as if by some *outside* force or will, but eventually I recognized that what had apparently entered me was actually *inherent* to myself, appearing alien to me only because of my long-time suppression of it. Gradually, I lost interest in my habit of assuming I had a distinct *inside*, an actual interiority wherein the true Glam supposedly dwelt! The division between inside and outside showed itself to be mere mind-play, as did all my moralistic divisions...

"At the same time, a deeper morality, one prior to all my concepts, slowly arose in me. *Very* slowly, for I was fascinated for a long time by what my embodiment of this so-called darkness was bringing to me — many unsuspected doors opened for me, presenting strangely attractive opportunities. Many, many times, I lost my balance, but out of that learned to settle into a deeper balance, one wherein my actions required *no* overseeing ethic, for they, more and more of the time, carried within their very momentum a profoundly intuitive resonance with Lantar, a keen and lucid appreciation of what was *essential* to each situation!

"I gradually and motivelessly shed my need to consult anyone or anything regarding my doings; this did not, however, make me impermeable to incoming messages and signs, but rather instead *magnified* my sensitivity to such influences, so that my doings were informed from many sources, but controlled by none. How arrogantly independent I may be making myself sound! I hope not...

"Put another way, I was in charge not of what came to me, but of what I *did* with it. The more I stood alone, the more open I became to seemingly alien influences, simply because I was less and less exploitable by them! In my very aloneness, I knew a deepening intimacy with the primal pattern of things. In my aloneness, in that powerful thrusting and anchoring of individuality, that very *crystallization* of selfhood, my heart expanded to include more and more, so that though I *appeared* alone, I was not at all!

"I know now that I could not have thus expanded without the grounding, the well-rooted centeredness, brought about by my unambiguous embracing of my aloneness. Forgive my meandering of phrase, but I want to say all this as clearly as possible, and to do so I must weave together many strands, all the while knowing that the tapestry they form is dense with Paradox! Everything keeps getting simpler, even as it grows more subtle; nothing could be simpler than complexity! Yet Paradox itself has all but ceased to be problematic for me — did you not, Xandur, once say that what appears as Paradox to the mind appears as living Truth to the awakened heart?''

Xandur's eyes were enormous and luminous now, ringed with an exceedingly diaphanous violet aura. His features would not hold still for Glam. Even so, Glam knew that Xandur had followed his every word and phrase, however circuitous. The Sirdhanan was listening with his whole being, without strain.

Glam stopped briefly, then declared, "Though he may superficially resemble the man who left Amula, this is *not* Glam who now sits and talks with you!''

"For me," said Xandur in a quiet but very penetrating voice, "you are *now* Glam. That cave was simply the place of your birth-pangs. What succumbed and metamorphosed in you then need not be viewed as an entity unto itself, a discrete *somebody* who let darkness in — it was none other than a *doing*, a self-protective habit, that insisted on referring to itself as *you*, a personified doing that resisted alteration. Your so-called darkness was but a broadening and brightening of that doing, a shattering of its grip, and, more importantly, it was an intensification and partial awakening of being. And is!''

"It is a fullness.''

"Yes! It is the fullness of love that denies no shadow, the fullness of passion that embraces *every* feeling, the fullness of *you*, initially appearing in its *dark* disguise, inviting you into self-transcendence. Doing so, however, is not a matter of spiritual escape or ascent, nor of disembodiment — to transcend yourself, you must *be* yourself, *fully!*''

Glam nodded, and Xandur tilted his head playfully, quickly adding, "But I am jumping ahead — go on with your story.''

Glam proceeded, speaking more and more easily, playing up the drama, letting insight and overview spontaneously arise from his narrative flow. Only once did Xandur interrupt, just before Glam described his arousal at the hands of Ezparya. "Do not," said the Sirdhanan, "leave anything out on Esmelana's account.''

Esmelana sat still, her hands in her lap, her face slightly upturned, her eyes wide and occasionally full of tears, her attention bathing Glam, again and again drawing him into unexpected detail. Though the content of what he was saying was more directed at Xandur, the feeling of it was given just as much in response to her as to the Sirdhanan. It didn't really matter that she couldn't follow his every phrasing; she was undeniably *with* him, both in his passionately vivid recounting, and in the *feeling* of his periodic conceptual flights. Sometimes he wept as he spoke, sometimes he laughed, sometimes he leapt up with fiery abandon, almost always infusing every unfolding scene with poetic accuracy, letting his entire body tell each story. As he revealed the intimacy he'd shared with Ezparya, he felt excruciatingly vulnerable, almost unbearably naked, crying so hard at times that he couldn't speak — how good it felt to tell them about her, to tell them all, even that he still sometimes missed her, missed her terribly...

Esmelana gasped when he described Tornellas's death, and cried when he told of his departure. As she listened, she remembered many of the dreams she'd had during Glam's absence, especially those in which she'd seen him in peril. The sound of his voice touched her deeply — it was so rich and alive, so shapely with emotion, so thrillingly stormy, so vibrantly calm! His gestures only added to his voice — it was as if all of him were speaking, no, not speaking, but *singing*, sending note after shining note into her core of being. What an amazing adventure he'd been on! But there was more — she couldn't help noticing a faint sadness all around him, a sadness that seemed to have nothing to do with his experiences. She had seen this sadness around everyone, even Xandur. Xandur had told her that it was simply an acknowledgment or sign, almost always unconsciously generated, that one *could* be feeling much better, even in the midst of the most captivating or ecstatic experiences. It was, he'd said, the grief of separation from Lantar, the grief of self-imposed bondage, however subtle, refined, or luminous, however rich with spirit-communion...

Nevertheless, Glam's sadness didn't seem to enclose or enwreathe him, nor to necessarily isolate him; rather, it appeared to her oracular sight to actually *be* him! It was a blend of many colours, woven from his reaching, his hunger, his restlessness, his unrelenting commitment to...

Suddenly, she knew, wishing she didn't. How obvious it was! Like everything else, her father would *use* this sadness, this ever subtler sense of separation from the Source, to catalyze his awakening, even if it meant... leaving her *again*! She unsuccessfully tried to hold back her tears, struggling to not yield to her anticipation's heartbreaking picture. If only. If only...

If only! The insight, though, was definitely there, wedging its way into her heart, sending an echo through her — he might have to leave *again*! Then she felt Xandur's hand take hers. She knew he knew. Solid and tender was his touch, steadying her without protecting her from her hurt.

Glam didn't finish until late in the evening. After a long, easy silence, Xandur went to Glam, and hugged him. Glam was surprised, for Xandur had never before touched him so; then he noticed a faint trembling rippling through the old man, and realized that the Sirdhanan was actually weeping. Xandur may have transcended the usual man, thought Glam, but he had not done so by distancing himself from his feelings — in fact, he'd immeasurably deepened his capacity to feel, without, however, losing himself in his emotion. How could one, as some had claimed to have done, truly reach or know Lantar without being profoundly *intimate* with one's emotions? Was not spirit-awakening a passage *through* feeling, rather than above, or over against it? In truth, there was *no* feeling that was in itself a hindrance to realizing Lantar, none! True feelings, not those generated by mind, nor those warped by notions from one's past, but spontaneous, non-reactive, organismic responses to what was currently happening, were neither positive nor negative, but only Lantar incarnate...

When Glam and Xandur separated, standing at arm's length from each other, they exchanged a long, open look. Xandur's eyes were achingly soft, yet also fiery, suffused with both peace and passion; Glam felt soothed and deeply supported by the Sirdhanan's liquid gaze, and, more importantly, *recognized*. A lone thought came: Xandur hovers at the very edge of Eternity, held back by...

"Goodnight, Glam," said Xandur, and left. Glam picked up Esmelana and stood gently swaying, holding her as close to him as he could, letting his head fall beside hers. Before she left, they agreed to spend the next day together at her favourite beach. He watched her run out of the house to join Xandur, her sprint so loose and free, as natural as the turbulent dance of the sea...

That night, he repeatedly dreamt that he and Esmelana were swimming at a beach that was neither of Amula nor of Anushet. It resembled the inlet where his canoe had been destroyed, except that it was much wider. Though they played happily, he felt a slight sense of foreboding, which he dismissed as self-doubt. Was not the sun bright, and the sky perfectly blue? Was not Esmelana a grace and a joy? Then, with abrupt force, gigantic stormclouds, bulgingly black, crowded the sky, whipping the waves into a rapidly rising fury. He knew exactly what was coming, but couldn't prevent it.

He and Esmelana were separated.

Desperately, he searched for her in the madly heaving waters, but in vain. The waves towered far above him, darkly hissing, their undercurrents gripping his legs. At long last, almost battered into unconsciousness, he was hurled onto shore, where he lay gasping and frantically blinking, looking for Esmelana...

Each time he awoke from the dream, he found himself calling out her name, his voice ringing through the blackness of his bedroom. During the final repetition of the dream, he once again lay wave-cast upon the shore, looking for Esmelana. Then, remembering that he'd already *dreamt* this, he pulled himself from the dream. The night was dense and tight. He ran his hands all over his face. His heart was pounding wildly.

What was that?

His bedroom door was creaking open! Someone had come into the room! Trembling, he sat up, lighting a candle. The room seemed distorted, its walls almost shuddering, as though in a dream. Perhaps it was just the candlelight. Again, he touched his face, finding only minimal reassurance in the familiarity of its features. Around and around the room crept the candlelight, at last settling on his guest...

In his doorway, his crazily wavering doorway, stood Esmelana, her face veiled by shadows. She was sobbing. But look, just look at how tall she was! And what was she doing holding a sword? And her hair, so, so white? And the tiny red feathers in place of her eyebrows, and the blood dripping from her sword...

He was, he realized with a shock, *still* dreaming!

Bursting into wakefulness, he lit a bedside candle. His bedroom door *was* open. He sensed that there was someone in his house, possibly in the kitchen. Taking the candle, he slowly walked through the house. He saw no one, but felt a strong presence — someone *was* there, in subtle form. Perhaps Esmelana was at this very moment dreaming of him...

Sitting on the edge of his bed, he closed his eyes and, after stilling himself inwardly, did something he'd done many times before — it was an inversion of ordinary sight, a willful entry into that inner locus where he *actually* experienced vision. When he finally felt his attention firmly established there, somewhere deep inside his skull, he focussed in on Esmelana. Almost right away, he saw her asleep, curled up on one side.

Looking more closely, he saw that she was dreaming. Her dream shimmered and shook within the field of his vision, opaque and amorphous at first, then gradually clearing to reveal her standing on a twilit beach, leaning into a fierce wind, reaching, reaching out for... him! He felt her struggle, her wrenching heartpain, knowing that she sensed herself to be reaching through an ever-shifting barrier, a densely billowing cloudiness. Suddenly, she stopped and turned around, her face brightening. She felt him looking at her! She *knew*!

He lost all spatial sense; no longer could he maintain his psychic positioning. Letting go of it, he fell back on his bed, overcome with ecstasy, feeling unqualifiedly united with Esmelana — now he need perform no trick or manipulation of attention in order to be with her, for she was *with* him, not just in some rarefied subtle realm, but substantially, essentially, fully! Even Death would not terminate their bond, but only alter its form. He and she were but tributaries of the same river, ocean-bound...

He arose, and walked down to the shore. The waves were barely visible. In a short while, the sun would rise. He sat on the sand, knees up, letting his thoughts drift about him. How bright were the stars, how eloquent their message! Venus blazed like a tiny sun just above the horizon. He was ready now, knowing to what he was drawn...

Did he not feel it in the upper center of his back, pressing into the rear of his heart? Did he not feel its virgin air awaiting his inhale? And its pristine slopes his feet? And its incandescent triangle hovering behind his eyes, radiating through his flesh, filling out his spirit — Aratisha!

He felt both exhausted and energized. His sense of time was hopelessly disrupted; events were succeeding and overlapping one another with stunning rapidity, far too fast for his mind to assimilate. However, he didn't feel at all hurried, or pressured — he was prepared for what was happening, even welcoming. He was ready! What foolishness it would be to resist this shaping and reshaping of his perspective! Was it not true that he could only have his heart's desire when he stopped fighting the preparatory fire?

He sat motionless, his eyes half-shut, his body given over to the touch of the dawning day. It was all very simple. There were no decisions to agonize over, no matters to carefully weigh. He knew what he had to do. The breeze was cool and moist, the sky a softly brightening dome. As surely as the sun must rise, he must attempt Mount Aratisha...

30

Xandur's Story

Glam waited in his house; any moment now, Xandur would arrive. All morning, Glam had been with Esemelana, playing in the waves with her. She was an excellent swimmer, courageous without being foolhardy. The one time he saw her misjudge a wave, she took its downforce head-on, then emerged unscathed and laughing from the topsy-turvy tumbling it had given her. He loved seeing her slim body and jubilant face leading the gleaming curve and downspill of a great wave, her movements as fluid as the ocean's...

He hadn't told her yet that he was going to Mount Aratisha. If she intuited it, she gave no sign. After his visit with Xandur, he would tell her. The door swung open, and Xandur entered, looking tired. With a solemn air, he declared, "I cannot stop you, and even if I could, I wouldn't."

Smiling, he sat. "Long before you returned to Amula, I knew you would attempt Aratisha, that you would have no other course. Always, Glam, always, you have been on the verge of leaving. Not escaping, not avoiding, but simply *leaving*, like an arrow, always on the verge of saying goodbye, even to what you love dearly. That is your pain, your grief, your perennial wound, the great price of your undertaking.

"Fortunately, you haven't distanced yourself from what you must leave, so as to minimize your hurt upon parting — you have, to a significant degree, made room for attachment and for deep human bonding, as well as for the *necessity* of letting it all go. Thus has your heart been stretched, tested, and ripened — you know that *everything* must be left, and yet your leavetakings, all of them, have been but a series of *returns*, all at essence just preparation for, and reflections of, the Great Return Whose Call now so clearly reverberates through all your doings.''

Glam felt deeply moved by Xandur's words. Leaving to return... Each return, part of an ascending spiral, an ever-brighter herald of a fundamental return, or just mere repetition, prolonged and glamourized by seemingly special experiences?

Both. And something more...

''Your accumulated doings, your wealth of experience, your entire adventure, *suggests* movement, evolution, a *progression* of sorts. But that is only from *your* point of view, however lucid it might be. From the Viewpoint of Lantar, none of this is *truly* necessary. None of it! From that matchless Standpoint, there is no need whatsoever to alter *anything*, though of course there is a need to awaken to the point where one's doings arise from one's core of being, in which case alteration or change occur spontaneously and *naturally,* without any ego-centered interference or ambition. Don't you see that *all* circumstances, all conditions, all doings, all appearances, are but expressions of Lantar, utterly meaningless, subject only to the laws governing the mechanics of manifestation? The Source and Substance of All is no more affected by what arises in and *as* It, than is the sky by its clouds.''

Glam felt irritated — why was the old man lecturing him so? Of what use to him was such parroting of spiritual doctrine? To realize Lantar, to actually *embody* that inconceivable Viewpoint, he must *be Glam*! He must live his Glam-ness fully, with nothing held in reserve, nothing! Only in that pure totality of passion could authentic self-transcendence occur; otherwise, spirit-awakening would be reduced to just one more strategy for rising above suffering, just one more attempt to exist in a state of unthreatened immunity, just an ever-more sophisticated *escape* from feeling!

His irritation vanished. What Xandur had said did not in any way actually deny him his Glam-ness, but only opened out its sky, inviting from him not annihilation of self, but rather the *complete* flowering of self...

"I cannot argue with what you have said," declared Glam, "yet I would not want to take it so literally that I made a virtue out of doing nothing, or simply abandoned my efforts. I would not only stand still and contemplate the Source! I am but a sapling; I must move as I meditate, and meditate as I move, as I fill myself out. As of late, my doings seem to be helping deepen my recognition of Lantar. My seeming *progression*, as you put it earlier, is *not* a strategy, but rather a *natural* byproduct of my deepening alignment with Lantar. My activities, inner and outer, do not so much absorb my attention, as *loosen* it up, so that it is more available to its source."

"My saying that all of this is fundamentally unnecessary does *not* mean that it is not worth doing," said Xandur, smiling slightly. "Nor does it mean that your activities have been fruitless. My point is this: let the Viewpoint of Lantar soak into your doings. Remember It in the midst of your whatever. Let It lighten your way, let It permeate and place in perspective your journey, let It teach you the wisdom of letting go, let *It* generate your intentions, until the artificiality of the gap between It and you is obvious to you! And why do I say all this to you? Why do I lecture you so?

"Because I *know* where you are going, because I love you, because I know your journey to Aratisha will test you severely, because I *ache* for you to go all the way! You must do everything you can to *feel* Lantar as fully as possible, especially when you are darkened by doubt or fear.

"Remember the One Who is beating your heart, the One Who is behind the scenes, the One Who is appearing *as* the scenes! Let that remembrance possess you, let its currents disrupt your assumptions about yourself, let it upend and bend you, let its fire consume you! Permit it to do its awakening work, and see what Wonder arises from the ashes of what you *took* to be yourself! That Wonder, that Joy, that Boundlessness of Being signals not the *end* of you, but the undying Truth of you, simultaneously individuated and seamlessly eternal..."

After a long silence, Glam gently said, "Xandur, why is it that you have not gone to Aratisha? Has it not been necessary for you?"

A grief-tinged, mistily glowing look drifted across the Sirdhanan's face, a look unmistakably conveying the spin of the seasons, the rhythms of birthing and dying, the bittersweet brevity of all that arose. At the same time, however, it was also a look of panoramic compassion, completely free of regret. It seemed to Glam that Xandur saw and felt the full range and depth of suffering, without protecting his heart from any of it, all the while rising from it like a great tree, aware of and caring for not only all its roots, but also its skyward intention, its green reaching...

Xandur, so, so luminously intimate with the aborted longing that underlay all the deluding and distracting activities of humans! Xandur, his wounded heart blessing all, ever clarifying the sacred doors! Xandur, his eyes simultaneously sad and detached, bright with awakened love... Glam felt Xandur as a father, yet he also now felt fatherly toward Xandur. The Sirdhanan was not quite fully at one with Lantar, although the Amulan populace liked to believe so. Glam knew Xandur now felt seen by him — there was a soft, almost teasing joy in the old man's sadness. Lost in neither his joy nor in his grief was Xandur; he was simply allowing them to occur, to take their natural course.

Finally, Xandur said, "It hasn't been necessary for me to go to Aratisha. My pathway is to serve the awakening of others, to be consistently available to them, day after day. Doing so is sometimes difficult, sometimes very painful, but never burdensome, for it is *innate* to me. But my way is nothing special — it isn't some sublime pinnacle of service or humanitarianism, nor some kind of exalted achievement. It is simply the way that best suits *me*.

"You, Glam, are a true wanderer. Existence is your territory. At times, your way overlaps mine, but it is quite different, at least for now. For you to live otherwise would only hobble your spirit. You are a wanderer, Glam, an explorer of the Great Wilderness from which humans seek to distract themselves. You are a flaming arrow of holy yearning, shot through experience itself, your flight spontaneously kindling others into knowingness, your journey a muscular yet fluid leap into welcoming light, your path a celebration of both day and night...

"Your way is no more selfish than mine — we are both using our circumstances to fuel our awakening. Our real gift to others is our commitment to being *fully* ourselves — what more can we give? That very commitment, when it no longer wavers according to our moods, *naturally* catalyzes actions and speech in us that *truly* serves others. Such is the essence of *real* help, however unhelpful or disruptive it might seem!"

He laughed boyishly, and, in a lighter voice, continued. "At one time, you probably thought I was in a condition of complete, unconditional awakening, unquestionably *enlightened*, permanently at one with Lantar! But none of the Sirdhanans are, and none, to my knowledge, ever truly have been, with the exception of Radenin, who was my grandfather, and he died but a week after his enlightenment. He was very ill for the last ten years of his life, often in agonizing pain. A man of exceptional courage he was, a true warrior, using the very intensity of his illness to spark and anchor his Great Realization of Lantar. His death was the greatest magnificence I have ever witnessed...

"But back to Aratisha: I *have* been there, but only to the lowest slopes. I was not much older than you when I went; I'd been a Sirdhanan for less than a year. As soon as I entered the forest that encircles the base of Aratisha, my plans went awry. It was much darker and thicker than I'd imagined; the vegetation was tangled and soggy, the footing very muddy. Often, the ground gave way, and I'd find myself up to my hips in mud, slimy, treacherous stuff with incredible suction. I was lucky not to have died in one of those holes. But the condition of the ground was only minimally problematic compared to the animals I encountered. There are animals in the Great Forest that do not exist elsewhere on Amula. Of course, you've heard the legends about them; so had I. But I'd met no one who had actually penetrated the Great Forest.

"I'd been in the forest for several days when I met a large black leopard. Already, I'd seen some bears and smaller creatures, but they had all avoided me. The leopard actually approached me, its fangs bared, its muscles rippling almost hypnotically under its shimmering velvet skin. How elegantly it moved! I immediately calmed myself and stood steady, spear in hand. I met its stare, driving my own gaze into the verdant liquid of its eyes. Such rare beauty there was in our meeting! A mesmerizing, strangely moving communion it was — but if I had not had the alertness of my Sirdhanan training, I wouldn't have felt the twin presences behind me! Without looking, I knew that two other leopards were poised behind and above me. The forest quiet trembled with barely contained power. I could feel the intense coiling of their coming spring; several more heartbeats, and they'd be upon me...

With all my force, I spun in a circle, my spearhead whistling out the circumference. At the same time, I released a tremendous shout. The cats hesitated, and I leapt to one side, showing my teeth; I hadn't killed an animal for many years, but I was prepared to do so now. For a long time, all three leopards just looked at me, with disarming ease. At last, they smoothly walked away, not looking back. I was, as you can imagine, very relieved, but not for long — I soon became aware that they were following me. This went on for days. More and more, I felt drained by my near-constant maintenance of heightened alertness.

"Also, as I penetrated more deeply into the forest, snakes began appearing, many of them twice the length of the pythons of coastal Amula. The snakes' colouring, combined with the dimness of the forest, made them difficult to spot. Several times, I brushed against some, mistaking them for swaying branches — how very fortunate I was to not have been stricken or grabbed by one of them! The insects were more of an irritation than a danger — centipedes as long as your forearm, and fat, bluish flies with a seemingly insatiable appetite for my face. I hardly slept. I knew I had at least three more days to go before I'd be out of the forest.

"And, true to Amulan legend, the air was crawling with the mouthless utterings of the disincarnate. These were entities of a particularly gross nature, drifting miasmically just above the forest floor, dank and turgid, completely lost in the illusory reenactment of their depraved rituals. They didn't really bother me, though they would surely madden any traveller who did not possess some mastery of the subtle realms — for such travellers, their fears and doubts would be rapidly magnified far beyond their capacity to deal sanely with them, to the point of such extreme paranoia and hallucinatory terror that suicide would become intoxicatingly attractive. Hence the taboo against entering the Great Forest. Very, very few are capable of moving through such psychic bombardment! Very rare are those who can deal easily and intelligently with their *own* nightmares, and the atmosphere of the Great Forest is an unbelievable intensification of those qualities epitomizing the very worst of nightmares! Yet even despite my ability to withstand the leechlike onslaught of the disembodied, I almost didn't make it through the forest...

"What probably saved me was that I finally stopped being so concerned about the leopards. I paid more attention to the snakes, and to my footing, and gave myself more time to sleep. One night, I spent a long time constructing a shelter high up in the trees, upon a thick interweaving of branches. Doing so exhausted me, but I slept through the rest of the night and much of the following morning, suffering no more than a handful of mosquito bites. I awoke refreshed. For the remaining three nights, I built shelters far above the forest floor.

"During my final night, I awoke to find a snake wrapping itself around my arm. It was as thick as my neck. Its head was directly above my face, its fangs less than a finger's length from my eyes. Somehow, I kept calm, though my heart seemed about to burst out of my chest. I put all my power into psychically pushing its head away, visualizing a wall of safety between myself and the fangs. Then, slowly at first, exceedingly slowly, and then as quickly as possible, I grabbed its neck, squeezing with all my might. It squirmed, tightening itself around my arm. I still remember its eyes right in front of mine, reflecting bits of moon. Finally, I managed to kill it, clumsily smashing its head against the side of my shelter, again and again. Needless to say, I slept poorly the rest of the night.

"When at last I left the forest, I was feverish. I crossed a small valley, and started up Aratisha, winding my way through dense shrubbery. The sky was clear, the footing excellent, but I only grew weaker and weaker. My fever came in sudden waves; once, I fell down in a full faint, something I had never before done. Just after sunset, I built a shelter beneath a wall of rock. There was a stream nearby, and the air was sweet and fresh. For two days and two nights, I lay there, barely able to move, utterly helpless to ease the fire raging through my body. I kept my attention concentrated in the center of my chest, feeling as though I were clinging to the wreckage of a boat spinning madly in an inferno of an ocean-storm. I knew there was a strong possibility that I might die on that slope...

"When my fever was at its peaks, Lantar was most obvious to me. There was a sublime, multilevelled humming in and around me, a vast humming within which the condition of my body was of no more consequence than the shapes of the bushes near me. Much of the time, there was only a wondrously soft ecstasy, an *effortless* absorption in the great humming, which actually was less sound than it was boundless *feeling*.

"I intuitively realized, and realized with my entire being, that what I sought, grand or small, wide or narrow, was not mine to seek, but mine to *presently* embody, mine to simultaneously be *and* transcend, mine to live, to fully live! I realized that I need not exclude *anything* in order to awaken, including what my seeking was an escape from; at the very moment I knew this, and *all* of me knew it, I felt an overwhelming compassion for others, an empathy far, far deeper than any sentiment or helpful intention, an irresistibly compelling drive to serve the inner life of others, to expose and brighten and ignite the spark of pure being that I could not help glimpsing in their eyes...

"And so I understood that I was to climb no further. I was to return to what I considered to be mundane, conventional, ordinary; that, however, no longer bothered me, for it, even in its most extreme dreariness and dullness, was now stripped of most of the familiarity with which I had invested it. Let me add that the realization I now describe to you occurred in one brilliant moment.

"I stayed on the slope for a week after my fever had passed, doing little more than eating, meditating, and sleeping. I killed a few rabbits, knowing I'd need their meat for my return journey. The thought of again passing through the Great Forest filled me with dread, but my passage back was surprisingly easy, at least compared to my initial trip. Each night, I built a shelter up in the trees, constructed so that snakes could not easily reach me. During the days, I walked quickly. The hanging snakes were not difficult to spot, the disincarnate avoided me, and I saw no leopards.

"Only once did I feel real danger. The ground suddenly sagged, and I was sucked down in mud, all the way to my belly. As I struggled to crawl out, I saw a massive bear approaching me. It stopped right in front of me. Two tiny cubs were trailing it, and a third appeared behind me, emitting sounds that drew forth low, distinctly menacing growls from its mother. I was stuck between them, which obviously displeased the mother; my extreme helplessness didn't seem to make any difference to her. Coming closer, she lifted a paw, presumably to strike me — I had no doubt that she was going to maul me, if not kill me. Then, all of a sudden, I ceased seeing her as a *threat*. I didn't manipulate myself into seeing this; it was in no way an act of mind. It simply happened. An understanding beyond any language passed between us. She withdrew, walking away with all three cubs — I can still see her lumber, her great head, her eyes — and I extricated myself from the mudhole, and continued on my way.

"And so I returned to everyday Amula, but it was no longer the same, for I was no longer the same."

After a lengthy silence, Xandur stood, breathing deeply. "Such was my journey to Aratisha, but where I reached only the very lowest slopes, you may attain the higher slopes. The peak itself is not out of your reach, unless you make it more important than the climb. Soon I will go, and you will not see me before you leave for Aratisha. I pray that you will not be misled by notions of ascent! In essence, ascent and descent are no more than *descriptions* of the movement of attention, just reminders of location. What is *truly* free has nowhere to go, not up nor down, neither in nor out, neither here nor there — you could say it has nowhere to go because it is *already* there in spirit, *already knowingly* established in Lantar, and *as* Lantar.

"The blissful visions and uncommon experiences that come when one has reached the uppermost peaks of attention have nothing whatsoever to do with the realization of Lantar, nothing! They are *not* signs of enlightenment! Like *any* other experience, they are here one moment, and gone the next, even though their particular moment can be, and often is, greatly extended through various manipulations of attention... Let such experiences spontaneously arise, rather than *expecting* your journey to produce them! But I have said enough. Perhaps I only burden you with my advice."

"No!" declared Glam, his eyes moist and radiant. "What you have given me is much, much more than advice! I feel both lightened by what you have said, and wonderfully warned. Many of your words are mine, yet your manner of giving voice to them went far, far beyond mere repetition of what I already know — hearing them thus spoken has strengthened me, and deepened my faith in my journey. I am ready."

Xandur smiled like an ecstatic child, his eyes innocently yet knowingly wide, lit with an intimacy both intensely personal and transcendent. "I will go now, Glam."

"Xandur, I cannot thank you enough for what you're giving Esmelana."

"Yes, you can," murmured the Sirdhanan. "By giving her open access to your heart, wherever you are, whatever your circumstances."

Glam watched the old man walk away, loving his straight back, his looseness of movement, his slight limp, his short white hair, his effortless radiance of being. Xandur had given him what he could, given it with generosity and trust, transmitting it with a love that was not in opposition to anything, a love that could not lie...

And what of Esmelana? Would her support for his going be obstructed by her pain over his departure? He imagined her watching distant sweeps of ocean for his canoe, while wave after wave of inconsolable hurt surged through her — but had she not, without any bitterness, opened to him upon his return, letting her pain and love and naked need spill out, like a sacred offering? Now, he must tell her he was leaving *again*, leaving very soon, and see her exquisitely unguarded face trembling all over, her eyes clouding...

Yet how did he know that her response would be such? All he knew was that he loved her, and that he must go; if he didn't, it would only dull their love, tarnishing it with both suffocating safety and subtle resentment. He was going. So many goings, so many goodbyes, so many deaths, all to be lived passionately, all to be taken to heart, no matter how sharp the wound...

Morever, was not *every* goodbye, however superficial, misguided, or partial, but a play upon, a version of, a rehearsal of sorts, for the *final* goodbye, that supreme letting-go that brought one into Everlasting, unexploitably obvious intimacy and union with Lantar? Every goodbye or letting-go not *fully* participated in, or denied, or resisted, only reinforced the quality of self that could *not* feel Lantar, that miserable little knot of unquestioned assumptions that so mechanically and insistently referred to itself as a *me*. Death upon death, none of it to be resisted, nor to be blindly submitted to! Goodbye upon goodbye, leaves falling without regret in worlds inner and outer, gross and subtle, blossoms bursting wide and lusciously fragrant, throbbingly alive, nectared sweet and jubilantly deep, shouting with a million tongues hello after hello after hello, as petal after petal withers and whispers goodbye, falling and fading, dying into Undying Life, dying into ever-truer recognition of the One Who is it all...

Human hearts would break all along the way.

Love must weep. Not out of sentimentality, nor out of shattered hope, but out of compassion. Otherwise, one would all too easily harden and set, becoming rigidly imbedded in the routines and rituals of a self-centered destiny, worldly or other-worldly. The meditator's escape into pure witnessing or into mystical realms was but a *strategic* shunning and avoidance of the heart-hurt of ordinary experience, fundamentally *no different* in its underlying motivation than that of the usual human's distraction-generating automaticities. In short, the exploitation of one's vital *or* subtle possibilities, however spiritually rationalized, was but a turning away from the demands of *real* love.

Love must also weep. Xandur, you stand stranded at the very edge of Eternity, yet still you choose to love, to uninhibitedly feel, to empathize with your *entire* being — you do not disembody or distract yourself in order to escape suffering. You are uncompromisingly intimate with the roots of suffering, but you do not forsake your happiness! The holy doors beckon you through, yet you keep one foot firmly atop Amulan soil, ever remaining luminously wounded, clearly demonstrating that nothing need be turned away from...

Tomorrow, he would see Esmelana. For now, it was sufficient to savour his time with Xandur.

Letting go was he, letting go without trying to let go...

31

I Will See You Again

Esmelana cried when Glam told her about his approaching departure, but only for a short time, her tears all but unblemished by reactive sorrow. Even in the midst of her strongest sobs, he felt her love for him.

"You already knew, didn't you?" He held her high in his arms, her face little more than a handsbreadth from his. As she nodded, he said, "Do you know why I'm going?"

"Only that you must."

"Yes," he sighed. "I surely must, and, at the very same time, it is my choice. I suspect that I'm not going in order to find something, but to *be* something, something that I already am here, but not fully — how silly my words sound, so stiff and hollow! So brilliantly insufficient, so solid with superficial conviction!"

He laughed, shaking his head, then looked directly at her, caressing her with his tone. "How I'd love to be able to *exactly* explain my going to you, to dress it up with such meaning that there'd be nothing else to say about it! But where I'm going, explanations are mostly time-wasters, indulgences of mind, comforting little reinforcers of everyday familiarity, mere *parodies* of living Truth! Even now, I make a complex blanket out of my words, words spoken more to me than to you, and wrap myself up in it, pretending to be warmed by it!"

He made a gesture of so enwrapping himself, peering around with a smile so false and sleepy that Esmelana started to giggle. "How much better it is," he continued, letting his body relax, "to sing to you of the magic of all this, the wonderfully natural magic, the forever and ever Heart of hearts, where happiness is brighter than *all* meaning! *That* happiness, which is not at all dependent on our moods or circumstances, is the truest and most difficult of all disciplines, is it not? There is no technique that guarantees its appearance, no method, no ritual, no promise, no thing, and no one! It is *not* produced by anything in particular! It is only *here*, always right here, when we stop looking for it elsewhere — real happiness is *not* elsewhere! Is it not crazy to look for it at all, when it is right here, right now?

"This kind of happiness is not a something, is it? It's us, isn't it, Esmelana? It's *us*, the truest us! Sometimes it cries, sometimes it laughs, sometimes it gets angry, but it *doesn't* stop shining, not for anything! It is everywhere — do you not feel it in the breathing of the trees, the white roar of the waves, the sudden turning of someone's head? Does not everything and everyone, even if they don't know it, throb with *its* great heartbeat?

"You are in my arms, and *we* are in the arms of that great happiness! Is this not wonderful? Is it not enough to feel and breathe the ease of it, the vast presence of it, the endless radiance of its boundless Mystery? I see it in your eyes, Esmelana, unclouded; I see it it looking through you at me, reminding me to love, no matter what, to love passionately, ruthlessly, openly and wisely, with nothing held back, *nothing*! And is not love the best magic of all? Real love, open-eyed love, is free of mind, free of ambition, free of needing any sort of permission, free to leave *everything* behind — yet it does not *really* leave, just as I do not truly leave you!

"Just listen to me going on, kissing you with my words! Perhaps I speak so because I know that soon, very soon, I will have no one to talk to!" He knew she was listening more to the sound of his voice than to its contents. And was he not doing the same? Grinning, he put her down, and, without making a sound, lustily threw himself into the role of one who talks excitedly and far too rapidly, exaggerating his movements to the point of contortion. Esmelana laughed delightedly, putting her fingers in her ears, thrusting her face right in front of his. He lectured, pleaded, begged, cajoled, threatened and scolded, all in acrobatic silence. Soon, Esmelana was helpless with laughter, inspiring him to further inventiveness. At last, still persisting in his spasmodic dance of mute oratory, he began to speak, but in gibberish, letting an excruciatingly earnest look overrun his face.

Esmelana could stand no more; she leapt upon him, squealing and shrieking, and over they fell, rolling and wrestling. He protested mightily, emitting jerky bursts of high-pitched nonsense sounds, while she did whatever she could to squelch his frantic phrasing...

Finally, they stopped and lay still, side by side, the only sound that of their breath. For a long time, they remained in silence, unmoving and unthinking, happily absorbed in each other's emanations, feeling as though they shared the same heart. They spent the rest of the day together, singing and playing, saying little. Rather than regretting their upcoming separation, they were grateful for their time together. At sunset, they walked to the temple where she lived. The very air seemed affectionate, the sunlight friendly; everything around them seemed to be offering its blessings. When they reached the temple gates, he dropped to his knees and faced her.

"Tomorrow," he said, "I'll prepare for my journey, and the day after that, I will leave."

"I will see you again," she whispered. "I know I will."

"Goodbye," he said. Other words came to him, but only evaporated before her beauty. No verbalizing of his love and appreciation for her was needed now. Even his goodbye seemed unnecessary, as did any lingering. Turning slowly, he walked away, knowing that she was watching him go. A dozen or so strides later, he rotated, looking back, sending his hands out wide to her, his arms unfurling like underwater stems, his body flooded with overwhelming longing. He let his arms float up high above his head, watching her do the same, her little body arching up on tiptoes. Love arced between them like a flaming rainbow, a love bursting with spirit-force and unspeakably deep recognition, a love simultaneously personal and universal, ashimmer with both grief and joy. A few moments later, their arms descended together, soft as a sigh, and he turned away, his heart aching with his last look at her...

He walked very slowly, meticulously yet effortlessly aware of every step he took, luxuriating in his bittersweet richness of feeling, not stopping until he'd reached a beach near his house. Removing his clothes, he sprinted straight into the sparkling waters, swimming out past the waves. So many things were for the last time — he might never again swim in these turquoise waters, these smoothly rolling, silken waves, this ocean so powerful in its intimacy, so, so deep in its welcome...

Must he say goodbye to everything, and everyone? Yes, but *without* such personal dramatization, *without* burdening doing so with any notion of "must" or apparently heroic self-sacrifice! That sort of farewell was but an egocentric badge, a bit of glorification for the self that insisted on clinging to itself. If a goodbye was not as natural and graceful as a leaf falling, then it was not a true goodbye, but only another facet of personal armouring, just one more brick in a wall that was of no real use to anybody. And was not a pure goodbye actually a kind of hello?

Death after death after death — one could dissociate from all that Death touched, but doing so was just the pinnacle of consolation, the ultimate flight from Life. *Willful* absorption in the Deathless was not Enlightenment, but only one more fear-fueled activity, the most sophisticated escape available to humans. Death after death — but why bother making a problem out of this? Did the waves complain about their upcoming breaking, their inevitable shattering against the shore? Did not their breaking, their death, feel more like a revelation of their essence than a mere dissolution of their form? A celebration and supremely eloquent acknowledgment of something prior to all shaping and all embodiment?

How vast were these waters he swam in, how effortlessly spacious, how forceful and how yielding, how abundant with unrestrained vitality! So, so uncalculating! So, so unlike those humans who sought refuge in primal emptiness, in Nothingness, deliberately excluding themselves from the passions and desires of Life. He had seen a rare few, three Sirdhanans in all, who had succeeded at this, and he had marvelled at their attainment, but he wouldn't now. They were peculiarly invulnerable, shut off to their own ordinary humanity, meditatively removed from the very intensity of desire itself — their state of being, however exalted or peaceful, was nothing but an extreme reaction, or solution, to their own suffering, a kind of disembodied, undifferentiated immunity...

Such detachment was *not* love, not even a pale imitation of love! It was but a sublimely engineered clinging, a subtly desperate hanging-on to Eternal Emptiness and Nothingness. However, Lantar was prior to such Emptiness and Non-Being, prior to all states of being and non-being, *already* present *as* all these states, all these conditions! The manifest and the unmanifest, whatever the level, existed simultaneously in *and* as Lantar, no more separate from each other than were the waves and the ocean.

He stayed in the water until well into the evening, then made his way to his house. Tomorrow, he would prepare for his journey.

And the day after tomorrow...

Part III

Give me your hand
And let me show you my land
Give me your eye
And let me show you my sky
Come with me into the shining night
Come let exploding stars deepen your delight
There are unborn storms and blue-armed glories
There is a brilliance throbbing inside
Give me your point of view
And let me show you what you always knew
Come with me into the Unknowable Now
Come let wonder widen your brow
There are children whose wombs wait for you
There is a land where mind cannot go
Give me your all
And let me show you the door through the wall
Come with me into the heart of the fire
Come leap speechless into open-eyed desire
Give me this
And let me show you your bliss
Come with me into every room
Come let the sobering joy bloom
Give me what you most miss
Is it not time to receive Eternity's Kiss?

32

The Great Forest

After ten days' travel, Glam reached a small village that was only a short walk from the Great Forest. It was a strange place, an outpost with no spirit, no frontier excitement. The side of the village facing the forest was completely windowless and painted a shiny white, because this would, as Glam was repetitiously and dourly informed, shield the village from the forest's evil. Whenever Glam asked if any of the villagers had actually entered the Great Forest, he only encountered shaking heads and downcast frowns.

What sourness, what sullen paranoia, what bricked-in fear, oozing out with every begrudging gesture and word! When he said he was going into the forest, they turned from him, muttering incomprehensibly. How easy it was, and not just for these villagers, to turn from and look down upon those who were embracing an adventure, inner or outer, that one *needed* to undertake for oneself, but wouldn't, with the excuse that one *couldn't*!

He didn't stay in the village for long. It reminded him of a repressed Anushet — give these people some displays of uninhibited bloodshed and carnivorous mutilations, and they'd surely begin to smile, however slightly! They might as well be sitting in Anushet's amphitheatre...

But there were no gory spectacles in the center; this amphitheatre was surrounded by the looming bulk and breath of the Great Forest, with its massive green jaws, its gleaming talons, its midnight eyes, its enormous, salivating shadows. In the very midst of this encircling nightmare huddled the spectators, numbing their terror with regular doses of bitterness, cynicism, and suspicion — they were faced inward, but without the alertness or spaciousness of a meditator, held securely in place by their unswerving commitment to their misery, their precious misery, their backs turned to what they feared. They were not, however, faced too far inward, for the festering, black-flamed *core* of their nightmare crouched there, waiting, waiting for... recognition!

Day after day, the villagers manoeuvred in their narrow space, on constant guard against any force that might push them in *either* direction. They seemed to believe that their self-entrapment was their lot in life, and were rigidly unyielding in their defence of this belief! No wonder he was such a bother to them, for he, without having to say anything, reminded them not only of their self-imposed dilemma, but also of their failure of nerve, their spirit-denial, their ritualized lovelessness — how very difficult they had made it for anyone or anything to jolt them out of their rut! How very thoroughly they had muffled the cries of what lay entombed *within them*, literally turning it into a monster!

As he left the village, a mob of children charged after him, raucous and violently chaotic, shouting out insults. Again and again, stones bounced against his backsling and legs. Finally, when one struck the back of his head, he spun around, facing his attackers, most of whom gripped stones in their hands.

"You are brave enough to stone me," he declared, "but are you brave enough to come with me to the edge of the Great Forest?" The children stood frozen, their faces far more vital than those of their parents, but just as miserable.

"Well," he roared, "either come or go!" Sullenly, they backed away, not looking at each other. Glam continued walking, free of followers. The sky was clouded but bright, and the air fresh, tinged with anticipation. He felt strong and healthy. His backsling held provisions and clothing, as well as a small axe and two daggers. Water-gourds hung from the bottom of the pack. Also, he had two spears, one strapped to the side of the backsling, the other in his hand, serving as a walking stick.

In front of him materialized the details of a dark green wall of trees, growing ever higher. Then, at last, he was in the Great Forest. Though there was more light than he'd imagined, it still was not easy to see clearly. The footing was terrible, just as Xandur had said, mucky and nastily unpredictable. Just before nightfall, he built a shelter far up in the trees. No snakes disturbed his sleep.

By dawn, he was on his way, feeling well-rested. The hiking was difficult, but not so difficult that he wasn't able to maintain a steady pace. Numerous small bogs and dense expanses of thorny undergrowth forced him to take a near-constant zigzagging route. Toward day's end, he came upon a stream whose banks provided by far the best footing he'd yet encountered in the forest. That night, he again built a shelter high above the forest floor, and again slept well.

The next day, he covered more ground than he had the previous two days. The stream gradually widened, occasionally sprawling out into blue-green potholes. Its banks were easy to walk along, being generously imbedded with large, roughly surfaced boulders. The psychic congestion Xandur had described was definitely present, but it didn't disturb him; the voices that whispered and growled and babbled from between the trees could not penetrate him, nor seize his attention. They could only bother him if he became permeable to them, and he wasn't about to let that happen. Basically, these spectral entities seemed no different than the beings who populated his darker dreams, beings he had long ago learned to recognize as *ordinarily* nothing more than phantoms arising within *his* own consciousness, phantoms masterfully embodying various leanings of his...

Nevertheless, he was wary. They were dense, but very persistent. If he were to slip in any way, he'd be inviting them into himself. Their presence was remarkably similar to that characterizing Anushet, except that it was more powerful, more slaveringly condensed — for all he knew, perhaps these beings were the disincarnate of Anushet! Once, when they were particularly thick around him, he stopped and shouted, "Parasites! Go from me! Go now! Too long have you been in limbo here! Go!" Immediately, the air cleared, but only for a short time...

He didn't sleep well his third night. Twice he awoke to find large snakes slithering along the outer edges of his sleeping platform, the waving movements of their heads barely visible. He knocked them away with the shaft of his spear, hearing their bodies crashing against branches below, then, a few moments later, dully smacking the earth.

In the morning, he discovered to his horror that the trunk of the tree upon whose branches he'd built his shelter was wrapped, densely wrapped, with slowly ascending snakes!

Amid the rising coils, he counted seven heads, all mottled purplish-red, all extravagantly fanged, blue tongues flickering hypnotically. The uppermost snake was only an arm's length below him. It was too far to jump to the ground, and too far to leap to another tree. Leaning over the edge of the platform, he killed the first two snakes with a spear, driving its tip through their mouths and out the back of their heads. The rest continued rising, but very slowly, their iridescent heads getting ever larger. After fruitlessly trying to dislodge them with hurled branches, he very cautiously lowered himself down the trunk, killing each snake in succession, driving his spear between each pair of glistening black eyes. When he at last reached the ground, he was exhausted and shaking, for it had taken all his strength to simultaneously climb down and manipulate his spear.

What Xandur had termed the Great Forest's disincarnate now milled around him, turbulent and repulsively insistent, wetly panting, mixing with the viscous stench of the dead snakes, pressing against him from all sides, hissing and licking and bubbling, pawing at him. His exhaustion had made him vulnerable to them; he could only partially shield himself against their clammy invasion. Parasites! Soul-suckers! What a slimy rustling was their combined voice, what ancient depravity in their clamouring, what sticky gluttony! He felt as though he were but the object of a vast, mouthless hunger...

But I am not here to gratify thee! I am not thy maggot-feast, nor thy flesh! And I do not yield to thee, thou who feel so trapped here! Thou who have fallen into this forest, this abysmal zone, like sludge sliding to the bottom of some filthy trough, thou who have accumulated here simply through habit, perverse, unillumined *habits* thou mechanically personified while physically embodied, know that I am no part of such gross weakness!

He knew his thoughts were heard. However, the air around him didn't clear at all. "Leave me!" he screamed over and over, but still nothing changed. A multiheaded fear wriggled up through his belly, madly darting here and there.

He knew what he had to do.

There was no alternative. Reluctantly, for he feared that doing so might make him vulnerable to animal attack, he let the surrounding entities enter him, and pour into his voice. They could not, however, merely speak through him, or use him as a medium to fulfil their intentions — he sang out their hideousness, their malignancy of spirit, their darkness of appetite. Shrieking and howling, he whirled and stumbled crazily. Protect me, Lantar, for I am utterly helpless!

He shook violently with the passage of the sounds. Searing pains raced through him, erupting within his skull. He felt as though his entire spine was being wrung out in a pair of huge iron hands, all of its inner substance being squeezed upward through his neck. Again and again, he screamed for release, as a blinding agony crowded the space just behind his eyes.

No more! No more, please...

And still his voice came, unhindered by the seizures that racked him. Though he was close to passing out, he managed to stay on his feet. Then, in one glorious moment, the pain disappeared, and he was filled to overflowing with blissful sensations. Now, he sang out the deeper truth of the Great Forest's disincarnate, wailing out their lovelessness, their loneliness, their heart's innermost pain. Within his outpouring there gradually emerged another sound, a brilliant filament of compassion, becoming more substantial with every breath he took. There was room in him now for these beings, room for all...

Finally, he was silent. The entities were still present, a short distance from him, but their malevolence and obsessiveness was in tatters; they were less a mob now, and more an assembly of confused individuals. He felt their longing, felt it being revealed to them, and felt akin to them.

"Do what you will," he said in a firm yet tender voice. "But know that you need not stay here. As strongly as you feel yourself to be called here, you are even more strongly called elsewhere. True wisdom consists of nothing more than joyously obeying that call, which is simply an invitation, and eventually a demand, to awaken from your dreams, rather than a directive to fulfil them!"

After a long pause, during which he surveyed the drooping greenery

all around him, he added, "May your future embodiment shine with
Lantar's Light."

He laughed — here he was, speaking to something his *eyes* couldn't
see, feeling very light and happy, marvellously unburdened, in the
depths of a forest so dense that only the palest of sunrays filtered
through its foliage. Perhaps his sounds had attracted some carnivores.
He didn't care; let them come! Soon, he was walking upstream again,
humming songs to Lantar, breaking into a trot whenever he could,
exulting in the purification catalyzed by his encounter with the Great
Forest's disincarnate.

Halfway through the following day, the stream became impossible to
walk along or beside, its banks now sheer cliffs over twice his height.
For a short while, he followed a course parallel to the stream's, then
had to move right into the tangled, overgrown thickness of the forest.
A number of times, he saw the centipedes Xandur had described,
huge and bristling black, undulating at the touch of his spear. But
where were the larger animals? The only sign he'd seen that might
indicate such a presence was a patch of flattened ferns — perhaps a
bear had recently slept there...

Just before nightfall, as he was completing his sleeping platform, he
saw two pairs of gleaming eyes directly below him. Though the light
was very poor, he had no trouble making out the forms of two
leopards. He dropped a handful of twigs upon them, and they backed
away, snarling. Then, flinging a large branch at them, he roared
ferociously. Gracefully sidestepping the branch, they retreated a little
further. He roared even louder, and the leopards disappeared into the
undergrowth, smoothly and silently.

It was a long night, too long. He slept lightly, on the alert for snakes.
None came, but the leopards returned again and again, several times
sharpening their claws on the trunk right below him. The next day, he
knew they were following him, though he neither saw nor heard
them. At least the footing was improving. Soon he would be through
the forest; he could sense the base of Mount Aratisha but a day or so
away. The leopards, however, were getting closer and closer — he
could feel them on either side. Maybe there were more than two.
Maybe they'd do no more than track him. Maybe, maybe...

Hadn't Xandur been followed for days by leopards without being attacked by them? Yes, but this felt very different — he strongly intuited that they were going to attack him. He must face them now, while he was still sensitized to them. He must!

In the middle of a small, mossy clearing he lay flat on his belly, feigning sleep, his backsling beside him, a dagger and spear beneath him, one in each hand. Patiently he waited, breathing through his fear, his awareness of his surroundings preternaturally keen.

Come to me, come...

He continuously felt the presence of the leopards, letting it enlarge and intensify within him, until its intent was throbbingly vivid. A sinewy power, lithe and surpassingly elegant, insinuated its way through him, filling him out until he felt as if he were a leopard. How soft and potently precise the padded feet, how simultaneously loose and taut the silken muscles, how streamlined the meaty desire, how graceful the arrowed poise, how fluid the spine...

When he sensed that they were very close, he felt an urgent desire to leap to his feet, but forced himself to lie still. Any moment now, he must face them. Too soon, and they might just back off, merely postponing their attack until his vigilance weakened, which it surely would. Too late, and he would probably die. Perhaps he ought to get up, and keep walking...

At that very moment, he knew without a doubt that he must arise, as rapidly as possible. He was up on his feet in one movement. The leopards were less than two body lengths away. There were three of them. One was poised to leap.

He screamed at them, but they didn't retreat. With all his power, he drove his gaze into one; growling and spitting, it backed away slightly, moving its head from side to side.

Come, come to me...

The other two attacked, their ivory fangs contrasting with the plush red of their wide-open jaws. He caught one full in the throat with his spear, and attempted to dodge the other. It knocked him over, and he rolled to his feet, dagger in hand, but it was too late — the leopard was upon him, its claws tearing into his flesh, its mouth descending toward his neck. Immediately, he took its drive to kill into his voice, and screamed the loudest scream of his life. The leopard hesitated, its eyes rolling upward, and Glam thrust his dagger up into its belly, pushing up with his knees at the same time.

The leopard roared in pain, rolling off him. The mute eye of the trees encircled him. At the edge of the clearing stood the third leopard, unmoving. The other two now lay dying. Taking his other spear, he quickly killed them, acutely aware of the stare of the third. A ragged breeze shuffled past him, pale and soggy, trailing a scent of wood-rot and ferny decay...

He had survived. Perhaps he had not needed to kill them; perhaps he could have just kept walking, and they would never have closed in on him. But those were just doubts, utterly undeserving of his attention now. He was bleeding, though not heavily, from gashes in his chest. He remembered his first time in Anushet's amphitheatre, when he had killed the white-maned beast. Suddenly, he felt extremely weary. He squatted, spear in hand, to face the third leopard. He didn't want to kill it, too, but if he had to, he would...

It gazed back at him in silence, its eyes dark and shining wide, full of forest and open sky, soothing and easing him. Brilliant black beast, supremely confident roamer of this knotted wilderness, sleek, shimmeringly coated dancer sitting so easily, so powerfully, so simply and so elegantly, that tears come to my eyes, my spear is not for you! Great cat with your noble head conveying both loss and acceptance of that loss, I will not kill you! Majestic lord of this shadowed domain, your liquid eyes dissolving and rejuvenating me...

At last, the leopard turned and walked away, its ebony curves subtly dappling in the pearly shafts of sunlight, its hips swaying with consummate ease, its flowing glide holding Glam's attention long after it was no longer in view. He sat still for a while, breathing deeply, then gathered his weapons, put on his backsling, and continued on his way, knowing that the third leopard would not attack him. For some time, images of the other two stayed with him, leaping and weaving through his mind, their deaths curling and twisting like smoky vines in front of him. He stopped at the first stream he came upon, washing his spears and dagger before cleaning his chest wounds, glad that his injuries were not serious.

Late in the day, he came through the Great Forest, descending into the small valley Xandur had described. How rapidly he'd passed through the Great Forest! Had it only been five nights? A dense cloud cover made Aratisha invisible. He slept in the open that night, not minding the traces of rain that fell, dreaming of swimming in pools of shadow-stained water, dark, faintly opalescent pools that reminded him of the third leopard's eyes...

33

Come Let
The Sobering Joy Bloom

At dawn's first light, he left the valley, winding his way up through the dense shrubbery wreathing Aratisha's base. Although the sky showed no blue, being fatly packed with black-bellied clouds, there was a lightness to the atmosphere, a subtly rejuvenating electricity. Other than the muffled thunder of two quick but heavy rainfalls, there had been no sound. Everything, even the smallest pebbles, seemed to be welcoming him, enriching and expanding his sense of exhilirating aloneness. By day's end, he could see over the Great Forest; an irregular, blackish-green strait it was, lying between him and the Amula he had left. Above him, there was very little to see, due to the drooping presence of a thick, multilayered mist.

In the middle of the night, he was awakened by a strong wind. Whistling and howling, it shoved at him when he sat up, pushing harder and harder. Where was his backsling? It had been blown some distance from him — he could barely see its wobbling silhouette. Hastily, he retrieved it, just before the wind rose to a full-throated fury. Stones rattled down the mountain, bouncing and ricocheting, their chaotic music eloquent with avalanche possibility. Lying as flat as possible against the ground, he held his pack as a shield between himself and the slope above — the stones were getting larger, and soon, he thought, they would be boulders! He must move!

To his right, maybe twenty long strides away, was what appeared to be an overhang, a small, concave cliff-face; if he could reach it, and press in against its base, the growing torrent of rocks would likely pass overhead, not touching him. Gathering up his backsling, he sprinted toward the base of the overhang, the gale full in his face. Once he fell, but quickly regained his footing, reaching the cliff-face in a single breath. He sat with his back flattened against the rock wall, watching the star-filled night through an erratic but thunderous waterfall of rocks, many of them as large as his head. A small outcropping to his right prevented the wind from reaching him.

What ferocity this wind possessed, shrieking and wailing like a monstrous birdbeast, so close that he could stretch out his hand and touch its speeding currents! So this was Aratisha, Seat of Lantar, and this gale was its voice tonight. Was he being welcomed, or warned? Both...

By daybreak, the wind had dropped to less than a rustle, and the mountainside was still. He began climbing, hoping he'd soon be on firmer ground. Gradually, the footing improved, firmed by lumpily serpentine crisscrossings of pine roots. He slept that night atop a bed of boughs in the center of an oblong gathering of dwarfish, thickly knurled pines, many of which were bent double, as if bowing. Soon he was dreaming he was in his original ocean canoe on a dark blue sea, within sight of a shore he yearned to reach. There was no wind, and, worse, there was a powerful undercurrent pulling him away from his goal. With an all-out oaring effort, he came within a stone's throw of the shore — its golden sands curved and rippled before him, hazily tender and almost unbearably soft, beckoning with all the promise of a long-awaited embrace. However, he wasn't able to come any closer! Desperately, he struggled with the canoe, using his every resource, again and again calling on Lantar...

None of it brought him any nearer to the shore, not even the sudden realization that he was dreaming. He cried out his longing with full-spirited abandon, yet still he could not attain the shore. After a while, he could sense pine branches poking through the fabric of the dream — now the dream was gone, but not his yearning. He lay on his back, gazing up at the branches and their intricate intermeshing, through which a few stars showed. The frustration of his dream hovered all around him — so, so close was he, yet so, so far! Yes, he had closed much of the distance, but it was *still* distance, wasn't it? The point was not the size of the gap, but the fact that there *was* a gap. How could he bridge it? He let the question seep into him, feeling the many levels of it, all the while knowing there was no answer that was of any real use. The leap required of him was beyond all philosophy, however spiritual; it was a leap without any spatial, temporal, or cognitive coordinates, a leap that was more surrender than journey...

The dream would be back. He had always had it, in one form or another, had he not? It was surely the loveliest of three-dimensional paintings, vibrantly aglow with Life's pageantry and drama and need, a stunningly complex painting ordinarily taken to be Reality Itself. And he, he too was in it, right in it, busily being the chronic center of attention, straining and sweating and apparently growing, artfully ennobling his lead role with rare experiences, ever seeking, like just about everyone else, to fulfil himself *within* the framework of the painting, as though that were his only option!

Occasionally, when his awakening had been deep enough to glimpse the true nature of his surroundings, he had assiduously tried to somehow paint himself *out* of the picture, as if such an experience would liberate him! As if the picture itself were the problem! As if there existed eternally obtainable security in *any* place, even a place of profound detachment from all possible scenarios! Much, much more was required of him than just enlarging or restructuring the frame, or departing for a more comforting picture within which to dramatize his presence!

Such a deluding infinity of hope, suffering, and consolation-seeking it all was, such a sprawling spectrum of bargaining for immunity from suffering, such a colourful madhouse of sleeping painters, adroitly and persistently painting themselves into corner after corner, dreaming that they were awake! He sighed. It all only grew more and more subtle as Lantar became the primary goal, the greatest of all destinations — but Lantar was *not* locatable! *All* of this was Lantar, even the dirtiest details of the painting, but it had to *be recognized* as such, not just mentally, but with one's *entire* being!

What foolishness to reduce this to mere metaphysics, to mere thought, to so-called religious belief! What insanity to substitute *belief* in Lantar for *direct*, whole-body communion with Lantar! And what suffering to cling to this belief, or to any other, as though it were a lifeline, or a remedy for suffering! Beliefs, like facts, were static, no more than frozen, emotionally-stained bleatings of frightened or ossified minds, obsessively consistent in form, providing through their very predictability and familiarity a *sensation* of security, a sensation of crucial importance to those who had turned away from their core of being...

Truth, on the other hand, was unmistakably alive and fresh, obviously originating from a source deeper than mind. Truth was consistent *not* in form, but *in feel*; it *spontaneously* arose, its phrasing, tone, and gestures in deep, empathetic resonance with what it was *currently* addressing, its moment one of *unrehearsed* creativity. Such fluid, multilevelled sensitivity was essential if one was to enter into real communion with Lantar — had not Xandur once said that Truth was the Logic of Lantar?

What was needed was *recognition* of Lantar, not a recognition to be just *added* to the rest of one's experience, but a recognition arising from *and* intimate with the *Source* of all experience. Such realization could not be brought about through any manipulation of belief, emotion, or body, for it required an uprooting of the very self who engaged in such activities!

It could only be allowed. To ask *how* was just more avoidance, however sincere or well-intentioned. It was of no use to be calculating about Lantar! Trust was necessary, unqualified trust, and love, and discriminatory intelligence, too, an intelligence unburdened by belief in *anything* whatsoever. What was asked for was nothing less than the totality of oneself — nothing could be held back or suppressed, nothing could be reserved, *nothing*! It was not just some little portion of oneself, some sort of seemingly self-contained inner sublimity, some spiritualized *personification* of interiority, that sought illumination, but *all* of one!

The next night, he had the same dream, but felt far less frustrated at its end. The stars were piercingly bright, the air full of sparkling chill. He could make a problem out of the *apparent* incompleteness of his dream, or he could make room for it! He awoke in the morning feeling exhilirated, and hiked upward at a tremendous pace for the rest of the day. Thick were the stands of pine, but easily passable, their upper branches adorned with small scarlet birds with long yellow bills. Chubby little rodents, inquisitively-snouted, appeared now and then, scattering at his approach. Clusters of multihued flowers glistened throughout the pale green grasses of plateaus and dips in the mountainside. All the while, the sun poured down on him — how very satisfying it was to thus climb, to play at the edge of stamina, to thrill with such fullness of breath, to simultaneously exhaust and replenish!

During sunset, he sat with his back against a boulder, looking out over Amula. The Great Forest was but a strand of dark green. Beyond it was a softer, brighter green, hazily and plumply stretching back into ever bluer shades, until it was but ocean. How far away was Esmelana, and yet how close! He felt as though she were beside him, gazing out of his eyes with him, watching the turquoise-streaked fire of the sky fanning and fading. Perhaps right now she was sitting at the ocean's edge, letting the sinking sun turn her hair to flaming gold...

He smiled. This was a lovely spot, the most beautiful gathering of pines he'd yet seen. The ground was soft and level. What a fine place to spend his fourth night on Aratisha! When he was halfway through constructing a shelter, he suddenly stopped, realizing that he wanted to do far more than just throw together a few branches.

He wanted to stay — why not make a home here? Why should Aratisha necessarily be any more auspicious at greater heights? Why should an increase in altitude be any more conducive to the realization of Lantar? He remembered Xandur saying that the way to Lantar was not a matter of ascent — were not the visions, blissful sensations, and resplendent states of being brought about by inner ascensions of attention just *more* experiences, here one moment, gone the next?

However, none of this meant not to climb, not to strive; it simply meant that Lantar was not attainable through *any* positioning or strategy of attention, not even the absorption of attention in the Infinite Formless. He began to laugh, louder and louder, knowing he couldn't possibly figure all this out, but that he'd probably try to! His laughter rang through the pine-sharp air — here he was, seemingly at the edge of himself, his mind frothing with multileveled nuances of meaning, his heart meltingly open, his entire being falling into deepening intimacy with this great mountain, and the trees, and the air, and the increasingly obvious Wonder that shone through it all...

Yes, let his mind think, and his heart feel, and his senses perceive! Let his intuition flower, and his being take root and take wing! Let all this be, high and low, extraordinary and mundane, and let Lantar be revealed through it all! Let all this, every last bit of it, inner and outer, dissolve in the Obviousness of Lantar! And let this very dissolution expose and incarnate the sacred absurdity, the unspeakable Mystery, of *everything*, born and unborn!

Nothing need be pushed away, nothing need be excluded, nothing need be risen above, nor otherwise avoided — was not all of this the play of Lantar, simply asking to be *consciously* known as such? How could he go on convincing himself that any of this *wasn't* Lantar? How could he possibly go on blinding himself to the totality of Lantar's Presence?

He wept freely, slipping into embrace with a Truth much deeper than knowledge or emotion, a Truth whose Presence was prior to any exercise of mind, a Truth that could only be lived and loved...

He would live here.

34

To Be Lovers
With The Calm and the Storm

His cabin took five days to build. Serving as its cornerposts were four pine trunks that even the fiercest of Aratisha's storms had not been able to budge. Over the top of the framework he stretched a piece of hide he had brought in his backsling; it was just large enough. He finished the sides and roof with finely woven strips of bush-fiber. He'd stay here until it was time to go, but he wasn't going to simply wait for that particular moment to show itself — he would *live* here, make his home here, make his stand here! How very dramatic that sounded...

Yet were not these gnarled pines, these waving grasses, these rocks and rodents and tiny flowers, *all* making a stand of sorts? Was not all that he saw here making its own stand, its own uncorrupted articulation of being, however ephemeral, however blurred or brief? Not a stand, or position, *against*, or even *for* something, but rather *as* something, as the fullest possible expression of itself. Such a stand, or embodiment of essence, was unsullied by defiance or compliance; it depended on no one's approval or applause. In its very arising, in its very purity of individuation, even in its dying, it naturally and spontaneously celebrated its Source.

He was not making his stand as a means, nor as a ladder to elsewhere, but because there was fundamentally nothing else for him to do. All other possibilities were overwhelmingly hollow or unattractive, no more than options he had already explored and even exploited, whether in action or in intention. So he would live here, based in a shelter barely big enough to stretch in, but so roughly cosy, so neatly and pleasingly nestled in the heart of the pine grove! Nearby was a clear, clean stream. Plenty of edible roots and plants, too. When his provisions ran low, he could always make a meal out of rodents — not a very appetizing consideration, but so what?

He rapidly settled into what would have once seemed to him to be an extremely lazy life. He ate when he was hungry and slept when he was tired, distracting himself from none of his needs, nor doing anything to make them more interesting. He made no attempt to meditate. Something was already astir in him, something that didn't require his interference *or* guidance for its fruition; it was afire with its own momentum, not needing any of his kindling skills. All that was actually needed was his cooperation, his wholehearted participation in what was happening to him. Whatever it was, he trusted it totally, knowing that to do otherwise would only harden and isolate him...

A graceful economy of action permeated all his doings, inner and outer; he only did what was necessary, delighting in doing it as well as possible. For every portion of time he spent sitting, walking, or working, he spent almost twice as long lying motionless on his back, letting his body and mind settle into deep relaxation, while his attention freely roamed, open-eyed and energetic. None of what he did distressed him, for he didn't burden any of it with the obligation to make him happy, or free, or at one with Lantar.

What he did felt utterly natural to him, occurring not so much as a series of events, but as an almost uninterrupted continuity. Months passed. He didn't bother to notice if he was progressing spiritually, or in any other way — no longer was he chained to the notion of progress. He did not, however, vegetate, but became more and more refined, more and more rooted in his true condition. Thoughts still came to him, sometimes quietly, sometimes with the insistence of mosquitoes, but none could seduce his attention for long — in no way was this a *deliberate* effort to abide as the witness of thoughts, nor to withdraw from identification with the thinking process, but rather was only what came *easiest* to him. What had once been a resolute, even monumental, effort was now happening as naturally as the gusting of the wind, or the opening of a flower-bud. He felt more substantial than he ever had before in his life, and, at the same time, more transparent, more *consciously* continuous with everything...

Lying on his back, he'd slip in and out of sleep, in and out of dreaming, more often than not maintaining awareness as he did so. The presence of the great mountain both inspired and steadied him, its wisdom of earth and stone saturating him, making him ever more porous, ever more receptive to rain and sun, to storm and calm, to rise and fall. He had come at the right time — any earlier, and he'd likely have tried to make something apparently significant happen on Aratisha; he'd probably have treated it as a very potent spiritual site, busily and ambitiously immersing himself in all kinds of goal-oriented attunements with it. Seeking, however, was no longer of interest to him — why run after surrogates of What was already here?

He was happier than he'd ever been before; even the most unpleasant of circumstances could not lure him from his joy. There was, nevertheless, a subtle discontent in him. He let it be — after all, it was such a minor aspect of his experience, certainly not something to worry about. But it didn't go away, no matter how strongly his expansiveness diluted it. Gradually, he saw it more clearly — it was a vague yet gnawing sense that he could be feeling even better. More to the point, it was *not* a hankering after experiences of deeper or more prolonged ecstasy, nor was it a desire to maximize pleasure, but rather it was a *reminder,* present even in the midst of his most exalted moments, of his distance from Lantar, a reminder that there *was* distance, however slight. And it was also a goad, a goad that suddenly intensified after his fifth month on Aratisha.

His time up to then had been remarkably peaceful, regardless of the weather or fluctuations in his health or moods. And not only peaceful, but extraordinarily energizing; he felt as though he'd accumulated the essence of Aratisha, becoming an immense reservoir of Life-force, overflowing with power. He had learned to contain and circulate within himself enormous amounts of energy. Now, though, his knowing that he could be feeling even better, which so far had not interfered with this vitalizing process, clearly and *consistently* demanded his attention.

He grew restless. It was no longer sufficient to continue as he had been doing. He was painfully full of force, of spirit-intensity. Before, he'd simply allowed it to overflow, giving it back to the elements, easily and gracefully. Now, that wasn't enough — there was obviously something else he needed to do with it, something else he needed to allow, but he didn't know what that was. He must find out! But how?

It wasn't something that could be figured out, nor reduced to a problem. He focussed on the intent of his restlessness, struggling to illuminate it, but it eluded his search, holding itself to no particular shape. Many symbols and visions appeared to him, but none fit. He let himself feel Xandur and Esmelana, entering into deep psychospiritual communion with them, but found no answer, not even a useful sign or clue...

He was more than willing to let the energy itself guide him, but it only seemed to accumulate, to ever intensify, to demand something of him that he knew not how to give. Doing nothing didn't work. The appropriate action didn't reveal itself, no matter how open he was. Powerful waves of Life-force surged through him, tempestuous and swollen, increasingly painful, seemingly seeking an outlet, but far, far more than just an outlet for energetic discharge, such as could be provided by orgasm or intense exercise or emotional catharsis.

There was no relief. He had come too far. Sometimes, the pain was overwhelming, and he could only lie screaming in spasms of agony, his body burning, stretching, and heaving, his eyes searing, his heart wildly beating. In the midst of even the most blinding pain, he looked for guidance, but nothing that came to him was of any use — nothing worked to ease him, not even letting go of seeking ease. He was helpless.

One day, he awoke shaking uncontrollably, filled with a force that grew more powerful with every moment. He barely managed to get to his feet, stumbling outside. The sky was terribly blue. There was no breeze. The very pines seemed poised, each one within a transparent, trembling sheath of pale yellow light. There was only waiting, only the barely-held breath of an incandescent silence...

Now, blessed now, forever exploding now, now...

Suddenly, it seemed that Aratisha itself was rushing up through his feet, streaming up through him in a million rippling rivulets, rushing up through him in an excruciatingly sustained climax of liquid granite and shrieking earth, up and up, ferociously bright — his entire being felt as though it were aflame, burning through its every name. He noticed that he was sobbing.

Now, blessed now, forever exploding now, now!

Was he to die in madness? A raving solitary, nerves terminally ablaze with the unrestrained Passion of Lantar? Lightning storms raging, raging blue and blindingly white inside my disintegrating skull, my throbbing ocean of mind! Wave after wave of ecstatic Force invading and fountainbursting my bewildered flesh, my flesh of mud and stars, my flesh now but patterned energy, my body gone, gone wide, gone deep, gone, gone to its elements!

Everything, including him, was clearly beating to a rhythm he could not see or grasp or explain, but could *feel*! And *be*! And express, and celebrate, and sing, sing, sing the fathomless Heart of, the Glory and the Wonder, the Everlasting Mystery, the Unspeakable Unity, the Love!

This earth, this dear, deep earth that his toes gripped and wriggled in, this air that kissed his eyes and bathed his ears, this achingly sweet flood of daylight that filled him and spilled him, this gone to forever day riddled so true with Death that Life poured in, and in, into him, through him, beyond him, ever brighter, ever more *him*...

He sagged at last and fell, still crying. Whatever he did or didn't do made no difference now. Once he had jokingly referred to his cabin as tomb and womb; now, death throes and birth spasms rushed together all at once, merging into one great current of being. All of him seemed to flood upward and outward, and yet, at the very same time, to coalesce at his heart. The pain passed. The intensity faded.

The sky was plump with clouds. Everything appeared utterly ordinary and utterly unfamiliar, fresh as if newborn. Its rhythm was none other than his...

35

Until The Fire
Is But Light

Weeks went by, and months, with graceful anonymity. Rarely did anything disturb him, not even his recurring dream of being in his canoe, within sight of a shore he could not reach. It seemed to him that each return of the dream only further eroded whatever was between him and his heart's desire. He felt no need at all to hurry, to somehow conjure up a shortcut — it was enough to let the dream be, to allow it space and time to breathe and settle, just as he was doing with everything that was occurring during the waking state. In fact, all of his states — waking, sleeping, dreaming — were existing more and more as a continuum, threaded through and through with an effortless alertness, an unsleeping presence. His waking and dreaming experiences mingled together more and more, both equally real to him, both equally transparent and illusory, both secondary to the luminous intensity of being he felt...

One night, he again found himself in the dream, fully aware that he was dreaming. As usual, nothing he did brought him any closer to the shore. He relaxed, noticing that he wasn't drifting further out to sea. He had crossed the ocean in his canoe, but he couldn't close this final distance, except in fantasy — how very near the shore now appeared, closer than in any previous repetition of the dream! Such a sublimely curving welcome, softer than sleep, warm as Esmelana's love, forever curving, containing within its starry folds all curves, all arcings of light and love, all bridges to the Divine, all the rainbowings of space, all the heart-leaps of pure promise...

Abruptly yet gracefully, he leapt from the canoe — he would get to shore without his craft! Warm and sensuously green was the water, intoxicatingly intimate, receiving him like a long-lost lover — never had he felt water quite like this! Its ecstasy, its seamless unity, its unexploitable flow, became *his*, and he no longer cared about getting to shore; perhaps these currents would carry him there, or perhaps not. It didn't really matter, for this water, or, more precisely, his *relationship* with this water, *was* the shore!

Then the dream vanished. He lay in his cabin, feeling excited, letting his gaze float along the vague outlines of the walls and ceiling — how very much his cabin now reminded him of his canoe! Immediately, he felt an overwhelming urge to climb further up Mount Aratisha. It was time!

At the first sign of daybreak, he left his cabin, donning his backsling. All he'd left behind were a few clothes, a spear and dagger, and one water-gourd. The trees quickly grew sparser. By noon, he was above the treeline. The wind was light but penetrating, the air crisp and piercingly blue. Finally, he stopped to rest. Far below was the grove that cradled his cabin, barely discernable. The Great Forest was but a wavering arc, the thinnest of moats, and the rest of Amula but a pale green, hazily undulating sea. And beyond that the ocean itself, and somewhere across the ocean, Anushet and Ezparya...

Ezparya. He let himself sense her, letting her presence touch him, until he could see her — alone she was standing, so, so alone, swaying like a storm-bent leafless willow high above a fatly writhing plain of ravenous, multiheaded flesh. Focussing more intently, he saw her eyes; they were clouded with contained pain, glittering black and fiercely hard, but there was a softness there too, a blurred, vulnerable trembling. Suddenly, a great longing, painfully sweet and poignant, coursed through him, filling him with images of her being here with him, upon this magnificent slope...

Ezparya! He yearned to embrace her, to hold her and melt with her, to say something to her, something of his love and appreciation for her, but no words were there for him to speak — their time together had already said it all, far more eloquently than he could now. He could not help but honour their separation, for it didn't tarnish their bond of being, but only affirmed and supported it. It would be folly to further extend himself over this gap to her — this moment's contact and communion was more than sufficient. How sweet was his longing for her, and how sweet was the Great Wonder that shone through his longing, the ruthlessly loving Brilliance that evaporated all nostalgia! He momentarily thought of Tornellas, feeling a pang of tenderness, and then nothing. Standing, he turned and continued upward.

The climb grew increasingly difficult. By nightfall, he was exhausted. He slept in a small cave, wrapping around himself a silk-filled blanket that had been a gift from Xandur. Several times, he awoke in the night, shivering with cold — how rapidly the temperature had dropped! By sunrise, he was already on his way up, hiking as quickly as possible; soon, he was warm and sweating, enjoying his exertion. Shortly before noon, the first traces of snow appeared, sparkling and precisely pitted. Never before had he seen or touched snow; its crystals melted easily in his mouth, but not until they'd stung his tongue with tiny stabs of cold. Soon, except on cliff faces, there was only snow, a bumpy yet elegant uprising of virgin white, blindingly bright in places. He couldn't see the peak, but guessed that it was at least three or four days away.

How could he possibly cross that much snow? He remembered a Sirdhanan who could control her body temperature to such an extent that she could probably melt snow with just body heat, but he didn't possess such control. Even if he did, he doubted that he'd attempt to cross such a vast expanse of snow. He could not go much further, but he wasn't sure he wanted to return to his cabin so soon.

Yet what could he do? He couldn't stay here, unless he found a shelter. For a while, he searched for a cave, but in vain; all he could find were a few small recesses, good only for emergency sleeping. Could there be caves higher up? Perhaps, but he felt no enthusiasm when he thought of actually looking for them...

The afternoon sun skidded across the snow, slanting and bouncing, more harsh than warm. The wind was brittle and aloof, chill enough to raise gooseflesh on him whenever he stopped moving. With only a trace of reluctance, he began climbing down, not looking back once. He slept that night in the same cave as the previous night. The next day, he descended the slope as fast as he could, leaping and twisting, spinning and crouching, remaining right at the edge of balance, enjoying himself immensely, singing songs to Lantar that were more lusty than devotional. Down he ran, down and down, his abandon matched only by his balance, his laughter skyflung bouquets of knowledgeless understanding...

So back he went, returning once again. It was getting to the point where it didn't seem to matter where he went — did not all journeys with destinations of self-betterment only tend to *reinforce* the assumption that there actually was somewhere to go, outer or inner, that would deliver one from what one suffered? What madness to place such primal responsibility on the shoulders of a *particular* place or realm, be it physical, mental, emotional, psychic, or spiritual!

None of this, however, negated the journey itself, but only put it in a perspective auspicious for awakening. Was not all movement, all doing, all effort, all experience, however degraded or automatic, but an expression of Lantar? Was not the dirtiest facet still Lantar? Was it not obvious? And if it all was *already* Lantar, then what point was there in *seeking* Lantar? None, except to *truly* know the folly of doing so — and then what purpose did he have other than to live in such a manner that he liberated enough energy and attention so as to *fully* know this with his entire being? To, in other words, *recognize* it so completely that Lantar's Light permeated all of his doings and non-doings...

Such had been the function, however obscured, of his travelling. The very passion of his adventure, the open-eyed risk and breakdown and breakthrough of it, had stirred up the fire, fueling its flames to such brilliant intensity that the non-essential in him had been all but consumed, reduced to embers, released to the elemental domain, the great crucible of manifest being in which his seeking was but one more offering!

Just more return, level upon level. Was not Existence, in *every* moment, inviting one and all into the Heart of such fire? Come, It seemed to be saying, come where you are called, come see the roots of your darkest desire, come look and leap at the same time, come meet the One Who appears as you, come journey by My Side, come love Me full, come love Me day and night, come deepen the roots and wings of your stride, come welcome What welcomes you, come! Come, come where you are called! Come, come ride with Me until the fire is but light, come, come home, come now, ever now...

Just more return, level upon level, ever more radiant with Infinite Mystery. Only Lantar does not return. Lantar had no place to leave, and therefore nowhere to return to. He, on the other hand, he who still stood self-enclosed in the midst of Lantar's Love, continued, in an ever subtler manner, to flirt with notions of personal destiny, denying himself *full* access to Lantar's Viewpoint. Yes, he had relinquished much to the fire, but not everything — he, despite his intentions to the contrary, would not surrender the position of Glam for that of Lantar, even though he knew that such a radical yielding would *not* be the end of him, but rather the complete flowering of him. What insanity to assume he could only be Glam *or* Lantar, but not both simultaneously! Ah, the dilemma of being oneself, and of transcending oneself! The *apparent* dilemma...

What precious musings these were, what well-dressed refuse! He laughed at what he had termed his dilemma — did not Lantar's Viewpoint *include* Glam's? That is, to transcend himself, he must *be* himself! Then just what was the sacrifice, the great sacrifice about which he was making such a crazily articulate fuss? It was none other than the self-conscious knot of assumptions and habits that insisted on referring to itself as Glam!

His madness, like that of any other human, was that he wanted to receive the benefits of a profound transformation of self *without* actually fully undergoing the transformation itself! Nevertheless, the he who wanted this was rapidly fading, already but the flimsiest of phantoms...

How readily humans sabotaged their own awakening and happiness, taking refuge in beliefs and behaviours that only weakened and dulled their capacity to see what they were really up to! How readily they deified *whatever* produced a convincing illusion of true happiness and well-being! How persistently and how automatically they made their happiness *dependent* on someone or something outside (or inside!) themselves, dramatically clinging to whatever that object might be, their very dependency itself only further contracting them into unhappiness! How then would they ever know a *healthy* dependency, one that was but a heartfelt acknowledgment of their true needs, as opposed to one that was but a *strategy* to snare happiness?

Humans would simply not do what they needed to do in order to have their heart's deepest desire, and so they suffered horribly, methodically impaling themselves on the ubiquitous horns of their apparent dilemma, writhing in pain, devoting their lives to searching for and possessing solutions to this pain, all the while almost never recognizing that *they* themselves were generating the very condition that was the source of their pain! The pain itself, however masked, numbed, or glorified, only reinforced the case of mistaken identity that was its origin, that misguided sense of self that was always trying to remedy its self-imposed suffering without going to the *root* of it. This self was but suffering incarnate, the very *personification* of disconnection from one's core of being — in fact, it wasn't a self at all, but only a self-bound activity, an ancient habit, a mind-complicated knot pulled tight between sternum and spine. All it could do, if uninterfered with, was spawn more and more of itself, seeding its environment with its habits...

And here he was, plunging through *his* habit and down to his cabin, barely keeping his feet, dazed with cascading insights, crazed with Lantar, drunk with utterly unreasonable joy, tripping over bushes and bumps and stones and, most of all, himself! He couldn't stop laughing, not at something, but *with* something — he felt as though he were charging through his viewpoint, even at its most expansive, breaking through all the mind-latticed arrangements that had once defined and bordered what he took himself to be... His laughter obliterated his thoughts. Understanding swept through him with ecstatic force. How powerful was this love he felt, how wonderfully merciless its exposure of pretension! Every wave of laughter both deepened his wonder and stripped it of all seriousness. The joke was not on him —

It *was* him! And was he not also the spaciousness uncorked by the punchline? The Eternity blooming inside every moment, the boundless Grace of the Source, the limitless Expression of Pure Being?

There was nothing to protect now, nothing! Only when nothing was sacred, was everything sacred. Paradox stacked upon paradox, now no longer problematic, but joyously and inexorably streaming together, dissolving in an exalted alchemy, reappearing as only Truth, undiluted, ever-virgin, and beyond all rehearsal...

He was ready.

36

I Have Been Waiting
For You

The sun was not quite overhead when he reached his cabin. Such a sturdy little place it was, so firmly tucked in amongst the pines, so cosily dappled with sun and shade! He was scratched, bruised, and happily exhausted, looking forward to a long sleep. Inside he stepped, swinging off his pack, looking —

What?

Against the far wall sat a man!

"A beautiful day," said the stranger, slowly and melodically.

Glam said nothing, breathing away his shock, studying his visitor carefully. A smooth, sinewy body, very loose and deceptively alert. Unkempt black beard and hair, enwreathing a fierce face, swarthy and high-cheekboned, dominated by large green eyes, eyes of remarkable luminosity and steadiness, eyes deer-wild and fearless...

"Not very talkative, are you?" gently chided the man. "I suppose this is your cabin."

Glam nodded, disliking the man's tone. After a short silence, he said, "What are you doing here?"

"What are *you* doing here?" declared the stranger, widening his eyes.

"Do not toy with me," said Glam, his irritation growing.

"Why not?"

"Continue to taunt me, stranger, and you will regret it." Glam dropped into a squat, his hand settling on the hilt of his dagger.

"My name is Josalna."

"And mine is Glam."

"So what brings you to Aratisha, Glam?"

Glam felt puzzled; the man's question appeared sincere, but Glam knew it was not what he really wanted to say. After a prolonged pause, he said, "I tire of your questions."

"They are not questions!" snapped the stranger, with sudden force.

"Let this cease," said Glam slowly and softly, readying himself to do battle. "Whatever your purpose here is, I do not wish to pursue, since you are so obviously unwilling to speak it truly."

"And just how will we know if I speak truly?"

"Enough!" roared Glam. "If you do not leave now, I will throw you out! I don't wish to fight with you, but I will if I have to — I will kill you if I have to!"

"Nobly said," sneered Josalna, shifting to a crouch with feline ease. "Come! Will you now kill me, just as you killed the two leopards?"

Hiding his surprise, Glam rose, moving closer to Josalna.

"Are you not going to ask me how I know about the leopards?" Josalna's voice fluidly boomed out, seeming to be launched straight from his belly. He made his face look like a snarling leopard's, full of carnivorous rage and murderous intent. Then, as Glam took another step toward him, he let his entire face soften.

Glam stopped, astonished. Josalna's eyes were the eyes of the third leopard, gleaming with savage innocence and sublime understanding, shot through and through with a peace deeper than grief, deeper than loss, a peace of supreme passion and ease, a peace that brought Glam to his knees. These eyes were pure, raw animal, gloriously wild, and yet as human as Xandur's, suffused with softness and heartbreakingly deep compassion. There was an extraordinarily fine balance to them, an evenness and spaciousness of emanation he'd never before seen in anyone's eyes. Such fierce yet humourous welcome there was in the verdant fire of these eyes, such speechless intelligence, such panoramic heart! Josalna's eyes were clearly stranger to no experience, inner or outer...

Glam began to cry, letting Josalna's gaze penetrate him. Relief swept through him, relief at being so clearly and completely seen — no, not just seen, but *felt*, imbibed, known, touched throughout his entirety, so that all he had been, and all that he had done and sung, came to one locus in the center of his chest, a budlike coalescence of immensely concentrated force. A short moment later, the bud quivered, its lips moistly parting, its exquisitely tender heart slowly unfolding and stretching, petalling out wider and wider, reaching and reaching, stretching without limitation, singing every colour ever brighter, winging every shape ever truer, embracing all, knowing all, being all, being...

"I have been waiting for you, Glam."

"I know," sobbed Glam. "But only *now* do I know!" Suddenly, he started to laugh, as he had coming down the mountain, his laughter only further amplifying his openness. Was there no end to this? Was there a beginning? And was there no silencing the one who asked such questions? His laughter obliterated it all, transporting him beyond himself, sweeping him out to sea, infinite sea, into a recognition eternally available to all who cease sabotaging their awakening...

This was Lantar, Lantar unmodified, Lantar from Lantar's Viewpoint...

Almost.

Josalna laughed a high, sweet laugh, then came forward and hugged Glam, holding him for a long time, softly yet firmly, until Glam was still and silent. Then they went outside, sitting just above the pine grove, looking out over Amula. Finally, Glam said, "You've been on Aratisha for many years."

"Yes."

"Have you been to the peak?"

"Twice. But it is but the peak." With a mischievous grin, he patted the top of his head. "Just as the lowlands are but the lowlands."

"And in between?"

"Ah!" laughed Josalna, leaning back on his elbows. "*That* is the heart of the matter!"

Glam smiled and, in a low voice, began singing a song about Aratisha, improvising almost all the words. Eventually, Josalna joined him, tossing in solemn aphorisms that steadily grew so ponderous that they both ended up laughing uproariously. A silence followed that lasted the rest of the day. It was more than enough to just sit with Josalna, to be in the company of such a one...

Late that night, Glam asked Josalna how long he would stay.

Josalna's voice was but a whisper: "Until you no longer need me."

37

Let Me
Show You My Land

A week passed, and nothing was said. Sometimes words gathered in Glam, but he'd no desire to voice them. Not only did his questions vanish in Josalna's presence, but also the very motive for formulating them ceased to interest him; the entire process of questioning and answering, of thinking and rethinking, of seeking to figure out and explain, weakened very quickly in its power to trap his attention, as though it had long been ripe to do so. This was neither a strategy nor a regression into a preverbal condition, but rather a spontaneous, utterly natural transcendence of the merely verbal, a full-blooded passage into a domain where mind was but pure servant to heart, where speech, inner and outer, was but an expression and enrichment of being, an artful, multidimensional play of nuance, an unrehearsed yet wonderfully articulate phrase-supplier for even the most intricate or subtle currents of being...

Everything that reinforced his everyday identity, be it thought-forms, states of emotion and mood, or rituals of desire-satisfaction, gradually ceased to bind him. There was, however, no need whatsoever to repress any of these activities, nor was there any need to further examine their contents or structure. His not taking them seriously did not trivialize nor empty them, but rather placed them in well-lit perspective, stripping them of their power to contract him, slowly but surely restoring them to their natural condition, to intimate and unthreatened continuity with their Source...

A welcome wildness infiltrated him, playfully undermining his sense of familiarity with almost everything. No longer did he care to resist what was happening to him. There was no point in explaining it to himself, however brilliantly, nor was there any point in reporting it —

to do so would only serve to keep him at the edge of himself, diligently occupied with the upkeep of his outlook! How very easy it would be to play spiritual hero, standing like an unblinking colossus at one's psychospiritual limit, mind frothing with meaning, making high drama out of every last detail of the ledge, ever *inflating* one's self! And how equally easy it would be to play the paragon of humility, feigning unworthiness, making a virtue out of obeisant piety and repressive renunciation, loudly proclaiming one's nothingness, ever *deflating* one's self!

Such stands, whether of self-importance or of self-impotence, were nothing more than ego-centered positionings, ritualized arrangings of self, branded with ambition, sustained by the propaganda of misaligned mindplay. Unhealthy stands they were, saturated with aborted flowering, forcing their roots down into the barren soil of disembodied abstraction, self-consciously posturing beneath an artificial sun, ever struggling against an inner wilting...

He needed no reason whatsoever for his doings, no purpose-bright justification. All roles were his to play, but none in particular pulled him their way — the days were just too magnificent, too magically ordinary, too alive with the Great Mystery, too full to be enhanced by *any* distraction or specific costuming of his individuality. And Josalna! Wildman, childman, madman, man beyond Man! Josalna, man of radiant passion and pristine calm, man of sacred eyes and no disguise, man of countless faces, man of unsleeping heart, pure man standing everywhere and everywhen, standing so free, teaching me without *teaching* me, again and again winging my stride and evaporating my pride, my here-and-now glide!

Josalna was a joy to watch, whether he was sitting motionless on a rock, silhouetted against the setting sun, or whether he was chasing down rodents, yelling and sputtering, smooth and supple as a leopard. Occasionally, Glam joined Josalna in his hunting sprints; he'd stumble and struggle, repeatedly losing his balance, but Josalna had no such difficulty, somehow maintaining his speed over the most treacherous ground.

Sometimes Josalna would, while sitting, give voice like no animal or human Glam had ever heard, his hands dancing in complex, ecstatic rhythm with his sounds, their every flicker, twist, thrust, and lift conveying both immense power and extreme sensitivity, historied with mythic significance. His sounds ran together into one great chant, cast in all directions, a chant at once multitudinous and solitary, none of its individual voices fully obscured by the others — it was the speech, the innermost singing, of the elements, and also of the forces governing them. It was the Breath of Lantar, given pure utterance! How very clear and closer than near Its awakening shout! Steady and enduring was Its Call to rise and shine, pouring down on the lowlands, down on all lands, outer and inner, streaming on and on, brightening the horizon of even the dullest of human dreams, Its Invitation all but lost amidst the hubbub of human slumber...

Josalna not only sang out Lantar's awakening Call and eternal Welcome, but also *uncalculatedly* embodied It in *everything* he did — he'd no particular destiny to dramatize, no specific scenario to fill out, no adventure of discovery to take, no dream to fulfil, for he was simply *awake*, no matter what his condition or circumstances, waking, dreaming, or sleeping. It wasn't that he was supremely conscious, a superman of alertness, but rather that he *was* wakefulness itself, wakefulness incarnate, *motivelessly* aware of itself even in the deepest sleep. Josalna did nothing to maintain his awakened condition; it was not some sort of achievement, but was *him*, gone to forever, not somewhere behind the scenes, but *present* as the Unsleeping Heart of every scene...

Glam saw this, and saw the gap between himself and Josalna, knowing that it was not actually a distance to be crossed, but only something *he* was doing, something that *he* was activating. This obvious yet elusive something, this primal habit, had, he now realized more than ever before in his life, been with him all his life, however subtly. But now, sweet, sacred now, it was weakening and thinning without his willing it so, its hold on him rapidly fading, all but disappearing when he was in Josalna's presence. Yet was he not always in Josalna's presence?

The ever-virgin Mystery of it all, including himself! The infinitely tributaried Wonder of it all, this sublime yet commonplace Magic so fluidly pervading everything! Everything! This boundless Mystery that both included and transcended whatever tried to figure It out, this ever-changing Foreverness planted in every heart, waiting and waiting, waiting for Its lovers, waiting to burst forth from Its seedcase, waiting to participate through each individual in the great alchemy of transformation, waiting and waiting, dying to live...

Knowledge was but one small facet of this Mystery, a mere knowing *about* things, a self-replicating complex of information and explanation. Knowing something directly, through heartfelt communion with it, was possible, but knowing *what it was* was impossible, for its mystery was deeper and more fundamental to it than *any* description or explanation of it! That is, the essentialness of anything transcended *all* knowledge about it — information was peripheral to Being, serving as the latticework of knowledge, but not of knowingness. And where did all this lead? Out of the labyrinths of mind! Out of self-containment, out of the promised lands of ambition and hope, out and out, out past all self-obsession, out past all alibis and all self-defeating cries, out past all *meaning*...

Was not meaning but a superimposition on Being, a consolingly fixated spasm of mind masquerading as *true* understanding? Meaning was not inherent to Existence, but was only something humans *added* to Existence, something that provided a comforting illusion of certainty, a belief-framed security, a buffer against the unavoidable insecurity of Life. Yet was not such insecurity to be embraced? Making a problem out of it only weakened one's impulse to awaken, covering it with compensatory activity, especially that of clinging to meaning.

What Josalna was transmitting to him was not meaning or knowledge, but *undiluted* Lantar, raw Lantar, presented without any packaging whatsoever. In no way did he attempt to make this palatable to Glam. What a joy it was to look into his eyes! What a joy it was to be so near him! Josalna did not burden Life with meaning, nor with any other such cramp of mind or feeling. Spontaneous through and through was he, his features excluding no face, his laughter streaming and rolling through every time and every place, playfully and profoundly intimate with What escapes all naming! See his smile, explaining nothing and including everything, radiant with unexploitable love and humour! Feel him, his heart spanning the Infinity behind human minds, his every move, however offhand, a bridge to Lantar! Feel him, feel him now, feel him waiting for the unknotting of attention, waiting for awakened love, waiting to be *truly* seen...

Late one night, Josalna finally spoke. ''Do not assume that I do not suffer. My joy arises not from an absence of suffering, but in the very midst of it! I cannot help but feel the heart-hurt of all, the loveless struggling, the pain and the obsession and the fear, and I feel it without protecting myself at all! I *feel* their condition as though it were *mine*, not mine to have and bemoan, but mine to unbind and shine! I cannot turn away from anyone or anything, not now, not ever, no matter where I am!

"I love all. This is not my choice, but a fact, an endless act. It is what I am, and what you are. Love is the great Law, the very substance of Consciousness, the eternal Prism of the Formless. We can only *be* love, not sentimentalized love, not abstract love, not manipulative love, but *unsleeping* love, love that cannot lie, love that shrinks from nothing, love that cannot sink or die! In such love, *we* disappear, and what reappears is the face of pure Being! Love is *not* so much our need as it is our *condition*, our ground and our sky, our heart's very breath! True love is revealed not in the fulfilment of our dreams, but in our awakening from them, *all* of them, every last one of them! Even now, you, Glam, *dream* of being where I am! But *where* am I?"

"Certainly not in my dream!" laughed Glam.

"And where is your dream?"

"Everywhere I go."

"And just how do you *know* that?" Josalna grinned impishly, his eyes burning into Glam.

"I feel it — it seems that I create the conditions for its appearance wherever I am."

"Yes, but *who* feels it? *Who* creates such conditions?"

"The one who speaks to you now."

"And *who* is that?"

"The one who is not yet fully awake, the one who is still fascinated by some of the possibilities within the dream," replied Glam stiffly, his tone slightly exasperated. Why was Josalna playing this metaphysical game with him? Of what use was it to talk of such things now? Had not enough been said already? Why reduce the Essential to spiritual wordplay?

"Such a crowd of you's!" boomed Josalna. "So neatly arranged and articulated, each sucking its own thumb and gorging on its own fruit, in its own little niche, ever seeking to colonize the rest! But tell me, and tell me true, where is the *real* Glam?"

Glam was silent.

"Where is the *real* Glam? Where?"

"I tire of your questions!"

"They are not questions!" snapped Josalna, his voice making Glam jump.

"Well, whatever they are —"

"Stop, Glam! Do you not see that what you are doing right now is *exactly* what is keeping you trapped within the dream? Do you not see how you are even now defending its perimeter? But why protect yourself around me? What you are protecting is not a *you*, but a habit, a habit whose mind you all too easily speak! Do you not see *me*? Do you not love *me*? Yes, now your eyes fill with tears, and your chest sweetly swells, and your brow beautifully brightens, and you do see *me*, but *what* just happened? Do not simply be glad it is over with, and that you are again open — learn from it so profoundly that you need never again indulge it!

"The real Glam appears here as all of these apparent you's, but is in fact *none* of them! Their referring to themselves as "I" is just everyday delusion — you already know this, and have for some time, but you are nevertheless *still* subtly bound by it! Look at how quickly you reacted to my questions, even after this marvellous series of days we've had! Your reactivity, however, is a gift, an immensely valuable gift, for it clearly reveals where you are still reluctant to be your full self."

Glam nodded. "Look," continued Josalna, gesturing at the silvery swirlings of mist far below. "See what is before you, and marvel at how readily *you* still stand apart from it, imagining it to be fundamentally different than you! Your *clinging* to selfhood is but a disease, a self-inflicted assumption that sucks your attention away from your true identity! Stop embodying your refusal to love all the way! Stop, stop now, stop throughout now..."

Glam began to cry. "Let go now," whispered Josalna, taking Glam's hands. "Let go of the you who glamourizes letting go. Let go now. Let go of your evolutionary show. Let go of growing and knowing. Let go of masterminding your leap, let go! Let go without trying to let go, let it *all* go, Glam, all of it!"

Josalna's words were far less instruction than they were evocation, flooding unobstructedly through Glam. "Let go now, let go of letting go, let go not to reach sainthood, but to outshine *every* should! Let go not to be a better *you*, but to reclaim your real ground, to stand true! Let go not to live *in* the Eternal, but to *be* the Eternal in time, your everything afire with sacred rhyme! Let go not to leave it all behind, but to make room for it *all*! Let go now, Glam, ever deeper into now, now, holy now, everlasting Now! Let flow What beats your heart and shines you bright! Let glow the Joy for which love must weep!"

Josalna stood, still holding Glam's hands, his eyes incandescent emeralds, his face ablaze with passion and love, his touch electric with spirit-force and welcome. "Don't bargain for later, Glam! Hear me, and hear me *now*, hear me with every fiber, corner, portion, every up and down, in and out, round and long, every last bit of you! Go beyond your every fascination with me! Feel *me*! Receive *me*! Realize the melting wonder of this sky, the star-gloried dome, the scarves of braided cloud, the unblinking eye of the moon! Feel the unworrying green of these trees, uninhibitedly assuming its full shape, filling out the imperatives of its leafy shout! See the Great Welcome written everywhere! Everywhere, Glam, everywhere! See the futility of avoiding or postponing this!

"Stop turning away from what gives you life! Stop now, in midthought, or in mid-breath, or in mid-feeling, or wherever you are! Breathe What is breathing *you*, breathe It full, breathe It wild, breathe It free of all history! Hear me now, Glam, hear *me* in the birthstirrings of your very next distraction or spirit-contraction! Feel *me*! Feel all of this, making room for its every face, even as you stand rooted in its Heart of hearts!

"Take me, Glam, take me in, take me to the weave of your true name, take me to the bottom of your pain, take me behind your face, take me to where you are sun and rain, take me soaring in place! Take me in, take me right to your core! Is there not just the breathing free of Love's Door? Just this everlasting Moment, nothing less, nothing more? Just the end of your search for a better deal, just the end of you looking for somewhere special to kneel? Take me past your past, Glam, take *me* in until there's no in and no out... Take me to us, take me past all the obsession and fear and fuss, take me deep, take me steep, take me right to the heart of the matter, regardless of the weather!

"Welcome me as I've welcomed you! I am your oldest ally, and I am your sky's deepest cry. I am the hello in grief, and I am the joy of each new leaf! Do you not recognize me? Have you not always seen *me*, not just this crazy man who now hurls words at you, but *Me*? The Me Who shines through all these gestures and impassioned phrasings, the Me Who is the Lord of your stride, the Me for Whom you've always cried? The Me Who is the very Heart of all this, the Me Who cannot help but forever love you? The Me Who is you?"

"Yes," sobbed Glam. "Yes! But I have made doing otherwise more important. I have sought to be in charge of my letting go; I have been ambitious about not being ambitious! I made You, wherever and whenever I felt You, into a goal, a worthy challenge for the mighty Glam, instead of allowing *You* to be my foundation! I insisted on *searching* for You, instead of —"

"Do not," interrupted Josalna, "assume that your search was mere folly. It carried within itself its own transcendence, its own dissolution; the very passion that you brought to it, the very intensity of surrender you permitted yourself in the midst of your seeking, readied you for this. That is, your seeking, not in of itself, but because of *how* you used it, actually *ripened* you! You used your search to *outgrow* the very motive for searching! The mirages of *elsewhere* thus ceased to seduce you — you found me when you stopped looking for me, did you not?"

"Yes."

"But I am not just this!" Josalna suddenly grinned, patting his whole body with exaggerated vigor, then opened his arms out in a gesture of thanksgiving. "See the land and the sky, the swirl and dash of it all, the rising and falling, the birthing and dying, the splendid flux of all this, the nothing and the everything, the exquisitely varied pulsations of Pure Being, speechless with Its infinity of faces, all the countless waves of Lantar's Current!

"All of this is a marvel, even that little self-important parcel of it that is obsessed with meaning! Such a wondrously fertile chaos of sound and colour this is, coiling and squirming and squeezing and leaping into shape after shape! Such appearances and disappearances, ever textured with mind, ever spinning out design! Flowers and flowers, showering out bouquets of uncompromised brilliance, unhesitatingly shouting out every colour, opening to sun and rain and every kind of weather, flushed and arush with differentiation, succulent with blossoming and the nectared swoon of sacred fertilization, such a vast glory of petals stretching wide, surrendered deep, exploding out and out, layer upon layer! Such rhapsody, and such decay! Flowers and flowers, Glam, boundless realms of them, dying in a blaze of pure trust, now but a scattering of wilted petals, each petal but a fallen offering to Lantar, a flimsy, extraordinarily fragile, utterly *unrehearsed* piece of a song older than pain and time, a song that beats out the rhythm of your heart, and all hearts!

"The flowering that you, Glam, are on the threshold of, exists but in seed form in almost all humans, all but forgotten, or merely reduced to half-hearted rituals. You are to help others remember. Your very presence will be sufficient, though not if solely confined to its passive mode; you will often be moved to take strong action in *response* to the slumber of those around you. Few will truly recognize your gift, and fewer still will receive it, but it is for those few that you will return to Amula."

Josalna's words burned into Glam. So he was to return. So he was not to stay with Josalna...

"You must return, Glam. Tomorrow, or the day after tomorrow, I will leave, for you no longer need me in this particular form, or in any other, for that matter. My humanness has served its purpose with you, regardless of how much it would love to linger with you. *I* will always be with you, as you will be with me, no matter what our current appearance or *apparent* identity, no matter what particular destiny or need we are embodying! And what else is there to say? Even now, my words fall far short of what is passing between our eyes...''

Moonlight bathed their faces, half-cupping their gaze. Without any resistance, Glam let in the gift of Josalna's presence, letting it radiate all through him, knowing that Josalna's upcoming departure signalled no separation, except peripherally. How could Josalna *truly* leave? What he and Glam shared, or cohabited and *were*, was not corruptible by any kind of coming or going; It simply abided as Itself, Its very Life utterly unopposed to Death, or any other parting.

They sat unmoving until daybreak was near full. Glam looked up, drinking in the sky, loving its brightening stretch, its achingly pure curve, its boundless transparency — its blue could be obscured by cloudiness, but not corrupted. When the clouds were gone, the blue was still there, intact. As was *he*, no matter what he did — but this was more than metaphor, for behind his eyes, he could sense a bright, pellucid blue, bluer than any sky. Into this blue he let himself be absorbed, even as he gazed at the sky. There was a Brilliance at the core of this inner blue, an uncoloured Intensity that he suddenly realized was illuminating all of the blue, fanning a million shining tributaries through it. Without a doubt, he knew that Josalna was living in this Brilliance.

And, more to the point, living *as*.

A boundless, intoxicatingly clear love filled Glam to overflowing — there seemed to be nothing happening except for the multidimensional creation and spinning of a vast wheel of sound and colour, the hub of which was his heart, or, more precisely, the *feeling*, the exquisitely naked feeling that flooded his heart, emanating from it infinitely in all directions. Effortlessly, he recognized it all as Lantar, knowing this with his entirety, knowing it, loving it, *being* it...

He felt Josalna's hands cupping his face.

"This is your birthright, Glam. And it is everyone's, if they would but claim it. Existence is revealing Itself to you now, in Its undressed purity. But do not settle for that revelation, wonderful as it is! Do not seek to reexperience it, nor seek absorption in it, not even when it is but Consciousness Itself! Go right *through* it, Glam, right through it! Go into That in which it arises! Do not stop short of Lantar's Domain! Go beyond Lantar as Being, and beyond Lantar as Non-Being, until Lantar is but Lantar!"

Josalna laughed. "Perhaps my advice is unnecessary caution — you must go on, and yet there is nowhere to go! Is it not all paradoxical? Yes, but *only* to those who are still looking for Lantar. Paradox is but Truth in the Light of Lantar. Ah, but just see my words slipping over one another, leapfrogging left and right, eager to be spoken before I finish with them altogether! What I speak of is unspeakable, and yet I have presumed to say it anyway! Foolishness is infinite. But so is love."

These were the last words Glam would hear Josalna speak. The sky was on fire.

38

Its Heartbeat
Shaping Our Truest Ground

Glam awoke in the middle of the night, hearing a low, melodic humming — soothing it was, deep and penetratingly warm, luxuriantly earthy and fecund, mother-soft, purring with liquid ease, rolling on and on, yet also lofty and bracingly cool, afire with fatherly force, gloriously crystalline. Tender yet roundly muscular was the sound, simultaneously nourishing and challenging, winged by its very depth, aromatic steam rising from its gallop, stars embroidering its flight...

Its source was Josalna. He was sitting cross-legged in one corner, his body gently swaying from side to side.

This was his last night with Glam.

How richly inviting was this music, how deep its roots, how spacious its sky! How vast and joyously poignant its passionspill, how bright its sweetly sailing crystals of soulsound! Did not its heartbeat shape humanity's deepest ground? Did not the tumbling hourglass forever live in the shout and whisper of this sublime humming, this timeless strumming? All around Josalna pulsed a diaphanous light, bulging wide whenever his voice rose.

The more Glam watched and listened, the more awake he felt, his body seeming to spread far, far beyond its edges, expanding in all directions. Finally, full of almost unbearable bliss, he arose and left the cabin, stumbling and staggering about as if drunk, laughing and weeping, still hearing Josalna's chant. How indescribably intimate he felt with *everything*, how effortlessly oceanic his embrace, how unspeakably obvious his understanding! All of this was now not so much his, as it was *him*, inviolably *him*...

With considerable effort, he climbed up to where he and Josalna had sat during the afternoon, his entire body shaking almost orgasmically.

Let It come! Let It do what It wills . . .

Wreathing the moon was a shimmering ochre ring, flamingly fringed with violet hues. The air was a delight to breathe, crisply cool and moist. Wrapping himself in blankets, he stretched out on his back. Gradually, his bliss-spasms eased into a light, finely-textured tingling, accompanied by a sensation of dissolving right into the very Energy of Which his body and mind seemed to be but a configuration — many times before he had felt this sensation, but never so compellingly as now...

And what of his perceptions? What of the world they had once so convincingly presented? That world's solidity and definition was now but an apparition... Before perception, *what* was there? Without physicality's perceptions, *what* was there? What remained? This! This Eternal Wilderness of Being, this Infinite Mystery! This Unknowableness, this Overflowing Emptiness, this Immutable Joy, forever Conscious of Itself, now appearing as *him*!

There was no going back now.

And no going ahead...

Perception was but the sensation of experience. And what was experience, but the association of the separative self with phenomena, with manifest existence itself? This vast interplay of forms, physical, mental, emotional, and psychic, level upon level, rising and falling, injected with meaning — such a dynamic, infinitely varied display it was! Such immense and touching complexity, resplendent with its cycles of birthing and dying, its cycles great and small, its peaks and valleys, all obscured by the clinging to knowledge, as well as by the craving to be distracted from one's suffering! But what sublime beauty there was in the cascading of the seasons, what effortless grace, what brilliant losing of face, what unambiguous fullness of celebration, what surpassingly eloquent art!

And there was a deeper Life, One that animated and fleshed out this interplay, a Life not at all subject to the laws governing the world of experience...

Such Life was none other than Lantar.

Long had he stood apart from Lantar, busying *himself* trying to close the gap, even as his very ambition maintained the distance. Habit it was, mere habit, insistently *personified* habit, the string through the beads of his experiences, now all but unravelled, existing only as the flimsiest of filaments, less than gossamer. Let the beads spill! Let them come unstrung! Let them rearrange themselves without pretending to add up to *him*, or to *house* him! Let them be unburdened by any meaning, or systematized gathering! Let them remain uncolonized, and let them be unambivalently transparent to their Source!

He began to weep, letting everything go, simply because there was nothing else to do, letting go and letting go, letting his love flood out, pour and stream and soar out, denying no experience, seeing and hearing and feeling humankind, and everything else, in its totality. Humankind, self-bound, lost in the mechanics of experience, gross or subtle, so dulled by needless repetition, so stubbornly committed to self-constriction and its compensatory addictions, turned away from the Joy and always-present Obviousness of Lantar, ever seeking refuge in surrogates of What it had turned away from, ever reaping the consequences of its self-entrapping rituals, blindly seeding its children with the same capacity for self-delusion. All too many humans desperately searching, looking for the Real in all the wrong places, settling for and *believing* in imitations of It, settling for mere pleasure and consuming abstractions, obsessively distracting themselves from their binding *act*...

No judgment passed through Glam. He only wept. The Awakening he now embodied was but a seed in almost everyone, all but unrecognized, buried beneath the debris of getting by... Glam did not resist his sadness; he cried not out of helplessness or hopelessness, but out of love. All of Existence seemed to weep with him, to join him in his unavoidable compassion, as well as in his joy.

Love must also weep.

Finally, when his crying had subsided, dropping into gentle waves no louder than a murmur, he felt a hand on his head, a firm, warm hand, a heartbreakingly *human* hand.

It was Josalna's.

In his touch there pulsed an empathy and knowingness beyond all comprehension. Glam lay still beneath Josalna's touch for a long time. Several times, he thought it was raining lightly, then realized that the drops falling on his face were Josalna's tears...

39

Room for All

There was only Lantar.

The pine grove breathing soft, the departure of Josalna, the mist-draped night, the unblinking eye of the moon, the undreaming Beauty streaming through every domain, the undying Love ever available, the unbroken Moment of Now...

There was only Lantar, and there was everything.

Sleep came without any break in consciousness. He was *awake*, doing nothing to maintain his wakefulness, for he *was* it. Nothing could be more ordinary, and nothing more human. The dream-play of Existence still arose, but he was utterly free of it, free to both participate in and transcend it, free to feel its every glory and every horror, free to *fully* live it, without losing himself in any of it, including his needs and attachments. He could not help but see it for what it was.

And he could not help but love it.

Late the next morning, he left his cabin, and began his downward trek. The bright green land beckoned to him.

Esmelana and Xandur would be waiting for him.

ROBERT AUGUSTUS MASTERS is a psychospiritual trailblazer and shamanic visionary, as well as a master therapist and teacher, an adept at getting to the heart of the matter, teaching only what he *intimately* knows, artfully, unswervingly, and potently serving as a multidimensional catalyst and medium for the awakening and embodiment of the full human. He is the guide of Xanthyros, a community both young and very ancient, in which awakening is the priority, not a dry, detached, or desireless awakening, but rather a vibrant, full-bodied, exquisitely practical awakening...

In Xanthyros, the difficult is not risen above, nor otherwise avoided, but is deliberately entered into *and* passed through with open eyes, until its energies, however dark or reactive, are *fully* and luminously integrated with the rest of one's being — this passage is simultaneously a solitary and communal effort, the structuring of which is neither prepackaged nor rehearsable, but is instead formed in earthy yet fluid correspondence with the *essential* imperatives of the *present* moment. This journey, which is not so much from here to there, as it is from here to a *deeper* here, honours no morality except that generated by awakening's alchemy. As such, Xanthyros serves the *real* needs of its members, rather than merely fitting them into an already designed system.

Xanthyros is an ever-evolving sanctuary for those whose longing to be truly free is stronger than their longing to distract themselves from their suffering. Xanthyros is also a fertile experiment, a passionate risk, a stand and a leap, an invitation and a sacred demand, a frameless doorway, a dynamic yet sweetly subtle crucible wherein the fire of the awakening process can do its work, not just in the transformative and revelatory meetings of Xanthyros, but also in its businesses, its children's school, and its ever-deepening transfamily intimacy...

A DYNAMIC, STRIKINGLY ORIGINAL BOOK FOR THOSE
WHOSE LONGING TO BE TRULY FREE IS STRONGER
THAN THEIR LONGING TO BE DISTRACTED
FROM THEIR SUFFERING...

THE WAY OF THE LOVER
The Awakening & Embodiment Of The Full Human

Robert Augustus Masters

THE WAY OF THE LOVER is not about fulfilling ourselves within our dreams, nor about finding a more consoling dream, but rather is about recognizing and awakening from *all* our dreams, without any recoil from passion, desire, attachment, intimacy, or any other facet of a fully human life. Through making room for all that we are, not metaphysically, but *literally*, level upon level, we contact and *embody* a very different kind of fulfillment, not one that just pleasurably sedates us, emptying us of the tension of unilluminated desire, but one that rejuvenates and alerts us, reestablishing us in full-bodied, radiant communion with the Truth of what we fundamentally are — thus do we become our own fulfillment, saddling nothing with the obligation to make us feel better, freeing ourselves from self-constriction and its compensatory addictions, breathing more and more integrity into our stride, giving our love without giving ourselves away, letting ourselves be a meeting-place of grief and joy, a potent and throbbingly human intersection of both the mortal and the Everlasting...

THE WAY OF THE LOVER reveals not a step-by-step path or system, paved with doctrine, idealism, and compulsive ritual, but rather an ever-new passage, not from here to there, but from here to a *deeper* here; as such, it provides not a bridge over Life's difficulties, but a conscious entry right into *and* through the very heart of them, a journey of gutsy luminosity, burdened by neither hope nor despair, honouring no morality except that generated by awakening's alchemy.

Its chapters include:

- The Inside & Outside Of Self-Fragmentation
- The Teacher Is Everywhere • The Impulse To Awaken
- True Center & Its Chief Surrogate
- Breakdown Precedes Breakthrough • Irony Undressed
- Egocentricity & Essence-Centricity
- Sentimentality & Cynicism • Hope Is Nostalgia For The Future
- Responsibility Is The Ground Of Freedom
- The Anatomy Of Eroticism • Masochism & Sadism
- Into The Heart Of Rejuvenative Orgasm
- Ecstasy Is Not Elsewhere • Jealousy Unmasked
- A Mirage Of Intimacy: The Cult Of Two
- You Are Being Tested, Now • Parenting, Freedom, & Responsibility
- Guilt Means We Don't Have To Grow
- Birthing The Man • Myth As Transformative Metaphor
- Guru-Worship, Cultism, & God-Communion
- We Are Not "In" A Body • Awakening Creates Its Own Morality
- There Are No Oscars For Awakening

The lover is not merely within, nor without, but simply *here*, living *as* the very heart of each moment, existing in essence as a quality, a condition, a choice, that cries out for *complete* incarnation. In the lover, dependence and independence are not in opposition, nor in parasitic collusion, but rather in juicy embrace, potently unleashing through their sensitive yet dynamic interplay a fecund, heartfelt resonance with the obviousness of Eternal interdependence and interrelatedness. Again and again, the Ecstasy, Suffering, and seamless Wonder of Existence are uninhibitedly *embodied* by the lover. The lover stays luminously wounded, innocently yet knowingly raw, avoiding the lure of indifference and "spiritual" detachment, inhabiting an intimacy both intensely personal and transcendent, clearly demonstrating that awareness and feeling need not be separated...

Spontaneous Talks
by
Robert

Dolby B Chrome Cassette Tapes

MAKING GOOD USE OF TURNING POINTS

Turning points are times of extra energy, times of fertile chaos and potential transition; when we try to *think* our way through a turning point, we only confine its turbulent force in our minds, thereby intensifying our confusion, instead of letting its energies *fuel* our leap into a more fitting level of being. This talk, given October 27, 1988, is about how we must *consciously* blend with the currents of our turning points — we won't necessarily know where we are being taken, but we will not need to know, for we will inevitably be carried to a truer shore. Turning points need not be turned into crises; they are *not problems*, but wonderfully visceral confessions of our ripeness for a certain jump, or shift...

RELEASING SEX FROM THE OBLIGATION TO MAKE US FEEL BETTER

This talk, given October 7, 1988, is about freeing sex from its all-too-common chore of consoling us, whether through stress-discharge, pleasurable distraction, neurotic sublimation, or romantic delusion. If we pay *conscious* attention to ourselves in the midst of sex, we will see the underpinnings of our suffering with remarkable clarity — we will literally catch ourselves in the *act*, recognizing that what we tend to do sexually is but an exaggeration of what we do (or intend) when we *aren't* being sexual. When we stop depending on sex to make us feel better, we stop making a problem out of dependency itself, finding in ourselves a strength that is utterly *unthreatened* by dependency or attachment. Come toward sex *already* unstressed, *already* established in joy, letting it be a celebration of ecstatic intimacy, unburdened by any goal whatsoever...

THE ANATOMY OF EGO & SELF-ENTRAPMENT

Ordinarily, we exist as a self-enclosed, uneasily governed crowd of fragments, each one of which, when given sufficient attention, tends to refer to itself as "I" — however, all of these "I's" are not really selves, but are only *personified habits*. This talk, given October 23, 1988, is about shifting from ego-centricity (or unconscious identification with our dominant fragment of self) to essence-centricity, the point being not to annihilate ego, but to illuminate and purify it. All too easily, we seek release *not* from our self-entrapment, but from the pain of being *in* the trap, not truly realizing that the trap-door is *already* open, awaiting our passage, asking only that we let go of the *security* provided by our self-entrapment...

INTO THE HEART OF ENDARKENED MOODS

Instead of trying to escape or distract ourselves from our endarkened moods (which only reinforces their *roots*), we need to consciously confess *their* point of view and intentions, doing whatever we can to illuminate their terrain. In this talk, given November 22, 1988, the emphasis is on clearly exposing what we are *actually* doing while in unpleasant circumstances (inner or outer). Real happiness is not in fleeing "bad" moods, but rather is in going right to the very heart of them. Pure witnessing is of some use, but all too easily creates an unnecessary withdrawal from passion — the key here is to blend witnessing with *direct*, empathetic participation in our *feeling* dimension, knowing that *everything* we are must be fully faced, embraced, and passed through...

HAPPINESS IS NOT IN HAVING, BUT IN BEING

Real happiness is not in having, but in *being*. The expectation that *having something* (a relationship, an object, a certain feeling, a spiritual breakthrough) will make us feel better only intensifies our suffering, by *addicting* us to that particular something. This talk, given December 12, 1988, is about the nature of having, the need to shift from having to being, and the sane use of possessiveness. If we insist on having something, then it *has* us; on the other hand, if we rest in and *as* our being, then we can both enjoy and *deeply* participate in having, without becoming addictive about it...
(Concludes with a poem)

EMBODYING THE PASSIONATE WITNESS

This talk, given December 7, 1988, is about carrying alertness into the labyrinths of self-contraction, without any recoil from passion, desire, attachment, intimacy, or any other facet of a fully human life. Trying to escape the pain of our self-entrapment only creates more pain and more craving for pleasurably sedating release. The alternative to this is not resignation, nor more sophisticated strategies of escape (including those of all too many "spiritual" paths), but is simply to make room for our pain, letting its energies come unclenched, until they are but *available* Life-Force — this is *not* a technique, nor a recipe, but an always-fresh *art*, the very essence of which is the spirit-bright embodiment of the passionate witness, the one for whom turning away is no longer an attractive option...

REAL RISK-TAKING

In this talk, given November 2, 1988, risk-taking is thoroughly explored. If we aren't willing to risk everything, then we'll only lose everything of *real* value. Sane risk-taking is not a matter of egocentric daring, but rather a matter of luminous intelligence and heartfelt gutsiness; it is a willingness to come undone, to let our binding familiarities come unstrung, and it is also a way of *directly* acknowledging the inherent insecurity of Life. It is crucial to dive into open-eyed intimacy, to dive deep, to again and again stretch to make the leap, to develop and honour relationships wherein it is safe to let go of being safe. Without risk, there is no ecstasy, no fullness of being...

FROM GUILT TO SHAME TO FREEDOM

Guilt is *not* a feeling, but a suppression of feeling, a psychophysical knottedness, a heart-numbing splitting of self that allows us to *continue* doing what apparently makes us "feel" guilty — put another way, guilt means we don't have to grow. However, guilt is but frozen shame. This talk, given November 16, 1988, describes the movement from guilt to shame to freedom, and from blame (the morality of guilt) to responsibility (the morality of *healthy* shame). Shame, when skilfully worked with, catalyzes a deep inner cleansing, a lucid, *heartfelt* acknowledgement of what was done, a warmly streaming catharsis of one's entire system, bright with both self-forgiveness and a return to wholeness, free of guilt's stalemated world...

TRUTH CANNOT BE REHEARSED

When we are committed to being other than ourselves, we are but beggars for applause, inner or outer, capable only of *re-acting*; we are haunted by stage fright, especially that of performing what *cannot* be performed. This talk, given November 21, 1988, is about acting, truth-telling, and identity. As we cease pretending that we aren't pretending, we become less and less concerned about others' approval of us, and our freedom of choice becomes more than just the dictates of our conditioning. We learn the art of giving ourselves without giving ourselves away, gradually ceasing to animate our reactivity, shining through our every role, realizing that there are no Oscars for awakening...

ECSTASY CANNOT BE PRODUCED

The assumption that ecstasy is elsewhere, at the end of a series of steps, or at the point of maximal sexual stimulation, is not true — ecstasy exists in the *heart* of each moment, in the very depths that we flee in our compulsive searching for pleasurable release. This talk, given October 7, 1988, explores both ecstasy *and* its surrogates, emphasizing our need to *literally embody* a life free of all escapism and compensatory activity. Ecstasy is *not* addictive; only when we've turned away from ecstasy do we become addictive, simply because we then create dependency-relationships with whatever promises to deliver us from our suffering. Ecstasy is not a reward, nor is it a product — it is but the open face of real happiness, the pure shout of the awakened heart...

(Concludes with three poems)

RESPONSIBILITY IS THE GROUND OF FREEDOM

This talk, given August 29, 1988, is about not permitting *circumstantial* happiness to obscure our addictions, including that of ego, and it is also about the relationship between freedom and responsibility. For *real* freedom to exist, we must be responsible for creating and maintaining the environment, both inner and outer, that best supports such freedom. Without true responsibility, freedom is but licence, just an exaggerated kind of permission; without freedom, responsibility is but joyless duty, a burdensome obligation, polluted by well-dressed *blame*. As we awaken, it becomes increasingly clear that for every increase in freedom, there must also be a corresponding increase of responsibility...

AWAKENING CREATES ITS OWN MORALITY

Prior to awakening, we are infested by moral codes dictated by authority other than that native to ourselves, literally enslaving ourselves to inner and outer shoulds, worldly or other-worldly. This talk, given September 9, 1988, concerns the art of opening ourselves to the morality generated by the awakening process. Instead of rigidly conforming to rules, we need to create conditions conducive to the stage of our awakening, *without* addicting ourselves to the replication of such conditions — our activities thus become not a means *toward* happiness, but rather an expression *of* happiness. Peace then is for us not a repression of violence and primal force, but rather a passionate, *full-bodied* yes that includes within itself *every* no...

Ordering Information

BOOKS: LOVE MUST ALSO WEEP $16.95

THE WAY OF THE LOVER   14.95

ROOM FOR ALL   7.95

AUDIOTAPES: (Dolby B Chrome Real-time tapes, each with two talks by Robert; average length 80 minutes)

AWAKENING CREATES ITS OWN MORALITY /
ECSTASY CANNOT BE PRODUCED

INTO THE HEART OF ENDARKENED MOODS /
EMBODYING THE PASSIONATE WITNESS

RELEASING SEX FROM THE OBLIGATION TO MAKE US
FEEL BETTER / FROM GUILT TO SHAME TO FREEDOM

HAPPINESS IS NOT IN HAVING, BUT IN BEING /
RESPONSIBILITY IS THE GROUND OF FREEDOM

TRUTH CANNOT BE REHEARSED /
THE ANATOMY OF EGO & SELF-ENTRAPMENT

MAKING GOOD USE OF TURNING POINTS /
REAL RISK-TAKING

(Each tape is $12.95; a set of all six is $69.95)

All prices are in Canadian dollars, and include postage.

Order from: **XANTHYROS FOUNDATION**
P.O. Box 91980
West Vancouver, B.C.
Canada   V7V 4S4